# *The* Seattle Office

# *The* Seattle Office

Good > Bad

Hard to Believe?

***Deane Addison Knapp***

authorHOUSE®

*AuthorHouse™*
*1663 Liberty Drive*
*Bloomington, IN 47403*
*www.authorhouse.com*
*Phone: 1 (800) 839-8640*



*Published by AuthorHouse 10/23/2015*

*ISBN: 978-1-5049-5419-8 (sc)*
*ISBN: 978-1-5049-5418-1 (e)*

*Library of Congress Control Number: 2015916280*

*Print information available on the last page.*

"THE SEATTLE OFFICE is a thought-provoking, fast-paced adventure that travels up and down the west coast of the U.S. and beyond. With an abundance of vivid descriptions of surrounding waterways and quiet towns, it lays the foundation for the ageless question of good winning out over evil. Does it? There are rapid romances, fierce fights, troubled towns, and two master-minds who oversee it all."

"It poses a question about loyalty as well – can it be bought? Or is it earned? I would recommend THE SEATTLE OFFICE for an adult who enjoys spy/adventure-type novels but who isn't afraid to examine their own thoughts about good and evil. This book will give you the chance to examine where you stand on the continuum of what is right and wrong. – Because sometimes destruction has to happen in order for justice to be had."

-----*Laura G. Johnson/Red Pen Proofreading & Editing*-----

# FROM THE AUTHOR

I want to say thank you to Laura G. Johnson for her kindness and expertise. Also, my wife, Dorine, is a big help. I could write a whole book just about her. My children would chime in with excellence from time to time, and then there are my grandkids! Indeed, another book!

How can one guy be so favored with all of you? Thank you again, each one!

*Deane Addison Knapp, Purdy, Washington, USA*

# Contents

What would you do if good men and women took the lead?

Would you throw darts, follow after them, or lead with them?

What would you do if you were free enough to make that choice?

# Part One

## 1

Ed was shaking his head. Unbelievable. The new guy was yelling at him. They learned everything they needed to know except respect for their elders. Ed was 55, this kid was probably 25. He remembered. He always respected and admired the railroad men, all of his life, especially when he was starting out. These were the men he looked up to and revered. Now, this kid was yelling at him.

He knew exactly how far he had to take the engine in order for the last car to clear the switch. How many times had he done it? Don't ask. He knew exactly what was needed, exactly how far; farther was inefficient, not unsafe. But no, the kid insisted on operating by the book. He was telling Ed to go farther, as if he held some sort of authority because he had just gotten out of school. Well, he wasn't going any farther. The older you get, the more respect you should get. Simple.

Now the kid was shouting into the walkie-talkie and running along the cars toward the engine. Ed could hear him with or without the 2-way. He was getting louder and more disrespectful. Amazing. The old truths always endure. Power tends to corrupt, and this kid was well on his way.

Okay, Ed thought. He was in the yard, and as Yard Boss the kid was technically in charge. As his mind decided, the feelings of anger rose, and his hand went to the throttle. As his fingers reached it, his arm went numb. Anger quickly turned to fear as his chest exploded in pain. Ed's last conscious thought was that he had waited too long to see the doctor about the symptoms he'd been having. He hadn't had time. He was a railroad man with work to do, and the work was important.

His hand managed to grasp the throttle, one last attempt at doing his job. His body fell forward heavily onto his hand and pushed the throttle forward, all the way.

*

Joe was finishing his day. He loved driving, and this little 5-speed Metro was fun to drive. Provided by the company for their couriers to drive, they had to make sure the gas tank was full for the next day's driver. The office part of his job done, he headed for the gas station. He was on empty. The business gas card went with the station two miles away. He knew the route well. First stop light: railroad tracks; second stop light: gas station. Fill up. Back to the office; card out. He'd be off early today.

Joe drove for a living. That made him a professional driver. A source of pride with him. As he stopped at the first light, the gray car ahead of him had its nose in the crosswalk. Sloppy. The car behind had a mom with kids strapped in. Hmm; cute, but had her hands full. Distractions, not good. Was that a cop behind her? Joe liked having cops around. When you paid attention to what you were doing, there was nothing to feel guilty about. Cops did not just notice bad drivers, they noticed good, smart ones, too.

The gray-nose in the crosswalk accelerated through the green light and Joe did also, leaving an appropriate length between them. Cute mom behind quickly ignored her kids as she noticed the cop behind her. Her mind, however, could not help wandering. It had been a busy day. Next thing was what to have for dinner?

As Joe started across the tracks, he remembered how bumpy railroad tracks were when he was a kid; but these tracks were recessed into the concrete and you barely noticed them. Three tracks. The first he felt slightly, the last two he never got to.

A motion in his peripheral vision caused Joe to turn his head. The speed of the approaching blur didn't make sense, and as a professional driver, when the feeling of being out of control came, you automatically checked ahead and behind, as you began reacting with your hands and feet.

The blur was coming quickly from the right, and he knew the gray car ahead would make it across the tracks. Joe would, too, if he tromped on it, but his mind sharpened instantly. A train?! No way. Hold it! He checked his mirror: cute mom and kids. Joe's mind just wasn't fast enough to keep up with the speed at which this thing was happening. His knowing what to do to save himself and the car collided with his need to attend to the welfare of others. Joe's military training reacted before his mind could reach a conclusion. It produced a split-second action. His right foot tromped on the brake, not the accelerator; his focus was on the mirror. The look of horror on the cute mom's face, and her body leaning forward meant she was braking. Good! For a second a smile formed on Joe's face. Then the uncontrollable arrived.

He felt the passenger-side door hit his right arm and the side of his head. Then his head bounced off the center post on his left side and he was tumbling. He thought there would be searing pain from broken glass and metal, but the sudden head trauma rendered him unconscious. The physical rolling of the car being bounced along in front of the train caused a feeling in his mind of tumbling. This sensation kept on going even though the car and the train soon stopped. His unconscious mind was sheltering him from the horror happening to him.

The sensation was like...he was surrounded by water, but he could still breathe. Wow! Was he in a thick fog, or had he been pushed into a river, or...? He opened his eyes as he continued to tumble, but there was no change, open or shut. He was tumbling slowly, evenly, like wet clothes in a warm dryer.

# 2

The cute mom saw the train out of the corner of her eye, also. She wanted to brake, but her mind said 'no'. The railroad barrier arms were not down so she had the right of way. The speed of the oncoming train changed her thoughts and she hit the brake pedal, but not too hard--the kids were on board. When she saw the brake lights a few feet in front of her, she changed her mind, and gave the brake pedal everything she had. She knew she had made contact with those brake lights ahead of her, but suddenly they were gone! Her car was turned sideways and the train was blurring by, inches from her babies! A quick prayer: "Jesus! My babies!", rendered the train gone. The loud roar that held her face in a grimace, and her body bracing, quickly went away down the track with the train. As she opened her eyes, her car was still rocking from the 'whoosh' of the train. She tried to breathe and mind her babies. Then she heard a knocking on the window. One look calmed her down.

*

John Hamilton had a humorous side that he employed at only the most appropriate times. It fit in well with his serious, professional side as a State Patrol Officer. He had started out in paramedic school and liked it for two years. However, his interaction with the Police, Sheriff, and State Patrol during traffic accidents and such, led him to his nineteen-year career as a Washington State Patrol Officer.

His thorough medical training, his humor, and his ability to project his intelligence won him respect from his peers, as well as his many daily new acquaintances. He comforted people when they were agitated, and he agitated people who were sleepy, drunk, or stoned. He saved lives on occasion, and smiled and said something funny when children were scared.

When John first heard the train, he thought it was the take-offs and landings from the nearby Air Force base. When his eye caught the fast approaching blur, his training kicked in. He braked hard, flipped on his blue lights, and grabbed his mic.

"Police emergency, 56$^{th}$ and BN tracks; send Fire, Aid, and back-up, NOW!"

He could only stare at the picture that played out in front of him. The bell had begun to ring, the railroad crossing lights flashed, and the barrier arms began to move down at the same time as the train smoked through the intersection, taking the white Metro with it. The Ford sedan in front of him got knocked sideways, but now sat still, parallel to the tracks, without any visible damage.

He had felt himself being rear-ended but didn't mind, because it was up to him to stop traffic one way or another. A glance to his mirrors showed the air bags inflated in the front seat of the car behind him. Good. The white Metro had been completely broadsided and rolled a couple of times and then stabilized, somehow attached to the front of the train. As soon as the train cleared the intersection, it noticeably slowed. John recalled trains having an emergency power cut-off at the front of the train, which activated when it came into contact with anything on the track. The ensuing fireball in front of the train was short lived. The lucky and/or unlucky driver must have been on empty.

One of John's hands went for his door handle and the other hand for his State Patrol Officer's hat. It was rule number one: always wear your hat if outside the vehicle.

Air bags in back, okay. Metro, done for. Immediate concern: the Ford sedan in front of him. As he approached, a mother and three car seats started the adrenaline flowing again, but there was no broken glass and no screaming. Good so far. He tapped on the window of the car door and the mom righted herself. He tapped again and her face turned toward him. Getting a full look at his uniform, she visibly eased a bit. As she rolled down the window he instructed, "Turn the key off, ma'am. Turn the key off."

John had the first medic vehicle tend to the mom and kids. The second he pointed down the track and said, "Don't get your hopes up."

A fire truck and medic vehicle turned down the tracks and pulled up at the front of the stopped engine with two attached rail cars. Two firemen approached the smashed car, while a medic climbed up into the engineer's compartment. The engineer had sustained no visible injuries, but had no pulse. Okay, it began to make sense. Slumped over the "gas pedal". Heart attack.

The firemen both grimaced and prepared themselves. A small car, very mangled. Maybe the door popped open and the driver ejected. Better odds. Nope. Blood. Smoke was dissipating. Apparently, the car must have been very low on gas. The body was still strapped in, just bent and pierced by metal and plastic.

"Head trauma!" one called out.

"Check for pulse!" the other instructed.

"Uh…I'm not sure where…to…Whoa! He just opened and closed his eyes!! Medic!!!" The next hour was heart wrenching: cutting, prying, bending, but amazingly the pulse never wavered.

The tumbling dryer made no noise, but was rhythmically steady. There was a background sensation of being pulled, pushed, and moved, but only in the background. He just kept tumbling, safe and sound.

After a while, Joe realized he had no way of measuring time in any accurate sense. He was starting to get used to thinking while tumbling. He couldn't assess whether a moment was a second, a minute, an hour, or a day. Maybe it was longer. He couldn't tell. The only thing that was steady was the tumbling, but he couldn't remember when it had started. As far as he could see there was no off switch.

Wait a minute. He couldn't remember who he was either. His thoughts searched everywhere. Since he was aware of tumbling, he should know who he was, but he couldn't remember; just a nagging thought that he should. The only thing that was steady was the rhythm and sensation of tumbling.

And then it stopped.

# 3

Days had passed since the body of the man was pried out, stabilized, transported, hospitalized, and monitored. His pulse was steady but he had not regained consciousness. His room was full of flowers but he couldn't smell them. His visitors were staff except for a journalist named Tom, who worked for the Seattle Times and came frequently to Tacoma. He had read the story about the accident and dropped in to see if the man had regained consciousness. The fact that no relatives or friends had visited made Tom wonder, but life was meant to be lived to the fullest, and most people had a lot going on. An hour to visit someone in the hospital was a generous gift in and of itself. The hospital was making money every day Joe was there, so they were stabilizing him, not trying to awaken him.

*

Kandee wasn't her real name. She made it up because she liked to be different, liked to be special. She wasn't what you would call gorgeous, but with the way her little nose turned up slightly at the end and her active personality, everyone thought of her as gorgeous. She kept her hair rather short in a variety of styles and colors. She could be very professional or in need of being loved, depending on the situation. Kandee liked people and people liked Kandee.

She was a nurse, and as such, she could always count on at least part time work wherever she was. She had recently moved back from the east coast to the Pacific Northwest where she had some roots. She had walked into one of Tacoma's many hospitals only a few months before, and right away was offered part time day, or full time night work. That was easy. Get paid all night and still have time during the day for normal things, including teasing men. That was one of the things Kandee liked and was good at: teasing men. She liked wearing green contact lenses. Men always did a double take, and women just stared, wondering how their life might change for only $89.95.

Room J-17 was part of Kandee's routine; one of the more pleasant parts. The bed was not unoccupied, but Joe was in a coma. She could stare at him while checking his vitals without worrying that he would notice. She lifted an eyelid once and saw normal blue eyes to go with his normal brown hair. She might slightly rearrange some features, but so far, knowing nothing of his personality, she decided he was close to perfect. Perfect men were pretty much nonexistent. Kandee had a good amount of experience in that regard. It was kind of fun to pronounce Joe perfect so far, except for his dull name. Kandee's perfect man fantasies all had names starting with K like hers. Joe's middle initial was K, and she decided it must be Kent, and she would call him that. As she brushed the hair off his forehead, she wondered if he might just have the slightest British accent, too.

*

Joe decided to open his eyes since the tumbling had stopped. He couldn't tell if it had been a second, or a minute, or an hour, but the steady cadence of the tumbling had indeed stopped. So, however long it had been, he opened his eyes.

It took a second to focus, but a woman, only a foot from his face, materialized. Wow! She was...well, not necessarily gorgeous, but…he was becoming lost in her green eyes. Five words were going through his mind over and over, making him feel wonderful. He forced them out of his mouth, but they came as only a whisper. "I must be in heaven!"

Kandee had noticed his eyes fluttering while she was arranging flowers in the room and had come close; she was staring at him when his eyes opened wide. His five words made her have to catch her breath, and her fingers covered her mouth automatically. He had said it twice, a little louder the second time, as if he wasn't sure he had said it the first time. Hmmm, heaven?

Kandee smiled sweetly and softly said, "It's a possibility," sort of teasingly.

"You're an angel," Joe forced the thoughts through his mouth, hearing himself speak for the first time. His mind was beginning to overdose on the lovely few seconds of awareness. He sensed the tumbling was going to begin again, but no, only a wonderful warmth, and he did not want to fight it.

Kandee noticed his eyelids fluttering again and said just above a whisper, with a full beaming smile, "I'll never forget that you think so…Kent."

He was asleep again. Her heart was pounding. Was he going to die? Was he going to exist the rest of his life in a coma? Or, perfectly, would he wake up again and be in love with her? Kent and Kandee! It sounded so romantic.

*

The cute mom woke up and burst into tears.

She had been joined by her husband at the tracks before the shock started to clear. The family all went to the hospital and got checked out. The doctors okayed them, and now they were home, safe and secure.

Now it was 3 AM, and she woke up realizing that the guy in front of her had jammed on his brakes so that the train would hit him and not her. All her emotions broke loose and her husband woke and immediately gathered her into his arms.

"It's okay, baby, just a nightmare. It's okay, I'm right here."

Through sobs she muttered, "Not a nightmare. I just realized. He chose to die, so me and my babies could live." Her husband didn't get it. He reached over her to get the medicine the doctor had prescribed.

"Here honey, let's take another one of these."

"No, Chad; listen. I'm okay. I just remembered something. Will you let me talk it through?"

"Sure, baby. Go ahead." She nestled into his arms and he pulled up the blankets.

"The last thing I saw was his brake lights. That's what made me tromp on my brakes!"

"That's good, honey, you did good. You saved our family." Chad was trying to think at 3AM. "That's why the train just missed you."

"Chad, that's why he died and we are alive! His car was already going over the tracks. If he would have kept going, he would have lived, and *we'd* be dead... Do you see what I'm saying?"

He adjusted her in his arms and tried to follow. "Okay baby, go over it again, slowly."

Grace's honey brown hair was so soft as she lay her head on his chest. He buried his nose in it as she played with his belly button and talked. After a few seconds he began focusing on what she was saying. After two minutes she was starting to make sense. After five minutes he became aware that her story changed things. Each time she mentioned the guy in front of her, and how he died for her and her kids, she sobbed for a few seconds. He adjusted his arms again as he realized, out of terror this time rather than relief, that he had just about lost his family.

She stopped fiddling when she stopped talking and after a while she said, "He's in heaven."

Chad reached over and pulled her hair away from her forehead and tucked it behind her ear. "Yeah, or soon will be. I think he's still in the hospital in a coma." Chad's voice was slow and soothing, but her body tensed.

"What?! You mean he's still alive?"

# 4

Ed had a marvelous memorial service. The railroad men, along with cops, firefighters, and teachers, were big labor. They all stuck together. Especially when one of them died in the line of duty. They all showed up at funerals. Paid, of course.

Ed's wife got the life insurance, and the mailman whom she'd been chummy with for some time. Ed's son got the house, all paid off, and his on-again-off-again girlfriends suddenly all got serious. Ed never had been nicer to his family than at his premature death. Everyone thought it, but no one said it.

Far from being held responsible, the kid was honored for averting a worse disaster. He called all the right authorities according to the book, and came out looking good for a promotion. America, the land of opportunity.

*

Joe, it seemed, was the only one who did not look so good, future-wise anyway. Actually his past wasn't very clear either. It made Tom Collier pause. As a Seattle journalist, he was playing with the south-end story in his spare time, which meant after he had accomplished the assignments given to him by his boss. In trying to look into Joe's past, it seemed he had always had part-time jobs strung together, and nothing you would call a career.

Plus, there were his four years in the army. Tom couldn't nail down how many months or years were spent where. Joe's life seemed very normal, but when you tried to go deeper, there were dead ends.

Tom was playing around with this story because his other stuff was so boring. He did his best at being consistent in his work like a baseball player. Taking walks or hitting singles was okay, because when his home run blast came, his bosses would see a solid foundation of work as the reason, and not just a fluke long ball.

Tom knew what his career work was. He would continue his excellence in the mundane, and work in the excitement carefully, and with control. He wouldn't want the big boys and girls to grab the limelight after his hard work of digging. So, Tom continued to work the angles, when he had time. The more time he gave to this story, the more it felt like the rumblings of a home run.

The shovel full that seemed to have something other than dirt in it was Joe, who had gaps of months sometimes, with no work, and yet no unemployment compensation. Was he independently wealthy and traveled every once in a while? If so, why work at all? Did he go on a drunken binge whenever he had some money saved? Tom didn't think so. He had carefully questioned a couple of Joe's past bosses and they couldn't say enough good about him. Also, Joe had no college education, only a high school diploma. What happened in the four years between high school and army? Probably just normal after-graduation travel, with no focus, just trying on the world. Once Tom asked a probing question of one of Joe's former employers, "Was he intelligent?" The guy had paused and reflected, "You know, I got the feeling with Joe that he had way more intelligence than the job required."

Tom was seeing the stitches on the fastball better with every few pitches. He let the excitement build, albeit slowly. He was starting to taste that pitch that would be met with such a sharp cracking sound, that everyone would look up, and the ball would be heading for the seats.

*

State Patrol Officer John Hamilton, usually the interviewer, had been interviewed at the scene by his peers. When the equipment and men attacked the smashed Metro, still a part of the front of the train, he headed that way. Could the driver possibly be alive? Yes, was the only answer that made sense when he saw the frantic, yet professional way the firemen were working on the car. When the ambulance pulled close, he had to hold himself back from helping out. He backed up and leaned against the side of the railcar and made his mind organize the facts chronologically, as he remembered them. As the sun was getting low in the sky, he was released and told to go home early, and take two days off. So he headed home via another officer since his car was being impounded.

He surprised Margie in the laundry room, folding dry towels to the sound of the washing machine. She burst into a smile and hugged him, and then tensed and stood back and looked him over from head to toe.

"Honey?"

"I witnessed an injury accident and they told me to take a couple days off. I need to calm down and remember just what happened. I'm sure I'll be called in to court by the insurance companies on this one."

"You want to go to the ocean."

"Yeah, you guessed it, but you better call Ginny, because I'm not going to be much fun."

Two phone calls and two hours later, they were checking into two rooms at their favorite ocean place. One for John and Margie, and one for Margie and Ginny. Ginny was Margie's fun partner and stabilizing influence when John had these work related episodes to deal with. Once, John had been shot at with a sawed-off shotgun while walking back to his patrol car after getting a driver's license and proof of insurance from a pickup he'd pulled over. Both he and his car got peppered. He landed on the ground face down and felt the man retrieve his info. John laid still and the man just left. It was all he could do to reach his radio. The man ended up crying drunk in a bar later that night, confessing what he had done to his buddies.

Ginny, a next door neighbor at the time, held Margie together, and was good at it. Ginny and Margie, Margie and Ginny; they were important for each other and John was thankful for the relationship. He and Margie both knew that death always lurked just at the periphery. As they unpacked, John put a couple of bottles of his favorite wine in the fridge. He only indulged when he was off for more than a day, and today he needed to relax and think seriously. After he built a fire in the wood stove, he sat on the floor, his back against the bed, with a notepad, pen, and a glass of wine. Margie and Ginny were heading for dinner in the downstairs restaurant.

*

Kandee knew she had to write on Kent's chart that he woke up and spoke. But she didn't think that the exact words were that important.

"Where am I?" She put as his question upon opening his eyes.

"In a safe place," she wrote as her reply, as he fell into a deep sleep a few moments later. That sounded more professional, more nurse-like.

*

"We've got to go see him, right now!" Grace was ready to get up and go to the hospital.

"Honey, it's 3:30 in the morning. Now take one of these pills, and when you wake up you'll be ready, and we can all go."

She settled back down. He was right. Her husband was a gem.

# 5

Joe slept well and woke up hungry. As he looked around, he recognized where he was, and it wasn't heaven. He chuckled thinking about the dream he had. Or was it a dream? Maybe he had died, gone to heaven, and got sent back. If he had been sent back, he suddenly knew what he must do. Hmm.

Among the lines of IVs and sensors, he found the button that summons the nurse. He ran his hand through his hair and pushed the button. A large smiling nurse trotted in and began to exclaim how wonderful it was that he was awake, and everything was going to be fine, and how did he feel, and where did it hurt, and...

Joe held up both hands; "I need to make a phone call and I'm hungry."

"Oh, I'll get today's menu for you and..."

"Phone first please, then menu."

A minute later she returned munching on something, and plugged a phone into the wall. She handed it to him along with the menu. "I'm going to call the doctor; he'll be excited," and she trotted out of the room.

Joe quickly dialed a toll free number. When the machine answered he said three words and hung up. Okay then, menu.

*

When Kandee heard from Shelly at shift change that J-17 had awakened from his coma, her whole body went through some funny feelings, but she continued on her normal routine, not wanting anybody to know how much she had let herself fall in love. And so, later that night as she approached J-17, she stopped and steeled herself. Kandee was nothing if not brave. She could count on herself to put her best professional foot forward even when her heart was swimming.

The door was already open and she slowly moved into the doorway. Kent was sitting up in bed, and a man was sitting by the bed with pad and pen, interviewing him. She slipped in, unannounced, and was hardly noticed. She began her routine of checking equipment and patient. When she came closer, to check IVs and such, she sat on the side of his bed. Then she took her pen light and softly said, "This way". She gently pulled his chin toward her while shining the light in his eyes. The conversation between the two men stopped abruptly, seemingly for only a moment, but it did not continue when she turned off her light. She watched his pupils go from big to small, and slowly back to big again. He was just staring now, and she didn't move. Just enough of a smile, she thought, was what was called for at this moment. Then she patted his hand and said, sort of playfully, "Thank you," and got up, turned away, and began checking his chart. She could feel him watching every move she made. This was fun.

Joe was stunned; the nurse's green eyes just swallowed him up. What he was saying to the journalist he had just met, was gone. When she said 'thank you' and got up, he realized he knew her and just stared after her. The nurse was the angel in his dream! He wasn't sure how many minutes had passed, or were they seconds, but it took that long to formulate, transmit, and enunciate a word.

"Hi."

She turned, raised her head and looked at him. He was stunned all over again. Her smile broadened and she said, "Welcome back." Her voice sounded like an angel's.

The only thing he could think of to say was, "Was I in heaven?"

She paused, smiled and said, "Well, we don't think so, but only you know for sure. What did you see?"

"An angel."

"Then… it's a possibility."

He was stunned for a third time. She had said the same words as in his dream! He intended to keep talking but his eyes and ears were saturated.

She turned and headed for the door, but over her shoulder she said softly,

"I'll be back."

His eyes followed her out the door and then didn't know what to do.

"Joe," his new journalist friend said, "Joe, do you know her?"

Joe moved his head toward Tom. "Yes," he said.

"From where?" Tom loved asking questions.

"Heaven."

*

State Patrol Officer John Hamilton took two big sips and held each in his mouth awhile before swallowing. The first sips always tasted the best. Then he repositioned himself on the floor and raised the wine again. This time a long slow sip and swallow, long slow sip and swallow, breathing through his nose. When the goblet was empty he put it down and sighed. "Okay now."

John knew the mellowness that was coming would allow his professional training to kick in, and he would write down the facts as he remembered them. An occasional sip to stay at that point half-emptied the bottle after about an hour. There, the facts were set down properly.

After a bathroom break, he strolled to the window and looked out through the tree branches to the ocean below. The wind was light, but there. The moon-light on the waves made the scene perfect. Then there was the roar, the unending roar of the ocean. He closed his eyes. The roar was almost as good as the wine.

A few minutes later, there was a soft tap on the door, and Margie poked her head in. She eyed John at the window, his empty goblet on the floor, and knew he was done. She waved goodbye to Ginny, picked up a second goblet, and joined him. The rest of the evening belonged to them.

John's professional training took a break.

*

Tom tried to digest Joe's answer. Did he know the girl or not? There was definitely something between them. He wrote "nurse?" on his pad, and addressed Joe again. "Joe, thanks for letting me introduce myself and talking. I just have one more question and then you should get some sleep."

Tom was going to ask his question, but Joe asked one first. "Did you happen to see what her name tag said?"

Tom slowly looked down to his pad and added a second question mark to the word nurse. "No, I missed it," he answered, "It seemed like you recognized her though."

Joe looked at Tom and sighed. Tom seemed easy to trust. "Either I died and went to heaven, and she was there, but I got sent back, or… I didn't die and she was just in my dreams, …or…"

"Joe, you could have woken up momentarily before coming out of the coma and saw her as she was checking on you."

That made sense. Joe inched his way down into his bed and spoke slowly as if he was sleepy. "Yeah, Tom, that's the only thing that makes any sense."

Tom stood, "Joe, can I ask one more question? Then I'll go."

"Shoot."

"You made a phone call after you woke up, before you ate. The nurse overheard it and said it only took three seconds. What was that?"

"Yeah..., thanks Tom..., I think you're right..., she must have..." Joe faded fast, so Tom patted his leg as he turned to leave.

"Sleep good, buddy. I'll be back tomorrow." Joe's eyes were closed but his mind was racing. His life of luxury here in the hospital was at an end.

# 6

Kandee knew her last round of the night shift to J-17 would be her last chance at love. She knew Kent was in love with her, most men eventually were, so she combined her bravery with her heart and formulated a plan. If Kent woke up with her in his arms, he would never want her to leave. Her new life would be launched.

She came to his room and listened at the door, then opened it, stole inside and left the light off. She made sure the "sleeping" sign was in position outside the door. She floated over and checked Kent's breathing. He was fast asleep. She glanced around the room and then went for the bathroom. As she closed the bathroom door, Joe opened his eyes.

Kandee flipped the bathroom light on and unbuttoned her uniform. She slipped out of it, took off her shoes and socks, and looked at herself in the mirror. Her light blue two piece undergarment had only been worn twice before but with wild results. She knew she was irresistible. Earlier in the evening, the guy on the floor below with the knee replacement had offered her a hundred bucks to climb on top of him that moment. She had smiled and touched his nose and said she would have to think about it while he got some more rest.

Kandee now took a deep breath and turned the door knob. She would slip across the room and under the covers and into Kent's arms and go from there. Oh, this was fun.

Joe knew how to sound like he was asleep and when he heard the door shut he opened his eyes. He carefully raised his head and looked around. All clear. He could see light from under the bathroom door, so he would open it a bit and in the half-light search the closets and drawers in his room for his clothes. He slipped his feet onto the floor and sat up.

Joe stood and made sure the light-headedness passed before he moved. Then he crossed the room and reached for the door handle to the bathroom. But before he could touch it, the door opened out toward him. He squinted in the light, but there in the doorway was his dream angel. She let out a kind of high pitched "Ohh," and the staring began.

"Hi." Joe managed.

His angel said, "Oh, Kent." And wrapped her arms around his neck.

She smelled so good. Joe instinctively held her and then walked her backwards into the bathroom. He reached back and closed the door and then held her at arms' length. Then he took her hands in his and could feel himself reacting as he saw her little outfit.

"Kent, I know you're in love with me, and I came to tell you that it's all right because I'm in love with you, too, and I was afraid I would never have the chance to tell you."

All Joe's senses were heading for the moon, but he reined them in and drew her into his arms again so he could think of what to say. "Well then, aren't we a pair. I... am in love with you, even though I don't know your name. And... you're in love...I'm not sure who Kent is."

"My name is Kandee," she said with a snicker, "and I'm calling you Kent because Joe is such an ordinary name."

"Well...Kandee and Kent...Sounds romantic," he said. She wrapped her arms around him tighter and buried her head in his chest.

Now Joe's mind was frantically searching, because he had to wrap this up quick. "Kandee...you were so...so right to come here...because I'm leaving tonight."

"What do you mean?" She looked up into his eyes.

"And...I need to...ask you...two things." Joe was trying to think first, then talk. There was a pause; Kandee said nothing for once. "Can you find me some clothes...ASAP, and...will you come with me?"

Kandee fell apart. She started crying and breathing like she was running, and said, "Oh Kent, I'm so happy; let's crawl into bed right now."

Joe rearranged his hold on her, putting one hand on her lovely hair. "Kandee, will you let me tell you something?"

"Mmhmm," she muttered.

"I've got to meet with my boss first thing in the morning, and it takes a whole day practically to get checked out. I've got to leave tonight. If you could find me some clothes, you could come with me... if you want."

She stood back, and looked up at him. Then she kind of curtsied. "So you like my outfit?"

Joe felt himself reacting again and reached for her uniform. "You make that outfit look lovely," he said. Handing her the uniform, asked, "Want to help me?"

Her green eyes were wide and he couldn't stop himself from kissing her.

She hugged him again and then came to life. "I know just where to get you some clothes. I'll be back in ten minutes." She put her things on, and turned to leave, then stopped. "You'll be here when I get back won't you?" After watching her dress, all he could do was nod his head with a big smile. Then off she went, closing the door to J-17 after herself.

Joe tried to settle his thumping heart down. Then he sat on his bed with his head in his hands. "What in hell?" was all he could say.

Minutes passed. In his mind he dealt with each fast-approaching problem and gave it a solution, wrong or right. Training from before kicked in and it felt like an old, wise friend. He could not stay here, he had to move...

# 7

Joe Cornish replayed the phone message just to be sure, and then deleted it. He was somewhat surprised, pleasantly so, and he let a deep breath out slowly. The three word message meant, "back on course". He recognized the voice, but they knew each other only by code names, not by real names. D. Charger was letting him know he was alright and back operating according to the last instructions. Joe Cornish did not know what the D. in the code name meant, but always thought of the D. as Dodge as in Dodge Charger, when dealing with this agent. Subsequently, he had chosen F. Mustang as his code name when communicating with D. Charger.

He appreciated the message because it updated the operative's status. Apparently he was out of his coma and now things were back to normal. Joe Cornish launched himself out of his desk chair, and fiddled in his file cabinet until he found the D. Charger file. Putting it in his brief case, he grabbed his coat and closed the door carefully, as the pane of glass in the door rattled dangerously if it was closed harder. As he walked down the hall away from his office, the beautifully etched glass pane was still intact. It read: Joe Cornish—Special Investigations—Seattle Office. The building Joe Cornish exited into a drizzly Seattle afternoon was the Federal Building which, everybody knew, housed his employer: the FBI. What nobody knew, not even the FBI, was that Joe Cornish had, in the past, worked for the CIA.

*

Kandee was walking softly back to J-17. Each time her feet started to run she slowed herself to normal speed. In her pocket was six one hundred dollar bills and in her arms a plastic hospital bag with clothes. She had taken the time to visit Mr. Knee-replacement, and sweet talked him out of all the money he had with him, and his clothes. He had said that his wife was begging him for an equitable divorce, and he just had to have Kandee. He was rich and she would never have to worry about anything again. She had told him she'd be back on tomorrow night's shift and they would work out all the details. He never really said she could take his money and clothes, but could only stare at her as she grabbed what she wanted, smiled at him, and left.

She had stopped in to see Mr. Knee because he had something she needed. But it was for her Kent, and she didn't care how much of a hurry Kent was in, he was going to be between her legs tonight, in this hospital, before they left. She was going to reel him in before he could spit the hook out.

*

Mom, her babies, and her husband had visited Joe in the hospital while he was still in a coma. She had talked to him and had brought her babies close to his ear to say their names and "Thank you." She explained that she knew what he had done and how grateful she and her husband were, and live or die, they would never forget him, and would pray for him daily.

Also, she had taken time to write all her feelings and thoughts down in a letter. She enclosed pictures of the whole family with names, etc., and left it in an envelope on his pillow next to his head. The nurse had put Joe's identity numbers on it and put it in the drawer by his bed, with his other valuables.

Now, as Joe was hurriedly finalizing his next moves, he put the letter and pictures into a larger envelope and addressed it to Tom, the journalist at the Seattle Times, with a note: "Please take care of this for me. I'll be in touch. Thanks." As he licked and sealed the envelope, the door slipped open and a smile exploded across his angel's face when she saw he was still there.

"Oh Kent, I'm so happy! I've got clothes and money for us!" This as she unbuttoned her uniform. "But first things first; I'm yours, right now."

Man, Joe thought, if she is an angel, she sure can fly fast. Then he countered.

"But Kandee, first things first." He took her hands in his and lifted them to his lips. "Will you marry me?"

Kandee was stunned momentarily. She had been in love before and had caused men to fall in love with her and passionately make love to her, but the sincerity and seriousness of Kent's eyes and voice stunned her. She shook her head as if to say no, but said "Yes, Kent, with all my heart, yes." She wrapped her arms around his neck and held on, feeling like a balloon that just had all the air let out. "I love you," she whispered almost cautiously as if she had never felt the feelings of vulnerability and security together before. What was happening to her? This was unknown ground.

Joe unpeeled her arms from around him and sat her on the side of the bed. "First, we have to leave. Now." Joe said this as he began to dress in the clothes she had brought him. She followed his lead and buttoned up. Within a minute they were hand in hand peeking through the door into the hallway. The coast being clear, they crossed the hallway and entered the stairwell, being careful to quietly close the door.

Now he held her face in his hands as if she were a child being given a task for someone much older. "Go get your purse and coat."

It took a moment for her to understand that this meant she would have to leave his side, but yes, she had completely forgotten her things. "Okay." She whispered without disconnecting their gaze.

"Then, take the elevator down to the garage and I will meet you there." She whispered, "Okay" again just as Joe kissed her on the lips. Then he opened the door to the stairwell and lovingly pushed her into the hallway.

Joe's countenance quickly changed to serious business. Instead of going down, he headed up the stairs. Round one went well enough. Now, he had to think out round two. He left the stairwell when he got to the top floor and moved down the hallway. This floor was unfinished and not in use. He went down the hallway until he found the women's restroom and went in, but left the door unlocked. He turned on the light long enough to get the layout and then turned it off and carefully sat down. Now, think.

# 8

Joe Cornish had headed uptown for three blocks and turned into a "mom and pop." He picked out a can of Coke and laid a five on the counter when it was his turn. The owner not only recognized the customer, but he recognized the Coke can and the five as a message saying that the customer was okay and was not to his knowledge being followed. The owner put the five in the till and gave back five ones as change. The customer quickly counted the ones and recognized the message that everything seemed normal from the owner's viewpoint, also. Joe Cornish stepped outside and paused to open the Coke and take two quick swallows. The owner of the outdoor newspaper and magazine stand across the street recognized the message and took out his cell phone and made a quick call. Joe Cornish hailed a taxi and headed for his condo on the west side of Lake Union.

His day was winding down, or so it seemed.

*

Joe tried to concentrate in the dark but he could not unhook from Kandee. He almost laughed out loud when the thought passed through his mind that maybe it was because he was in a women's restroom. Security would not give an unlocked, dark, women's restroom a second thought when looking for a missing male patient.

Why was he having trouble unhooking from Kandee, despite his professional training? There were beautiful women all over the place.

As he forced his mind to boil down his feelings to the root reason, he remembered his first encounter with her. Was she an angel? Had he seen her in heaven, and then got sent back and saw her again as a nurse? It had meant something. He needed to not unhook from her. That's why he was having trouble doing it. He remembered, when he had realized he might have died but been sent back, that something came to mind very strongly which he needed to do. It was very possible that Kandee was part of doing this and didn't know it, even though she might have been an angel. Or...maybe it...was only the trauma he had gone through... What was he doing in a women's restroom with the light off anyhow? Now he did laugh out loud. He had to find Kandee and move on. With her, not without her.

Joe headed for the stairwell again and descended to the garage without meeting anyone. When he looked out the small window of the door into the garage, he didn't see anyone. Opening the door and entering the garage didn't help. Kandee was not there. He quickly scanned the whole area and for some reason noticed the restrooms. He suppressed a chuckle, then forced his mind to go back to his training. The training made him look at the restrooms again and he quickly moved to the door marked Women, knocked gently and called, "Kandee!"

She was in his arms like a small explosion. "I didn't know what to do. I thought maybe..."

"I know, it took longer than I thought. Kandee, I'll always come back for you. Remember that." Joe had made a decision. She heard the words but had never had anyone speak to her with such sincerity and love. They turned around and arm in arm they found her car, got in, and drove out. It was morning.

After Tom got back to his Seattle Times office, he couldn't sit still. He felt Joe was part of a bigger story, and Tom wanted to bite harder, not loosen up. He told his boss that a one hundred and two year old veteran was in a Tacoma hospital and he wanted to interview him before he died, just in case.

"Just in case what?" his boss had bellowed.

"Exactly," Tom countered evenly, "just in case what."

Tom knew his boss would jump at the chance to publish news that others had overlooked from a lack of hard journalistic work. His boss moved his stare from Tom to the clock, to the window, and then said slowly, "Yeah, go get me something."

Tom had decided early wasn't early enough and set his alarm for 3:30 AM. At 5 AM he was at the Tacoma hospital cafeteria with a cup of coffee in hand. He quizzed a table of nurses about the 102 year old and got enough info for part of a story. Then he described the nurse in Joe's room and one of the nurses said, "You mean Kandee. She's finishing up J wing. She must have gotten delayed because she's usually here with us." Tom bit on that one like a Seattle sea lion after a salmon.

With Joe on J wing and the nurse working late, Tom wanted to check it out. He thanked the nurses and headed for the elevator. The nurse's station in J wing said Kandee was helping J-17 get cleaned up before leaving later today. Tom thanked them and casually walked toward Joe's room. Listening at the door, he heard nothing. A turn of the handle and the door eased open to a semi-dark room. Nobody visible and no sound. He walked in and checked the bathroom. Empty; and so was the bed. He glanced around once more and noticed an envelope on the side table and moved for a quick look. It had his name on it! He glanced at the back, then read the name on the front again and pocketed the envelope. No Joe and no Kandee. He had better leave before he got blamed for something. He casually walked past the nurse's station to the elevator. On a whim, he punched the garage button and zoomed to the bottom. As he stepped out, a car went by with a man and a woman in it heading out into the morning light.

Tom had a nose in him that was a lot bigger than the one on his face. As he glanced around the garage again, he turned to look at the car just leaving. The driver was adjusting the rear view mirror. The journalist nose kicked in. Joe and Kandee? Her car, him driving, adjust mirror? Quick, look again. He took a mental snapshot of the car as it turned and entered the street. He closed his eyes. P.T. Cruiser. Yes, that's what it was. Now his nose went to work again. Into the elevator, up and into the cafeteria again. The group of nurses was just breaking up.

The plump one, who was also rather cute, saw him and said, "Hey, did you find Kandee?"

Tom closed in on them and said, "Yeah, she was down in the garage fixing a flat tire on her Mustang."

Plump and Cute said, "Mustang? She doesn't have a Mustang. She's got a...ah..."

Another nurse chimed in, "Kandee drives a PT Cruiser."

"Oh yeah," added Plump and Cute, "it's a pretty blue."

Tom had scored and began to extricate himself. Sheepishly he muttered, "Oh... I guess I didn't see her then."

But PC wasn't done. "So what does a reporter want with Kandee?"

Tom stopped and turned around to face the question. He looked down and tried to look embarrassed. "Well...uh, I saw her yesterday upstairs while I was interviewing J-17 and...I thought she was cute." Tom looked up and kind of raised both hands in a busted kind of way, and produced a dumb looking smile. The nurses all laughed and giggled and began to dissipate. Except for PC. She took a step closer to Tom and smiled one of the prettiest smiles Tom had seen since his mother had smiled at him, said she loved him, patted his bottom, and pushed him into his first grade classroom on the first day of school a few years back. Tom's nose and brain were quickly overcome by his heart. He was momentarily stunned by the smile and the memory, and opened his mouth, but nothing came out.

PC saw his reaction and spoke first. "Kandee is cute. Where does that leave me?"

Tom couldn't believe it. This girl was plump and cute, and brash in a kind of exciting way; his heart bubbled over. "That leaves you...as my lunch date." He reached for her hand, barely knowing what he was doing. Tom was now lost in her eyes.

PC's charm just kept coming. "All I had was coffee. I'm going home and making breakfast. You look hungry."

"Yes...yes, I am," he said.

# 9

Joe Cornish checked the various security devices he had arranged as he approached and entered his condo. Everything looked good. He checked the spare bedroom; yes, someone was asleep in there. Joe's condo moonlighted as a CIA safe house and had agents crashing there if they needed to disappear for a while. He wasn't sure who was in there just now, but whoever it was deserved their sleep. He silently closed the door.

After doing some light housework he settled into his favorite chair in the den, first opening the window to the lake and turning on some classical music. On his desk to the right was a cigar box, lighter, and an ashtray. To his left was a small refrigerator with clean glasses on top. He grabbed a carton out of the fridge and poured a nice cold orange juice. Ahhh. Then a cigar came to life and out of his briefcase he took the D. Charger file.

The absence of a photo didn't bother Joe Cornish. He had never met any of the undercover operatives that he handled. Agents, yes, but not those operatives who came when a job needed doing and then were reassigned. The first page was facts, the second was history, but the third listed tendencies, and that's what interested Joe Cornish. D. Charger, it seemed, had a tendency to fall in love rather easily, but was capable of stopping his feelings when he had to disappear. He was also chivalrous. He was not afraid to lay his life down for the right situation. He would sooner wreck his car than run over a dog. Also, he tended toward religion or spiritual stuff. Basically he was a romantic. One thousand years ago he would have been a monk; five hundred years ago, a knight; three hundred years ago a patriot, and today? D. Charger was an undercover operative for the FBI, but not really one of their agents. He loaned himself out and was recommended by high level operations officers. Joe Cornish had never met him but enjoyed handling him. He was easy to handle.

The file said D. Charger had never not finished a job to the satisfaction of his superiors, whether they were military, civilian, or badged. The last few pages outlined D. Charger's current instructions, and a schedule for contact between D. Charger and F. Mustang. It seemed that new bad guys were trying to lay foundations in Washington State's Puget Sound area, and D. Charger's current operation was getting a low-profile assessment of their progress.

D. Charger had apparently been recruited right after high school by his best friend's father. The father was a community college professor of science and a CIA man. This professor had taken special care of D. in the years of his training in various parts of the world. D. had learned a lot from the man's wisdom and had stayed clear of the bureaucratic tar pits of the organization. The professor had recently died following a heart attack.

It was a good file. Just enough for a handler to know. Also, Joe Cornish noticed D. Charger's birthplace was right here in the Puget Sound. He hoped that didn't complicate things.

*

Tom and PC had a wonderful morning together. PC's house was on a city side street not far from the hospital. When they got there they opened all the blinds, letting the sun flood in. Since the neighbors were all at work, PC turned on some music louder than normal. Then they stepped into the shower together and let their desires take over. At breakfast, dressed only in towels, they ate heartily and talked excitedly. PC had 4 days off and Tom was working on the story of his life. PC said she wanted nothing more than to be his right hand man all through her long weekend. She grabbed a pad and pencil and his hand. The towels fell off as they climbed into her king-size bed, and spent the rest of the morning playing and planning their next four days.

Tom recounted most of the story about Joe and how he thought Kandee fit in. PC lit up all over again because she loved mysteries. The excitement of Tom's life as a journalist, and his volunteering to let her be a part of it, made her even more amorous. Finally, PC began to get sleepy, having worked all night, and Tom had to check in at work and do some writing. He kissed her on the lips and the nose and said he'd be back in about 6 hours. PC closed her eyes as she tucked the sheets around herself and fell asleep with a smile of luxuriousness that was real. Noon was just arriving as Tom headed for Seattle.

*

Driving and thinking. Joe was at ease doing both. He didn't know if anyone was looking for them, yet his training always considered it probable. Joe was heading for Seattle, but got off at Federal Way and stopped at the Goodwill store. No one would think of looking at Goodwill stores for them.

"Come on, will you help me do some shopping?"

"Of course, I'd love to," Kandee was being very careful and it made Joe sort of chuckle inside. Kandee was in the passenger seat but leaning her head against Joe's shoulder with her hand on his bicep. She had not said much as if afraid she would say something wrong, or that he would leave her if she let go.

They bought a suitcase and enough clothes for them to be comfortable, and an umbrella, just in case. If they could get to Seattle before missing persons and missing car reports on Kandee got out, they would be alright. He knew where they could hide for the night and headed up Highway 99 toward downtown Seattle.

*

Joe Cornish finished his cigar, got up, stretched, and walked to the window. Looking out at the boats in the various marinas, he realized again how much he enjoyed living on the waterfront in the middle of a city.

His job at the FBI, in charge of special or unusual investigations, was left up to him to run. His proven ability to plan and execute covert operations was recognized as a gift.

But something was wrong. He could feel it.

Joe Cornish lived by his sixth sense of being aware of something not right. It had served him well, so he began assessing everything. He was handling D. Charger and five other agents and operatives in the Western Washington area. He looked at his watch. One hour till D. Charger would check in. He would have to wait till then to find out if that was where the trouble was.

Shutting the window and turning off the radio, he listened. The shower off the spare bedroom was being used. He left the den, turned down the hall, and peeked into the bedroom again. This time the bed was empty and the clothes lying around were women's clothes. So he backed out, but right into the barrel of a gun.

"One move and you'll be joining the angel chorus." It was a woman's voice, low and sultry, and he recognized Gretchen. She was one of his agents working undercover as a stripper at one of the bad guy infested nightclubs in the area.

"Is that your finger?"

"Yep, and nothing else." Joe Cornish began to turn, but stopped when he noticed the 'nothing else' part was true.

"What are you doing?"

"Just finding out for sure you were you. I'm back to work at nine and I'll check in on B schedule." She slipped past him toward the shower and he tried not to look.

# 10

Joe realized that he and Kandee had to kill some time. She said she liked Taco Bell, and so after driving through, he spied a car wash and got into line. They ate and watched the car wash do its thing, then pulled across the block and got gas. Heading for Seattle again, she wouldn't let go of him. All she said in that half hour was, "Kent, I love you."

He smiled and kissed her on top of the head. "I know...I'm glad."

Arriving in Seattle, Joe pulled into a Diamond parking lot, four blocks from the Four Seasons Hotel in downtown. He parked as out of the way as he could. He put forty dollars in the slot and they walked hand in hand, with suitcase and umbrella, up to the finest hotel in Seattle. Three hundred dollars bought them a small but very nice corner room on the eighth floor. Joe figured no one would look for them here. Yet a window on both streets would keep him aware of anything unusual.

Kandee had worked all night and had snoozed only slightly on the way up to Seattle. Once in their room they got ready and crawled into bed. The woman who knew how to excite guys and demand love making, had turned into a kitten that purred and only wanted to be held. Kandee fell asleep with the feeling of security beginning to overcome the feeling of vulnerability. She woke up five hours later to find Kent lightly snoring. She got up, went to the bathroom, and then curled up next to him again. This time she felt safe and quickly fell asleep.

Joe had stayed awake a couple of hours, thinking and listening to Kandee sleep. He always worked alone, but it was so nice to have this lovely creature curled up to him needing safety and companionship. He had till between eight and nine o'clock tonight to check in, so the best thing to do when well-hidden was get some sleep. He fell asleep and dreamed of his angel.

*

Joe Cornish moved his thoughts to the delights of having an occasional lover, one not related to any of his work, and off of the sound of Gretchen splashing around in the shower. He readied himself to go out to dinner and went downstairs to checklist his forty-two foot Tiderunner. It had a double bed up front and a relatively large galley and dining area under the pilot house. The back one third was, of course, for sun tanning.

He made sure everything was full: gas, propane, food and water for three days. One peek in the wide drawer under the bed revealed an arsenal of unimagined variety.

Joe Cornish still sensed something amiss, so with his best yachting outfit he donned an ankle holster with a .38, a Beretta behind in a waistband clip, and a shoulder holster with a .357magnum just in case he needed to change the direction of a charging elk.

*

Joe woke up and remembered his situation immediately. Kandee was awake so he said, "Hi."

She looked up, smiled, and said, "Hi," then kissed him.

"Will you go out to dinner with me?" he asked.

She punched him in the ribs. "Of course I will. What did you think I would say?", she said tenderly.

"Oh, I just wanted to hear you say 'I don't ever want to leave your side', or something like that."

Now she began to cry. He could feel her tears on his chest. Not expecting this reaction, he just held her.

An hour later they were dressed in their Goodwill best and waiting downstairs for a taxi.

"Who did you call?" Joe had made a quick call and she was just curious.

"I made a reservation for dinner with my boss. I need to talk to him and I want you to meet him." As they got into the taxi Joe said, "Lake Union, Karl's Boathouse."

*

Joe Cornish finished dressing and accessorizing just as his cell phone rang. A man's voice left a number. It was D. Charger's voice so Joe called the number right back.

"Yes."

"F. Mustang for D. Charger."

"Mustang, I need advice. I want to meet face to face tonight and talk." There was a bit of a pause.

"Okay, I'll be at the dock at Karl's Boathouse in about an hour. We'll dine aboard."

"Good. I'm bringing a date."

"She better be clean and untainted."

"Don't worry, I scrubbed her back myself." Spy lingo.

Joe Cornish ended the call. Something was still wrong and it wasn't with D. Charger. He went to the den and emptied his safe into a large briefcase. He grabbed a handful of cigars and put them in his sports coat pocket. He looked around the den and then realized he didn't hear the shower. Going to the spare bedroom, he saw Gretchen was not only done, but gone. He saw a note on the table beside the bed and read it. "I love you," it said with the "you" underlined. The note from Gretchen was in a code he had taught to all his agents. She was telling him she had to betray him in order to stay undercover. "You" meant Joe personally was the target and the underline said, "Move fast." Because he was always at least three steps ahead of disaster, Joe never cursed. Cursing would mean he had screwed up.

Joe Cornish was on his boat and pulling away from the dock in less than sixty seconds. He headed for the fuel dock at the end of the lake, and had the attendant fill the extra gas tank and add it to his bill. He didn't have to leave the pilot house which was equipped with one quarter inch steel reinforced walls, and bullet proof glass. While there, he called Karl's Boathouse.

"I'll be docking there in fifteen minutes, and dining onboard with two of your guests. I'd like Jeff to be our personal waiter for the evening as I'll need him to pilot us around a bit."

"Very good sir, of course. And the name of your boat, sir?"

"*Cascade Islander A*."

"Ah, Mr. Cornish, we are always pleased when you can visit us."

Joe ended the call, and proceeded up the east side of the lake. As he was docking at Karl's Boathouse, an explosion of medium proportion came from across the lake. Joe finished docking and monitoring the dock boys as they tied him up. After handing them each a twenty, he turned his attention to the other side of the lake and saw smoke billowing out of what had been a rather luxurious condo. His.

As he turned back to the dock, Jeff was standing almost at attention in his white waiter uniform, on the dock next to the entry railing. Jeff was one of Joe's agents.

"Good evening, Sir."

"Good evening, Jeff. Please step on board for a moment." Jeff came aboard and remained standing while Joe Cornish dropped down a few steps, pulled two thousand dollars in cash from his briefcase, and gave it to Jeff. He spoke from the stairs so no telescopic lens could have access to his lips and continued, "Four of your best chicken dinners, a half dozen bottles each of champagne and merlot, plus a nice dessert. Give this to your boss and ask him to say he can't remember the last time I visited, if anyone asks. Oh, Jeff, get your duffle out of your car. We're heading south tonight. Also, a couple will be joining us. They should be walking through your doors shortly."

"Yes, Sir. Very good, Sir. Please excuse me while I tend to your needs." Jeff played the part in case anyone was reading his lips. He was a professional and walked up the dock and into the restaurant without the slightest hint of his anxiety.

Half an hour later, he had the manager taken care of and a rolling cart filled with his duffle and the orders. He stepped into the bar and asked the waiting couple to join him, and together they walked down the dock to the *Cascade Islander A*.

# 11

The taxi was making its way through traffic tolerably, and Joe was debating what to tell Kandee before they arrived at Karl's Boathouse. He opened his mouth to begin, but a muffled explosion drew his head to the left and toward the lake. Through the buildings and other obstructions he saw smoke coming out of a lower unit condo of a big building across the lake. The driver noticed also, and quickly checked his mirrors and surroundings. A few minutes later they entered the drop off parkway of the restaurant. They got out and Joe paid the driver.

Pulling Kandee to the side, he took her by the arms so that she looked at him. "I love you," he said. She broke into a smile. "We're going to talk to my boss; he owes me a lot of money, and then we can disappear for a while. Okay?"

"I love you, Kent."

"I'm so glad. Stay close." She grabbed his arm and held on as they entered the restaurant.

"We're dining aboard this evening, with..."

"Yes, sir, you are expected. Please follow me," they entered the bar to wait.

"I've selected a table by the window for you. There will be a short wait." He walked them over to it. "May I seat you?" Joe nodded and the waiter pulled out Kandee's chair for her. "Your dining room tonight is that white and blue one there." The host pointed out the window and down to the dock. "I will be back for you in no more than ten minutes. My name is Jeff." Jeff offered his hand to Joe and they shook hands. It was sort of an unusual thing for a host or hostess to do, but he looked up and said, "Thanks." Joe recognized the look in Jeff's eyes as he turned to leave.

Joe reached across the table and took Kandee's hands. He forced a smile until Kandee smiled back, and only then did he carefully take in the room they were waiting in. He was on alert.

"Is that your boss's boat?" Kandee asked.

"We'll see. I think so." Joe's eyes went from the boat to the scene across the lake. The smoke was dissipating, and he could see flashing red lights about a mile away, on the move.

"I don't even know what kind of work you do," Kandee caught his attention again.

"I know. Isn't it fun? All I know about you is when I woke up and you came into my room, I recognized you from a dream. Or else I was in heaven, and you were an angel. Kandee, are you an angel?"

"It's a possibility!" They both laughed and fell another notch closer in love.

Joe's smile went from forced to genuine, to fading, as if he were ready for the next explosion. He caught himself and let the genuine smile out again as he looked fully at Kandee. He liked her. He was struggling with what that feeling meant. Part of him wanted to say it was that 'at home' feeling, but another part balked and reminded him that that particular feeling was locked away forever, and not accessible.

Joe caught himself again and went back on alert. Right away he noticed a folded slip of paper on the table to his left. Opening it showed only an arrow pointing down. He replaced the note precisely where he had picked it up, and slowly moved his hand under the table. He swung his eyes back to Kandee's, and then to the entrance of the bar where Jeff had just entered. With his left hand he felt a small, flat, round metal object attached to the underside of the table, and recognized it as a homing device. Jeff was motioning to them, and Joe waved with his right hand, as he pocketed the metal device with his left. It was for his protection in case something happened and they got separated. He was on high alert.

*

Tom spent the afternoon writing up a story about the hundred-and-two year old in the hospital. It was part fiction and part non-fiction, but it was good reading. He printed it out and entered his boss's office after a quick knock. His boss was on the phone as always, but handed Tom a piece of paper anyway. Tom dropped his story on his boss's desk, took the paper, and left. The note read:

*SLUTT – first anniversary. Run it tonight.*

SLUTT stood for South Lake Union Transit Trolley. It was a light rail train powered by electricity and it encircled the lake. This could be fun. Tom grabbed his things and headed for Tacoma as fast as he could.

PC had gotten Tom's call and was ready for a night out when he arrived at her house. On the way back to Seattle, they tried to speculate where Joe and Kandee were. PC got on her cell phone and tried three or four friends. Tom had found that the number Joe had called in the hospital was an unlisted Seattle number. Why had Joe and Kandee hit it off so well and so fast? Did they disappear together on purpose? Tom's cell rang. He handed it to PC to answer.

"Tom's phone. I'm his secretary, how can I help you?"

Pause…then slowly, "…Tom doesn't have a secretary…," the voice said.

"Well… then I'm his well-endowed lover and he's busy at the moment."

Tom grabbed the phone. "Tom."

"Hey man, they found the PT Cruiser you were looking for. It's parked in a Diamond a few blocks down from the Four Seasons in Seattle. There was enough money in the slot for three days, so the cops just left it there."

Okay, Tom thought, one question answered. "Thanks man, my treat next time." Tom kept his contact at the Seattle Police Department happy. "Bingo, they're in Seattle, downtown. I bet they are hiding in plain sight in the Four Seasons." PC clapped her hands together like a little girl. "We'll swing by and look at it, then catch the SLUTT and check it out, and then stop on the lake somewhere to have dinner."

They found the Diamond parking lot, and Kandee's car, and hopped out for a look. The hood was cold and nothing in the car gave any clues as to Joe and Kandee's whereabouts. Tom's journalistic nose was running. "Let's stay at the Four Seasons tonight, what do you say?"

"Yes, yes, and yes. That's where serious gentlemen take their lovers to propose, you know." PC was just being PC.

"You know, you've got to be more careful with the men you hang out with; you might find yourself married someday soon."

"Tom, I've been waiting for you all my life," PC said a bit more seriously.

Then Tom said, "Today's been so much fun and we've moved so fast, I can't remember if you told me your name."

"Patricia Chandler Bronkowski," she said. He looked at her, but only quickly, as he was pulling into the Four Seasons. "Please call me PC."

The valet was at the car door but Tom looked at her again and said, "You're kidding!"

"Nope! Why, what's wrong with PC?"

"Nothing. It's just the nickname I gave you when I first saw you with the other nurses in the cafeteria..."

"Okay. 'Fess up then. What did PC mean this morning? And remember I can tell if you're lying." The valet knocked softly on the door window. Tom held his hand up but kept looking at PC. This is it, he told himself.

Slowly he spoke, "PC means 'Plump and Cute'." They kept staring at each other.

Then PC said, "You don't really love me, do you?" PC was being PC again.

"I'm going to make you marry me." Tom was dead serious. They both just stared at each other until the valet knocked again.

Tom got out and handed the valet a twenty dollar bill. "Don't park it. I'm going to check in and be right back." Pointing to PC, he said, "Will you keep your eye on her? She'll cause trouble if you let her out of the car."

"Yes, sir. I'll guard her with my life."

It took ten minutes, but he was able to bill the room to the Seattle Times. It was the Four Seasons' anniversary month so they didn't ask questions. He returned to the car. As they were pulling out of the hotel, Tom's phone rang again.

"Fire and Aid cars responding to Lake Union. I assume you're already there and writing the story."

"Yes, sir. That I am," Tom hung up because he knew that was all his boss would say.

He headed uptown toward Lake Union. Parking behind Burger King, they walked to the main SLUTT terminal. There was a haze over the lake, coming from the west, same as the breeze. One of the SLUTT trollies was just coming to a stop and unloading. They boarded and sat on the lake side. Within minutes they could see the red lights of the fire and aid equipment and residue of what looked like a small explosion in one of the condos. Tom looked for the name of the building. The Bluff at Lake Union. He grabbed his phone and speed dialed his office. "Jimmy! Anyone of significance living at The Bluff at Lake Union?" Tom was playing a hunch. He loved to let his journalistic nose go and follow it.

"I'll call you back," Jimmy was a second cousin of the boss at the Seattle Times and made himself useful by helping reporters in any way he could. Otherwise, his job was emptying the waste baskets.

As the transit trolley continued around the lake, Tom and PC chatted about the appearance of the trolley, the scenery, etc., putting together the SLUTT story. The trolley moved along the water until it crossed the ship canal at the Fremont Bridge. Then it headed east along the north side of Lake Union, past Gas Works Park, up to the Mountlake Bridge, then crossed back over. It went by the University of Washington Arboretum, under I-5, and along the east side of Lake Union, on the opposite side of the lake from the explosion.

Tom decided they'd better get out and hit a nice restaurant or else they'd end up back at Burger King. They got off at the next stop and walked towards Kay's Lake Pantry. They were seated inside with a view of the shoreline docks down the lake. Each table had a pair of binoculars on the window sill, and PC began to take in the sights. "How does an open-face salmon burger with mushrooms, grilled onions and a side of potato salad sound?" Tom was hungry.

"What?" PC was busy looking through the binoculars.

"What kind of wine do you like?" Tom thought this question might get her attention.

"Tom!" PC was now staring at something through the binoculars.

"Red, white, pink, yellow, champagne? Want me to just order for us?"

"It's Kandee!" PC blurted out.

Tom grabbed the wine list. "Candy...wine? What do you...?" Then he looked up at PC, and then in the direction she was looking. "You mean Kandee?"

PC kicked him under the table. "Of course I mean Kandee. What else would I mean?"

Tom's nose started twitching. Could it possibly be? "Well, give me a look; show me where," PC pointed and Tom looked. Sure enough, a couple of docks away, were Joe and Kandee walking down the dock with a waiter toward a medium-sized blue and white boat.

# 12

Jeff led the way, pushing the cart. Joe and Kandee followed arm in arm. Joe was on high alert because he didn't know what was going on. As they came even with the front of the Tiderunner, Joe Cornish started the engine. Joe practically jumped out of his skin. It only took half a second to realize that what sounded like an explosion was indeed the engine starting. Joe took a couple of deep breaths to counteract the adrenaline rush. Reaching the entry railing, Joe helped Jeff with the cart. When all were aboard, the dock boys undid the lines and Joe Cornish moved out into the lake. "Jeff! Come up here and take over." Jeff stepped up into the pilot house. "Take us down toward the Locks." Then Joe Cornish moved everyone inside to safety.

He held out his hand and said, "Ford Mustang."

Joe did the same and said, "Dodge Charger." Then he looked at Kandee and smiled. She was holding onto his arm, "And this is Kandee."

"My pleasure, Kandee. My name is Joe Cornish." Joe Cornish was a gentleman most of the time. He turned to D. Charger and asked, "What would you like me to call you?"

"Joe. Just call me Joe."

"Thank you, Joe. I must say we may presently be under attack."

Smack!! A bullet hit the pilothouse glass but left only a mark. "Boss! Someone's aiming at me," Jeff's cool was gone.

Joe Cornish spoke graciously to Joe and Kandee, "Sit down please." Then yelling to Jeff, "Stay on this course and speed."

Smack!! Another bullet from the other side hit just below the glass.

"That probably will be all," Joe Cornish announced, and no more bullets hit. After five minutes, nerves were loosening and Jeff yelled, "What happened back there? Why just two shots and nothing else?"

Joe Cornish responded thoughtfully, "Apparently I only rate two assassins and the bad guys are not the only ones with sharp shooters." The meaning of this took a moment to sink in, but Joe Cornish continued, "the only way to scare the enemy when he is trying to scare you, is to be ready for him with a bigger stick."

Joe looked around the lake at the other boats, buildings, etc. Boy, this guy really plans ahead, he said to himself.

"Boss, we're a sitting duck out here," Jeff wanted to keep talking. If bullets didn't work, maybe a heat seeking missile was aimed at them.

Joe Cornish again calmly responded, "Yes, and we've survived quite nicely. Would you like to suggest a different plan or should I take your place and you prepare our dinner?"

Jeff shifted to waiter mode and said, "Very good, Sir. Dinner will be served in fifteen minutes."

Joe and Kandee went up to the pilot house with Joe Cornish, and were captured by the view. A busy city surrounding a beautiful lake. They were heading west down the waterway now, which narrowed and led to the Locks, which led to Puget Sound. Shilshole Bay to be exact. The boat was moving along at moderate speed as cool as if this had all been planned out.

After a while, Joe said what he was thinking. "I like working for you."

"Good, because I can use both of you quite well." Seriously, Joe Cornish continued, "We're alive because I spend more time planning ahead than doing anything else." Then, "And I do believe it's time for dinner."

Jeff heard that, and was just finishing pouring wine into glasses made with heavy bottoms so as to not fall over on a boat. "Dinner is served in the dining room, sir." Then he took over piloting again.

Joe, Kandee, and Joe Cornish ate and drank as the boat waited in line, entered the Locks, and waited again as the water levels changed. As they slowly moved through and out into the bay, their conversation was light, and Kandee just blended in.

*

Tom put the binoculars down and then picked them up again. "Here, put these in your purse."

"What?" PC said.

Tom now spoke into his phone. "I need a taxi for Tom at Kay's Lake Pantry, now. Thanks." Then looking at PC he said, "Come on." Tom left a twenty on the table and escorted PC toward the door. At the desk he apologized and said he got called into work. Outside, a taxi was already waiting, so they got in.

"Mr. Hansen?" asked the driver.

"Yes, thank you, driver. Will you drop us at our car at the SLUTT terminal?"

"Of course." The driver checked in and was on his way. It didn't take long.

In their car they headed for the Aurora Avenue Bridge, then got off at the Fremont exit. Then down along the water. "See if we can see the blue and white boat." They finally saw it lined up at the locks. Tom pulled into the parking lot and they got out and walked down to the locks' observation spot.

"There's a snack bar inside. Get us a couple of hot dogs and coffee. Hand me those binoculars first." Tom was excited and was being bossy. PC liked it. As she headed for the snack bar, Tom yelled over his shoulder as he brought the binoculars to his eyes. "You better come back!"

"I'm not going to come back," PC yelled back.

Tom scanned the boats in the locks. The blue and white one was in the rear. As it came into view, he suddenly smelled coffee. "Oh, you're a life saver."

PC smiled and said, "No, actually I resemble a strawberry. And I taste better dunked in chocolate."

Tom made a mental note. After a bite of hot dog and a sip of coffee, Tom focused on the boat. "...Can only see the driver... no one else. There must be bird poop on the window. I can barely recognize..." Pause... "Wait, I think it's a rock chip... Unless... Hey, I think they've been shot at." As the boat went on past, Tom read the name: *Cascade Islander A*. Tom stopped. –C-I-A-? He took out his phone. "Jimmy, what did you...?"

"Yes, Joe Cornish, FBI: Special Investigations Office, lives in the Bluff at Lake Union."

"Jimmy, find out if he owns a boat called *Cascade Islander A*, and also if there is a boat with the same name, but with a B or C."

"Gotcha."

Tom put down the binoculars and they sat on a bench to eat. "What are Joe and Kandee doing on a boat owned by an FBI guy, heading for Puget Sound, piloted by a restaurant waiter, and why?" They talked the subject over for a while, then suddenly the phone rang.

"There's a *Cascade Islander A/B* at Shilshole and Tom, it's big!"

Bingo, score another one for the nose. "Thanks man, see what else you can find out about Cornish."

"Okay."

"Come on, we got to go again." Tom's journalistic nose was having a field day.

"Where this time? I thought you were going to propose?" PC quipped.

"Shilshole Marina. I think that's where they're going." They ran for the car and followed the ship canal to Shilshole Bay. After entering the marina and parking, Tom got out and stood on the hood of the car with the binoculars. He eyed the area where the big boats were and then got back into the car.

"We've got to move down some more." A quarter of a mile farther, they pulled off again. This time there was a marine supply store with a restaurant and wide deck on the second floor. "Come on, we're hungry again."

"Oh good, I was just going to mention that." They asked to be seated on the deck by the railing, and through the binoculars Tom saw the name he was looking for on a yacht that was at least seventy-five feet long: *Cascade Islander A/B*.

A pretty little waitress came and PC ordered a cobb salad figuring they could share. Tom looked at her, "I guess we have dinner and wait."

*

During dinner on the boat, Joe changed to more serious matters. "I just wanted to make sure you knew the whole story and that I'm okay now, but I'd like to request some time off."

Joe Cornish smiled, "Of course I knew. Who do you think sent you all those flowers? Your relatives and friends?"

Joe thought for a second, "Oh, I didn't even think about it." He hadn't even wondered.

Then Joe Cornish spoke more seriously, "I think we're done down in Tacoma anyway. It's a good time to pull you, with the wreck and all." Joe Cornish was hinting at something, but Joe wanted to speak his mind.

"Sir...I'd like to bail out when possible, because I found someone whom I want to spend time with." Kandee perked up and stared at "her Kent".

"I hear you, Joe," Joe Cornish responded, "but we are neck deep in an operation and I'm glad you and Kandee are here."

A curious and concerned look came over Joe's face. "What are we in the middle of?"

Joe Cornish filled in some of the blank spots Joe was not aware of, even though his work as a courier driver had to do with surveillance of the new bad guys who were establishing a toehold in the Puget Sound area. He outlined the undercover work being done and the results. He also explained that the two attacks on his life tonight were orchestrated by these people. "They are out of San Diego. When someone tries to scare you, you scare them back, but with a bigger stick." Joe Cornish lived by certain rules.

"What are your plans?" Joe asked, but wasn't sure he really wanted to know.

"I'm planning Alaska right now. You and Kandee might fit nicely there, but first we head south."

South? Joe thought, "South? How far?"

Joe Cornish answered, "San Diego."

"San Diego? With what?"

"A bigger boat."

# 13

The salad was delicious, but the two kept looking at each other as if waiting for the thrill of their day together to wear off and disappear. "I think I'm genuinely in love with you, Patricia Chandler Bronkowski..." Tom started, but PC jumped in before he could finish.

"I *know* I'm genuinely in love with you, Tom, and I don't even know your last name. And what's with this 'I think' stuff? Don't use my full name ever again. And sit up straight, you're slouching. You like bossy women, right?" PC was sending that beautiful smile. Tom's heart was melting. He realized that the thrill was around to stay and he wanted to finalize this moment. He opened his mouth but the waitress interrupted, bringing back Tom's credit card and receipt.

"Have a nice evening," she said with routine pleasantness.

"Thank you." Tom looked through the binoculars again. Now there was activity on board the *Cascade Islander A/B*. Cargo was being loaded and people were stirring about. Suddenly, the *Cascade Islander A* came into view and docked just across from its sister ship. Tom stood and adjusted the binoculars. He could see Joe and Kandee on the back of the boat. "There they are. Joe and Kandee, and that must be the FBI guy."

PC was finishing her ice cream and asked, "Where to now, boss?"

"Come on, we've got to move again." He lingered for a moment longer and watched as the pilot/waiter of the smaller boat disembarked and headed up the dock. Then Tom grabbed PC's hand and quickly left the restaurant. Returning to their car, they parked at the main entrance. The dock gate appeared unguarded as they strolled towards it, trying to time their approach with the pilot/waiter coming from the other direction.

Tom began to quietly talk fast as if he was excited to show his girl his boat. PC caught on and went along with it. As the pilot/waiter opened the gate on his way out, Tom and PC caught the gate and went in, brushing by in their own little world.

A moment later PC whispered, "Where did you learn how to do that?" She was proud of him.

"I'm a journalist, my dear. We are born with many such gifts that only come out when needed."

"Wow. What's our next step then?"

"I don't know."

"I like this. This is fun."

*

Joe and Kandee went to the back of the *Cascade Islander A*, and sat down. Joe Cornish ended his phone call and seemed to be satisfied that they were all safe. He went up and talked with Jeff as he docked the boat and killed the engine. Jeff immediately jumped to the dock and headed toward the entrance gate.

"Let's move to the house," Joe Cornish made a grand gesture toward the entry railing. Joe and Kandee casually followed their host around the dock area to the yacht and walked up the gangway to the main deck. With wide eyes, they were about to take the tour, when they heard yelling.

"Joe!! Kandee!!" Turning around they saw a couple being detained by two of Joe Cornish's men at the head of the dock.

"Joe! It's Tom from the Times! It's good to see you again!"

On the yacht, Kandee grabbed Joe's arm and said, "Kent! That's PC from the hospital."

"Who?" Joe didn't recognize the female.

"One of the nurses; we're friends," Kandee lit up and waved. PC decided to get into the act, "Hi, Kandee!" And she waved back.

Joe Cornish put a hand on Joe's shoulder and said, "Explain, please."

Joe tried. "Tom is a journalist from the Seattle Times. He tried to interview me at the hospital, but I didn't say much. He somehow found out about the three word call I gave you as soon as I came to. He's smart. I like him."

"What's he doing here?" Joe Cornish asked, although not really irritably.

"I talked to him yesterday afternoon. And the girl is a nurse friend of Kandee's. I don't have a clue how or why they're here."

"Okay, be happy to see them and invite them aboard."

"What? Why? He's a reporter."

"If it would be easier to make an appointment for a visit with them at a later date, go ahead. We are leaving presently."

"We can't take them with us!?"

"Why not? They might be useful." Joe Cornish spoke softly into Joe's ear with instructions.

Joe then took Kandee by the hand and ran down to the dock and greeted Tom and PC. The men noticed a nod from Joe Cornish and allowed things to unfold.

"Tom, I'm surprised to see you. Kandee and I are going for a cruise. Please join us." Kandee and PC hugged and then smiled at their men, then whispered back and forth.

"Kandee, tell me you're alright," PC whispered.

"I've never been better. Kent asked me to marry him but we had to visit with his boss first. Are you alright?"

"Yeah, I'm really good." She hugged Kandee again and at the same time kicked Tom in the leg, for not proposing yet.

"Ouch!"

"I've got a promise but no proposal yet," PC said this a little louder.

Tom attempted an explanation, "Joe, this is PC. I'm going to marry her, but she doesn't believe me."

"Well, Kandee and I are going to be married, too." Joe then got a quizzical look on his face. "Tom, how long have you known PC?"

"Ah... since early this morning. Time flies, you know. How about you and Kandee?"

"You remember. It was just before I woke up."

They all just looked at each other and laughed and smiled. As they walked toward the boat, their questions and answers were genuinely as friends. Kandee was glad to see someone she knew. Tom's nose was hitting home runs, and Joe felt good around Tom.

At the entry railing, they stopped and Joe spoke as Joe Cornish was standing just on board. "Joe Cornish, this is Tom from the Seattle Times and his fiancée, PC. Tom and PC, this is my boss, Joe Cornish."

Tom jumped in first, sticking out his hand, he said, "It's a pleasure, sir. You're FBI aren't you?"

"I am indeed. You've done your homework, Tom. We are about to sail, but I wonder if you and PC would join Joe, Kandee, and me for a quick refreshment and just a moment of your time?"

"It's our pleasure, sir." The group boarded and went into the living room. As they sat around a large coffee table, Joe Cornish whispered to the female attendant. Almost immediately she brought glasses and served Merlot.

"Tom," Joe Cornish started. "I have a...request to make of you. Even though your presence was not anticipated, I would like to offer you and PC a week's cruise with us right now...as sort of an early wedding present. Does that interest you at all?"

PC cocked and got ready to kick, but Tom didn't hesitate. "Yes, sir, uh...it does. However, my journalistic nose is twitching like hell... could I ask a question?"

Joe Cornish smiled and held up his hand, "Yes, of course. But first," raising his glass, "let me welcome you both on board my new home."

They all took a sip and Tom interjected, "The smoke on the lake was from your old home, was it not?"

Joe Cornish rose, lifted his glass towards Tom as if to say 'touché', and said, "Tom, I believe I like you already. If you'll allow me a moment to instruct my crew…by the way, is there anything in your car you might need for this coming week?"

Tom and PC looked at each other, "My briefcase and laptop; I need to lock the car."

Joe Cornish had his phone out. "Jeff, on your way back could you retrieve a briefcase and laptop from…," he looked at Tom and repeated Tom's info, "the back seat of a gray Honda Pilot and lock it up? We will leave as soon as you arrive." Closing his phone, he addressed the four again, "Please relax and I will return shortly with your things, and with answers a-plenty."

Tom held his glass up and said, "Thank you, sir."

PC jumped up and plopped down next to Kandee. "Isn't this fun?"

Kandee smiled a secure and comfortable smile and agreed. She had never felt this feeling of safety and fun without being in complete control of everything. It was wonderful, and at the same time she was giddy about having PC around.

Joe got up and went to the side window. Tom followed. "Joe are you FBI?" Tom's voice was low but inquiring.

"No, but I do undercover 'ops' for them sometimes," Joe was being truthful.

"Is this more than just a pleasure cruise?"

"I think so… I'm sensing our skipper's going to be very revealing here shortly… How in the hell did you find me? I can't for the life of me figure out how you arrived on this dock at the same time as us." The two men chatted a bit.

After a moment, Joe Cornish returned. "Friends, I want to take you into my den where we can talk privately." Joe Cornish gave Tom his things and led them down a hall and into a snug but very nicely appointed room on the left. "Please make yourselves comfortable. The bathroom is down the hall farther on the right."

PC and Kandee glanced at each other, and arm in arm they headed down the hall.

When seated, Joe Cornish began. "Tom, Joe and Kandee are joining me on an operation which my bosses don't know anything about. However, it is within the scope of my capacity as agent in charge of Special Investigations, so my bosses tend to leave me alone, unless something bad happens of course, and then their job is to skewer me." Tom and Joe's eyes met. But Joe Cornish continued, "What I need is some public awareness of this operation that is truthful or even slightly slanted towards my viewpoint. If you are agreeable with that, I'd like to continue with a short outline of our destination and plans."

"Yes, sir, PC and I need to make a few calls to cover our absence, but yes, sir, please continue."

Joe Cornish stood and walked around a bit as he continued. "You may or may not know that the Puget Sound area is being infested with a bad influence that builds itself with intimidation and fear. My office's undercover investigations of this past year have touched some 'private parts,' if you will, and have resulted in two attempts on my life in the last few hours. I have a sign which hangs on the wall of my virtual office which reads, 'If someone scares you, scare them back with a bigger stick.'" Joe Cornish paused and sipped his wine. "That is what this cruise is about."

As the men talked for another half hour, the female attendant caught the girls coming back and offered to show them the boat.

Presently, Joe Cornish stood and announced, "Gentlemen, let's break and return at ten. Please relax and refresh and I'll see you in the dining room then." He left as Joe and Tom stared at each other. Tom felt like he was at the ball park, bat in hand, and ready to rip the cover off the ball on the first swing. Joe had been in the army, and felt a bit trapped on a boat.

Tom broke the silence, "I guessed right. My nose told me you were a bigger story when I first interviewed you."

"Yeah... well... Right now I'm a bit spooked on this boat."

"Oh, quite a nice play on words. I might use that in my column."

The girls knocked softly and entered, "Come on, we'll show you guys our rooms." There they made their calls and relaxed.

# 14

Gretchen worked hard her first hour wanting to please her bosses and her customers, too. At break she grabbed a short robe, her phone, cigarettes and lighter, and sat out in the beer garden. The youngest of the three brothers who operated the club sat down with her and lit her cigarette.

"You like to work hard," he said.

She looked at him and replied, "I like the work and do what I get paid for."

Gretchen had a little half-smile that tended to suck the air out of men's lungs. "How's business?" she asked, changing the subject from her to him.

"Business is fine. We're just running into some opposition and it's not sitting so well." The little brother was fidgeting.

"You don't look like you're panicking. In fact, I've never seen you scared." The youngest brother was a talker and she could draw it out of him. "How come?"

"Because I think way ahead, not like 'you know who'. They think they're smarter because they're older, but they're not." He paused and then said, "Gretchen, when I think ahead, you are in my plans, you know that, right?"

"Of course I know that. And I kind of like that." She reached for his hand and asked, "Where were all the guys coming back from when I got here?"

He played with her fingers and hardly knew what he was saying. "Oh, somebody screwed up a hit and got clipped themselves.

Stupid northwest wanna-be bad guys. We got some real muscle coming up in a couple of days. The guy you gave me got away..."

"What!?" Gretchen was relieved to hear it but acted and sounded scared.

"No, it's okay baby. Your info was good, and you know I keep my eye on you. No worries."

"Thank you, Jack. You know I wouldn't work here if it wasn't for you being around."

"You and me, baby. I'll be back." He got up and left. It was ten-thirty. Gretchen saw the chance to use her phone and took it.

*

Jeff's errand was to buy some boatwear and beachwear for Joe and Kandee. Not knowing sizes, he bought many different sizes.

At ten, Joe Cornish greeted everyone and laid out all the purchases.

"Please help yourselves, all four of you, and Janae will handle laundry service. We are presently heading north and west out the strait, and when we hit the ocean we'll turn south. The weather might get a little nasty, but we have a small pool that we can draw the roof over. Also, a theatre at the end of the hall. Breakfast though, will be at six AM, because I want us to get into the habit in the next few days of getting up early."

"Kandee and I are used to working the night shift, so no problem with us," PC was perky.

"Fine. Well, let me unfold my plan just a bit more so you won't feel overwhelmed. Our destination is San Diego, the heart of the beast, if you will. We are going to anchor somewhere outside the port and send in all four of you for a tactical strike." Joe Cornish eyed everyone, just to take their temperature so far.

Kandee's voice was small and serious, "That sounds dangerous."

"Indeed it is, my dear, but only for those who don't know what is coming. For those who know, it will be similar to a walk in the park." Joe Cornish was just warming up. "However, just in case I am wrong, and these next few days are your last, I would like to offer a gift, if it is to your liking." Joe Cornish liked being ahead of things and staying ahead. Joe and Tom exchanged glances again and Tom said,

"Sir, your gifts so far are extravagant, with a touch of danger included."

"Yes, Tom, and this one is quite the same. It is sometimes said this gift is equal parts extravagance and danger." Now they all looked at each other, speechless.

"I am primarily a peace officer, have been for quite some time. I am also the captain of this ship, and offer to you the services I am authorized to render if asked." Silence.

PC's mind happened to be on the same wave length, so she started screaming. Then she jumped up and started bouncing. She took Tom's hands and pulled him to his feet. She yelled, "Ask, Tom, ask him." Then she kicked him in the leg. "Ask!!" Tom opened his mouth desperately, but nothing came out. Joe and Kandee looked at each other, and as their eyes met they understood his meaning at the same time. As they embraced, Joe Cornish's phone rang, and he quickly went to his den and answered it.

Gretchen spoke softly but quickly. "Thank God you're still alive. I'm fine. They're mad as hell and bringing in some muscle from down south day after tomorrow. I'm switching to schedule C."

"We're on our way to visit their family down south. Brace yourself for this weekend." He and Gretchen kept their conversations brief for the sake of security.

Joe Cornish then made a short call to San Diego and returned to his guests. They were huddled together and all talking at the same time. He came in, sat down and waited. After a few moments they calmed down and Joe stated, "You have the ability to marry us."

"Indeed I do. Also, please let me pass on some good news. Our survival of the attempts on my life earlier today has opened a hornet's nest in Seattle, and as we speak, they are sending additional muscle up from San Diego to Seattle. I appreciate it when the bad guys cooperate and make the plans we already have in motion easier."

Tom spoke, "You have had this planned from beginning to end?" Tom suddenly realized he needed his note pad on him at all times if he was going to accurately report what was happening.

"Yes, and... seeing it's almost eleven o'clock and 6AM comes next, I suggest we all retire for the night."

PC's turn. "We want to stay up a little bit longer."

Then Kandee. "Sir, we'd like to get married before we go to bed." The girls were pretty good at quick planning themselves.

Joe Cornish looked up with surprise on his face, but it turned into a broad smile. "You folks delight me. Any time my plans can be improved on, I am impressed."

A half hour later they were married. PC and Kandee each had a ring on another finger, so the ring ceremony was Joe and Tom taking the ring off one finger and putting it on the appropriate one. The fit wasn't perfect but that could be dealt with. On PC's insistence, the papers were signed by all before bed, as well.

Joe Cornish ended with a Seafarer's benediction. "May Almighty God, who created the seemingly unending abundance of this ocean we are traveling on, do so also in each of your lives." They all said 'Amen' together without really realizing they would. They laughed, kissed, and then hugged Joe Cornish, and headed off to bed.

At 5:30AM, Joe Cornish was pacing outside around the deck. A middle of the night call from San Diego had him thinking.

Joe had slept well after their wedding night bliss. Kandee had not slept much, but kept luxuriating in the safety and comfort of Joe's love and care for her. She had laid still beside him so she wouldn't wake him.

Tom and PC enjoyed themselves for the second time in 24 hours. Tom consequently fell asleep quickly from the exhaustion of a long, fruitful day. PC dozed and woke early to the sunlight and ocean breeze coming through the screened porthole beside the bed. She cuddled closer to Tom to make sure he was warm enough.

The sound and smells of the ocean, together with the smell of a wonderful breakfast, woke everyone up. All four were showered, dressed and in the dining room shortly before 6AM.

Joe Cornish arrived from outside at exactly 6AM; smiled and greeted each one individually. As he sat down, Janae finished serving coffee to everyone. Holding up his coffee cup, Joe Cornish offered, "This promises to be a wonder-filled day with addendums to our plans." Everyone else raised their cups and sipped.

"Were there overnight developments?" Tom wanted the whole story. Joe Cornish caught Joe's eye as he addressed Tom's question.

"Yes, there were. It seems, even as we are traveling south, the enemy's journey north will make our operation more effective, and at the same time less dangerous. However, let's right now journey to the galley, and breakfast cafeteria-style." Janae waved them in and hugged the girls as they entered. There were many selections offered and each took what they wanted, then got settled back into the dining room.

Joe offered first, "That news is bad for Seattle, but sort of leaves a vacuum for us to fill down south."

"But a vacuum is never good in nature unless it's planned for," Tom countered.

Joe continued, "Exactly, and with the Cornish plan already in place, we just have to adapt or even expand it to exploit the vacuum to our advantage."

PC didn't want to be left out, "Do we have to kill people?"

Tom playfully kicked her, then continued, "So we could apply an even bigger stick than planned, in other words, a bigger scare, and still leave room to not hurt anyone." He was thinking this through as he was talking.

Joe again, "Yes, not killing is the plan, but hurting their stuff is an operation where sometimes people get hurt, if they choose to interfere. It depends how quickly we act and how quickly they respond."

"Okay, but is the vacuum filled permanently or just temporarily? In other words, do we know what the effect of our operation will be? What will complete success look like?" Tom looked at Joe Cornish.

Joe Cornish was delighted at the interest and involvement he was hearing and seeing. "Part of planning is considering how big of a bite to take and how long it will take to chew. Sometimes eating fast is good if you concentrate on what you're doing. Remember the invasion of Iraq. The bravest commanders drove their tanks through the enemy's lines and made it all the way to downtown Baghdad before pulling back to their supply lines. It uncovered the lack of resolve of the enemy. Anything could have happened to them that far into enemy territory, including being gassed. But they took that chance and won. The more cautious commanders concentrated on holding the territory they had won, and both strategies worked well together. I plan to do both also, and we," he gestured inclusively with his arm, "are going to be the brave commanders. I have elements on the ground to take over when we leave and the dust settles. Tom, I can guarantee success will be sweet, but the scope of it can only be measured upon completion."

"If we are the brave ones, do you have plans for us that go far beyond what we should be able to accomplish?" Tom asked.

"This is what I've been contemplating all morning. How can we give the biggest scare and safely retreat?"

Joe then asked, "The operation the enemy runs, is it mainly drugs?"

Joe Cornish: "Yes, but they seem to buy into night clubs and such and then squeeze the other owners out. Drugs are their product, but night clubs and topless bars are their sales and advertising arms. Plenty of customers. The other thing is, our undercover gal in Seattle says she is seeing more younger girls. They are usually hooked on drugs and are a bigger and bigger draw for private parties and expensive private dates. Drugs are always a part of that scene."

"Ugh!" PC spoke what she thought. Kandee sat with her mouth closed and her hands over her mouth. Tears began running and Joe saw PC staring at Kandee. He turned and quickly wrapped his arms around her.

"You're with me now, Kandee. You are my wife."

PC jumped in, "Crying helps. You go for it, girl." Kandee began sobbing and Joe just held her.

After a minute, Joe Cornish said, "Why don't we move outside to the deck chairs?" Janae began cleaning up as soon as they all got up.

The sun, the ocean, and the breeze calmed things. They took deck chairs, formed a circle, and sat down.

Joe Cornish began, "Kandee, this is uncomfortable for you."

Kandee took a few deep breaths. "When I was fifteen, my first boyfriend was twenty-five. He taught me how to make love in order to make a man happy. Then he wanted me to make all his friends and acquaintances happy, and I just barely got out of that whole thing. I saw girls that were younger than me getting trained, too, and I wanted to take them all with me, but I couldn't." Then tears began again but she continued, "I got away, and made it on my own. Someone told me Jesus loved me, but I couldn't figure out how to find him. I grew up never knowing what having someone actually love me was until..." She looked up at Joe and a smile broke out. He hugged her tighter and came close to tears himself.

After some silence, Joe Cornish said, "Kandee, you have provided me with some direction. This is excellent." He was thinking and talking at the same time now. "I have access to a church man and his wife who have developed a strategy to rescue girls like you have described. He claims to have safe houses up and down the west coast. He told me if I find young drug addict/ prostitutes that ask for help, he would place them in safe houses and provide for their rehabilitation. I have never actually done anything in that regard. If we find any young girls and they want to be rescued, are you interested in helping?"

"Yes, sir, I'd be very interested," Kandee suddenly felt worthwhile.

"Me, too!" PC added, "Me, too!"

"Alright ladies and gentlemen, I have some additional planning to do and some calls to make, but another piece of the puzzle is in order. We are planning to dock in about two days, up the coast from San Diego Harbor, at a deep water dock belonging to an exclusive housing community. Our boat will fit in with others there and we have a house reserved from which we will run our operation. We are going to cause mechanical and electrical difficulties in various night clubs, all in a matter of minutes. We will leave a message for the bad guys that what we did was simple and worse could be done if our demands are not met. They will probably ignore the threat since the problems will be easily fixed. Then we bring the second round, and they will not know what hit them. In this confusion, we may be able to rescue some girls. Now think on these things, but please have some fun and let's meet for lunch at noon." Joe Cornish rose and headed for his den.

Joe said, "I think we'll go to our room and read, or something."

Tom said, "Yeah, or something. Us, too. See you in the pool in an hour."

# 15

Jeff had done alright in the swim suit department. Kandee was less full figured than PC, but both were incredibly cute. The sunshine, the pool, and the gentle rocking of the ocean were soothing, and enjoying them brought the group up to lunch time. Jeff greeted them and then said, "Mr. Cornish had to visit Monterey, but he'll be back for dinner at 6PM. Janae has lunch ready."

He continued, "Joe, he left this list for you. Will you go over these things with the others so you are all comfortable with these procedures?" Jeff handed Joe the list. Then he looked toward Janae and then went back to his other duties. Janae served lunch.

The afternoon was spent lounging and talking about operational protocol, like silent signals, what to do if this, that, or the other thing happens, and a phone number to memorize. Joe also took them into the den and showed them how to operate a handgun.

At 5:30 while in the deck chairs, Joe grabbed the binoculars and saw a boat heading right for them. He excused himself and went to find Jeff. He stopped at the den to get the gun. Jeff was there, busy.

"Jeff, there is a boat heading for us."

"Yeah, I know. Joe's on it and plans are changing. Bring the others into the den here, will you, Joe? I've got to leave when that boat gets here."

"Jeff, tell me what's happening."

"Joe will tell you. All I know is my part starts now."

Joe found the gun, loaded it, and stuck it in his swim trunks under his shirt. He went back out onto the deck and saw the boat only a hundred yards off. Grabbing Kandee's hand he said, "Come on everyone, follow me."

When they got to the den, wine had been set out and they helped themselves. They heard the boat come up alongside, and Tom and Joe looked out of the porthole. Joe Cornish was stepping onto the yacht, and Jeff and Janae were leaving, each with a suitcase. Joe Cornish could be heard in the hallway, and as soon as he entered the den he began to talk.

"Well, aren't we the lucky ones," Joe handed him a glass of wine. "Thank you, Joe! Well, I remembered hearing the reverend say that Monterey was a bad area, so I found the most expensive night club and visited it just after it opened at one o'clock. I arranged for a private party at the club for my 'son,' Jeff, since it's his twenty-first birthday. I ordered three of the youngest females available. I paid double and told them Jeff needed privacy if he was to enjoy the evening and want to come back with his friends. This will be a trial run. When Jeff gets them alone he will tell them they can be rescued tonight, if they want to be, and never have to be around these people again. Meanwhile, Janae will sabotage their HVAC unit with a timer that will activate tomorrow when all the ones in San Diego do. Then she'll be ready to drive Jeff, and whomever else comes, to the boat and out to us. Kandee! You might have some girls to care for tonight. Okay?" Joe Cornish was visibly excited.

"Yes, sir, that's very okay."

Joe took the gun out from his swim trunks and laid it on the desk…he felt the boat picking up speed and was about to ask why when Tom jumped in.

"Why were you carrying that gun, Joe?" Joe was about to answer Tom when Joe Cornish jumped in.

"When Joe saw things happening that he didn't know were part of the plan, he reacted according to his training. A reaction that I like and approve of very much. If someone unknown to him had accompanied me off the boat and onto this yacht, he would have hidden and listened at the door until he was satisfied I was not being coerced. When I send you four out tomorrow, you will be in good hands." This time PC stayed seated and Kandee jumped up and gave Joe Cornish a kiss on the cheek and then sat down on Joe's lap. Joe tried once more.

"Sir, you said 'tomorrow.' You've shortened our arrival time by one day, what's up?"

"The bad guys are moving faster, so we're going to, also. Let's have dinner, I'm hungry." Joe Cornish caught Joe's eye for a second. "I'm going to freshen up; I'll see everyone at dinner in a few minutes."

Joe recognized the phrase "I'm hungry," as something's not right. He herded the other three out the door as he scooped up the gun and put it in the band of his trunks again. The first thing he did on entering the dining room was pick up the binoculars and scan all around the boat for any sign of traffic. His training kicked up another notch and he said "I'll be right back." Joe climbed to the pilot house and recognized the pilot as one of Joe's men. "Anything on radar?" he asked.

"No sir."

He thought 'food.' He went back to the dining room and peeked into the kitchen. Same chef. He asked the chef, "Are you hungry?"

Knowing the lingo, the chef said, "No sir, I'm not hungry," slowly looking around to see if something was boiling over or burning.

On entering the dining area again Joe saw through the doorway to the back of the boat. Joe Cornish was helping one of his men in scuba gear into the water. The boat slowed to a stop, faster than normal.

By this time Tom's nose was twitching. "What's going on, Joe?"

"Tom, pull a couple of life vests out of the side chest there and try them on the girls. Don't take them off till I tell you."

"Joe!!" Tom sensed something big was up.

"You can swim, can't you, Tom?" Joe was evasive.

"Joe!?" Tom began again. Joe motioned two fingers to his lips and patted down with his other hand. Tom remembered the meaning from earlier in the day. Stay calm and quiet. Tom gently corralled Kandee as she started to follow Joe.

"Joe asked me to fit you two with life vests as a practice drill and for us to keep calm and quiet. Kandee, he used the motions we learned this morning. Can you help me keep PC from becoming anxious?"

"Sure, yeah," Kandee moved to PC as Tom got the life vests. Kandee made the calm and quiet motions for PC to see and whispered, "It's a drill, get it?" PC stood still as Tom helped them put on their vests. The three sat down as Joe scanned the horizon again. After a few minutes, Joe joined Joe Cornish at the back of the boat and helped the diver get out of the water. Tom could see a serious discussion ensuing and then the men turned and headed their way.

Joe Cornish spoke, "Thank you for your patience. We've a small problem and will have it fixed soon. Just stay calm and please be seated."

Both Joes, then, searched the whole ship and didn't stop till they found what they were looking for. Having found it, they came back and set it on the dining room table. It was a small plastic box with six AA batteries taken out.

"Well then," Joe Cornish said loudly, "Let's eat dinner." The guys helped the girls out of their life vests and put them away. Dinner was served to them this time, and it was delicious.

During dinner, Joe Cornish was truthful and thorough in the tale he told. The pilot had felt something odd in the handling of the ship ever since they left Seattle. In calmer waters he had decided it wasn't his imagination and had told his boss about it, as soon as he had returned from Monterey. A diver went overboard and found an explosive package secured to the bottom of the boat. It had a sound sensitive detonator. Basically it was waiting for a loud noise of a certain decibel to detonate. The diver detached it from the boat and let it drop into the ocean. Then upon searching the ship, they found a battery operated noise making device that was waiting for an electronic signal of a phone call on a certain frequency to make it work.

"They've tried to kill me three times now. I would at least like to steal three of their girls."

"Yes! Let's do it!" Kandee was excited.

Joe Cornish drew a deep breath and let it out again slowly. No one understood that he did it because he could. Once again, he was still alive.

"Tomorrow, Tom and PC will be the tip of the sword. My men will sabotage the electrical boxes at six locations. They will malfunction at 5AM so nobody will notice until noon or after. The food in their fridges and freezers will go bad, it will be sweltering when they open up. A pin prick, but at six locations at the same time--it will get their attention. Meanwhile, Tom and PC will stroll into the district attorney's office and hand her an airtight case against the head of the organization. He will be arrested by the time we get back to Seattle."

Tom blinked and asked, "What do we do after we leave the DA's office?"

"Go for a walk in the park or go shopping. Just be back here by noon. That's when we leave."

"Sir…I'm curious…when…How is an air tight case against a serious bad guy just sitting around at the FBI until a reporter happens to get it to the DA?"

"It's not FBI."

"What makes the evidence so airtight?"

"An eye witness that is dying to testify."

"Testifying eye witnesses tend to die before they testify."

"Yes. This one already did," Joe Cornish was enjoying Tom's inquisitiveness.

Tom thought for a moment. "You've made a tape recording."

"Yes. A video tape in the presence of a State of California Supreme Court Judge."

Tom thought about this, then said, "Wait, why would a Supreme Court Judge allow a case like this to sit?"

"The judge was one of the people the witness saw breaking the law."

Tom was stunned but his nose kept him going. "How in the world did you get a judge to hear an indictment of himself?"

"He was the last one on the witness's list."

"Wait. The FBI would have arrested him on the spot."

"Yeah or soon thereafter," Joe Cornish answered each question truthfully, and at the same time tried to lead Tom.

"What do you mean by "not FBI"?" Tom was doubling back now.

"Well,...let me see if I can give you a brief run-down on this investigation since as a reporter you are undercover, in a covert operation."

"A certain United States law enforcement agency was investigating our 'Mr. Serious Bad Guy,' and his activities in other countries. When they led to this country, they gave the info they had to the FBI and it landed in my lap as Agent in Charge of Special Investigations. Since I had worked for this other agency in the past, I kept them in the loop. They appreciated that and let me know what they were finding out, outside our country. When we found this witness, not only did he know a lot of inside stuff, but he was dying of cancer and wanted to come clean before he died. We had him tell all in a video with the judge present. The judge knew he was a dead duck when the witness included him with the accused at the end. So we made a deal with him. The judge swore on the video that it was true, and confessed his part and spilled what he knew. For that we gave him one year to get his stuff in order. He retired, traveled with his family, and after the year was up, he disappeared before we could arrest him. His body was found in San Francisco Bay," Joe Cornish paused.

"You know, I think I'll just quit asking any more questions, since this is getting more complicated, not more simple," Tom had gotten an ear full.

"Well then, Jeff and Janae are going to start us off tonight. They'll catch up with us probably between 2 and 3AM, so I for one am going to enjoy the sunset and get to bed early. Kandee, I may need your help in the middle of the night."

"Please come and get me whenever they come. My mind is still used to being awake through the night."

*

Shortly after 2AM a boat pulled up to the yacht. Kandee heard it and got dressed. As she headed to the back of the yacht, she saw Jeff and Janae and a young girl get aboard. Kandee moved closer and eyed the girl. The girl saw Kandee and took a step toward her. Kandee opened her arms and reached out for the girl without even thinking. The girl jumped into Kandee's arms and they hugged.

Joe Cornish helped Jeff and Janae transfer their gear into the dining area. He said softly, "Welcome, young lady. You are safe here," and then to Jeff and Janae, "Tell us what happened."

Janae began, "Sir, my part was successful. I put the device in the electrical panel and set the timer for tomorrow morning."

Jeff continued, "When the three girls were ushered into my room and we were alone, I simply explained who I was and what I had planned, and that it could include them if they wanted. At first the girls were shocked and worried that it was a trick, but asked me to explain again. When I did, including that Janae was outside waiting for us in a car, they put their heads together and talked amongst themselves. Sir, this is Janis by the way. She and the girls came up with a plan of their own. They decided that Janis would come with me and see if it was a trap, or what. If it was a real rescue, they wanted to up the ante." Jeff hesitated as Joe entered and sat down.

"Please continue," Joe Cornish was interested to hear.

Jeff continued, "Me and a friend of mine will pay for another party tonight, with three girls each. Then we'll just do the same thing, only with all the girls."

Joe opened his mouth, but Janis spoke up. "We all want to leave. We just didn't know if anyone was concerned about us enough to come and get us." Kandee hugged her again.

"Who did you have in mind as your friend?" Joe Cornish asked.

Jeff looked at Joe. "Yes." Joe Cornish said, "Good thinking. I love it. So, Joe, Jeff, and Janae will leave in the morning and handle the Monterey operation, while we dock and run the San Diego operation. We'll rendezvous at a point in the ocean and head north as all hell breaks loose down here."

Jeff turned more serious. "Sir, there's one tough spot." Both Joes raised their eyebrows. "The girls will only come back with us if Janis shows up back at the club again. Either we just drop her off a few blocks from the club and she walks in and says she went home with me, or I could bring her back and say I took her with me, and pay extra. Then I could line up tonight with them for Joe and me. Either way there's no guarantee Janis will not get punished, or worse, disappear. So I'm thinking I should go in with her and offer to pay any penalty."

Joe Cornish addressed Janis, "Do you trust the other two girls to not rat you out for more favor with their bosses?"

Janis took a moment to understand the question. "Yes, but if I don't show up, they won't trust Jeff and will spill."

"Okay. Jeff, you better go with and explain with money. If they don't buy, we'll come and get you, but it might take a day or two."

"Yeah, I think it will work."

"Okay, let's get some sleep. We'll talk more at breakfast and then send you on your way. Janis, Kandee will stay in your room with you. Please give her all your personal information, and that of any of the other girls who might want to be rescued. Sleep well, everyone."

Kandee took Janis and headed for a spare cabin. Jeff and Janae went to get cleaned up and sleep. Joe followed his boss to the den, where they talked through all the plans and made some calls. Then bed. As morning was breaking all were safe and rested.

At breakfast, plans were finalized. Jeff, Janae, Janis and Joe boarded the small boat and headed to Monterey again. Kandee felt like her life was leaving, but PC hugged her and told her the best was yet to come.

# 16

That afternoon, the yacht docked just up the coast from San Diego. Leaving two men on the yacht, the rest disembarked and moved up through the upscale community and into a big house. Joe Cornish's men readied their gear and left for their assignments. They'd be back around dawn.

The sabotage operation went well. The phone and electrical lines were set with small explosive devices timed to all go off at 5AM that morning. Joe Cornish had told his men to do anything else that was doable as long as they got away with it cleanly. They spot welded the dumpsters and their rollers so they wouldn't open or roll. There were also retractable gates that were closed when the club was closed. They simply added an expensive padlock to each gate that was bullet proof and hard to saw through and squirted super glue into the key hole. When all was accomplished they returned to the house. Dawn was just breaking; they had some breakfast and then went down to the dock, boarded the yacht, and got some sleep.

Tom and PC were in the house, just waking up, excited to get going. At breakfast they talked more with Joe Cornish and he gave them a briefcase with the evidence in it for the DA.

"The District Attorney won't be there till after nine o'clock. Only give it directly to her. Tell her, 'Joe Cornish regrets not being able to say, hi, in person but sends his best wishes from his family to yours; and good luck with the case.' If you use those exact words she won't ask you any questions, and you can be on your way."

"Sir, while we're there, can I ask some questions?"

Joe Cornish looked Tom straight in the eye and said, "You don't want anybody to remember you. When I let you write your story, don't say you two were the couriers. Remember, things could go wrong, so leave time to deal with trouble if it comes." With that they were on their way. Kandee helped Joe Cornish and the staff get packed up and moved back onto the yacht.

Tom and PC walked out to the highway and caught the bus. It brought them to the transit center and then they boarded the one to downtown. The DA's office was on the bus line. They arrived at 9:15, were able to walk in and take care of business without any trouble. On leaving the building Tom steered PC up the sidewalk. A couple of blocks up was the newspaper building and they went in.

"I'd like to speak with Colin Jones," Tom answered the receptionist when she offered help. She made a call.

"Please wait. He's on his way down, or up actually. He's in the archives," she gestured to some seats.

"Who is Colin Jones?" PC wanted in.

"A reporter friend from school. I want to reestablish our friendship, so we can pass scoops to each other."

Ten minutes later, Colin Jones came up extending his hand. "Tom, what a delight. Do I owe you or you owe me?"

"Colin Jones, this is my wife, PC. PC, Colin is one of the few friends I have in the newspaper business," Tom half smiled.

"Well, I'll take that as a compliment. Hi, PC. You're gorgeous. Tom, how long have you two been married?" Colin was wondering what was coming next.

"Ah… about 40 hours," he looked at PC for confirmation. She nodded.

"Oh, wow. And I wasn't invited?"

"Colin, where can we talk?" Tom changed the subject.

"Follow me," Colin swung around, nodding with his head. They entered a conference room across the lobby and sat down.

"Give me something juicy, Tom."

"You'll read my story in next week's Seattle Times, but your story started a few hours ago at 6 different nightclubs here in San Diego. It will continue with the DA indicting the owner of the nightclubs," Tom was giving just enough to hook Colin.

Colin was jotting notes, then looked up. "Yeah, keep going."

"I'm done, and you didn't get this from me. I'll send you inside stuff from Seattle, and you send me inside stuff from San Diego."

"Tom, give me a name or an address."

"I honestly don't know either, but clubs usually open at or around one in the afternoon don't they? Check out a few at opening."

"Is it an FBI raid?"

"If you can find the answer to that question, it will really juice up the story. I'm going to work it on my end in Seattle. See, the same guy who owns the clubs down here owns a club in Seattle. Probably other places, too. I honestly don't know."

"How did you find out about this? Tom, hang on!"

Tom and PC were up and leaving. "You wouldn't believe me if I told you, but I'll put some of it in my story. Gotta go."

"Tom! Tell me you're going to keep in touch," Colin wanted more.

"I'm going to keep in touch," Tom yelled over his shoulder. He and PC left the building hand in hand. They caught a cab, which brought them to the bus terminal again. PC plopped down next to the window on the bus, with Tom next to her.

"Was Colin part of the plan?"

"He is part of my plan. This story is going to explode and I need eyes down here."

"Aren't we going shopping?"

"It's 10:30. We better head home," he quickly moved his legs away from her.

PC then asked, "You think the DA had us followed?"

Tom didn't answer right away. He looked around the bus carefully; then whispered, "I think it's the bus driver. Wasn't he our cab driver, too?"

PC broke out laughing and kicked him in the leg anyway. "You know someday you're going to believe that I love you."

"Yeah, maybe. Someday," he leaned toward her and noticed the ocean out the window. This was even better than a dream.

*

Joe Cornish had been talking and making phone calls all morning. The operation seemed to be going well. He had his San Diego men hidden across from each club with video cameras, in order to capture the whole episode. He looked at his watch and saw it was 11AM. The day shifts at the clubs could be opening any time. Joe was thinking Tom and PC were probably shopping and he was just wishing they would come back sooner, when he looked out and saw them coming down the sidewalk toward the house.

When they walked in the door, he asked, "You're both okay?"

"Yep. Everything went smoothly."

"Okay, let's get on board and we'll talk there."

They walked together down through the beautiful homes with sculptured lawns and yards, to the dock and onto the yacht. Joe Cornish had left instructions that the boat be untied and ready to move as soon as he stepped on board. His instructions were carried out smoothly and to the second. Champagne was served in the dining area as the boat cast off and headed out into the ocean in a northwesterly direction. "Come, let's enjoy the view," Joe Cornish grabbed the binoculars and they all headed to the back of the boat and sat on the cushioned seats along the sides. Joe Cornish stared through the binoculars at the fading dock and landscape. He didn't see anyone looking their way, or anything out of the ordinary.

"Well, I think I shall first propose a toast to success and then tell me what happened," they all lifted their glasses and drank.

"Well, she was skeptical at first, but when we gave her the briefcase with your greeting and your regrets, she changed her tone. We got out of there as fast as we could and then took in some sights. We came back early in case there was any trouble at this end."

"Did your contact at the newspaper believe you?" Joe Cornish inquired. Tom's whole face dropped along with his jaw. Then he looked over at Joe Cornish who was looking through the binoculars again.

"You had someone follow us," it was a statement, not a question.

"No, I did not. I was going to suggest you contact someone down here if you knew anyone. Then I decided to just see what you would do. It was a hunch. Guessed right, huh?"

"You sure did. A friend from school works at the paper down here," Tom began to think Joe Cornish must have an IQ close to genius level.

"Did he believe you?"

"Oh yeah. I bet he's out there right now snooping around."

"Good, very good. The more publicity the better. Be sure to work on your story when you have time. We'll get it out when we get back to Seattle," then his phone rang.

Joe Cornish answered his phone, listened, and a smile began to break out on his face. It was a smile of satisfaction. He looked at his watch as he listened and then ended the call. "We are videotaping each club as the people come to work. They are going nuts," he said. He explained to Tom, PC, and Kandee what had been done. Their plans were having the desired effect.

# 17

Quite a ways north of San Diego, at Monterey Bay, Jeff, Janae, Joe, and six girls were stuffed into an SUV. Jeff was driving and Joe was riding shotgun. Jeff was trying not to speed but it was mighty hard. They had made a clean getaway and wanted to get far away as fast as possible.

Jeff and Janis had smooth-talked their way back into the good graces of her boss. Jeff's money and plans for another night along with a friend did the trick. He left Janis only after he made her boss promise that he could have her again tonight and said he'd be back around midnight.

About 11:45 Janae had entered the club first and sat at the bar. Only a minute went by before a nicely dressed but half-drunk man sat beside her and said, "May I buy you a drink?"

Janae turned, smiled, and said, "I'd like that."

"My name is Chet. I'll bet your name is...Samantha."

"Call me Sammy. That's what my mom calls me."

"You're kidding! Boy, I'm on tonight. Bartender, a white wine for Sammy and my usual.

"I like white wine best."

"I knew it. Let's get a table," he took her hand.

As they moved through the crowd, Janae noticed a couple who were arguing and pulled Chet to a table near them. As they sat down and were served, Janae saw Jeff and Joe coming in. They disappeared into the private area, and Janae began her diversion by becoming agitated.

"Chet, that woman keeps looking at me. I think she's talking about me!" Janae acted upset.

"No, no, no, no, Sammy, relax. We're going to have fun tonight. Let's get you another glass of wine."

Janae ignored Chet and turned to the couple that was arguing. "Why are you looking at me?!" Janae was yelling, "You think there's something wrong with me, or what?!"

The couple at the table were already mad at each other. They both turned and eyed Janae.

"What's your problem anyway?!" Janae was even louder.

"Hey, shut up. I'm not looking at you. There's nothing to look at!"

"Hey now, that's no way to talk!" Chet felt obligated to defend his date.

Janae stood up and took a step toward the woman. "Look, I don't know what your problem is, but I'm going to solve it for you!" Janae shouted.

The woman bounced up and lunged at Janae with both hands and pushed her into Chet who was struggling to get out of his chair. Janae let out a scream and man-handled Chet around to her front and pushed him into the lady as hard as she could.

"Hey, buddy, you can't do that to my girl," the lady's husband got up. The ensuing fight encompassed three more tables and became quite a ruckus.

Janae slipped out as soon and as fast as she could to get the car started.

Jeff and Joe were in adjoining rooms and the girls had been brought to them. When they heard the sound of the brawl they came out into the hall with three girls each. Jeff pulled the fire alarm on the wall. After that they simply moved with the panicking crowd out the doors and got in with Janae who was parked across the street. Bam. They were gone just like that.

When they reached the dock, they slowly walked toward the boat they had arrived in as if they were coming back from a wonderfully relaxing night out. They casually got into the boat and motored out of the marina. Joe and Janae got the girls comfortable and Jeff slowly picked up speed until he was going full throttle in a southwesterly direction. Southwest from Monterey Bay, and Northwest from San Diego, the two boats would rendezvous out in the ocean.

# 18

Things were heating up in Seattle. Everything except the weather, which was overcast and somewhat drizzly. The sun? Well, everyone knew it was up there, just beyond the clouds.

Gretchen was being lovey-dovey, giving Jack almost all he wanted. There was a sudden loud knock on the door.

"Jack! Now!"

Jack got up, splashed water on his face and looked at himself in the mirror. He quickly got dressed. His mind was frantic, but he consoled himself with the fact that he had disagreed with his brothers and had told them so. He was not to blame for the fiasco in Seattle a few days ago. He would stand up for himself. He left without even acknowledging Gretchen. Business came first.

Jack hurried down the hall to the inner office. It was used exclusively as a guest office. Beautiful in every way and kept that way for use when the bosses came north to visit. The body guard outside the door stopped him, searched him, knocked lightly on the door, and opened it, letting Jack in. Jack straightened and willed a confident look on his face as he took in the room. Two more body guards, his two brothers, the big boss and his right hand man. Jack was waved over to where his brothers were sitting.

"Sir, we're glad you could come," the middle brother offered.

"Shut up. Sit down, all of you."

After regaining control of the room, the right hand man poured coffee for the boss and then sat down.

Now the boss began, "You guys have pissed on me. I hate Seattle; it's too gray and wet. But I let you boys talk me into making a foothold here. You said you would take care of everything and not give me any problems." His voice grew louder with every sentence, "Now I'm up here in the clouds and rain. What the hell is going on?" He paused and calmed himself by taking a drink of coffee. "At least the coffee's good."

"Sir, we've analyzed the situation and what went wrong and –"

"Shut up!" The right hand man yelled. Jack's older brothers looked at each other in terror.

The boss continued, "Your dad did a good job of running things for me. Even in the last years of his life, from prison. What are you guys, adopted?"

Jack wanted to smile, but didn't dare. His brothers glanced at him and then attended the boss again. Almost nobody but the three of them knew. Jack was adopted, but he would press the point that he was the smart one.

"Sir, we've analyzed what went wrong and have changed things. We can show you all that we've done," the middle brother said.

"You learn from your mistakes?"

"Yes, sir," the two older brothers said in unison. Jack kept his mouth shut. There was a pause while the boss was thinking.

"You think I learned from my mistakes. You think I became boss of this organization by making mistakes?" Jack noticed the body guards lifting their guns out of their holsters and holding them at arm's length, pointing at the floor. The boss reached his hand over toward his right hand man while saying, "I don't make mistakes!" His right hand man handed him a gun. "And when I do, I take care of it immediately," he reached out his hand again. "I didn't come up here to this "fog bank" to analyze the situation," the right hand man fumbled in his pocket and then handed the boss a silencer. "I came to fix the problem, boys, not make it worse." He calmly attached the silencer.

The oldest brother now spoke, "My boss, tell us from your wisdom what to do and we will accomplish it for you to the letter."

"Thank you for that. You are finally making my job easier. Just do this one thing for me."

"Yes, sir," the older brother said.

"Yes, sir," the middle brother said. Jack kept silent.

The boss paused as he finished preparing the gun and in an even voice said, "Hold very still; I haven't done this in a while."

The brothers' eyes widened and the middle one reached for his older brother's arm.

"Sir..." the older brother tried respectfully.

"Shut up and sit still!" The right hand man shouted and pulled his gun also.

The boss aimed and shot the older brother in the chest. He plopped back against the couch. Then addressing the middle brother, "You think you can handle things without mistakes?"

"I know I can, sir."

"Wrong answer," the boss shot the middle brother in the chest also. He fell back against his dead brother. The boss then looked at the third brother, Jack. He thought for a moment and then handed the gun back to the right hand man who pulled out his handkerchief and cleaned the prints off the gun. The boss looked at the youngest son, and spoke once more. "Son, you think you can handle the operation here in Seattle or do I need to shut the whole damn thing down?"

Jack glanced from the boss to the right hand man and back again. Apparently they wanted him to speak. He stood up even though he had soiled himself. "I'd like to try, but I'll need your direction and wisdom."

The boss pursed his lips and relaxed them, then pursed them again as if trying to make a decision. He looked up at his right hand man and then back at Jack. "Son, I'm going to let you try, but I don't ever want to come up here again. If I have to, it won't be to kill you. I'll keep you alive. You'll just wish you were dead," he paused and looked Jack up and down as if considering changing his mind. He stood and addressed his right hand man, "Explain things to him." Then he left the room with one body guard in front of him and one behind him.

The right hand man walked across to the closet and got two black zippered body bags. He brought them over and laid them out on the floor. He emptied the pockets of both brothers and put everything in a briefcase, except the ring of keys. He tossed those to Jack.

"Get the shoulders, I'll get the feet." When the bags were zipped up the right hand man sat at the desk and explained how to run the business, including what to do with the money and how to account for it. He handed Jack a card. "This is my name and number. Don't bug me. Just call if you don't know what to do. Now get to work."

Jack didn't say anything, he just left. In the hall, four men passed him heading for the office. Jack headed for his room. Opening the door, Gretchen wasn't there. Then he heard the shower and went into the bathroom. He undressed and cleaned himself and then entered the shower. He took Gretchen and held on for dear life as the water washed, and washed, and washed over them. It was a while before he quit shaking.

# 19

After about two hours Jeff's GPS said they had arrived at the rendezvous coordinates. Dawn was just breaking and the only thing on the horizon was a tsunami buoy, a hundred yards away. Jeff motored for that and tied the bow rope to it. He shut down the engine and surveyed the horizon again. Joe, Janae, and the girls began to wake up as the sound of the engine quit. Joe immediately got up to check on Jeff and saw him searching the area.

"A-Okay?" Joe asked.

"Yep. We're here, now we just wait. Let's grab some breakfast and then I'll get some sleep."

Janae fixed breakfast with Janis helping while Joe carefully quizzed the other girls about their information. Jeff stood guard and ate. Then he handed the binoculars over to Joe.

"Get some sleep, Jeff. I'll wake you if I see anything on the horizon."

"Okay. Thanks. It will probably take a while for the yacht to get here," Jeff stepped down into the sleeping area, and knelt down at the foot of the bed. He pulled out the big drawer underneath, this boat being identical to the one in Seattle, took out a .45 and loaded it. Then he closed the drawer, visited the bathroom, and put ear plugs in. He kicked off his shoes, put the gun under his pillow, and quickly fell asleep.

Janae and the girls were finishing breakfast and they began to get giddy. The sun was rapidly becoming warm, the ocean was calm, and the breeze--perfect. Joe figured the girls would be scared to death, but they were acting like they were at Disneyland, looking around and wanting to do everything. Joe began cleaning the galley as Janae glanced at him and scooted the girls to the back of the boat. A minute later she came back.

"They want to go swimming," Janae said. She felt like she was trying to corral a handful of newborn kittens.

"Swimming?!" Janis came up to Janae and Joe as he exclaimed the word. He lowered his voice and spoke to Janis, "This is the ocean. There are sharks out there."

"We've dealt with sharks before. Every night. You tease so they want more. Then if they hurt you, you stop and yell, 'No, that hurts. If you hurt me I'll tell my boss.' Then you start teasing them again and soon they learn the rules and enjoy their time. We teach the sharks that they can be wild and still be careful not to hurt us."

Joe just looked at Janae. His mouth opened but nothing came out. Janae looked around and then said, "Wait a minute." She went back out into the sunshine and searched the compartment under the cushioned seats. She began pulling out life vests and the girls started putting them on.

"Janae!" Joe managed to get out.

"Hold on. Here, come help me." Janae was fumbling with a bunch of floats with wire mesh holding them all together.

"What is this?" Joe began helping.

"I think it's a floating pool with a wire mesh bottom and sides. I just remembered seeing it in here before but never got it out to look at, much less use it." One of the floats had a rope tied to it so they tied the rope to the boat. Then they started throwing floats over board and the mesh went with it. Janis had a life vest on already and jumped into the middle of the floats and started to push them into a wide circle. The connecting mesh was their protection.

Before Joe could object, the five twelve, thirteen, and fourteen year olds, jumped in wearing life vests and underwear.

Janae was holding in her excitement by holding her hand over her mouth. But her eyes couldn't hold back; they began flowing at the sight of these girls having so much fun. Joe frantically looked around for shark fins, imagining one in each little wave. After a few minutes, when nothing bad happened, he remembered he was on surface watch and climbed up to the pilot house. He saw Janae watching over her kittens and settled down to concentrate on his job. Donning sun glasses, he scanned the whole area. It was hot and bright.

After a while he noticed the girls climbing back into the boat. Janae found towels and sunblock. She sat them down, applied sunblock and brought them water bottles. Joe couldn't help but smile. Any passing boat would think he and Janae had six kids, all girls, and...

Joe stopped short. He remembered suddenly that he was married. He and Kandee could have a brood just like this in a few short years. His heart had just now changed. He felt a fatherly, protective aspect to him that he hadn't known before. He shook his head. It felt like he had just found something he had been looking for, for a long time. He went about his business again but somehow it was more important now.

Janae had the girls go to the bathroom one at a time, then sat down to talk. The sun was bright so they hooded their heads and shoulders with the towels.

"Janis, you girls have been on drugs, right?"

"Yeah, it will start wearing off pretty soon, but we're used to it. They would forget to drug us and feed us sometimes. Some aspirin and lots of water will help."

"What about sleep?"

"No! Nightmares! Keep us up and our minds active."

Oh boy, Janae thought. How do you keep these girls interested in something on a forty-two foot boat in the middle of the ocean?

"Oh!" Janae said it out loud.

Joe glanced down. Janae's got another bright idea. What now?

"Listen up everybody! We just escaped from a bunch of bad guys. You all have been part of their operation. Let's plan a secret spy operation to attack the bad guys and send them to jail where they belong."

"Yeah, yeah, yeah, yeah," they all erupted.

The girls spent the next few hours planning, coming up with silly ideas and laughing their heads off, planning some more and forming some serious ideas. Janae kept them interested by bouncing off their ideas, playing the devil's advocate, and telling some stories about real things she had been involved in. They kept going right up to noon when they all realized they were hungry.

Jeff woke up hungry about the same time, and checked in with Joe in the pilot house, glancing at Janae first. Janae just smiled.

Jeff greeted Joe, "I was going to say it's about time for the stuff to hit the fans, but the fans are all off along with the rest of the electrical service both in the San Diego and Monterey clubs."

"Yeah, if nothing went wrong, that is," Joe didn't like waiting especially if something was delayed. He never knew when to act, or sit still and wait a while longer. "We might be waiting for nothing. And we've only got enough gas to go straight back to land."

"Even if things went perfect we still got a couple hours to wait."

"Yeah, I guess so."

"Go ahead, take a break and have some lunch. And bring me something, too, will ya?"

"Sure," Joe handed Jeff the binoculars, then headed for the bathroom. When he got back, the girls were converging on the galley.

This time Joe got a bright idea, "hey, let's all play restaurant."

"Okay, I want to play!" all said at the same time.

"I need three volunteers to help me in the kitchen, and Janae and the other three will be old ladies stopping at a sandwich shop with an ocean view," Joe tried to sound playful and it was coming easier than he expected.

"Okay, you three come and help me in the kitchen. You other three help Janae find a seat in the restaurant. She's a ninety year old great-grandmother, you know," screams of laughter erupted as suddenly Janae needed help walking and seeing.

Joe got one girl busy making sandwiches with him and sent the others out to take orders.

"We have any kind of sandwich they can imagine," under his breath he said to the girl helping him, "As long as it's tuna fish. Check the refrigerator and get all the goodies out."

"Yes, sir, Pop!" Joe felt like he was working with a daughter.

After a couple of minutes he said, "Here you go, princess. Take this upstairs to Jeff. He's starving."

"Aye aye, Captain, I'll be right back," tuna fish with lettuce, mayo, and a pickle on the side headed up to Jeff.

Then the waitresses returned with their orders. "One Spanish sandwich on rye, with a sword on the side of the plate," giggling all around.

"One giant squid sandwich, no seaweed," more giggles.

"One lamb sandwich with goat cheese and plenty of wool."

"And one special of the day, as long as it is not tuna fish."

Soon they were all served as many tuna sandwiches and pickles as they could eat. They were wondering what to do next, when Jeff yelled, "Ho, Joe! I got something."

Joe bounded upstairs. "It's too early…"

Just then Jeff's phone rang. "Are you hungry?" The voice on the phone asked.

"No, sir, we just ate. How about you?"

"Not at all, we're all fat and happy. I think I see you. Can you see me?"

"I believe so," Jeff said looking through the binoculars.

"Okay, be there soon."

Janae heard Jeff's side of the phone call so yelled from downstairs, "We are all going to freshen up. If you two got to go, or get something out of the bedroom, you've got five seconds."

Jeff and Joe looked at each other. "We're good."

An hour later the yacht had come to a halt. Joe had untied the line holding them to the buoy and Jeff maneuvered up to the port side of the yacht. A rope ladder was plopped down to the boat and one by one the girls stepped on board. Kandee and PC greeted each one with a hug and seated them in the dining room. As Joe and Jeff came aboard, two of Joe Cornish's men boarded the smaller boat and they were over the horizon by the time the yacht was under way.

"Well, good to see everyone. We have iced tea," Joe Cornish motioned with his arm to the person in the galley. "We've all gone through a lot in the past few days. I'd like to just sit and have introductions, and hear from each one, if you want to, about your part in this operation. Also, what your dreams are for the future, or whatever else is on your mind." Tom had pad and pencil out and was busy taking notes.

The whirlwind of conversation took them into the late afternoon. The farther north they went the choppier the ocean got, but the larger boat compensated and all were comfortable and safe for now.

# 20

"We've been attacked!" was the message over the phone.

"What?!!" The right hand man had his phone up to his ear.

"All six clubs here in San Diego and the one in Monterey Bay had electrical failure and other damage done, all at the same time, early this morning." The man on the phone from San Diego was trying to sound competent, not nervous.

"Keep talking," the right hand man was in Seattle at a Seattle Mariners versus San Diego Padres baseball game. He was sitting next to the big boss, who was trying to enjoy the game. San Diego was losing.

"Everything is fixable, but the food in the freezers and refrigerators all had to be thrown out and repairs kept us from opening on time."

"What!!? You can't not open on time!" A loud whisper.

"It couldn't be helped. The security gates were all padlocked with expensive locks filled with glue or something. It took an hour just to get past the gates and then, when we realized the power was off, we went slow in case of booby traps. Sir, we did not want to make matters worse so we used caution."

"Okay, okay. You keep me posted!" The right hand man was about to hang up.

"One more thing, Sir."

"What!"

"A card in an envelope was left at each location. They all said, 'Leave Seattle now.'" Now the right hand man was livid.

"Dammit, I want results on this by tomorrow morning," the right hand man hung up and contemplated what to say to the big boss. Finally he leaned over and said, "We should head out and fly home tonight."

"What? What are you talking about?"

"Some things at home need our attention."

"What things?!" The big boss's question was just met with a stare. Then the boss realized this was not the place to talk. "Damn Padres," was all he could say. The right hand man spoke to the bodyguard next to him, "Possible imminent danger. Get us to the car now." The guard spoke into his lapel mic and six others jumped into action. As the big boss and his entourage left Safeco Field it began to rain.

*

Gretchen was a big girl as girls go, but Jack was only medium sized for a guy. As they were embracing in the shower, she noticed they were about the same height. Also, Jack was sobbing. This was an open door for her to ingratiate herself further and she took it.

"Tell me what happened, babe," her voice was soothing. Jack sobbed harder. She reached back and turned off the water and reached for a towel. She helped him step out and said softly, "I'm here with you and nothing will drive me away. I'm yours. I want you in my arms anytime, day or night." Talking usually gets a talker to start talking.

"He killed my brothers...point blank...right next to me," he was trying to stop sobbing but was having trouble. "He wanted to kill me, too...but instead he put me in charge. Gretchen, you've got to help me...I can't do this alone, not with his wrath hanging over me."

"It's okay. I'll help you, don't worry," she was soothing.

"Gretchen, we've got to work harder than we've ever worked before. And I don't want you dancing anymore. You'll work right along with me, making decisions and seeing that they're carried out."

"It will work. I always thought you could run this place by yourself. If you want me with you, I'm yours," they finished drying off and then he took her to bed and finished what he had started earlier. Ten minutes later he was getting dressed and ready to take on the world.

*

In the bulletproof limo, the big boss simply said, "Explain!" Within five minutes his head and neck were red and bulging.

"I'm going to find out who is behind this and cut his heart out and eat it in front of his wife and kids." He could hardly talk coherently, "Head for the plane," he yelled. And to the right hand man he said, "Send a couple of guys to get our stuff at the hotel and tell them to take a commercial flight back. We're leaving right now. If someone thinks they can play with my things just because I'm not there, they are going to find out personally that they are wrong." The right hand man made a couple of calls. When he was done he noticed he had gotten a message while he was on the phone. He pulled it up and listened, hoping for a good news update.

"Somebody took videos of our guys trying to get into our own clubs and sent them to the press. It showed us trying to move the dumpsters closer to the service doors to put all the bad food in. They wouldn't roll and the lids were welded shut. All our guys were cussing and frustrated and that's all over the news. The whole city is laughing at us. We are working on it. I'm just keeping you informed." The right hand man clicked his phone shut. He wanted to kill someone.

"What was that?" The big bad boss wanted details, and his bare hands around somebody's throat.

"An update from home. Things are back to normal, we're open for business, and they're working to find who did this."

"They better be. I want the person responsible to be sitting in front of my desk when I get down there. I never should have gotten involved up here in the first place, but now if I pull out it will look like I'm being driven out." The boss settled into his chair in the small office area in back of the plane and, with his favorite drink in hand, turned on the TV. A half hour later the plane took off from Boeing Field, in a steady Pacific Northwest drizzle. The plane was headed south.

*

The yacht was heading north. The water kept getting choppier. After a delicious dinner, Kandee and PC, as nurses, gave each girl a routine physical examination, and then got them safely tucked into bed. Kandee slept in one room with three girls and PC in another room with the other three. Janae was in her own room, conked out after a long day. The four guys huddled in the den and watched the video tapes of the effects of their handy work. They roared with laughter. When they finished it was 11PM.

"Time for a phone call," Joe Cornish dug out a prepaid phone from his desk. He opened it up and dialed.

*

The plane had descended through the clear skies of San Diego and landed about 9PM. The big boss and his right hand man headed straight for the main club and ordered dinner in their private room. After dinner and some light amusement, they got down to business.

"What did our surveillance cameras show?"

"Nothing, the power was cut off."

"I want to talk to the editor of the TV station. How dare he run those damn tapes!" Right then the right hand man's phone rang. He looked at it and answered.

"Yeah?"

"Is your boss with you?"

"Who is this?!!"

"If your boss is with you, turn on your speaker phone."

"Who the hell is this?!!"

"You and your boss are going to want to hear what I have to say."

The right hand man held up the phone and said to the boss, "I think it's the guy who attacked us." He pushed the speaker phone button, "We're listening."

"You have 24 hours to get your little drug and prostitution ring out of Seattle."

The boss exploded, "Who are you? You coward! Tell me who you are!"

"Call me Batman. Seattle is my Gotham City. I want every filthy part of your operation out of my city in 24 hours or I'll drop the hammer on you. And I think you know now that I can do it," Joe Cornish was talking slow and tough.

"I got people looking for you and when I find you, I'm going to find your wife and kids and torture them in front of you. They'll cry out for your help but you won't be able to do anything. I'll crush you, you SOB coward. Nobody threatens me!!!"

Joe Cornish laughed into the phone. "I'll tell you this, big bad boss, this was a courtesy call. I know you're not going to pull out in 24 hours, but when those hours are gone, your freedom will be gone. I warned you." Click.

The right hand man turned off the speaker. They both looked at each other. "Let's get out of the country for a few days."

"Hell, no. Nobody's going to push me around," he was Boss.

Joe and Jeff were looking at Joe Cornish. Tom was writing furiously. Joe Cornish closed the phone and stood up. He walked onto the deck and threw the phone into the ocean. Then he said, "Let's get some sleep. We've had one fun-filled day." The gentle rolling of the boat afforded everyone a sound sleep.

At 5:30 the next morning Joe Cornish was dressed and at the back of the yacht looking out onto the ocean. His phone rang.

"Yeah?"

"The big boss shot both of Jack's brothers and then put Jack in charge. He begged me to be his right hand man, not to mention lover, so I told him I was his. I think over time I can turn him. He's scared of his boss, but I think I can turn that into hate. I'm back to schedule A."

"Well done. Down here, the trap snapped and we're heading home." Gretchen was some girl. He wished he could reward her somehow.

# 21

Their newfound freedom started the girls giggling as soon as they woke up. PC and her girls went into Kandee's room and started a pillow fight. After a while things calmed down and then there was a lineup for the bathroom. Janae was in the galley making pancakes and scrambled eggs. The four guys grabbed breakfast first and joined the pilot on the bridge. When the girls sat down for breakfast, Janae served them OJ and aspirin.

"Good thinking," said PC, "Anybody feeling super bad?" Janis looked around and said, "No, we'll be fine. By now they've figured out we are gone. What will happen?" PC and Kandee both looked at Janae.

"They don't know how you left or where you are. We got away clean. When they figure out that you're gone, which they might have by now, they'll clamp down on security and keep a closer eye on the rest of the girls."

Janis broke in, "We want to help them, too, not hurt them."

"When we get back to Seattle, we'll turn you over to a group of Christian workers who rescue and care for girls that have been in the same situation as you girls. They will help you get in touch with family or get you settled safe and sound, and get you back into school. At that point some of you might want to help with the organization's ongoing rescue and rehabilitation work. The sky is the limit on what you can do. Just learn, work hard and grow. Kandee and PC are nurses, and I work for a government agency.

We all spend our time helping people. You can, too." After a good breakfast it started to rain.

Kandee and PC got them all safe and warm into the theatre room and handed out paper and pens.

PC instructed, "I want you all to write a letter to your parents. Just put down what you would say if you were sitting at your kitchen table with them." Kandee noticed PC was good with kids. She wondered if she would be with her own if she had some.

*

Breakfast for the big bad boss had caused indigestion. His right hand man had broken the news that six of the youngest girls he had paid good money for had disappeared, all from the Monterey Bay Club. One hundred twenty thousand dollars' worth, up and gone. He wrote in his notebook: new leadership for Monterey; think about Seattle; new security for San Diego; alert clubs in other cities that had not been affected. Yes, he had to start thinking ahead. He had just been reacting to what was happening to him. Someone else was thinking ahead and he was paying the price for it. He poured himself a drink. He was under attack. He kept hoping the attack was over, but in reality he had no idea if it was over or not. Maybe there was more coming. What should he do...? He was being played... The attacks got him so angry he couldn't think. All he could do was react. Revenge was all he could think of. Meanwhile, the attacks could continue.

"James! Get in here!" The boss's right hand man came from the office next door through a side door. "These attacks might not be over yet. You were right last night. We need to disappear for a while. That guy on the phone said something about my freedom. Get the operation back up to speed with added security. You know what to do. Then let's leave, at noon."

"Where are we going to go?" James had a number of places in mind.

"We are going to go somewhere where no one will think to look for us."

"Where would that be?"

"Some place we've never been. Some place we've never thought about."

"Okay..."

"Get the jet ready. Get us packed for a week at least. We'll each take one of the girls with us; you pick. Meanwhile, I'll get some money together. I've got an idea."

*

Noon brought a recess to the hastily called grand jury. They had seen and heard enough evidence to indict Jason Everett Samuelson. The indictment read for six pages. Drug trafficking, human trafficking, and other lesser offenses. Multiple counts.

The DA knew Mr. Samuelson had been indicted before, but not in the United States. He had never done time in jail. This was her big chance and she knew she had to hurry. Bad guys could smell cops coming. She got the paperwork organized and signed by the right people. She had a private eye at Samuelson's main club to try to keep an eye on him. By 1PM she and her briefcase were in a squad car with the vice detective and plenty of muscle.

Jason Everett Samuelson was a name that this particular bad guy had invented. His real name was Antonio Aragapo. He grew up in Italy, faced murder charges at fifteen, fled to Ecuador and came under the tutelage of Ecuador's main drug boss. The rest was logical history. He began operations in the United States probably twelve years ago. He was brutal, not afraid to kill people, and had a head for finances.

The DA checked with her PI and then instructed her driver to pull right up to the front of the club.

"You and I go first," she said to the detective. "Send a car around back and tell your guys to be ready. We'll call for back up when we need it." The DA and the detective got out and approached the club's door.

"It's 1:15, they should be open. We go in and announce ourselves. Then see what happens."

"Roger."

The big door opened wide and it took a few seconds to see in the dark interior. A hostess greeted them.

"I'm the District Attorney for the San Diego area. I'd like to talk to your boss."

"One moment please, ma'am. I'll go fetch him."

A minute later the man who approached them was not who she wanted.

"I'm the District Attorney for the San Diego area and I have a warrant to search these premises, and a warrant for the arrest of Jason Everett Samuelson. Please bring me to him.

"Ma'am, respectfully, I'm sorry, but he is not here. You've missed him by a little over an hour. I don't know where he went."

"Thank you. I'm handing you a search warrant for these premises. I don't doubt you, but I have the right to search, so I will. Please accompany us and be prepared to open any doors I ask you to." The search took an hour and no Jason Everett Samuelson, but the searchers noticed everything as they went room to room.

*

James knew that when his boss said that he wanted to leave at noon, he did not mean five minutes after. The jet was loaded by 11:45 including two twenty-something blondes who appeared to be quite the female equivalent to first prize at the county fair flower arrangement contest.

"The jet's ready, what are those?" James asked.

"What do you think they are?" The boss had his briefcase in one hand and picked up one of two suitcases in the other. James picked up the other one which was heavy. Oh, he realized, money. They walked into James's office, through a concealed door in the wall, and downstairs to another door. A short hallway led to another door and steps up to a restaurant across the alley from the club. Exiting the front of the restaurant, they got into a plain sedan with a driver.

"Tell the jet to take off and meet us at Montgomery Field in half an hour. Somebody might be watching it where it is."

"Yes, sir." James made the call and then instructed the driver where to go. The boss was thinking ahead; he wondered what was next. At Montgomery Field the driver headed for the boss's jet which he recognized. Jason Everett Samuelson, plus James and company, got comfortable after they boarded the jet.

When the jet was in the air, the boss announced to James and the two blondes on their laps, "I want to go to Paraguay and buy a ranch! Anybody want to come?" Laughter and cheering erupted and turned into kisses and hugs. The flight south was enjoyed by all.

*

It was raining again in Seattle. Normal. But other things were hopping. Jack, with Gretchen in tow, peeked into the guest office and saw nothing amiss. Not a clue as to what had happened earlier. They then went to Jack and his brothers' office and looked around. Gretchen grabbed a pad and pencil and trying to keep things light yet focused she announced, "I'm ready; instructions, sir?" Jack sat at his little desk and thought a moment. Then he started listing for Gretchen what he wanted done.

"I want the biggest desk. Get rid of the other two. We have got to get some sunshine in here," there was only one window. "Make the window bigger, or better yet put a sliding glass door with a small balcony. And see if they can install some solar tubes; one in the bathroom and one right here where I want my desk to be." An hour later Gretchen had a list of changes for the office and a call in for a cleaning lady to deep clean the guest office. Gretchen kept encouraging Jack, saying she thought his ideas were good, and adding a few of her own. So the next few days were busy for her and fun, working with Jack, planning the remodeling, and learning the business. She didn't have to dance anymore, but her real dance became more complicated and more dangerous.

*

Late lunch for the DA didn't taste so good. She had missed him by one hour, but had to go through the motions anyway. She wrote down her thoughts and compiled her notes with the notes from the other searchers as to what they saw, while searching for Jason Everett Samuelson.

Thus the manhunt began. All the pertinent law enforcement groups within the United States of America were brought on board and everyone kept everyone else updated, or at least they were supposed to. Everyone shared information, or they were supposed to. The cooperation between agencies was impeccable, or so everyone hoped. Worldwide groups were included, too. In other words the process began and ground its way through until the person was caught or everyone gave up. Usually when everyone gave up, it would find its way to the desk of the agent in charge of Special Investigations at the FBI's Seattle Office.

The problem: Jason Everett Samuelson of the United States was missing.

# 22

The trip north on the ocean was reaching its end. They weren't in a hurry, but they did have a destination. As they passed the boundary between Oregon and Washington states, the Columbia River entrance, they moved closer in so the eastern horizon included the Washington Coast. The farther north they went, the rockier the coast became. Flattery Rocks National Wildlife Refuge were the coastal waters and the yacht gave a wide birth to the Cape Flattery Lighthouse. After the lighthouse, the boat turned east and a bit south down the Strait of Juan De Fuca, which separates the U.S. from Canada. Past the crescent of Neah Bay, and paralleling Hwy 112 which ran along the beach, and past the crescent of Clallam Bay, they continued. Past the small protected cove of Crescent Bay, on down past the larger Freshwater Bay and to Angeles Point, where the Elwha River spills its cold Olympic Mountains water into the Strait. Then suddenly, Port Angeles, the biggest U. S. city on the Strait, just a ferry ride across from Victoria, Canada, the most beautiful city on the Strait, located on the southeast tip of Vancouver Island. Then out a bit and around Dungeness Spit, and on past Point Wilson Lighthouse and south, by Port Townsend and into Puget Sound. Before the yacht reached Foulweather Bluff, at the top of the Kitsap Peninsula, it turned southwest leaving Puget Sound and entering Hood Canal. Around Hoods Head, suddenly loomed the Hood Canal Floating Bridge. Having called ahead, the middle of the bridge opened, to the consternation of car and truck traffic both ways, to let the yacht through. Then southwesterly more as the canal narrowed, past the Bangor Trident Submarine Base, around Hazel Point, and into a little cove called Seabeck Bay on the Kitsap Peninsula side of Hood Canal.

The dock and marina jutting halfway out into the cove from the Seabeck General Store were new. The dredging allowed a craft of this size to dock at the outermost pier.

The rebuilding of the dock and marina, and the remodeling of the closed elementary school one quarter mile south of the store, were a pleasant surprise to the area. Nobody questioned where the money came from. Joe Cornish and his churchman friend had worked together in their younger years in the CIA, and sometimes drug money that had been seized had a way of doing good when it ended up in the right hands. The U.S. Congress had approved the money inadvertently, the authorization hidden in the legalese of appropriation bills. The renovated elementary school was now a safe house of unusually large dimensions including a gymnasium and a ball field. It gave troubled young girls a beautiful, safe place to rehab.

Janae, Kandee, PC, and six girls stepped off the yacht when they arrived and descended on Bobbi's Café on the old dock attached to the back of the Seabeck General Store. One of the young girls had once visited relatives in Western Washington and remembered wild blackberry pie. When she saw it on the menu she insisted they all have it with ice cream and cold milk. Seeing them coming off the yacht, Bobbi and crew treated them like princesses. She had no idea where they had come from, but knew that they might be neighbors for a while.

Joe Cornish had called his reverend friend while still in San Diego and said he had a six pack to deliver to the ball field in two days. The reverend was excited and said he would meet them there. Now he dialed again and said, "I've just docked and we are at Bobbi's."

"I'll be there in five minutes," the director of the rescue organization answered. A fifteen-passenger van pulled up to the

General Store and he and a driver got out. Joe Cornish with Joe, Tom, and Jeff met them and all sat down together at a table at Bobbi's away from the girls.

The girls all yelled at once, "Order the wild blackberry pie!"

Joe Cornish nodded at Bobbi and held up his coffee cup, and soon the men had wild blackberry pie, ice cream, and coffee.

"Let's all go up together and get the girls settled, and then you can dine with us on the yacht tonight. We'll fill you in on the details."

"Sounds good. It's been calm around this neck of the woods for years. How was the ocean?" The reverend's question led to pleasant conversation.

When the girls were done and all were loading into the van, Joe Cornish gave Jeff a list of instructions, including five hundred dollars for Bobbi for the snack and a dinner order for six to be delivered to the yacht. The instructions also included things from the General Store, as well as pizza for everyone at the safe house. Seabeck Pizza had multiple locations around the Kitsap Peninsula, but the original store was right here in a little building next to The Seabeck General Store.

Jeff took care of business and returned to the boat which was being refueled, cleaned, and resupplied.

Joe Cornish, Janae, Kandee, PC, and the six girls along with Joe, Tom, the reverend, and the driver arrived at the safe house and unloaded. All the girls were excited, including the older girls, when they saw the beauty of the refurbished school, the playgrounds, and the surrounding forests. Each girl was given her own bedroom with empty closets. Afterward they all met in the gymnasium and were introduced to the ten girls who were already living there. Then they were brought to an old classroom that looked like a clothing store. The six wandered through the racks and shelves and shoe boxes and picked out what they wanted. The three ladies kept their eyes on the young girls but felt like giddy school girls themselves. The six were given a schedule which included a debriefing time after dinner. Each girl was to tell her story privately to a counselor on staff and give all her private ID info. Kandee and PC were asked to stay the first night and then to return to the boat for an 8 AM departure.

When pizza came, Janae, the reverend, Joe Cornish, Joe, and Tom took the staff sedan down to the dock. The evening sun was dropping behind the Olympic Mountains, but it painted a violet hue to the patchy clouds mirrored on the calm waters of the bay. It was a perfect evening. The forecast called for rain.

# 23

The pilot/bodyguard that opened the jet's door and stepped out into the sunshine was as excellent as a bodyguard as he was as a pilot. Actually a cousin of Jason Everett Samuelson, he went by his given name of Nicolus Aragapo. He had seen so much violence in his life, he could smell it before it came. He stood on the top step of the stairs of the jet. He looked around at the airport and breathed in and out through his nose. Asuncion, Paraguay. New ground. Nobody knew them here. They knew nobody. However, they had two suitcases full of the universal language of respect. Nicolus stepped down onto the tarmac. His 9mm was holstered under his arm, and a .38 in a holster attached to his boot under his pant leg. The other boot had an eight inch knife that was concealed down a slit between the inside leather and the outside leather.

The man at the bottom of the stairs was not the problem. He led Nicolus into the airport security center. The machine gun toting guards he passed were not the problem either. Inside the building the lady in uniform at the counter looked as tough as nails, but he knew how to deal with her. She was not the problem. He walked over and stood across the counter from her. Her eyes were dark blue, almost black, and everything else about her was hard. Tall and muscular, she was almost as tall as Nicolus. Her straightforward gaze right into Nicolus' eyes was her mistake. His cold steel gray expression held her until she blinked. Then he said, "Your boss, please." She kept staring, but her body was weakening in a female sort of way that she had trained her body not to. She said nothing and left him standing there. She walked a few steps to the door behind her and entered without knocking. Less than a minute later she reopened the door, and standing to the side of the door, just stared at Nicolus. He moved around the counter and walked by her into the room. He smelled the slightest scent of perfume as he went by, but closed the door without looking back.

The uniform at the desk was the problem. He did not look up until he was done with his phone call. A call for a truck load of troops. The man was older than Nicolus and maybe wiser. He leaned back in his chair and sized up the pilot standing before him.

Nicolus spoke slowly, "Sir, we are in Paraguay to purchase a ranch and hide for a while. We bring no trouble and will create none for you. We would like to be cleared through your customs where we sit without problems."

"Who are 'we'?" The uniform asked politely.

"Two men, two women, and myself."

"That's all?"

"Our belongings and our jet."

The uniform pursed his lips, thinking. "I like your straightforward request. Why should I grant it?"

Nicolus pulled a package from behind his back that was tucked into his pants. It held twenty bundles of fifty one hundred dollar bills. He laid the package on the desk.

The uniform watched him and then eyed the envelope.

"And this is…?"

"This is why you should grant my request." The uniform looked at Nicolus for ten long seconds then dropped eyes to the envelope. Then he opened one end of the package and took out a bundle. He saw the one hundred on the top bill and then fanned through the bundle to see if they were all one hundreds. He glanced at Nicolus and then at the package again as he dumped the rest of the package onto his desk. He counted the bundles, lifting and stacking each one. Then, without eyeing Nicolus, he put the bundles back into the envelope, sealed it, and put it into a side drawer of his desk and locked it with a key.

Then he stood up and with a slight smile said, "I would like to personally walk with you to your jet. I will inspect it."

Nicolus turned and walked out, back around the counter. He got a whiff of perfume again, but this time it seemed a little stronger. He led the way out to the jet with the uniform following. The army truck that was summoned screeched to a halt as the man simply held up one arm even as he kept walking. At the steps to the jet Nicolas stepped aside to let the uniform go up first, but the man stopped, gestured with his hand and said, "Please." Nicolas led the way and they stepped inside. He turned toward the back and parted the curtain revealing James, the boss, and the two girls.

The man looked them over and nobody spoke. Then he said slowly, "Welcome to Paraguay. My name is Rolando. I am allowing you to enter my country. I would like to make your stay in my country more pleasurable by inviting you to dine with me as soon as you are settled."

Everybody stared at each other. The boss rose to his feet, respectfully, "Rolando, my name is Samuelson and I am glad to be in your country. You might have heard of me."

"Yes, Mr. Samuelson, I have." There was a pause as the two men looked each other in the eye.

Then the boss extended his hand slowly and said, "Then, I accept your invitation with gratitude." The two shook hands, both bosses who had men under them.

Rolando lifted a card out of his pocket and placed it on the small table beside him. "My personal number. Gentlemen, ladies, welcome."

Nicolus turned and escorted him down the stairs. At the bottom he said, "Sir, the woman at the counter…?"

"She is my daughter. Perhaps I will invite her to our dinner also."

Nicolus's body stirred at the thought of this woman. Before he disappeared, Rolando spoke into his phone briefly and then handed Nicolas a card with another number on it.

"Rodriguez. He will watch over you. Ask him anything. He is my best."

"Good day, sir," Nicolas walked back up the stairs and into the jet, closing the door. He called the number.

"Rodriguez."

"My name is Nicolus..."

"Yes. I will be at your hanger shortly. Please wait for me."

Nicolus hung up and joined his boss. "Rolando has assigned what he called 'his best' to accompany us. He will be here shortly."

"Have him come in and sit and talk with us. Do you think we can trust these people?"

"Yes, sir, I do. One hundred thousand U.S. dollars is worth many times more than that down here."

"Okay. Girls, iced tea for six."

Shortly, two SUVs pulled up outside. A man in his thirties got out and walked to the bottom of the stairs. He had the look of fitness. Nicolus stood at the opened door of the jet as the man climbed up the stairs.

"You are Nicolus?"

"Yes."

"I am Rodriguez. My wish is that we will be friends for life."

"Thank you. It is also my wish. Please come in."

James, the boss, and the girls were standing when Nicolus and Rodriguez entered.

"My name is Rodriguez. I am delighted that your safety has become my responsibility while you are here in Paraguay."

The boss gestured as he replied, "Please sit down. You've met Nicolus, my best man. This is James, my business partner and our attendants." The girls immediately handed out iced tea and all sat down. "Rodriguez, please convey our thanks to your boss when you have a chance. We feel welcomed here in Paraguay. It is our wish to purchase a ranch, perhaps out in the country, but not too far away from the airport here."

"Sir, we have a large ranch about an hour away from here that we use as a guest ranch for visiting dignitaries and their entourage. We would be delighted to sell it to you if it meets with your approval. It's in the hills above Nueva Germania."

"Yes, we would love to see it. Please show it to us."

"May I suggest that while we are gone, we have your plane backed into a hangar so as to be out of the sun, and the prying eyes of the satellites?"

"Excellent. Thank you, Rodriguez," the boss appreciated when he didn't have to think of everything.

The rest of the afternoon was spent riding in the first SUV with Rodriguez driving, followed by four bodyguards and a virtual arsenal in the second. The ranch was magnificent and came with its own caretakers for the horses and the cattle, and had cooks and workers aplenty. The view was beautiful, the air clean, and even the water from the well tasted good.

"Rodriguez, it's perfect. I shall call my banker tonight, and tomorrow we can sign papers. What is the price?" The boss liked doing things fast.

"One million U.S. dollars."

"An excellent price for all this beauty," the boss was excited, the girls were wide eyed, and James was tired after a long day. Nicolus remained vigilant.

"Now back to the office in the plane and we'll spend the night there," the boss said. Rodriguez spoke briefly to the caretaker and then they left.

Later, as they pulled up to the open hangar, Rodriguez offered, "Tomorrow then, we shall conclude our business, and spend the evening with my boss at his restaurant."

"He owns a restaurant?" The boss was impressed.

"Sir, the city of Asuncion owes a lot to Rolando. I will leave the second SUV here along with these men. They will take you shopping or wherever you want to go. Please allow them to do their job. They will be discreet as they answer to me. Please enjoy your evening. I will call you tomorrow." Rodriguez paused to talk to Nicolus, and then he got into the first SUV and was gone.

Then the boss said, "It's hot out here. Let's get on board and see what's for dinner." The plane was plugged into the hangar's power so it was cool inside. Nicolus spent ten minutes talking with the four guards, making sure they were all on the same page. He was impressed with the caliber of men that Rolando employed. He then climbed the stairs and stopped at the door for one more look around. He breathed deeply through his nose, and then went inside and closed the door. Dinner was delightful and after dinner it was bedtime. The boss took his girl and headed for the bedroom in the back of the plane. James and his girl folded the seats down in the living area, which made into a bed and crawled in together. Nicolus positioned himself in the pilot's seat. He would snooze off and on, but as long as he could breathe he could sense danger. He would not let his guard down until they were settled at the ranch.

# 24

Jack and Gretchen heard about the mess in California. The reverberations hit Seattle in the form of tighter security, twenty-four hour manned surveillance and, of course, higher prices to pay for it all. After a week of intense work they felt they had a handle on the business side of the operation. The drug pipeline was flowing. The prostitute/escort/dating side was growing, and the younger girls brought in the most money. Jack and Gretchen had basically lived at the club since the big boss had left.

One night after making love, Gretchen whispered, "I have part of an idea. You need to help me with it. Can I talk it out?"

"Yeah, baby, go. I'm listening."

"Well, girls like me, we dance, get tipped, do private parties for customers if they ask for us. We prostitute ourselves and everybody makes money and customers come back. But we are all over twenty-one and are responsible for the choices we make."

"Yeah, I already know that," she elbowed him in the ribs playfully. "Okay, Okay, keep going. My mouth is closed," he said.

"I'm just talking out what we're doing, trying to find an angle to make us more successful," Gretchen was trying to ease into it. "The young girls...we buy them, drug them, and work them until they give up hope of being anything but a prostitute."

"Are you going somewhere with this?" Jack was still listening.

"We are responsible for the direction of their lives, and it's ruining young girls' lives. Their potential is gone."

"Their potential is sky rocketing and we're living the good life because of it. You turning soft?"

"Jack! What if we could increase our income, reduce the number of laws we are breaking and not force girls to do what they don't want to do?"

"You fell asleep and you're talking out loud in your dream."

Jack wasn't getting this. So she reached down and got a handful of his testosterone makers.

"Jack! I'm serious!" she whispered loudly but kind of playfully also.

"Okay, okay, okay, I give, I give. Where are you going with this?"

"I'm not sure. This is where I need your brain, too. I want to double our income at the same time we clean up our act. That's my idea. Now are you going to trade me in for someone better with less of a mouth, or what?"

"No, no, no, baby. I crossed off all the names in my little black book. You're it. And I like it that way. If you want to go and live on a deserted island forever, just you and me, I'd be good with that. You're the best I've ever had. You're mine."

"Okay! This is fun, isn't it? We think up things that work better and make more money than your murdering boss. Why be attached to him if we're smarter? We are constantly under a death threat if we don't perform. What's with that? He's treating us like we're treating the young girls. Why should we put up with that? And why should the girls put up with us just because we are older and stronger?"

"What do you propose, turning over to the FBI and getting into the witness protection program?" Jack's attempt at being helpful.

"No, any dummy can do that. I want to make oodles of money and at the same time clean up our city. This is our home. Why let guys from out of town run our lives? We're smarter than that. And those guys don't deserve to live!"

"Shhhushhh. Don't say that too loud. Somebody might be listening."

"I just want to know if you're listening," Gretchen sounded serious and meant to.

"Yeah, baby. Go to sleep. I promise we'll talk more about your ideas. I love you," Jack had to process this.

"Me, too," Gretchen fell asleep; but not before she argued with herself. I'm supposed to help these bad guys get arrested, not make them into model citizens.

*

On board the yacht in Seabeck Bay, dinner was waiting for them. Joe Cornish, the reverend, Janae, Joe, Tom, and Jeff sat down to Hood Canal geoduck, Dungeness crab with vegetables, and Riesling from Eastern Washington. It was superb. After Tillamook ice cream and coffee, all were stuffed.

Then commenced the debriefing of the whole operation by Joe Cornish, letting each one chime in on their part. Janae helped by taking notes. The reverend was pleased as could be with the results of their work. This group was putting into action something that desperately needed doing. When the evening ended, the reverend gave a prayer of thanks for their safe return and for the successful rescue of six girls. He ended with, "God bless you and keep you all in His love." Joe Cornish walked the reverend up the dock to his car. When he returned to the boat, he called the others together and told them what he didn't want the reverend to hear.

"Our inside operative in the Seattle club scene sent us some remarkable information. The boss, whom we gave the DA information about, was up here while we were down there. He murdered two of the three brothers who ran the Seattle operation because of the bungled attempts on my life, and left the youngest brother in charge. Our operative is working as his right hand man. But instead of ratting him out, the operative thinks turning him is possible."

The four looked at Joe Cornish, and then at each other, shaking their heads. Could that really be possible?

"What does that mean to us?" Tom's nose was twitching. No one else was jumping in, and Joe Cornish just waited, so Tom continued. "Now let me think this through. While we were messing with his stuff in Monterey Bay and San Diego, he was readjusting things in Seattle. When he found out what we were doing, he headed back south as we headed back north. By the time the DA jumped on our info, she missed him. He must have found out he was indicted and hid, or left the country."

Everybody's eyes were on him. No one jumped in. Joe Cornish had a look of enjoyment on his face, so Tom continued. "The short term result of our actions is forcing the other side to play defense instead of offense. This is a good thing that wouldn't have happened without our actions. We, a group of private citizens, affected the relationship between the good guys and the bad guys through a private covert operation that had no connection with law enforcement, except for Joe Cornish." He looked at Joe Cornish as he finished his thoughts. So did everyone else.

"Well stated by the journalist from Seattle," Joe Cornish paused to see if anyone else would continue the thought. Joe did.

"Success breeds success. We are now a team, with a leader who has access to law enforcement intel, and assets from who knows where. Anyone up for another operation?"

Tom laughed out loud, but he was the only one. Joe Cornish still had that look of enjoyment on his face. Tom realized he was the only outsider here. He looked at everyone else, then addressed Joe Cornish.

"You already have another operation in mind," it was a statement.

Joe added, "He has another operation planned and ready." It donned again on Tom that Joe Cornish was exceptional at planning ahead.

Joe Cornish then spoke, "We'll be leaving in the morning and I'll tell you about my plans at breakfast. Let's say breakfast at seven, boat leaves at eight. Get a good night's sleep and pray that the reverend is right." The others all looked at him. Joe Cornish got up, said good night, and left for the den. Then they all looked at each other. They realized no one had a clue as to what Joe Cornish had meant by hoping the reverend was right.

At seven in the morning the girls at the safe house were all up and at breakfast. They had slept well and were ready for the day. Kandee and PC were eating at the staff table and enjoying their company. PC was impressed with their professional training and their genuine care for the girls, while Kandee was excited by the possibility of her future involvement in rescuing young girls from situations that she had barely escaped from herself.

Then it was time for the girls to head out and do chores. Kandee and PC looked at each other and realized they might not see Janis and the other five again. They jumped up and ran to them and gave hugs all around. Tears flowed and love was exchanged, but the schedule must be kept. So after a moment that would never be forgotten, they were gone.

Kandee and PC packed and decided to walk to the yacht, so by 7:40 they were headed that way. They stopped at the Seabeck General Store and bought some fresh flowers. The two popped in and said goodbye to Bobbi, and then ambled down the dock to the yacht. They put the flowers on the coffee table in the dining/living area in a heavy bottomed vase. After depositing their belongings in their rooms, they knocked on the door to the den. Inside, Tom and Joe both jumped up and opened the door to kisses and hugs. The engines were already running. Joe Cornish spoke into his phone and they were underway.

PC asked, "Where are we headed now?"

"Seattle is our destination," Joe Cornish stood as he spoke. "Joe, why don't you and Tom update the girls on our plans and discuss where your futures lie. I want to instruct the crew as to our arrival at Shilshole Marina."

The two couples headed for the back of the boat to talk and enjoy the beautiful scenery. Joe Cornish instructed the crew, and the yacht sailed. The rain never materialized.

*

After arriving at the marina in Seattle, Joe and Kandee went with Tom and PC to her house in Tacoma. Tom dove into writing out his story while the others went to the hospital where Joe officially checked out and the girls gave notice of quitting.

Tom brought his story to his boss later the next day, but after reading it, his boss's comment was, "This is fiction."

"Not only is every word true, I was part of the story myself."

"Then write it as a first person account."

"No way. I'll endanger myself. Print it or throw it away; it's all true."

"Nobody will believe it."

"Boss, the only reason I became a part of this story was that I followed the leads right into the middle of it. The reason they included me was because they wanted someone to write an accurate account. This is it."

"Did they tell you what to write?"

"You read it. Is that my writing?"

"Is there stuff they told you not to write?"

"Yeah. There were a few points they didn't want included. Stuff for safety's sake."

"I want to talk to the leader."

"He's not going to let you interview him; I can continue to be a part of this, if I am accurate in what I write. There's more coming, you understand? He will keep playing as long as I cooperate."

"What's this going to cost me?"

"I don't know. Probably plenty. But what's a Pulitzer worth? Or do we have a bunch of other stories going as good as this one?"

Tom's boss turned and looked out his office window. "What do you need?"

"I need this to be my only assignment, and a free hand to follow it where ever it goes."

"Okay, but dammit, you keep in touch with me!"

"Thank you, sir. I will."

When Tom got back to PC's, they all went out to dinner. Pacific Grill in downtown Tacoma provided them with a big private booth so they could talk freely.

"Joe, when I met and interviewed you in the hospital, your three word call was in code to Joe Cornish?"

"Yeah, but I'd never met him. He was my handler when I did certain jobs."

"He's brilliant," Tom was always fishing.

"I knew he was smart. But either he's very lucky or he's gifted in the planning and execution departments."

PC jumped in. "We have less than two weeks before we leave again. Kandee and I will be working. What about you guys?"

"Joe Cornish will keep us busy, I imagine," Joe said.

Tom added, "We'll just always keep in touch with you gals. Just remember the code words we learned on the boat."

PC bubbled, "This is so fun, and I'm married, too!"

"You're darn right you are, and don't you forget it," that earned Tom a swift kick under the table.

"I never would have believed I could be so happy," Kandee meant it.

Over dinner they reviewed the plans Joe Cornish had told them about. During dessert they each told something about themselves that the others didn't know. They had a wonderful time and got back to PC's house in time for the girls to go to work. Tom and Joe got some sleep. They had a 6 AM meeting aboard the yacht with Joe Cornish.

# 25

Jason Everett Samuelson awoke with a nightie wadded up in his hand. It's owner was sprawled on her tummy under the top sheet of the king size bed. The big bad boss got up and entered the adjoining bathroom. A few minutes later he dressed and opened the bedroom door, walked through the small office area and into the living area. Someone was in the forward bathroom taking a shower. It must be James because the other blonde was on her back only half covered. He bent down on the way by and gently covered her up. He couldn't help noticing and comparing her dimensions with those in the back bedroom. Then he pulled back the curtain and saw that the entry area was empty. Moving forward he knocked on the cabin door and opened it. Empty. Out the window of the pilot's seat he looked down and saw Nicolus talking with the guards who were still stationed at the opening of the hangar. As he moved to the jet's door, a van was pulling up to the hangar.

Nicolus glanced up at his boss and held up one hand to stop him from coming down. Then he eyed the van, and the guards approached it as if they knew who it was. Nicolus drew his 9mm and held it down at arm's length. The four guards reached into the van and each headed back to the jet with a breakfast tray. Nicolus stayed at the bottom of the stairs and ushered the guards up. The boss had each one put their tray on the table in the entry way. Nicolus kept his back to the stairs and eyed the van and the open hangar. For a moment, he was the only line of defense.

After the guards came down they returned to the van and unloaded five more trays and put them on a table just inside the hangar opening. Nicolus and the guards ate their breakfasts with a view inside and outside the hangar. An hour later, Nicolus climbed the stairs and entered the plane. The boss, James, and the girls were dressed, done eating, and sitting in the living area.

"Thank you, Nicolus. The breakfast was excellent. We have an appointment at the bank at ten o'clock. Then a closing with Rolando at noon. Lunch and some light shopping in downtown Asuncion and perhaps a tour of the city, then dinner at Rolando's restaurant at six."

"Then we're spending the night here again," Nicolus stated.

"Yes, I think it would be safest, don't you?" Nicolus agreed. As they spoke, Rodriguez drove up in another SUV.

The day went by as planned for the two couples. Nicolus was constantly aware of everything. He began to relax as they arrived at Rolando's restaurant that evening and Rodriguez stationed himself outside. They entered, and there she was. That tough expression had a hint of a smile as their eyes met. Rolando introduced her as his daughter to the two couples. Nicolus watched. He noticed she knew how to be gracious. As Rolando ushered the two couples to a huge circular booth and sat down with them, she turned to Nicolus.

"Please sit with me and dine," she said; Nicolus was impressed.

"I'll follow you," he answered, and they sat at a table right across the aisle from the five. Sitting across the table from each other, they each had a view of either approach to the booth. They each eyed the approach behind the other, then their eyes met and held.

Nicolus sensed the perfume again, not overpowering, but it stirred him. He noticed a slight bulge under her uniform blazer that was not her bosom. He knew a shoulder holster when he didn't see one. She saw his recognition and moved her foot under the table up his boot till she found his boot holster. He backed up only slightly when he felt her foot.

"You are as prepared as I am. I'm pleased to meet you again," she was straightforward, but not aggressive.

"My name is Nicolus."

"I know. My name is Nickolaea."

Nicolus was momentarily stunned but didn't show it. "That's a beautiful name," breathe, he ordered himself.

"I had a twin brother named Nickolas. He was gunned down along with our mother a few years ago."

Nicolus decided not to ask why. What should he say? He was rapidly falling in love and not used to it. "I'm sorry, I'll bet your mother was as beautiful as you are. Your country carries with it surprises, some pleasant, some not."

"You are strong and kind," their eyes held again. "Your wife must be very happy," Nickolaea was searching him as if she had him at gun point.

"A wife would have a hard time being happy around me," he looked away up the aisle, then across at the booth, and then back to her. She was just finishing the same thing. "A woman who understood my life and still wanted to be married to me would be an amazing woman."

"I would be a good wife for you, but you could not love me," she said evenly.

"Why not?" His thought came out as words before he could stop it.

"Men fantasize about strong women, but they don't marry them. Men marry women who need their strength."

Nicolus was amazed. This was the woman he wanted but knew he could never have. So he would impress her and then never see her again.

He continued her thought, "Women fantasize about strong men who they would be submissive to, but they marry men who will be submissive to them."

Now Nickolaea was impressed, "You are strong and kind, and intelligent."

Their eyes were locked and he couldn't control his heart anymore.

"I think it would not be hard for me to love you," there, he had satisfied his heart.

"I would delight in your love," she said.

She hadn't slammed the door in his face. Had he heard right? Boldly his heart was taking over. He opened his mouth again, "Then you are the only woman I will ever marry. When I am free to do so, I will come back and find you." There. He said it, and meant it.

"May you find me wherever I am." She meant it. They finally unhooked eyes and went back on surveillance.

The waiters brought bread, then dinner and wine, then they brought dessert and coffee. The conversation in the big booth was of the kind friendships are made of. Rolando and his restaurant were at the service of the big bad boss whenever he should visit Paraguay and his new ranch. As a token of his friendship Rolando would give the best he had. His daughter was strong in body and mind, and superb as a security bodyguard. Rolando would sleep better at night knowing that Nickolaea was protecting his friend. Rolando rose, reached across the aisle and took his daughter's hand. She stood and faced the two couples.

Rolando said, "I give you my daughter to help provide for you a secure future."

The boss rose slowly. He glanced at Nicolus and said, "Sir, you show honor to me. I accept your kind gift. Your generosity must be known all across South America."

Rolando gave his daughter's hand to the boss and he in turn gave it to Nicolus and said, "Nickolaea, I give you to my best for as long as you choose to serve me."

"Sir, I will work for you beside Nicolus as long as you wish."

The solemn occasion would be remembered...the evening was over. The night was still warm.

Out at the SUV, Nicolus reached for Nickolaea's hand. He opened his mouth but she beat him to it.

"I will go home and pack. I will meet you at the new ranch tomorrow."

"Yes," he let go of her hand and she left. He had business to attend to. Rodriguez drove them back to the plane while Nicolus remained ever vigilant.

The night aboard the jet progressed as the previous night had, except the boys traded girls. Nicolus snoozed in the pilot's seat again, this time setting his cell phone alarm for every two hours. He was used to excelling at his job until he collapsed and he had gone longer than this before.

After the same routine at breakfast, Rodriguez came with a third SUV and a refrigerated box truck. They all packed up what they needed and loaded into the SUVs. Rodriguez spoke like a tour guide as he drove out to the ranch. Nicolus was in front with him. At the ranch, the box truck backed up to the kitchen and unloaded a month's worth of food and drink into the refrigerators and the small walk-in freezer.

Nickolaea was already there. She opened the front door and nodded to Nicolus. Rodriguez went to check the workers and convey to them the boss's request: a runway long enough to land on and a hangar for his plane. Nicolus ushered the two couples into the house and Nickolaea led them slowly to their rooms. First, she stopped at her bedroom door and said, "Sir, with your permission, I will attend you and Nicolus will sleep."

The boss nodded and eyeing Nicolus said, "Yes, thank you," Nickolaea turned her eyes on Nicolus until he entered her bedroom and closed the door. He slept until breakfast the next morning.

# 26

In Seattle, Joe Cornish sent Tom with Jeff on an assignment to the club where Gretchen worked. They entered and sat at a table and noticed the dancers right away.

Tom asked, “Which one is she?”

“None of the above.” They ordered a late lunch with beer and watched. A while later, Gretchen entered the room wearing a revealing business suit. The guy with her commanded respect. They stopped at the bar and talked to the bartender, then looked around. Gretchen whispered, “New guys, I’m going over to say hi,” Jack continued out the other side of the room and Gretchen walked over to Jeff and Tom’s table. “You boys hungry?”

“No, we’re not. How about you?” Jeff had worked with Gretchen before.

“Me neither. Please stay as long as you like.”

“We’ll be leaving one week from today on the B.”

“It’s a date. I’ll bring a friend,” Gretchen reached across their plates and grabbed their beer bottles. Tom got an eyeful without intending to. “I’ll get a couple more for you,” Tom looked at Jeff, eyebrows raised. Jeff looked back and said, “Keep eating.”

Joe Cornish sent Joe to Juneau, Alaska, on an Alaska Airlines hop. He followed instructions in Juneau and was back by dinner time. Joe and Tom headed for Tacoma, and walked with the girls to the hospital cafeteria. The place always brought smiles to Tom and PC. As they were eating, a couple of nurses stopped and asked excitedly, "Are you two actually quitting?"

Holding up their ring fingers they answered, "Yeah, we got our hooks into a couple of rich guys who promise to love and obey us. So we're gone in four more days."

"Got any brothers?" Everybody laughed as the nurses headed for work.

"Okay, see you guys in the morning," Kandee and PC kissed their hubbies and left to work the night shift. Joe and Tom sat for a while.

"Where did you go today?"

"Alaska," Joe was always careful with what he said. "What did you and Jeff do?"

"We had a short talk with Gretchen. Have you met her?"

"No. She's a gal that Joe handles. What's she like?"

"Oh, definitely not a 10. I'd say 9 and three quarters."

Joe looked up. "Really?"

"Yeah, I saw her with my own two eyes," Tom was smiling.

Joe took another sip of coffee, not knowing exactly what Tom meant, but not really needing to know.

"Jeff and her were talking code, but I think she and a friend are leaving for Alaska with us on the yacht next week."

Joe put his cup down, "Hmmm. That could be a big deal. Maybe that's what this trip is about."

*

The DA heard a knock and looked up from her desk, but the visitor barged in without waiting. "Samuelson's in Paraguay!" he blurted out. She stared at the guy she had known for a long time, but seldom saw in person.

"Paraguay? How did you find that out?" she knew it was a dumb question as soon as she asked it.

"He bought a ranch, and we happened to have one of our guys working at the ranch that he bought!"

The DA just sat with her mouth open.

"He bought the ranch that the Government of Paraguay used for housing foreign dignitaries. We've had a guy there for years."

The DA wasn't sure which intelligence agency her cousin worked for but his info was usually good.

She stood up, walked over to the door and closed it, "Can we extradite?"

"Not from Paraguay," he was still excited.

She was trying to think, "What can we do?"

"I don't know. But I can tell you what he eats and drinks at each meal when he's at the ranch." She looked at him again and a hint of a smile formed on her face. She pointed him to a chair and grabbed the Samuelson file. In it she found the file left by the couple Joe Cornish had sent. Joe had left a number at which he could be reached. There it was.

Joe Cornish was in his den on the yacht taking a siesta. His feet were on his desk, he was leaning back in his office chair, and the little gas fireplace was going. It was raining in Seattle. Joe's hands were folded in his lap and his cell phone was in his hand, set on vibrate. The vibration woke him up.

"Yes?"

"Whatever the hell you said to Samuelson, he took seriously. He just popped up in Paraguay."

"Jennifer! What a pleasure to hear from you!"

"Just trying to pay you respect for the humanitarian award of the year that you earned."

Joe Cornish typed "Paraguay-map of-" into his computer.

"You must be hungry?" He asked if she was in any trouble.

"No, how about you?" She knew his spy lingo.

"Nope. Now what have you got in mind?"

"More of the same. You know, if it worked once..." Jennifer offered.

"Please continue," so she did. She shared what her cousin had told her. Joe Cornish listened and a smile began to form on his face. By the time the conversation ended ten minutes later, Joe had given Jennifer some instructions and then asked, "Who does your cousin work for?"

She looked at her cousin in kind of an annoyed way and answered, "He always neglects to tell me that, but he always has good intel."

"Jennifer, you'll keep me posted?"

"Of course, Joseph. When are you going to visit me again in person?"

Joe Cornish had already hung up. She shook her head. Typical Joe Cornish. Always wants to be a surprise. Jennifer then explained to her cousin Joe Cornish's instructions, and handed him the exact message he had dictated. "Is that too long?"

"No, I don't think so."

"Good. Thank you, Jim. You help me look good to my bosses."

"Glad I can help, cuz. I'll keep you in the loop," his exit was just as quick as his entrance.

*

Two days later the big boss was at his ease. Morning horseback ride. Afternoon in the pool, with the girls wearing one piece suits (the bottom piece). After a while everyone got hungry. Chinese was on the menu, one of his favorite dinners. They all got dried off and dressed for dinner. Everyone enjoyed it immensely, but when they opened their fortune cookies, the girls suddenly had a quizzical look on their faces. They looked at the men. Sudden terror had struck both. All four fortunes read- YOU THINK YOU

CAN HIDE FROM BATMAN? YOUR ONE CHANCE IS UP! SAY GOODBY TO FREEDOM-

The boss erupted, "What in hell?!" He pushed back his chair and looked to the kitchen. Nicolus was at hand immediately.

"Sir?" The boss handed the fortune to him.

"Stay seated, please," Nicolus spoke into his lapel mic. The ranch was soon in a lock down, as Nicolus had taught everyone when they had gotten there. Nickolaea's place was in the surveillance room, monitoring all the equipment and the radar which reached out ten miles.

"Everything is clear," she said into Nicolus's ear from the next room. Nicolus was standing beside his boss's chair with one hand on the boss's shoulder. The other held his 9mm pointing down at arm's length. Nicolus was listening, looking around and breathing through his nose. Out the window he saw guards at the doors, and others making perimeter checks. Once again he heard that low, strong, but feminine voice, "still clear."

"Sir, we have no sign of imminent threat, but I'd like to keep to my plan if only for practice sake."

"Yes, Nicolus, continue with your plan."

He spoke into his mic again, then after a moment said, "Everyone please follow me." The four got up and followed Nicolus to the door and then out to a waiting, running SUV. They all got in and Nicolus said, "Go." As the SUV sped off, that voice spoke in his ear again, "Still clear."

Nicolus turned and addressed the four in the second and third seats.

"When danger arises, my plan, if all is clear, is to get you away from the ranch. This is in the case, however unlikely, of a smart bomb from above, which would show up on our radar with only ten seconds before impact."

One of the girls blurted out, "What about Nickolaea?"

"Thank you. An excellent question. There is a bomb shelter underground off the wine cellar. We installed a trap door from the surveillance room where she is, directly into the wine cellar. She could be in the bomb shelter within ten seconds if the incoming alert sounded. Also, if for some reason we could not leave, it would be our destination also." Nicolus faced front again and directed the driver. The SUV slowed and turned off toward a cattle barn which was beyond some rolling hills and not visible from the ranch. The driver drove right into the barn and stopped.

"Let's exit please," Nicolus was calm as though practicing a drill. They walked through the tack room and opened a door at the other end of it, where stairs led down to a bomb shelter. As they entered through the heavy door, their eyes widened. It was huge, almost as huge as the ranch house, with many rooms.

"Who built this?" The boss was awestruck.

"This ranch serviced heads of state and had to have a plan for every contingency."

"That's why the million dollar price!" The boss thought it was cheap for the U.S., but expensive for down here.

"Our stay here should be brief. Sir, could I show you the command and control room?"

"Yes! James, will you see that the girls are comfortable?"

Nicolus led the boss into a soundproof room that was filled with communication equipment and a desk big enough for a head of state to do business at. Nicolus shut the door.

"Wow! What is the government of Paraguay going to do now for visiting dignitaries?" The boss was genuinely impressed.

"They have built a bigger, better one closer to Asuncion, and Rodriguez says, with a smile, that all the bad guys still think this ranch is where their targets will be."

"Oh, I see. He better have been smiling."

"Sir, tell me of the message on the fortune cookies."

"Oh. The guy that caused all the ruckus in Monterey Bay and San Diego had the guts to call me and tell me to get out of Seattle. When I threatened him and called him a coward for not identifying himself, he said to call him Batman and that Seattle was his Gotham City. I wonder if he had something to do with the indictment, too."

"The immediate question is how did he get those fortunes into your hands?" Nicolus was thinking.

"Yeah. I know. We better question the kitchen help," Nicolus picked up the phone that had an underground line to the ranch surveillance room. He spoke into it and listened, and then pursed his lips and made a decision.

"Let's head back, Sir. All seems clear, but I'm glad for the opportunity to drill our security detail and to show you this place."

"Sounds good. Is there anything else I don't know about around here?"

"Yes, there are some more minor things. And I thought we might put a bomb shelter under the new hangar when we lengthen that small runway."

"Yes, good! I think I'll call my new ranch Fort Aragapo."

"Ah, yes. An excellent choice."

They collected the girls and James and got back into the SUV.

The drive back to the ranch was slower. Cattle and horse pastures were evident. The evening was starting to fade as was the excitement of the day. They remained in the SUV until Nicolus questioned the house and perimeter guards. Nothing out of the ordinary. Nickolaea opened the big door, and eyed Nicolus. She could tell by his expression that all was well. The group entered their home away from home and settled in for a movie before bed.

Nickolaea whispered to Nicolus, "You sleep now. I'll wake you up early."

"I can't wait!" They both smiled and kissed.

# 27

Gretchen and Jack kissed good night. It was four o'clock in the morning. Their day had ended.

Gretchen whispered, "I want to talk some more when we get up."

"What about?" Jack yawned and spoke at the same time.

"I've found a very private cruise, on a yacht, that I think we should take this weekend. No telling anyone. We have capable hands to leave the business in for a weekend. We've been working hard and we deserve a break."

"Where?"

"Where what?"

"Where does the cruise go? Mexico, Caribbean, Mars, where?"

"I'm not going to tell you until we get aboard."

"No way. End of conversation. No cruise."

"Alaska."

"Alaska?! It's cold in Alaska, and snows there like it rains here."

Gretchen slowly teased, "Then we'll just stay in bed, on a yacht, all weekend long."

Jack bit, "Sold. I'm in, all the way."

Gretchen giggled at the pun. "Okay. We'll take Friday, Saturday, and Sunday off. Boat leaves Friday at three PM. I'll finalize the plans. You line up workers for our absence."

"Can I go to sleep now?"

"Oh, you don't like me anymore?"

"Give me a break. If I'm going to be in bed with you all weekend..."

"Sleep good, baby."

They both fell asleep quickly after a full day, each of their minds soothed by the anticipation of something good; albeit, different things.

Gretchen woke up early, but acted sleepy while Jack got up and dressed for work.

"Hey, get that little fat butt out of bed," he teased.

"Oh, you think I'm fat? Show me where."

"Look, you crazy girl. You got me now so I can hardly wait for this cruise this weekend. Let's get our work done, maybe we can leave earlier."

"Yes, boss," she got up and went into the bathroom. She quickly dialed her phone.

"Yes?"

"Hey, we're on for the cruise."

"Oh yeah? You hungry or anything?"

"Not at all. Three PM."

"See you then."

That day flew by because they were both so busy. Friday morning Jack was up earlier than normal, went through everything with everyone workwise and came back to a packed-and-ready-to-go Gretchen.

"Let's get out of here, baby, before something goes wrong."

"I'm ahead of you. We have a cab waiting outside."

And so they left. Gone before they were needed, to a place where they were not needed.

The cab dropped them off at the Shilshole Marina and they walked to the gate. Jeff was down the dock a ways and waved. Gretchen waved back, smiling, holding onto Jack's arm.

"Hey, isn't that one of those new guys you went over to talk to the other day?"

"Yeah, that's how I heard of the cruise. He said some other couple had to cancel and if I knew anyone who could go on short notice, he'd cut the price for them."

"Hi, Gretchen, welcome aboard!" Jeff saw a smile on Jack's face.

"Hi, Jeff," Gretchen smiled, waved, and continued, "this is Jack and we're both glad to be here!"

Jeff smiled broadly and offered his hand. Jack was staring, but smiling, and then shook hands.

"Hey, nice to meet you, Jeff. Uh, thanks for this weekend."

Jeff ushered them through the gate and down the dock. "Oh, it's our pleasure to have you two with us. Somebody had to cancel so we kept their deposit so you guys didn't have to pay one." They continued to chat as they wound their way toward the yacht. "Ever been to Alaska, Jack?"

"No. Is it going to be snowing up there?"

"Nope, no snow. Actually this is the best time of the year to go. Mosquito's aren't out yet. But the winter's over."

Jack began staring at the yacht as soon as they got near. It was a suspicious stare. Jeff led them to the entry rail but Jack kept looking, trying to take in the whole thing. He took a step back and then walked to the back of the boat. He looked at the name: DUTCHESS II. He walked back to Gretchen and Jeff and shrugged his shoulders.

"What's the matter?"

"Nothing, I'll tell you later."

They went on board, and Jeff gave them the grand tour. They were underway before the tour was even half finished.

"Are we the only ones on board?" Gretchen asked.

"Yep. Except for a couple of businessmen heading for Juneau who refuse to fly there. If you've ever flown into Juneau... well, for some people it's best by boat."

When they got settled in their cabin, Gretchen wrapped her arms around Jack and kissed him. She could tell he was still wondering about something. "Now tell me, what's up."

"Oh...just..."

"Just what, babe?"

"Well...you know that guy you gave us and we missed getting him?"

"...Yeahhhh...what about him?"

"Well, one of our guys followed his boat after we missed him and he came to Shilshole, too. He got onto a yacht very similar to this one, only the name was different."

"Whoa, Jack, wouldn't it be crazy if...no, that is crazy."

"Hey, I'm the one who's crazy around here and I'm crazy about you." He pulled off his polo shirt. Then she pulled off hers. Dinner wasn't for another hour.

For dinner they dressed nicely. Gretchen wore that business suit that was quite revealing. They entered the dining area and only the two businessmen were eating, and discussing something quite animatedly. When they saw Gretchen they stopped talking and stood up, staring. Jack smiled.

"Good evening," both men said.

"Good evening," Jack replied.

"Hi," Gretchen just smiled and looked around. She nudged Jack and pointed to a table toward the back of the boat. "Let's go sit there." And off they went. Dinner was superb, the wine excellent, dessert and coffee, the best. The view was ever entertaining, from ocean cargo ships, to other boats, to early season water skiers. As the sun began to set, it got a little chilly so the lovely couple headed for their room. The two businessmen were relaxing with coffee and waved. Jack waved, but Gretchen blew them a kiss. The younger business-man almost spilled his coffee. Upon entering their room they found fresh flowers and a nicely chilled bottle of champagne. A card simply said, "Enjoy", so they did.

They slept late into the morning as was their custom. Then they got up, showered and dressed, and went together to the dining area. However, the tables were gone, and a coffee table with two couches on one side and one couch on the other, took their place. Jeff greeted them, and waved his arm toward the single couch and said, "Good morning, please join us."

Jack looked around; there was no place else to sit. Gretchen took his arm and they sat down. A lady brought in coffee and scones, put them on the coffee table, and seated herself next to Jeff on one of the couches across from Jack and Gretchen. Then the two businessmen, and one other man, filled the remaining couch.

"Please help yourselves. We've already eaten," the older businessman said, but he seemed different from the day before. Jack sensed something was wrong. Gretchen began fixing a plate and a cup of coffee for Jack and then for herself, as the businessman continued.

"Jack, you don't recognize me, but I'm the man you and your brothers were supposed to kill earlier this month," Jack bolted upright but felt a hand on his shoulder from behind. He turned and saw two men standing there.

"What the hell is going on here?" Jack demanded.

Authoritatively, but not loudly, Joe Cornish replied, "Sit down and enjoy your breakfast. You are not going to be harmed. I have introductions to make."

Jack was seething mad and glanced at Gretchen. She had an odd smile on her face that he had not seen before. He sat down.

"My name is Joe Cornish. I work for the FBI, among other things. Tom, at the end, is a journalist for the Seattle Times." He spoke slowly, "Joe, next to me, Jeff, Janae, and the gentlemen behind you are some of my operatives. So you can see you are in the hands of the good guys."

"I don't know who you think..." Jack started.

"Jack!..." Joe Cornish said loudly, then softened, "I think you will like what I have to say, will you please listen?"

Jack waved his hand, as if saying 'whatever'. Joe Cornish continued, "Your boss from San Diego has fled this country and is now, as we speak, hiding in Paraguay. My associates and I were responsible for the trouble your boss had in Monterey Bay and San Diego. After he killed your brothers, I called and threatened him if he did not pull his operation out of Seattle within twenty-four hours. He did not comply with my wishes, so I sent evidence to the District Attorney in San Diego that will put your boss away for good, if not get him the death penalty."

"A grand jury looked at the evidence and immediately indicted your boss. He barely slipped out of the hands of law enforcement. And now, he is buying friends in Paraguay. He is a fugitive, on the run from the laws of the United States of America. Although we can't extradite him from Paraguay, I know his every move, including what he is having for lunch this very moment." Joe Cornish paused and poured himself some coffee. Jack looked like a caged animal.

"Jack, for the next sixty minutes only, I am offering you a way out of your entanglement with your brothers' murderer. If you fulfill all my requirements, I will give you immunity from a wide range of charges that will be brought against you in court Monday morning. And believe me, the evidence is fool proof."

"You're bluffing," Jack was cold and hard.

"I have an eye witness, with names, dates, and places," Gretchen stood up and slowly moved around the coffee table to Joe Cornish's side.

Jack's mouth dropped open, staring wide eyed in disbelief. "Gretchen... no..." he was demolished in an instant.

"Gretchen is one of my best operatives, has been for quite a while."

Jack's blood began to boil. Angrily he spat out the words, "You said you loved me and I believed you."

"Jack!" Joe Cornish was loud again. "I can also give you what you want most."

Jack sneered back, "No you can't."

"Do you remember the things Gretchen talked with you about this past week? Getting out from under your boss, working hard, not to break the law, but prospering under it?" Jack's eyes were burning holes in the floor.

Joe Cornish looked at Gretchen, handing her the ball, and she spoke softly, "Jack, you can do all those things. And I talked about them with you because I want to do them with you." His head began to rise with a quizzical look.

"I *do* love you. The sky's the limit for us in doing lawful things, and only death awaits you when you're working against the law." A ray of hope barely started to grace Jack's face. It was time for Joe Cornish to close the deal.

"Is there some loyalty you feel you owe to the man who murdered your brothers? Or is it that you don't think you owe your brothers anything?"

Gretchen finished with, "Jack I'm the same person you fell in love with. You know how hard I can work and play." She went back over and sat next to him. "I'm not ever going back to the club again. Think what we could accomplish together," she took his hand. "I am a law enforcement operative. I am on the side of the law, and I want to continue to do so with you, as husband and wife. Please. Listen to Joe Cornish, and listen to his requirements, but think of me."

Jack looked at her. He could feel his anger crumbling. She was worth everything to him.

"I guess...it's better than a...deserted island," Jack's voice was weak but desperate.

Gretchen broke into a huge smile and wrapped her arms around him. "I love you, baby. I love you, I love you, I love you." Jack couldn't hold back his emotions; he began to sob.

Jack spent the next hour alone with Joe Cornish in his den. Gretchen huddled with Janae, Kandee, and PC. Tom was writing furiously, Jeff was making his rounds of the whole ship, making sure everything was working properly. Joe didn't know what to do. He poured himself a cup of coffee, sat down and decided to think ahead. What was Joe Cornish thinking and planning next?

# 28

When Joe Cornish had finished with Jack, Gretchen grabbed Jack and headed for their room. They had plans to talk about. Joe Cornish went into the dining area and, seeing Joe, sat down and poured some coffee for himself. Jeff came around the corner and the three huddled.

"Gentlemen…" Joe Cornish started but his first sip was not hot enough. He rose and put his cup in the microwave in the kitchen, and turned it on. Nobody said anything. It was obvious Joe Cornish was still thinking. On returning to the couch with the hot coffee, he poured in some creamer and then picked up a spoon and stirred. He was staring at the coffee.

"You see, gentlemen…" he took a long sip, "Just like putting creamer into strong coffee, and stirring it around a bit to get perfection, we put Gretchen into a dark situation run by Jack, stirred it up a bit, and I do believe we have a perfect solution to this particular outbreak of darkness in Seattle." He sipped again and continued, "Jeff, our destination of Juneau was in case Jack didn't cooperate. I wanted a nice cell far enough away from Seattle to keep him safe and quiet. Now that he is on our side, I do believe we can change course and head back." Jeff nodded his head and left for the pilot house.

Joe Cornish sat back, sipped his coffee and asked, "Joe, what would be the best and fastest way to shut the whole Seattle club down?"

"Raid the place with warrants and make enough arrests so they couldn't open back up."

"Very good. I've e-mailed the evidence from Gretchen to the DA in Seattle and he felt Tuesday afternoon would be enough time to get things lined up. I'd like you, Kandee, Tom, and PC to go along on the raid in order to rescue and take into our custody all the under-aged girls working there. We will have an escape route and destination, probably Seabeck, planned out for you by then. Don't be afraid to stay a day or two to help make sure the girls are comfortable."

"Where will you be?" Joe asked, as Joe Cornish took another sip.

"Oh, I was thinking of taking a trip."

"When?"

"As soon as we get back."

"Where are we going?"

"Uh... not you, Joe. I need you to be in on that raid. Especially to make sure Gretchen stays safe and generally keep an eye on things while I'm gone."

"Where are you going?"

"Paraguay."

"What? With whom?"

"Jack and a cousin of Jennifer's."

Joe's mouth opened but he didn't know what to say. Obviously Joe Cornish was planning way ahead as he usually did. "I don't know who Jennifer is, much less her cousin, but are you sure about taking Jack?"

Joe Cornish put his coffee cup down and turned more serious. "We've had success so far in Seattle, and I say, why not push on until we get stopped. Evil sometimes has a soft underbelly. If I put a guillotine over Jason Everett Samuelson's neck and lay him under it, and then offer him a way out, he just might take it. And Jack's revenge for the murder of his brothers might be a sharp enough blade."

"Joe..."

"I know Joe, it's risky. That's why I need you here. If I fail and there is a massive retaliation, I want you to protect the safe house in Seabeck at all costs. The reverend's work of rescuing young girls has to keep advancing. Cache enough firepower close by the safe house so if my regular calls quit, you can be ready. Remember, in the safe in my den on the yacht, is a letter for you to open upon my death. If I miss one check in, consider me dead and open the letter. There will be instructions for you and funds for carrying them out."

Joe sat back on the couch. What if Joe Cornish didn't come back? It sounded like he was being put in charge.

Later, everyone assembled for dinner. As they were all seated and dinner was being served, Joe Cornish tapped his water glass and announced, "I'd like to thank the Almighty for making us one big happy family. Jack how are you feeling?"

"Uh…I…I've never felt the way I do right now. Gretchen says it's called freedom. Not free to do whatever I want, but free to do what's right with no limit."

"Excellent. Jack, I know you have an overwhelming desire to thank me for putting Gretchen into your life…"

"Yes, sir, I do.

"…so, I have concocted a plan. One that kills two birds with one stone. I am going to go to Paraguay and visit with your old boss. How would you like to accompany me?" There was a pause so Joe Cornish continued, "Do you think you're ready for that?"

"Do I get to kill him?" Jack was as serious as the coffee was black.

"No, you don't get to kill him, but you do get to make him think you will."

Then Gretchen blurted out, "Hey! You're going to bring my Jack back to me, right?"

"That is the plan, my dear. By the way, would you two like to get married?"

# 29

Gretchen and Jack would tell their kids that they got married and had one wonderful honeymoon night aboard a big beautiful yacht out on the water. Now, as the boat returned to the marina in Seattle, everyone was dispersing to their respective jobs.

Tom submitted another story and his boss chaffed again saying it was just that, a story. Tom's reply was the same as before, "I was an eye witness, and part of the happenings, because the guy running it wanted an accurate account published." It seemed Tom's boss wanted to be convinced, but was being stubborn.

Joe and the four girls drove out to Seabeck in a large van loaded with many items of usefulness taken from the big drawer under the double-bed in the forward compartment of *Cascade Islander-A*. Joe dropped the girls off to help the staff in teaching the young girls a drill in case of an attack from the outside. Joe drove around to the back of the property and opened a gate in the fence. There was a storage shed inside the fence and he unloaded the gear into it. They also gave the staff a heads up of more girls coming in the next few days.

Jeff's job was staying in contact with those who were conducting the raid. Joe and Jeff would be part of it and Tom and the girls would be waiting outside in two fifteen passenger vans, ready for any young girls.

*

Joe Cornish and Jack, immediately upon docking, walked up through the gate and entered a cab waiting for them.

"Boeing Field, yesterday," Joe Cornish told the cabdriver, handing him two hundred dollars. The cab driver alerted his dispatcher and at the same time found the gas pedal. He put his seat belt on tight and turned his Mariners cap backwards. Fifteen minutes later, Joe Cornish was giving the cabdriver directions to the hanger he wanted at Boeing Field. Arriving, they got out and headed toward the door labeled 'office'. There was a holler in the background from the cabbie, "Thanks, man!"

After some brief paper work, Joe and Jack were boarding a business jet which had luggage with their names on them belted into two of the seats.

The beautiful Puget Sound region, Mount Rainier, and what was left of Mount St. Helens, disappeared behind them as the jet sped south. Two hours later they were on the ground at San Diego's airport. The pilot opened the door to Jennifer and her cousin. Jennifer had one suitcase and her cousin had two -- large ones. Joe Cornish welcomed them aboard. He introduced Jack as one of his operatives from Seattle. Jennifer introduced her cousin simply as Jim from the east coast. Joe Cornish seated them, then served lemonade.

Jennifer spoke, "When I asked you over the phone last week, 'When are we were going to spend some time together," you hung up on me. Then you call this morning and leave a message to pack for a few days and meet you at the airport this afternoon. I laughed until my boss called me in, half an hour later, and said a rumor had surfaced that a contract was out on my life and I should disappear for a week, 'and be sure you don't tell anyone where you are going', he said."

She looked at Joe Cornish and he looked as though he hadn't heard her. So she paused and then looked at her cousin. He slowly produced a broad smile. She looked back at Joe again. This time he was smiling also, and reached out to bump fists with Jim.

"Ohhh! I didn't know you two were so closely connected. Silly me, I thought you had never met." Jennifer was enjoying the surprise and the feeling of being out of the loop, because she had very pleasant memories of time spent alone with Joe Cornish in the past, and her cousin was always full of surprises.

"I won't ask which one of you talked to my boss. I just wonder where it is we are going and if I packed right," she was enjoying acting peeved, and inspected her fingernails as if she were a jet-setting actress.

"Paraguay, my dear, Paraguay," Joe Cornish was playing along. Jack had almost stopped breathing at the talk of a contract, and now sensed something more serious underlying the banter between Joe and Jennifer.

"Paraguay!" She said the word as if it was a red apple and she was a teacher. "Why, I think the only person I know in Paraguay happens to be the guy who wants me dead!" Now Jack was all ears. Who was this lady? What did she know about his boss, or former boss, he corrected himself.

Outside, a car screeched to a halt at the stairs leading to the jet. A man got out, grabbed a suitcase and climbed. Joe Cornish met him at the door, welcomed him aboard, and then said to the pilot, "Let's go!"

Joe Cornish directed the man to a seat and announced, "This is a dear friend of mine. Reverend, I'd like you to meet Jennifer, who happens to be the District Attorney from San Diego, and her cousin, Jim. Jack here is with me."

The reverend spoke, "Everyone, it is my pleasure to meet you all," Jennifer's mouth hung open and she looked at Joe Cornish.

He held her eyes for only a second and then said, "Let's all buckle up."

The jet flew southeasterly for another two hours and then began a descent. The five enjoyed light conversation and the view of Mexico beneath them. As the jet landed and drew up to the airport buildings, Jennifer noticed the name Cancun. She was still playing along and enjoying the surprise trip. It sure beat the stress of her job. Jennifer sensed that this reverend was in on the surprise so she said, "Pray tell, what shall we do in Cancun?"

"Well, have dinner of course. First however, the reverend has a wedding to perform here and I'm going along. Care to join me?"

"A wedding!" Jennifer said excitedly.

"Yes. Just put on the best outfit you brought; the bathroom is through that door," Joe said pointing to the rear of the jet. Jennifer got up, took her suitcase and glanced at her cousin. He was fiddling with something in his pocket. Okay, he knows what's going on, she thought, and stepped into the bathroom. All four guys had changed into their best and were standing, waiting for her when she came back out.

"Somehow I feel like the lucky one," Jennifer offered. Her cousin burst out with a laugh, but quickly caught himself.

"My dear, you are stunning. Shall we go?" Joe Cornish always kept things moving. As they descended the stairs, a limousine was waiting for them. The trip was short, and ended at an old mission-styled chapel. The crowd was sparse, but the chapel was flooded with flowers.

"Oh, look at all the gladiolas," Jennifer said as they walked up the aisle to a seat. "They're my favorite, you know."

Joe Cornish looked directly into her eyes and said, "I do." Then he seated the four of them with Jennifer on the aisle so she could see.

Soon the music began and the reverend walked in from the side door and stood at the altar, beaming.

"Boy, your reverend really knows how to make everyone feel welcome."

"Yes, he's very good."

Jennifer was enjoying the music and the reverend was waiting peacefully. She took a quick glance up the aisle and saw no one.

Joe Cornish leaned over near Jennifer and whispered, "Do you remember the last time we spent the night together? I think it was in Vegas?"

"Yes, it was," she turned and eyed him.

Joe Cornish continued, "Do you remember what I said that night?"

"Yes, as a matter of fact I do." She paused and looked around to make sure they weren't missing anything. "We were both half drunk, and you said you would never marry anyone but me!" She emphasized the last word and looked into his eyes boldly as if to remind him. That was her undoing. His eyes were serious and sincere. It only took her a second to read his eyes, and one more to glance up at the smiling reverend again. Understanding began to dawn; could her secret dream be turning into reality? Right here, right now?

Joe Cornish got up and stepped into the aisle. He looked down at Jennifer and offered his hand. Then he spoke out loud, "Jennifer, may I have your hand?"

She offered him her hand as her other one automatically covered her mouth in surprise. He drew her to her feet as tears began flowing down her face, but she hardly noticed. All she could see was Joe's face as if framed in a picture.

"Jennifer, I do not want to be parted from you from this day on."

Now all she could do was wrap her arms around his neck and sob, her eyes flooded with tears of joy and relief. The past years of on the job stress found a release, one so wonderful, all she could do was hang on.

After a minute Joe Cornish gently brought her arms down and, holding both hands, looked intently at her. "Was that a yes?"

Now she began to laugh and cry. "Yes, my dearest Joseph, that's a yes!"

The ceremony, the dinner, the night in Cancun and an early morning walk on the beach, left Jennifer with waves of peace and safety overflowing her like waves of the ocean. Later that morning they all boarded the jet again and were ready to continue their trip.

# 30

Six hours brought them to Brasilia, Brazil, after a lunch stop in Caracas, Venezuela. That evening in Brasilia they acted like tourists. They slept in late and then flew down to Campo Grande, Brazil. From there they packed into a rented Suburban. Joe Cornish had the pilot fly on to Ponta Pora near the border with Paraguay, and wait for them. The five drove down in the Suburban and made it in about five hours; they were tourists. After securing the biggest room in the Ponta Pora Inn, and a room on each side of it, they settled in for some planning.

"We are only about an hour away from our target, as we sit here," Jim announced. "I have a man working at the ranch that Mr. Samuelson bought and I can communicate with him." Jack realized now why Jim was with them and was a bit more confident that he would get out alive after killing his former boss. Yes, Joe Cornish might be in charge, but if Jack found a gun in his hand, he would kill Jason Everett Samuelson at first chance.

"We are going to cross the border and drive south for about half an hour. We'll take a dirt road off to the right and wind around a few hills and down into the back side of the ranch." Jim was in charge of getting them there and making contact.

Now Joe Cornish took over, "Reverend, you're staying here and being our communications guy. If things go bad, get the pilot and get out. Fly home. If things go well, we'll have a big fish on the line and we'll need everybody to reel him in. Jim, Jack, Jennifer and I will establish a forward base of operation; then Jack and I will go on from there. For the rest of today, Jennifer and I are going to play tourist, scoping out the city and familiarizing ourselves with the roads, etc. Jack, I want you to go with Jim to a local pub and try to hear any news which might be important to us. Jim speaks the language. Do more listening than drinking. Get a good night's sleep. Let's be prepared to leave at 8 AM. This will be fun." Joe Cornish was optimistic. It was based on his planning.

Next morning, the reverend, Jennifer, and Joe Cornish breakfasted together while Joe filled them in on his plans. Jack and Jim had got along okay and just had coffee for breakfast in their room. They were ready by 7:30 AM. At 7:50 AM, Joe Cornish tapped on their door, and they joined him and Jennifer in loading the Suburban and heading out.

The border crossing from Brazil into Paraguay was not difficult; Jim took care of talking with the border guards. Traveling across the ridge and down the hillside to the south, the road eventually descended into the rolling hills of Paraguay. Here the mountains of Brazil seemingly petered out, as if the border had not allowed them access. It was warm and beautiful and the view from the border down across the lowlands of Paraguay was exceptional. When Jim suddenly pointed out the dirt road to the right, things got serious fast. They quite rightly remembered that they were on a covert combat mission behind enemy lines. Their best weapon: the element of surprise.

As they continued on the dirt road, the hills turned into rangeland and pasture areas. Soon a large branching tree came into view. Jim pointed to it and said, "Park under the big tree." Then he checked his watch and said, "Let's have a picnic." The four quickly got out and spread a blanket on the grassy ground. They set out a cooler and sat down. Just as Jennifer was about to ask her cousin what the heck they were doing, the sound of a vehicle was heard. From around the side of a low hill it was suddenly upon them. Jim eyed the car as it stopped and his undercover man from the ranch got out. He motioned for everyone to quickly get into his car. They put the picnic back into the Suburban, and leaving it unlocked with the key in the ignition, they loaded into the ranch car and headed back the way the car had come.

As the car wound its way along an ever-descending path, through low hills, and fenced pasturelands, the driver spoke, "I will stop at the barn and show you the underground rooms."

"Yes, excellent. Well done," Jim was pleased things were going as planned, when they were initially planned half a world away.

The main barn for the surrounding pasturelands came into view. It was bordered on all sides by low hills and was quite protected. The driver slowed and stopped as if he owned the place, and the few ranch hands working in the area took no notice of him or the passengers. The group got out and moved into the barn and through the tack room. This led to stairs down into a huge area with a side room of surveillance gear, phones and monitors. They entered this room and closed the door.

Joe Cornish announced, "This is our base. Jennifer, you and Jim will monitor Jack and I as we run the operation. Should we run into trouble, your exit strategy is to saddle two of those horses and ride back up the road to the Suburban and head back to the Ponta Pora Inn. If you miss the pilot, the jet and the reverend, just continue up into Brazil further and work your way home. More importantly, if we are successful, we will be busy." Joe Cornish went over the equipment with Jim who already was familiar with it.

Assured that base camp was set, Joe Cornish and Jack began the assault. They got into the ranch car with the driver and headed to the main ranch house. As they approached, Joe and Jack crouched down in the back seat. The driver pulled into one of the open bays in the large carport housing all the ranch machinery and equipment. He got out and ambled over to the kitchen door and went in. His break was over and he had checked what needed checking at the big barn.

Joe listened to the comings and goings of the ranch. Soon a group of horses thundered into the big yard and the riders dismounted. Ranch hands hurried to their assistance.

The booming voice of Jack's former boss was heard above the others, "Let's cool off in the pool before lunch." Jack's eyes widened in recognition, but Joe's deadpan stare calmed him down. As the commotion died down Joe pulled a 9mm out of his belt and handed it to Jack, "Can you use this if necessary?"

"Yes, sir," and Jack was sure it would be necessary. Joe peeked out; the coast was clear. He motioned Jack to open the door and get out. As Joe got out, he pulled his remaining fire arm and left it on the floor of the back seat. Suddenly standing up by the car, they took on the air of belonging to this scene and ambled to the kitchen door. Joe grabbed the door knob but it was locked. Only a second later it was opened from the inside by the undercover worker.

# 31

Tuesday afternoon saw one of the biggest line ups of law enforcement vehicles in the history of Seattle quietly pull up to Jack and Gretchen's club. The temporary management was in chaos because they expected Jack and Gretchen back. Not only were they not back, no one had heard from them, nor could they get ahold of them. Law enforcement covered every exit and then a group of detectives went in the front door with the warrants. Joe and Jeff were in the second wave and led detectives to the rooms where, according to Gretchen, the girls were kept. Bingo! There were a dozen girls, and ten were underage. They were photographed, fingerprinted and put into the custody of Joe and Jeff. As each girl was processed, Joe led her to one of the two waiting vans.

When Joe brought out the ninth girl, he put her in with Tom, PC, and Janae. They now had five girls in their van and Joe said, "Tom, you drive. You know the route and destination. You guys take off now and we'll follow soon. Janae, you're packing, right?"

"Yes I am," and she knew how and when to use a weapon.

"Okay. Drive normal, but try not to stop. The girls all used the bathroom before I brought them out, so you should be good till you get there." Joe closed the door and slapped it. Tom moved out and rescue one was underway.

As they drove away, Janae heard gunfire. She looked back and saw Joe on the ground, but he looked alert like he had just ducked at the sound. Tom slowed up, but Janae turned and spoke, "Keep going, keep going."

Joe heard the shot from above and ducked, then scooted behind a car. A deputy sheriff was on the ground, bleeding. He had taken a bullet without warning from the upstairs office window. The shooter and his accomplice were soon surprised by law enforcement from inside. Joe later learned that the shooter was the person left in charge and he freaked out thinking he would be executed by the big boss if he didn't put up a fight. One chose to give up and live, the other one chose death by a police bullet.

Joe moved into the building again and Jeff met him with the last underage girl. "Here. Keep your heads down out there. I'm staying and monitoring the raid through to the end. You guys go ahead and leave. Be safe," Jeff's professional training was keeping his emotions in check.

Joe took the girl's hand. He couldn't believe how young and vulnerable she looked. Outside the door he paused and looked around. Then with a good hold on the girl's hand, they dashed around the side of the building to the second van. Gretchen unlocked the door and Joe and the girl jumped in. Gretchen pointed the girl to a seat with Kandee near the four other girls. Joe jumped into the driver's seat. Pulling away, Gretchen suddenly grabbed Joe's arm and yelled, "Stop!"

Joe hit the brakes. "What?" He looked at Gretchen.

In her passenger side rear view mirror she saw a female walking up the alley, alone. Gretchen rolled down the window and yelled, "Joni, what are you doing?"

The female trotted up to the van, hearing a familiar voice. "Gretchen... I'm getting to work late, sorry... what's going on?"

Gretchen jumped out and opened the middle doors of the van, "Joni, get in quick. I'll explain in a minute."

She got in and eyed the young girls and Kandee. To Kandee she said "Hi," and sat down. Then eyeing Gretchen she asked, "We got a private party going?" As they rounded the street corner, Joni saw the lineup of law enforcement vehicles and ducked down on her seat. As Joe drove carefully away, Joni sat back up. "What was that?" She was wide eyed.

"That's a police raid. All the over-age girls are being arrested, processed, and will spend one night in jail. They will probably be released tomorrow." Gretchen was not exaggerating or making light of the situation.

"Why are they letting us go?" Joni was asking her boss as if Gretchen had obviously paid someone off and was getting away.

"They're letting us go because I'm an undercover law enforcement officer. If I would have let you walk into that, you'd be arrested and then released with no job to come back to. Joni, I can help you start a new life if you want to," Joni just stared with her mouth open, so Gretchen continued, "We're taking these young girls to a safe house where they will be taken care of and gotten back to their parents or someone who loves them. You can help us if you want to, or I can stop and let you out."

Joni then found her voice, "No, no, no, don't stop. Gretchen, I've always liked you. I'll help if I can. Please...just keep going," Joni covered her mouth with her hands. Tears were forming. She felt them coming and wasn't sure if they were from fear or relief.

Gretchen reached back and touched Joni's forearm. She said, "I'll help you, and you can help me. Tell the young ones back there they will never have to live this type of life again." Joni turned and saw all five young girls looking at her as if for wisdom or comfort.

Kandee saw that Joni was about to break into tears. She wrapped her arms around her and let her break. That brought tears to Kandee's eyes, and the girls joined in, too. Pretty soon the whole van was crying, with the exception of Joe, of course. Joe kept driving.

About forty-five minutes later, as they were crossing the Narrows Bridge to the Kitsap Peninsula, Joni asked Gretchen, "Where's Jack?"

# 32

The kitchen help minded their own business. The undercover kitchen man let Joe Cornish and Jack in the door and out into the dining room. The horseback riders were now all frolicking in the outdoor pool, just outside the dining area. The kitchen man quietly led them across the dining area, unlocked the door to the surveillance room, and ushered Joe and Jack in.

Nickolaea stood suddenly at the sight of unfamiliar faces. Her hand unsnapped her 9mm and had it out in a flash. Joe Cornish calmly held up his ID and badge which he had ready in his hand instead of a gun. Nickolaea automatically eased and then said under her breath. "I need you now, code blue," Joe Cornish knew code blue didn't mean what code red meant. So he and Jack stepped aside of the door and waited. Nothing was said; Joe Cornish just kept holding his ID and badge up like it was a shield against any harm.

"Who are you?" Nickolaea demanded. She held her gun in her hand, but pointed down at arm's length.

"Nickolaea, we are from the USA and I'll explain just as soon as Nicolus gets here," Joe Cornish was as calm as if he were in charge of everything. Jack just stared at Nickolaea and her gun.

Nicolus was at his boss's shoulder. His boss was in a patio chair by the pool watching the girls. He was trying to hold in his ample stomach but it wasn't working. James had not come outside yet, but the girls were putting on a show in the pool.

Nicolus's eyes were on the surrounding hills and the sky. He was listening for anything out of the ordinary. He ignored the girls because he was working, and he took his work seriously. As he heard the whisper in his ear piece he tensed and then relaxed again at the words 'code blue'. He put his hand on his boss's shoulder and said, "Stay here, I'll be right back."

"Okay," his boss understood that when Nicolus touched him in any way it meant something was up.

Jack felt the gun in his waistband and wondered why Joe Cornish wasn't going for his. The door opened, partially hiding Joe and Jack.

Nicolus stood half in and half out of the doorway. The first thing he noticed was Nickolaea standing with her gun drawn but pointing down, confirming 'code blue', and staring at something beyond his field of vision. She kept her eyes on whoever it was without acknowledging Nicolus. His gun was already drawn and leveled at whoever was behind the door. Then he heard a voice.

"Don't shoot me, Nicolus. At least not yet," Joe Cornish was calm and under control. As Nicolus slowly closed the door, he pointed his gun at Joe Cornish who slowly raised his other hand, not out of fear, but just acknowledging Nicolus. Jack followed suit.

"On top of your head, please. I'm going to search you. She will shoot you if your eyes give away the least spark of evil intent," they both obeyed, ID, badge, and all.

"Please do. I am clean. Jack here has a 9mm in his waistband, but it's not loaded."

"What?!" Jack burst out without thinking. Nickolaea raised her gun. Nicolus searched Joe, and then carefully searched Jack. He found the gun right away and confirmed that it was empty. He finished searching, and found no magazines or bullets at all.

"Now, tell me who you are," Nicolus was all business.

"Joe Cornish, Federal Bureau of Investigation. Special Investigations Office, Seattle. My badge is in my right hand,"

Nicolus carefully took the ID and badge from Joe's hand. It was authentic.

"Please put your hands down. And this is...?" pointing to Jack.

"Jack worked in Seattle for your boss until a couple of days ago. Last week your boss gunned down Jack's two brothers at point blank range as he was sitting next to them on a couch. He almost shot Jack also, but decided to leave him in charge instead. Your boss thought Jack would be sufficiently motivated to do what was required of him without excuses. Your boss was wrong. Jack changed sides over the weekend, and now he is here for revenge," Joe Cornish said it evenly, not threateningly. He did not try to stare Nicolus down. He just told the truth without fear or anxiety. Nicolus saw this and saw the fear and anxiety in Jack. So far the explanation made sense.

"How do you know our names?" Nicolus was still deadly, but he was moving toward calm seriousness.

"The same way I knew when you would be having Chinese food for dinner."

This brought the deadliness back into Nicolus's eyes, "What is it that you call yourself?"

"I identified myself to your boss only as Batman, and that Seattle was my Gotham City. I have not hidden the truth from you and Nickolaea."

Nicolus took a deep breath, "Am I making a big mistake by not killing you both right now?"

"Your decision right now will follow you the rest of your life, for good or for bad."

Nicolus breathed through his nose again. "I am going to let you sit down. Give me your word you can control him," nodding toward Jack.

"Jack will do what I say, won't you Jack?"

"Yes, sir," Jack began to feel less scared. He realized he was witnessing a man without a gun disarm another man with a gun. He suddenly felt a bit of pride for being on the right side.

"Sit down," Nicolus pointed to two chairs. "Nickolaea, please check the boss and the perimeter, and put everyone on alert except for the boss, James, and the girls." He paused and then gently grabbed Nickolaea's arm as she passed by him. "One moment, please," then he addressed Joe Cornish again. "The name of your undercover accomplice!"

"I believe his name is Michael; he works in the kitchen here. You know him. Please don't kill him, as he will be valuable to you after you hear what I have to say."

Nicolus turned to Nickolaea, without taking his eyes off Joe and Jack, "Find him, handcuff him, and bring him here please."

Joe and Jack sat. Nicolus eyed them and waited. Joe did not speak out of respect for the fact that they were in Nicolus's territory. After a moment, Nicolus heard something in his ear and opened the door. Michael was pushed in, in cuffs. Nicolus guided him to a chair. Nickolaea left again, closing the door, and began her check around the premises.

She peered through the glass wall out into the patio and pool. The four were in the pool cavorting. The girls had bunny-ear head bands on and not much else. She moved to the main door and alerted the guards outside. All seemed normal. She scanned the horizon outside. Nothing. She relayed a message into Nicolus's ear piece, "Normal."

As the four men waited silently, Joe Cornish noticed Nicolus's eyes change slightly.

"Now, tell me who else you have out there preparing an attack."

"The District Attorney for San Diego and her cousin, who I think works for the CIA, are in the surveillance office like this one in your barn bomb shelter. A reverend friend of mine is at our hotel waiting for good news or bad to pass on. I have a private jet and a pilot close by, also. I'm telling you the truth. If you can believe me, you can see our plan is not to attack."

Nicolus spoke softly into his mic, and a few seconds later Nickolaea entered again. The three were trapped by two armed bodyguards.

"Please," Nicolus gestured with his arm, inviting Joe Cornish to speak.

"There is a worldwide warrant out for your boss for murder and a lot more. He will soon have to run again as your money will not be enough to hold back the pressure of the world law enforcement community on the Paraguayan government. Your boss's assets are being frozen. If he tries to access foreign accounts through a local bank, the FBI will know. Your boss would have to go in person to wherever he has his money hidden, and law enforcement would be there waiting."

Nicolus's blood slowly began to boil. "You think you can so easily convince me to betray my boss with your talk?"

Joe Cornish now spoke with authority, "Nicolus, I am counting on your honor as a man to do everything in your power to protect your boss, even at the cost of your own life." Joe Cornish paused and let that sink into Nicolus. "I want to list your choices. First: Shoot us and flee with your boss. Eventually he will be caught and you and Nickolaea will be prosecuted for helping a fugitive, or perhaps die in a shootout. Second: You can give up now and surrender yourselves and your boss to law enforcement, and face a long jail sentence. Third: You have a third option only because I am here. The third option is the only one that will give you and your boss freedom. Not freedom to do whatever you want. You have that now, and it's not working. But freedom to do what's right and legal, with the sky as your limit under the law. I am your only option that has with it a future for you and Nickolaea, together. Will you choose life or death?" There was a pause.

"You can offer me no guarantee except your word, your talk. Even if I would agree, at the first opportunity you would rob us, shoot my boss and me, and take his frozen assets, too. You are foolish and naïve to come here. I have a fourth option that I will now take. I will shoot you all right now as you sit," Nicolus drew his gun.

"You are doing the right thing," Joe's voice was confident. Nicolus reached out and pointed his gun at Joe's head.

"You like my fourth option?" he cocked the gun.

"Yes, this is exactly what needs to be done," Joe's voice did not waver. Jack gave up. He was close to feeling like he did when his brothers were murdered. Might as well get it over with.

"Nicolus. Do you hear me? What you are doing is what *we* must do."

Nicolus's stare could not stop the confidence he saw in Joe Cornish's eyes. "What do you mean?"

"You are taking all my options away except death. At this point even the strongest man would do or say whatever is required to live." Joe was talking slowly and taking a chance, but he paused to let what he said sink into two minds that were trained to protect to the death. Nicolus was ready to shoot. At the first sign of fear in Joe Cornish's eyes he would pull the trigger. He had work to do. No time for games.

The pause became a pregnant time, needing action one way or the other. Nicolus had never backed down or blinked before. His stare broke most men. He curved his straight trigger finger and touched the trigger. No change in Joe's eyes. Nicolus intended to take a quick glance at Nickolaea, but she was looking at him and their eyes held. His training blinked. A sudden feeling of what it would be like to live with Nickolaea without being bodyguards, ignited in his mind like a struck match.

"What magic are you offering?"

Joe continued slowly, "I offer only what is true. Your job is to protect your boss and keep him alive at all costs, even if it means your death. If your boss felt he was about to die with no way out, he would agree to my third option. It would be his decision, not yours. You would not be betraying him," Joe paused, and then kept on slowly, "You and Nickolaea, your boss,--everyone would live. Live a good life with abundance, not a bad life with abundance. You have never imagined this before. I am offering this to you now."

Nicolus could see Nickolaea's eyes soften. He was in uncharted waters. He tried to think.

"Tell me how my boss would be better off, and not have me killed when I'm not looking?"

"I can arrange for him to live well off by his own hand under the law rather than opposed to it." This ignited Nicolus.

"How? You are not telling me how!" he was shouting.

Now Joe Cornish spoke out louder. "The same way I sabotaged his clubs without being seen. The same way I survived his assassination attempts on my life. The same way I knew just how and where to find him and you, even on the other side of the world. Nicolus, I'm not a beginner, this is not just dumb luck. I have assets that I choose not to reveal to you, but that you can clearly see are operationally effective. I offer you and your boss this, because I don't want his bad business to flourish. Because good can attain much more than bad."

"This is not law enforcement."

"True, it is not. Yet, in my capacity as a law enforcement officer, I can make this happen legally."

"You have just barely begun to make me understand you. My training and experience tell me to shoot, and then go about my business. I have no good reason not to."

"Nicolus," Nickolaea's voice was patient, not pleading, not more than a whisper. "If there is a chance for us...let's listen."

Nicolus did not look at Nickolaea this time. He knew her eyes would melt him. He waited, pursed his lips, weighing things, then looked at Joe Cornish again. No change there.

Jack looked up at Nicolus. He had seen that look before, when his boss decided not to kill him. Wow! Maybe he would not die today.

Nicolus straightened his trigger finger, thought for a moment, and lowered the gun. He replaced the safety on the weapon and holstered it. Nickolaea knew to keep her gun trained on them until Nicolus told her not to. He glanced at her and spoke with his eyes. She, too, holstered her gun. Nicolus and Nickolaea sat down, knowing they could easily overpower the three in a fight. They looked at Joe Cornish.

"Speak to us of your plan. Convince me I'm not a fool."

For the next ten minutes, Joe Cornish had the floor. Everyone listened, including Jack. Then it was time to act.

*

Nicolus and Nickolaea emerged with Joe Cornish between them in handcuffs. They walked across the dining area and out onto the patio. The big boss and James heard the glass door open and turned to see who it was. Immediately they stood up and faced the three.

"Nicolus?" The boss wanted to know if it was time to panic.

"Sir, this is your 'Batman'. We caught him as he was entering the house."

The boss began to panic, looking around to find a place to run or hide. "Nicolus…how in the hell…"

"I don't know how he got here, but I have him under control. He says he has an accomplice who is setting a bomb in this area. I think he is lying but I'm not positive."

"Shouldn't we go to the bomb shelter in the barn like you planned?"

"No, not yet. As long as he is here with us the bomb will not go off," The boss, then, stood up straight and slowly walked toward them. He began to boil as he looked at Joe Cornish.

"Who the hell do you think you are? I'm going to make you die slowly with a lot of pain."

"Jason Everett Samuelson, I am putting you under arrest and placing you into my custody."

The boss glanced at Nicolus and then said, "You are, are you?"

"An FBI SWAT team is less than an hour behind me. They are in two vehicles."

Nickolaea added, "Sir, I have two incoming cars on the radar."

"You think you can sneak in here and bluff me into letting you arrest me? Go ahead and blow the bomb. We'll all go together. Nicolus, where is the accomplice?"

"My guards are out looking for him, sir."

"Well, Mr. Batman, I'm going to tie you to a post outside and let the sun by day and the cold by night drain the life out of you!"

Suddenly a voice from behind them spoke. "That's not a bad idea, boss." Everyone turned to see who spoke. Jack had a gun in his right hand pointing their way, and a device in his left hand held over his head. "Shoot me and I automatically let go of the button. The button makes the bomb go boom!"

"Easy boy," The boss suddenly recognized him. "What are you doing here?"

"I traded your friend, Batman, here, some information about you, if he'd let me be there when he arrested the one who murdered my brothers. He works for the FBI, you know," Jack was enjoying this even though it was an act.

"Jack," the boss offered, "that was business; you know that. I have plans for you," The boss was stalling to give Nicolus time to do something.

Jack moved closer and stuck the gun in Nicolus's face.

"This is just business, too. I'm going to plug your two bodyguards and tie you to a post and watch *you* die slow. They'll pay for my brothers, you'll pay for the trauma you put me through."

"Now wait a minute..." The boss began to squirm.

"Jack, you promised me you would not interfere," Joe Cornish spoke slowly and deliberately.

"Yeah, and you believed me. Whether I watch this murderer die slowly or we all go together, the blood of my brothers will be avenged. That's the only thing I care about."

"Jack, I've got lots of money. You would not believe how much," the boss offered nervously.

"No, you don't, you stupid bastard. The FBI has frozen it all. The only money you've got is what's with you, and I will enjoy all of it, including the blondes, if they want to live. You're done," Jack was convincing.

"Batman, do something! You're the law here!" The boss was cracking, fast.

"Jack. I have a one-time offer that can give you revenge and let us all live."

"What are you talking about?" Jack asked.

"As the arresting officer, I have the leeway to make an offer in a life or death situation. Here's my offer: We all leave alive before the SWAT team gets here; I have a way for us to do that. You all remain in my custody long-term. You go back to work in accordance with the law, not breaking the law. I'll always be watching and I'll be helping. If you were all smart enough to prosper as bad guys, then you are smart enough to do it as good guys." Joe Cornish continued, "No indictment, no trial, no prison, no death penalty, as long as you remain under my custody and care."

Jack shouted, "What about my revenge?"

"We leave, then blow the house before the FBI gets here. Jason Everett Samuelson will be pronounced dead, his assets confiscated by the government. He'll have to start out clean and broke. All of you will. But you'll be alive, with only me to answer to."

Silence reigned.

The boss, who had the most to lose, couldn't keep his mouth shut, "Jack, you know a good offer when you hear one. Come on, I was wrong to kill your brothers, I admit it. There's no reason for you or me to have to die."

Joe Cornish knew a closing time when he saw it, "Jason Everett Samuelson, do I have your word for accepting the terms of this offer?"

"Yes, yes, you do."

"And your right hand man?"

"Yes, him, too. James, give him your word."

"Yes," James wanted in, too.

"And your body guards?" Joe Cornish was being thorough, closing the deal with precision. The boss looked at Nicolus. He hesitated, then nodded.

"Okay, we're all in."

"Okay, this is how we do this. Jack hands his gun to me; I get to have a gun as arresting officer. Everyone else drops their guns. Jack disarms the bomb. Then Mr. Samuelson, you and your people quickly grab what you need, and we all load into two vehicles and head toward the barn bomb shelter. Questions?" Everyone looked at each other in silence. "No? Okay. Jack, you first."

Everyone did as instructed. As the big boss walked past Nicolus on his way to his room, he patted him on the shoulder.

"It's okay, Nicolus. It's the only way."

The four went down the hall to pack. Nicolus and Nickolaea followed. Nicolus glanced back at Joe Cornish with a rare smile. Joe winked.

Moments later, two vehicles left for the barn. One was driven by Jack with Joe Cornish in the passenger seat. The other was driven by Michael, the undercover man. They were at the barn in ten minutes. They quickly moved inside the bomb shelter. Without any introduction, Joe Cornish spoke to Jim, "Do we have the ranch house on a monitor?"

"Yes, we do."

"Any activity?"

"None. In fact there seems to be no one around, inside or out."

"Okay, Jack. Rearm the bomb and blow it," Jack fumbled around and then, with a pause for ceremony, pushed the button. No one except Joe Cornish saw Jim push a button under the table simultaneously. There was no sound, but the ranch house on the monitor was obliterated in smoke and debris.

The boss saw his ranch blow up and then looked around at everyone. When his eyes landed on Jennifer he blurted out, "Hey, what the..."

Joe Cornish began introductions. "Jason Everett Samuelson, may I present Jennifer, the District Attorney from San Diego, who you probably recognize," Joe leaned over and kissed Jennifer on the cheek. "She's also my wife, I might add. This is her cousin, Jim, who was very helpful in locating you here in Paraguay. Jim and Jennifer, Mr. Samuelson is the object of your indictment; however, he and his attendants are in my custody."

Jennifer offered her hand to the boss. "You're getting off with only a slap on the wrist," she offered not really smiling.

"No, ma'am. I'm getting set free to work with the law instead of against it. You won't even see me getting a parking ticket."

Then Jennifer addressed her husband, "My dear Joseph, how do you do it?"

"Believing the truth about life is what sets people free, remember?" Joe Cornish had proved it again. "Let's load up and get out of Paraguay."

*

Rolando had gotten a note from his boss saying there was a warrant from the USA for the arrest of the guy who just bought the visiting dignitary's ranch. "Get up there and find out what his intentions are."

Rolando, Rodriguez, a second SUV with soldiers and weapons were almost there. They heard and saw in the distance, a huge explosion. As the two vehicles approached the ranch house, they could see it was obliterated.

They couldn't see it, but two other vehicles were leaving the barn a few miles away and heading up into the hills. Joe Cornish and crew stopped at the tree and picked up the SUV they had left there. Jim drove that one and they all headed for Ponta Pora, Brazil.

At the inn, the reverend was introduced and a lavish dinner was prepared for them, and served in the inn's dining room as per instructions from Joe Cornish.

Jason Everett Samuelson, or Tony Aragapo, as he now preferred, raised a toast, "To freedom, may it ever remind us of which side of the law we are on."

Nicolus and Nickolaea were sitting together. James and the boss had the blondes between them. Joe Cornish and Jennifer were together, with the reverend next to her. Jack and Jim came next, then Michael the kitchen spy and the pilot of the jet. They all responded, "Here, here. Freedom."

Joe Cornish now addressed everyone, "I suggest we don't wander too far, get a good night's sleep, and have an early flight. Could we eat breakfast aboard?"

The pilot responded, "Yes, sir, we can eat breakfast aboard. The plane will be full, but we'll make it."

Nicolus got up and walked over to his boss, bent over, and whispered in his ear. Tony listened and then looked at Nicolus, then at the reverend, and then at Joe Cornish. "Let's ask. By the way Nicolus, just call me Tony from now on."

"Mr. Cornish, Nicolus and Nickolaea would like to be wed. Would the reverend be available tonight?" The reverend and Joe Cornish immediately stood and the reverend said, "It would be my pleasure."

Joe Cornish started clapping and everyone joined in. Jennifer hopped up and ran to Nickolaea and gave her an arms-around-the-shoulder hug. Nickolaea had never had a woman, other than her mother, hug her before.

The reverend waved for silence and mentioned he had seen a chapel just down the road. "I will go make preparations," as he got up to leave, Joe Cornish grabbed his arm and whispered something in his ear. Less than two hours later, Nicolus and

Nickolaea were wed in a short but sweet ceremony. The chapel was filled with flowers and a sizeable offering was left in the offering plate at the door.

Sundown saw everyone in bed, and sunrise saw everyone buckled in and wheels up. The runway was just long enough for the loaded jet. When Jennifer got up to tend to breakfast, Tony motioned for the two blondes to get up and help her. Being underway and heading home caused everyone to relax. As Nicolus breathed deeply through his nose, the smell of violence was noticeably absent. Joe Cornish took a deep breath also, and let it out slowly. Nobody knew it, but he felt glad to be alive.

After breakfast, Nicolus went forward to join the pilot. The jet was heading north.

# 33

The two vans from Seattle both made it to the former elementary school, now safe house, in Seabeck. The staff there debriefed the young girls with Kandee, PC, Janae, and Gretchen looking on. Joni just hung out with Gretchen. Joe, Jeff, and Tom strapped on weapons and patrolled the perimeter while the staff served dinner. Soon afterward everyone went to bed for a very much needed night's sleep. The ladies mixed in with the younger girls to make sure each was cared for if they awoke with nightmares or the like.

As dusk settled into darkness, all was well over the little village of Seabeck, WA, on the shores of Hood Canal. Peace is always appreciated most at night, when the Almighty keeps watch through the darkness.

As dawn was breaking about 5:45AM, Joe sensed trouble. Jeff stayed on site while Joe went scouting. The newspaper was bagged and on the ground at the entrance as usual. Joe turned to the right at the road and walked past the small volunteer fire station located next to the safe house. As he continued, he crossed over to the water side of the road. The tide was all the way in. As the road curved slightly, the businesses at Seabeck came into view. The only one open at this hour was the little coffee shack. Joe continued to walk toward it, his weapon covered by his windbreaker.

There was a slight breeze with the chill of a morning by the water. The light of day had now completely conquered the night, but trees filled the hills which rose up to the east and hid the warmth of the direct sun for a while longer. Seagulls, crows, herons, and an occasional eagle, were all busy looking for breakfast. Up the road past the buildings, Joe could just see a doe with two little ones following her, crossing the road. There was very little traffic as Seabeck was on the way to work for only a few.

The dirt shoulder of the road, only a foot above the high tide, changed into a boardwalk connecting the shore with the buildings built out over the water. There were some small shops first, then the General Store, then the main dock out to the marina. Bobbi's Café, along the dock behind the store, was not open. Not yet. The marina was quiet.

Back out at the beginning of the dock, Joe continued his walk through town. Seabeck Pizza was in the building past the dock, then an on-again/off-again real estate office. A few paces later was the coffee shack. Joe climbed the two stairs and opened the door. A woman was busy getting the machinery warmed up, but yelled, "Good morning."

"Good morning. Glad you're open. This probably isn't early for you," Joe breathed in the delicious smells.

"Oh, no," she laughed. "I open every morning about this time, so this is normal." She turned around and then said, "Hi, I'm Tammie; you're new. Come in by boat?"

"No. I got here yesterday evening and stayed at the old elementary school," Joe was interested to see how much the community knew about what was going on at the old the elementary school.

"Oh, you mean the girls rehab center. Wonderful place! I have some of the girls come down and help me. Job training, sort of. What am I making for you?"

"Twenty ounce white chocolate mocha with a shot of peppermint."

"Oh, my favorite Christmas drink! I like it better than eggnog."

"Yeah, me too. I never got unhooked," Joe looked out the small windows. All seemed normal. "Is the marina where you get most of your business?"

"No, actually there are a lot of retired regulars from out and about that come here almost every morning. We hear all the gossip. I just thought you came in on the three small cruisers that docked last night."

"Nope. Where were they from?"

"Shilshole, I think. They had dinner at Bobbi's. My daughter waits tables there at night," she handed Joe his drink.

He gave her a ten and asked, "I feel like canoeing or rowing. Any boats for rent here?"

"Thanks. Sure, first slip on the left at the marina is a boat rental. Jerry leaves a boat tied up. Just put ten dollars in the slotted box and help yourself. See ya tomorrow?"

"Um..., yeah, for sure. This is great." Joe took another slurp, thanked Tammie, and headed out to the dock again. First slip on the left there was a row boat and, what a deal, it had a coffee cup holder attached to the seat. Joe stuffed ten dollars into the slotted box, untied the boat and got in. He figured out the oars and quietly headed out toward the deeper end of the marina. It didn't take long to find the three boats. They were all the same design and color as if they were rented. Hmm. Three rentals from Seattle in a group. Nothing odd, probably a family reunion or office party or hit squad of bad guys. He chuckled to himself. Then he remembered. Gretchen had said young girls were sometimes worth twenty thousand dollars apiece.

Joe rowed on past the boats keeping about twenty feet away. No sign of life. Reaching the outer end of the marina, he doubled back a little farther out. Then he saw something he'd missed on the first pass. The middle boat was riding a lot lower in the water than the one ahead and the one behind. It was loaded with a lot of some ones or somethings. As he was passing the third boat, he noticed a light on inside an open porthole window. He stopped rowing and coasted. Part of a conversation carried out over the water.

"Yes, sir, nine o'clock... about an hour, sir... uh, about 3 PM, sir, if everything goes as planned."

Joe only heard half of the conversation, but it was enough to start him rowing again. Five minutes later he was tying up the boat. He looked at his watch; 7 AM. Forgetting his coffee in the cup holder, he hurried back out to the road. One glance at the coffee shack stopped him in his tracks. A Kitsap County Deputy Sheriff's car was parked out front. Joe stared at it for a moment, then headed that way. It was empty, so he bounded up the stairs and opened the door. Once inside he stopped and stared. The uniform was about five foot ten inches tall, and well built in the feminine way. Tammie and the officer had abruptly stopped their conversation and were staring, also. At Joe.

"Hey, you're back already? It was that good?" Tammie broke the ice.

"Yes, yes it was, Tammie," Joe tried to sound friendly, "Good morning deputy." A pause.

"Good morning. Is there something I can help you with?" She was very professional. She turned toward him and faced him squarely.

Joe closed the door behind him, and became serious.

"Yes, ma'am; yesterday the King County Sheriff's Department, in cooperation with the FBI, conducted a raid on a Seattle night club. You may know that."

"Yes, I heard about it. How does that involve you?" She became serious as well.

"Ma'am, I'm attached to the FBI. I helped transport ten underage girls from the raid, in the custody of the FBI, to a safe house here in Seabeck. I have reason to believe the safe house will come under attack in approximately two hours. These girls are worth twenty thousand dollars apiece on the human trafficking market. I'm requesting your help and presence at the safe house until the danger passes, if indeed I'm right."

The deputy looked at Tammie, who didn't have a clue. Then she addressed Joe, "May I see your ID please?"

Joe got his wallet out. He dug out his driver's license and handed it to her.

"I'm undercover, attached to the Office of Special Investigations, FBI in Seattle. I go by Joe." The deputy studied the ID.

"Who's your boss over there?"

"Joe Cornish."

"Okay, I've met him," the deputy made a decision. "Please step out into my car," she and Joe stepped outside and she opened the back door for him. He got in and looked at his watch. She got in the driver's seat and introduced herself. "I'm Deputy Sharon Madison. Joe, you have identified yourself to me as an undercover agent attached to the FBI, Seattle Office. You are requesting my help, the help of the Kitsap County Sheriff's Department, in protecting the people and property of the girls rehab center housed in the old elementary school a quarter mile up the road from here. Am I correct so far?"

"Yes, Deputy Madison. The information I have gathered suggests a 9AM attack this morning on the facility."

"Okay, we're going to drive over there and you can introduce me to the staff." They pulled out and headed up the road. As they turned into the main entrance, Jeff saw the sheriff car with Joe in the back. Deputy Madison rolled down her window but before she could speak, Jeff walked up, bent over and looked into the back seat, "Joe, what did you do now?"

"Please identify yourself," Deputy Madison was polite and professional.

Jeff pulled out his driver's license and handed it to her and said, "My name is Jeff, and I'm an undercover agent attached to the FBI Special Investigations Office in Seattle."

"Jeff, I'm Kitsap County Sheriff Deputy Sharon Madison. I notice both you and Joe are armed. Is this normal procedure for you?"

"No, ma'am, but we've been armed since we got here last night, in the event of an attack from the bad guys because of the raid on a Seattle night club. We have two female agents here with us along with ten under-age girls we brought from the raid under the custody of the FBI. Also, there are about twenty more under-age girls already housed here that have been rescued previously, and about a dozen or so staff.

"Thank you, Jeff. Joe spoke to me as having knowledge of an imminent attack and has asked for my assistance until this situation can be resolved. I understand that there are about fifty people here at this rehab center, and at the most four who know how to use a weapon."

"That's correct, ma'am," Jeff nodded.

"Do you have any weapons other than the ones on your persons?"

Joe spoke next, "Yes ma'am, we were instructed by our boss to bring enough firepower to defend this property, and we did."

"Where are the additional weapons?"

"In the tool shed at the back of the property," Joe explained.

"Joe, did your intel say what the attacker's strategy might be?"

"No, ma'am. Just the 9AM start and an hour for the operation."

"And have you familiarized yourself with the property enough to assess what their tactics might be?"

"Yes, ma'am. There are two main entrance roads leading to the same unloading area here at the front of the old school, and a third entrance leading to the ball field. A dirt road leads to a gate in the back fence, inside of which is the tool shed. Other than that, the property is all fenced, with woods outside the fence, except for on the north side where the fire station is. I would assume their plan is a frontal assault, killing whoever they have to in order to get the girls. Also, I did not see any vehicles attached to the three boats that came in last night, which is where my info comes from. So either they have help coming, or would commandeer this facility's vehicles to transport the girls to the dock. Then anyone seeing them might think the boats are here to pick up the rehab girls for an outing." Joe's training was coming through. The deputy was impressed.

Jeff jumped in, "Good thinking, Joe. So why don't we pack everybody up and head for Silverdale? The Sheriff's office is there. We'd get everybody out of harm's way."

But Joe continued, "Yeah, except maybe that is their plan, to scare us onto the road and then hijack us between here and town at their choosing. We would be safest in Silverdale at the Sheriff Department's buildings. The second safest option is right here. The third option would be on the road or someplace else."

Then Deputy Madison made the decision, "Okay, then we stay. Let me make a few calls. You guys prep your people."

"Yes, ma'am," Jeff liked this gal's guts.

"Thank you, ma'am. Probably better not to use the police band; they might be monitoring it." Joe was hitting all the angles.

"Good thinking. I'll use my cell phone," Deputy Madison called her boss and filled him in.

Meanwhile, Joe and Jeff huddled with Gretchen and Janae. Breakfast was just finishing so they instructed the staff to implement the drill they had been practicing. Joe and Jeff then left Gretchen and Janae on guard at the front of the building, retrieved the arms cache, and brought it to the main building.

Deputy Madison finished her call to her boss. An alert was sent out by cell phone to the other deputies in the area, to be ready to respond via police band if an attack happened. That way if the bad guys were listening, they would hear that help was coming.

The deputy then called a friend of hers, "Chief Monroe? Deputy Sharon Madison...Hi, I need a favor, ASAP...I need you to get to your Seabeck fire station with as many volunteers and friends as you can by 8:45 this morning. I need you to act as busy as you can, like you're doing drills or something...Yes, sir,...We have intel of a 9AM attack on the girls rehab center and I think it's legit. If you guys are busy on the north side of the property, that will limit their tactics...Yes, please do, but hand guns and shotguns only... Thanks, Chief. Thank you very much."

Deputy Madison then parked her cruiser parallel to the sidewalk in front of the main building, with the window rolled down and the loud speaker on. She entered the building with the ability to talk into her lapel mic and have it go out over the car's loudspeaker.

Inside the rehab center, the drill put the staff and girls in two classrooms across the hall from each other. The drapes were pulled and the desks were turned on their sides and lined up as protection. Janae was at the door looking down the hallway. Gretchen was across the hall at the other door, looking up the hall. They each had a mic and earbuds connected with Jeff and Joe. The two women each had a shotgun and a handgun. Jeff and Joe each had hand guns on them, plus a shotgun and a sniper rifle. They took up position on the right and left of the front entrance inside the building.

Deputy Madison crouched behind an oak desk that was put on its side up against the main door entrance. It was 8:30AM and Joe and Jeff were glad that Deputy Sharon Madison believed them and was taking a stand with them.

Tom was moving back and forth, checking on the girls, and reporting to the front entrance. He did not want to miss a thing. He had been writing about the raid in Seattle, and had sent the story to his boss via computer. His boss had quit complaining because the single copy racks were consistently selling out when Tom's stories ran, so now he was determined to keep the ball rolling.

With their sniper positions staked out, Joe and Jeff headed down the halls to the north and south to make sure the doors were locked and secure. Jeff noticed the firemen were arriving next door and making noise. Good.

*

At ten minutes to nine, a boy on a bicycle rode up to the entrance and stopped at the sheriff's car. He laid his bike down and walked toward the entrance like it was a school day. Deputy Madison recognized him and opened the door and pulled him inside. He was one of the local boys who made money at the marina running errands and helping with the boats.

"Robbie, what are you doing here?" Deputy Madison asked as she walked him in and around a corner out of harm's way.

"Hi, Deputy Madison. One of the boat owners asked me to run this envelope up here to the girls rehab center. He gave me a twenty!"

Robbie and two other boys, all about fourteen years old, had discovered they could make good money by being on the dock when a visiting boat came in and tied up. They would catch the ropes and tie them to the dock, run to the general store for whatever was needed, and answer questions like tour guides. The boys loved it, made good money, and couldn't wait to get to work each morning. Usually before noon, they would spend some of their earnings at Seabeck Pizza's all-you-can-eat lunch special for $4.99. Sometimes, when they were stuffed, there was a pizza or two that needed to be delivered out to a boat. Life was good.

Deputy Madison took the envelope and said, "Okay, Robbie, sit here on the floor for a minute," Joe joined them as Jeff kept watch.

The Deputy read the letter and then handed it to Joe.

Joe read it and took a deep breath, "Tom! Keep an eye up front for a moment, please. Jeff, come here!" Joe handed the letter to Jeff who read it, and then looked from Joe to Deputy Madison and then back to Joe again. Everybody's mind was racing. Joe spoke first with an idea, "Robbie, which boat was the person from?"

"The three on the outside dock. They must have come in after we went home last night."

Joe continued, "Okay, good. Now, did they give you anything else?"

Robbie looked down and started to say something as if he were trying to think. "Uh... well..." Then he looked up at Deputy Madison. He had fallen head-over-heels in love with her the first time he had seen her last year. He did not want to disappoint her in any way.

"Robbie, this is important. We need your help. Did they give you anything else?" Joe noted that she could be tender as well as tough.

Robbie stared into her blue eyes, "Yes, Deputy Madison," he pulled his hands out of his pockets. "They gave me this and this." He held a one hundred dollar bill in one hand and a small black plastic box in the other. All three looked at the contents of Robbie's pocket, and then Joe took the box.

"Okay, thank you, Robbie. Very good. This makes sense. Did they say what the one hundred was for?"

"Yes. It was to make sure I didn't show anyone the black box." Telling the truth felt good, especially to Deputy Madison; but he felt like he had betrayed the boat owner. "Do you think I could still keep the one hundred?"

Deputy Madison smiled as she pulled him up by the hand, "Yes, you can keep the money. Thank you for being so helpful." She gave him a hug. Robbie noticed he was only a couple inches shorter than the deputy. She smelled good.

"Robbie, did they give you any other instructions? Did they want you to report back to them as soon as you could?" Joe asked.

"No, sir. That's all they said," Robbie crumpled the money in his hand and put it back into his pocket.

"Okay, this makes sense," Joe seemed to understand something no one else did.

"Keep talking," Jeff said.

"Let's join Tom. I want him to be in on this. I don't think they will attack till we answer. First I've got to try to contact Joe Cornish."

# 34

The plane's northerly route retraced its trip south, stopping and refueling in the same places. Everyone was relaxed and talking about the future. The overnight in Cancun was a delightful time for Joe and Jennifer Cornish.

At about two hundred miles before touchdown in San Diego, Joe Cornish took a phone call.

"Yes? ...Yes, Joe…No, not a bit. Things went extremely well. How about on your end?..." Joe Cornish's face went from happy to serious as Joe spoke from Seabeck. Everyone in the group on the jet could see the change on his face and became quiet.

"Okay…Joe, how long do you have to respond?...I see… Okay…Let me try something on this end. Just hang tough; I'll call you back shortly...Yeah I see what you mean. I'll make it quick." Joe Cornish ended the call and faced the group. Nicolus joined them from the co-pilot's seat when he heard the noise die down.

"Tony, as I mentioned, we raided the Seattle club and shut it down. We brought ten under-age girls from there to a safe house over at Seabeck on Hood Canal. I left four of my people to protect the safe house in case we failed to turn you and you retaliated. The safe house is under imminent attack as we speak. A note has been delivered with a small transmitting device. The note demands they bring all the girls from the safe house to their boats at the Seabeck dock or they will launch stinger missiles at the safe house. They would home in on the transmitting device. The note ended, 'you stole our property, if we can't have possession of it, nobody will.' Tony, is there anything you can..."

"Damn it, those bastards. I'll fix this!" Tony Aragapo was digging for his phone. He misdialed a couple of times, he was so mad. Finally he got who he wanted.

"Matty! What the hell is going on? ...Yeah, it's me. Tell me what you're doing! ...I know you've been calling. I didn't call back because the feds would be able to trace my call ...I'm out of the country. Now what's going on up there?" Tony listened and began to calm down. "Okay...Okay...listen, Matty...I'm not mad at you. That's good thinking and a good plan. But...I know, it sounds good, but listen to me...Matty, listen! Something big has happened to change things. I'll fill you in soon. I got good news! But for right now, call off the dogs... Matty, stop the operation, just shut it down and get the boys back...No, I'm not saying this because there's a gun to my head...Look, Matty, you've done good. But who's the boss? ...Okay, so abort the mission now! I'll fill you in when I see you...Matty, I got to get off the phone before they trace me...Okay," Tony ended the call, caught his breath and looked at everyone. "Matty's a good smart guy. I think I'll keep him working for me. He's calling the guys off right now."

Joe Cornish relaxed a bit, "Do you really have stingers?"

"Damn right we do. What do you think you're dealing with here, a nickel and dime operation?" Then Tony shouted while holding up his glass, "More champagne, girls." He liked being boss, but he loved this new feeling of being free to live on the right side of the law without limits.

*

Deputy Sharon Madison, Joe, Jeff, and Robbie were tense. Tom was writing on his note pad, furiously. Ten minutes had gone by. A long time when you're waiting. Then Joe's phone rang.

"D. Charger," Joe said in answering, just for old time's sake, and because this was serious business.

"F. Mustang, are you hungry?" Joe Cornish sort of chuckled to himself, but was still serious.

"Not any worse than last time we spoke."

"Good. Listen, the big bad boss," Joe Cornish winked at Tony, "contacted his guy in charge and called off the attack. They should be leaving about as quickly as they can get their lines untied."

"You're sure?" Joe wanted proof.

"As sure as we can be. Send out a scout, and drop that black box into the nearest toilet bowl."

"Okay, thanks boss. See you when we see you."

Joe almost hung up, but Joe Cornish continued, "Yeah, why don't you hang out there till I call in a couple of days. I'm going to go on a honeymoon."

"What? You're going on a what?" but Joe Cornish had ended the call.

Joe filled everybody in and said he'd go down and make sure the boats were leaving.

"No, you stay here," Deputy Sharon Madison was angry now. "I'll go, with Robbie. Come on, Robbie." She began muttering to herself, "If those bastards think they can pull something like this while I'm on duty, they're going to find out they were wrong. I'll give them a piece of my mind, if not my gun-right where..." The door closed behind Robbie and Deputy Madison, so Joe, Jeff, and Tom couldn't quite hear the end of her rant. But they all smiled.

"Boy, if I rob a bank, I'll first make sure she's off duty," Joe laughed. Tom kept writing as they all headed to the two classrooms.

Deputy Madison opened the rear door of her car and helped Robbie put his bike in the back seat. "You ride up front with me," she said. Then they left the property. After a short pause for a word of thanks at the fire station, Deputy Madison pulled into the dock entrance, with lights flashing.

"Stay here, Robbie, until I come back. Guard my car."

"Yes, ma'am."

Kitsap County Deputy Sheriff Sharon Madison opened her trunk. She put a flack vest on and got out her shotgun. Having called for backup on her way there, two more Sheriff cars pulled in about the same time, lights flashing. The two men got out and suited up, also. The three began their trek down the dock, shotguns in hand.

They could see men frantically untying ropes and starting engines. As the deputies got within thirty yards, the three boats began pulling away. They could see men scurrying about stowing gear, and getting below deck. The three boats hit high speed heading out toward the Hood Canal floating bridge. The three deputies stepped to the edge of the dock where the boats had just left, and stood staring after them, shotguns in hand.

A moment later, Deputy Madison said, "Let's go." Back at the cars she said, "You guys cover my beat for me; I'm going to have some fun. I'll be back in about two hours." Then, opening the rear door of her car, she took the bike out. "Robbie, I'm taking you to lunch tomorrow. Thanks for all your help." He got out and took his bike. Deputy Madison got in and backed out onto the road, leaving a couple of tire marks as she headed north with siren on and lights flashing.

Joe's phone rang as he was embracing Kandee and thanking the staff and girls for a great drill workout.

"Joe."

"Deputy Sharon Madison, Joe. They're all gone. I'm going to make sure they clear the bridge. Then I'm going to call the Coast Guard and ask them to do a routine stop and search. It might be interesting to find out what's on board those boats. I want to touch base with you tomorrow. Everybody okay there?"

"Yes, deputy, everyone's good. Can't thank you enough for your expert help. See you tomorrow, and don't have too much fun on the bridge."

"I'm going to try not to. Bye," Deputy Madison burned a hole through traffic all the way to the bridge.

# 35

About that same time, a private jet was landing at the San Diego airport. It taxied into a hanger and shut down. Joe Cornish asked the pilot to close the big door and thanked him for a job well done. The group on the plane got off and entered an office and conference room attached to the hanger. Joe Cornish got everyone sat down in the conference room and spoke to the former big boss.

"Tony, I'm going to set you up as a private eye. Your company will work mostly for my office. You have a wealth of information on drugs, drug dealers, drug routes, and how they're used. We're going to spread the word that Jason Everett Samuelson died in a fiery explosion at a ranch in Paraguay. I suggest you lose some weight, change your hair, your clothing style, etc., and enjoy working with the good guys for the rest of your life."

"Joe Cornish, I think I'm going to enjoy working with you!" Tony answered.

Joe Cornish opened the door to the office and grabbed a set of keys off the wall. He tossed them to Tony and said, "I'm going to leave you six, so you can talk business. Those keys fit the red SUV outside. Go have dinner and find a place to stay the night. Let's head north again in the jet with wheels up at 8AM. I want you to go over the Seattle club with me, on site, so I get an inside picture of the goings on in one of those clubs."

"Yes, sir. See you tomorrow." Tony was setting up his business in his mind already. He tossed the keys to James and said, "Prepare a place for all of us tonight, and make dinner reservations, but don't use your name. Remember everyone, we're all dead. Now, you girls go with James. I want you to buy clothes for James and myself that are a different style. Then find a hairdresser that you don't know who will come here with you to do all of our hair different. Got that?" He handed James a bundle of hundreds.

"Got it. But I got a question: when are *we* getting married?" the one blonde asked the question, but they both wanted an answer.

"Oh, for the love of God," Tony blurted out. Then, realizing it was a legitimate question, he said, "Well, you know, we'd be married by now, but I can't figure out which one of you I like best. James and I will just have to flip a coin. Now get going." The door shut and Tony turned to Nicolus and Nickolaea. "I hope you two are alright with this. I think we just pulled our heads out as the guillotine let loose!"

"We're good, boss...I mean, Tony."

"Okay, let's talk organization and security," and they did just that.

*

Over a thousand miles to the north, Kitsap County Deputy Sheriff Sharon Madison wheeled her car onto the eastern high rise of the Hood Canal floating bridge and pulled over, stopping at the highest point. She kept her lights flashing and got out with her shotgun in hand and her vest still on. She was just in time. She carefully stopped traffic for a moment and crossed to the opposite railing. The three boats were just coming under the high rise. She stood tall and held her shotgun up over the railing so it would be visible.

The men on the first boat saw her immediately. Their eyes widened in fear, but they just kept going. The second boat did the same, and the third boat's pilots ducked for cover. The deputy crossed back through traffic as the boats went under her. Half a dozen guys were drinking beer on the back of the first boat. When they saw her staring down at them with her shotgun, they stumbled over each other to get below deck. When the second boat came through, one of the guys reached up offering her a can of beer. She raised her shotgun and aimed at them. It took barely two seconds for them to scramble below, tripping over each other. The third boat was slower and must have had their arsenal on board. There was no one to be seen on the back of it.

Deputy Madison returned her shotgun and vest to the trunk. She hopped in and carefully did a U-turn, then headed back to her office. As she drove, she dialed the number of her sister-in-law, who worked at the Coast Guard station in Seattle.

*

Jennifer's cousin Jim, and Michael, the undercover spy, said a quick "good bye" as was their custom. Joe Cornish had simply said, "Let's keep in touch." Jim had quipped, "Hey, we're relatives now." Then he was gone.

Joe and Jennifer drove to her office building and parked in the underground parking garage. They rode up the elevator and stopped at her office. Nothing new. Then up a floor to the boss's office.

"Hey, you're supposed to be disappeared. Your life is in danger, remember?"

"Hey boss, I love you, too. The danger is gone. Jason Everett Samuelson went up in smoke when his ranch house in Paraguay blew up."

He looked at her. "How do you know that? I suppose you were there when it happened?"

"Heck no, boss, of course not. I was at least three miles away," they both looked at each other. The boss shook his head. Then he stood and extended his hand to Joe Cornish.

"Hi, I'm her boss."

"Hello, sir. Joe Cornish; I just replaced you." The hand shake was cut short. Jennifer's boss dropped his hand with an astonished look across his face until Jennifer held up her ring finger in front of his eyes.

"Hey, congratulations, Jennifer! Joe, it's a pleasure to meet you. That was fast."

"Yes, it was, but we've known each other for years, and this week was the right timing," Jennifer said what she felt. "By the way, sir, Joe was right. He works for the FBI and has hired me to work with him. The Seattle Office."

"Where am I supposed to find someone to replace you?" Her boss was serious and seriously overworked.

"You know Janie, my assistant. She's chomping at the bit. She'll be better than me," Jennifer knew it was true. Janie was good.

Jennifer's boss breathed in deeply and let it out slowly.

"Alright, go on, get out of here you two. Go have fun, with all my love. By the way, did you know it rains in Seattle, all the time?"

The door was already closed. They went back down to her office. She grabbed her essentials and then poked her head into Janie's office. Janie looked up. Jennifer showed her ring finger.

"Jennifer, let me see that," and seeing Joe behind her, added, "and him."

Jennifer introduced Joe Cornish and then said, "You're up to bat now. I just hit a homer. I'm done. Moving to Seattle.

Janie was stunned, "You're not kidding." Her hands went to her mouth. "You better buy a rain coat," Janie's mind was soaring.

"Bye, have fun. I'm going to!"

"Thanks, Jennifer, for everything," and they were gone, back to the car.

"Where are you taking me to dinner tonight?" Jennifer decided she was hungry, for real.

"McDonald's," Joe's face was deadpan.

"McDonald's?!!! I haven't eaten at McDonald's in probably ten years."

"Yeah, fifteen for me. You make me feel young again. My treat," and so they did.

After dinner she asked, "Are we going to spend the night in the back seat?"

"Heck no, I've got a private jet parked where no one will disturb us. The office in the back turns into a bedroom at the push of a button."

"Oh, this I've got to see."

# Part Two

## Introduction

A private army of forty. Wow. It really was quite impressive. Usually not more or less than that. An army of forty, where each one was a specialist.

I remember when I first found out about them, or THEY as they were called. I was excited and wanted to know more about them. Well, back then I hardly had a clue, but then nobody did. For instance, when some good thing happened for the sake of justice, or setting something right that was wrong, people began to say THEY did it. Just THEY, because nobody knew who *they* were. It was always something good that happened and no one knew who did it.

Forty specialists and no one knew about them. A secret of forty. Wow. Religion, science, combat, economics, philosophy, street sense, mathematics, geology, armaments--THEY had it and THEY put it to good use.

I'll never forget one example. A girl in school, way back when, had a father who was a bad guy, and he took his wrath and his pleasure out on her. Well, years later it was reported in the paper that her father had an accident and died. She inherited a huge sum of money. The article made it sound like her father had saved it all so that she could enjoy it when he died. She knew better. Someone else had put the money into his account after his death, but took no credit for it. THEY did it. The girl used the money to fund a safe house for abused girls like herself.

Wow. What good could be done with a private army and enough funds. The sky would be the limit. Back then, I was captivated by the thought. I wanted to know how they actually did those things. Co-ordination, logistics, secrecy. You know, with an army of forty.

Well, back then I decided I had to find out, come what may. Now, as one of the forty, this narrative can never be written down. It can only be remembered. The only copy, in my head, even while my heart yearns to tell it to you, my dearest love. And this is what I've learned: the best and most effective way to contain the longing I have to be with you again is to continue to commit acts of justice and goodness. I don't want to lose those feelings about you, just contain them.

When I found out that to become one of the forty I would have to die, we had been together just a short time. I'd done years of research and accomplishment, and meant to continue, then you came along. Why did I have to meet you? I'm forever so grateful and blessed to have had you in my life for that time. Yet, the hurt that I caused you when I died, the hope that was so evident in your eyes, gone...Yes, I saw you then, after my selfish commitment to continue. Having to die, at least in your eyes and in everyone else's...I had to. Why do people make decisions, and why do decisions have strings attached, and why do those strings seldom get cut off? I love you so dearly, so deeply. No, I don't love you. I can't love you. It won't work. I once was so over my head in love with you...but that's on the shelf, where it belongs. Forgive me, sometimes I take the volumes down and go through them and...I had to do it, my love.

I have kept track of you, though. You've gotten over me. Memories get put on a shelf, yet I know you take them down sometimes, too. I've watched you from an appropriate distance a few times and I've seen us in your eyes. By the way, I like your new love. He seems to be a better man than I. Good job!

Commitment. It's a decision to follow through on a dream, come what may. You see, when I finally made contact, and was granted an interview, the cost was death to all that I knew. I agreed and THEY took care of everything, including you, my love. THEY found and introduced your new love to you, and I was glad. And I wept. You are well taken care of, and I am one of the forty, which was my dream. We are both happy. And our bookshelves rarely get dusty.

I love puzzles. That's what I specialize in, you know, puzzles. Solving them and inventing them. I noticed a pattern, and the pattern led to a potential formula that I pursued and got lucky with. I anticipated their actions and showed up when THEY did, and witnessed things only THEY could know. I was the first ever to do it, so THEY said. When I contacted them and THEY agreed to an interview, my life ended, and began.

My first assignment was much like the one we finished just last week. A prison inmate, guilty, but a humble man who wasn't being treated well. Too many hard men. Not enough understanding, wisdom, etc. Well, they asked me to make a plan to help him, and I loved it. A few bad guys got injured permanently, and one good man, though guilty, gained more influence. Justice for the unjust. Puzzling, but it tasted good; I wanted to do more. So my planning worked well and that's where I fit in as one of the forty, and to my good fortune, good planners are not easy to find.

The Boss. Nobody suspects him. He spends millions on liberal causes, but has a secret army of forty, which is about as right wing as you can get. Ideas count and count big. This man said, "Justice is its own reward, when pursued." A short, easy to understand idea, and an army of forty to implement it. Stealth, secrecy, and good planning. Actually, stealth and secrecy take good planning. I pushed that idea and it took your place in my heart and my life. If a man, such as this Boss, has enough money, he simply decides what he wants to do and does it.

The origins of his thinking were simple. He was in love when he was young, but she ended up marrying someone else. They all remained friends. Later she was killed by a drunk driver.

Justice was not served, at least in his mind, so he used part of his inheritance to put together an army of forty. After dealing with her situation, he simply continued. It just felt so good to him to make a difference, and injustices abound.

My two moms who adopted me, raised me well. They were better parents than most of my friends had. But when I met this man, I reached out to him like the dad I never had and he liked it, or liked me, and let me into his life and inner circle. I went for it full throttle, except for you, my love.

When I first communicated with him, I made it short. "I figured you out. I want to be a part of your forty." I deliberately did not give any information about me. He had to wonder how I knew where to send it. After figuring out his next mission, and witnessing part of it, I described what I saw and again said I wanted to be a part, and signed my first name. So now, having left no clue as to my identity the first time, and only my first name the second time, I had him hoping for a third communication just to find out more about who I was. I almost missed the next mission because his tactics changed. I think he hoped they could lose me. I wrote, "Not bad. It almost worked. By the way, I like your style of justice," and signed only my first name again. I wanted him to feel slightly punished for trying to lose me. I think it worked. The next mission I witnessed, I was grabbed, handcuffed, blindfolded, and brought to him. Before the blindfold was taken off, I was grilled about events I'd witnessed and the notes I'd sent, until they were satisfied that I was the one who had sent the notes.

His first question after the blindfold came off was, what was my reason for the notes? My answer was one word: his last name, because it was the same as mine before I had been adopted. I remember his eyes. My answer made no sense to him, but I could see that he noticed I was sort of toying with him. No one had probably ever done that before, so he toyed back after a minute.

"Same question?" he said

"Same answer," I said.

We were putting a puzzle together about who I was.

"It is not computing," he said crisply, with a hint of annoyance.

"My answer is completely logical. Think about it a minute longer," me again, instructively.

Now he just stared at me, but he was adding and subtracting in his head. Our eyes were locked when suddenly the pencil in his hand dropped to the floor. The three men in the room began to move toward me, then stopped as the pencil bouncing was the only movement from his side of the desk. Then a softening in his eyes and face, and his voice, too.

"Your last name at birth?" I think he noticed we had similar eyes.

Slowly and softly with our eyes still locked, I said, "Same answer."

Then he closed his eyes and I wasn't sure what was going to happen next, but after about thirty seconds of silence, tears escaped from his eyes, and he immediately rose and left the room. My gaze followed him and then moved to the three men. They had no clue what was going on, so one of them finally followed him into the next room. Five minutes later, he came back out, holding the door, simply motioning with his arm for me to go in to the Boss alone.

Over the years, we've had many good talks. He has told me about some of his most meaningful missions. One was about a drug lord. A very careful and meticulous man. A man who never used drugs himself, but supplied thousands of Americans with especially pure drugs. He kept the purity high and the supply steady in order to not flood the market. Thus the price rose steadily as the demand rose for the good stuff.

A team from the forty kidnapped this drug lord and held him for a year. They took him right out of a top level meeting with all his senior men. They were simply told, "You will never see this man again. The business is yours." They fought each other over it and it ended up breaking apart. The drug lord, in the custody of the forty, was introduced to his product and kept addicted until his system was full of the stuff. He ate very little and slept most of the time. Then cold turkey was served and he suffered for a long time the agonies which he made countless others go through in order for him to become wealthy. When he started to get better, the head man had a talk with him.

"I'm as wealthy as you used to be. I will let you get wealthy again if you do it legally, and help people instead of hurting people." He is a changed man today, earning money and helping to sell the antidrug message. Incognito, of course. Justice. It takes hard work.

In that room alone together, when we realized we were father and son, he told me some history about my mother. He had thought they were in love, but he had gotten her pregnant and he began losing her. She gave birth to me and adopted me out, then called it quits with him and married someone else, only to be killed later. I asked him if she had any other kids from that marriage. He didn't think so, but could not be sure. He never quit loving her, as I can never quit loving you, my dearest love. It's too hard to try to stop loving you, so I put you on the shelf.

My father designated me as his beneficiary and successor. As he drew his last breath, he spoke of the possibility of a half-brother. My mother might have had and adopted out another son. I shall search and find him and see if our mother shines in both our eyes.

I must leave you in my thoughts again, my love. My work and its excellence are the reflection of my love for you; so it shall continue. I shall give every good thing to you and your family, without you knowing it, as often as I can. You have my love. I have my memories of you. I will go wherever I have to and take you with me, sitting on the shelf, wherever I go.

# 1

Jonathan was gifted with the ability to think intricately and plan accordingly. The plans were only a result of his ability to think in small detail. Each step and the possible actions and reactions were easy for him to calculate. He could have been a premier chess player, but had no time for games. Why use your skill to play a game when real life was there to use as a chess board? Since taking over the reins of the forty person army of covert operatives, which his father had established and honed to a justice-producing machine, Jonathan had added to its quantity. Where his father had only initiated the number of jobs that could be completed successfully, on time, and very satisfactorily, Jonathan had increased the number with the exact same results.

Some of his successes were in Africa, where warlords committed bloody genocide with impunity. When the corruption and bloodshed suddenly stopped, there was nothing more of interest for the world press to report. So the world quit hearing about those areas. Meanwhile, justice had been calculated and achieved and the people lived better. Relief supplies could now be brought in without fear of confiscation or the supplies ending up on the black market. Defunding the bad guys was a critical part of this action. Sometimes bad guys could be turned into good guys when their source of funding their life style ended abruptly. Others would not give up so easily and would fight for their dwindling empire with disastrous results.

Around the world, the treatment of women and children presented a seemingly unending array of situations needing justice. Every culture and even religions had dark sides to them, although they might not be readily noticeable.

Since there was no law against doing good, the sky was the limit and the opportunities endless. Justice was its own reward.

However, Jonathan had no son of his own. In fact, the only possibility of a relative was the deathbed pronouncement of his father that a half-brother might be a reality somewhere. As time passed, this item became more important to him. He put more time into finding out if it was true that his mother had birthed a son besides himself, albeit by another father. Surely he would be able to recognize, with one look, his mother in the face of a brother. Though he had never met his mother, his father had supplied many pictures of her to Jonathan and he could easily see himself in her pictures. The idea that this half-brother might have been adopted out also made his search more complicated.

His first moves in this area were simple like the first moves of a chess game. A child could do them with great success, but each move became exponentially more complicated and the results depended upon the planning involved. This Jonathan was good at.

While keeping his army busy, Jonathan played his personal chess game deftly. He realized that what any adopted male wanted more than even meeting their biological parents, was to have a blood heir of their own. He, of course, couldn't have this, for his heart was occupied with the past. Jonathan knew that if he had a younger half-brother, and his half-brother was aware that he had been adopted, his foremost desire would be to have a son. This knowledge constituted the positioning of his knight.

Secondly, his father had told him the name of the town where he himself had been conceived, born, and given up for adoption. This place would also be where his half-brother's birth and adoption took place. This knowledge placed the bishop in his game precisely where it needed to be.

Next, the rook was positioned to cover the escape routes. Jonathan knew that like himself, a brother with similar blood in his veins, knowing he was adopted out, would be a loner no matter how smart he was. Like Jonathan, he would tend to work alone, maybe covertly, maybe for the military, and, if similar to Jonathan, he would be outstanding in whatever he did. This then set up the checkmate move and Jonathan set it in motion.

The first of his final moves was to send out a query to his many acquaintances worldwide for a list of three of their known operatives who were the most outstanding in their field. He did this whenever he had to replenish his army, so it was not an unfamiliar request. Most figured he was assessing the worldwide capability to deploy a response team to troubled areas. He published an article every year on just that theme and everyone thought that was what the inquiries were for. Jonathan used this list to pick his secret army, and in this case used the information to search for his half-brother.

When the information got back to him, he added it to past information of the same kind. Then he looked for names that were mentioned more than once by his acquaintances worldwide who did not necessarily know each other. With this combined information, one name came up more times than any other in the past three years in the area of excellence in working alone covertly.

Then he began an exhaustive search for information on this man. He found that his place of birth was in the Puget Sound region of Washington State. Specifically, a town which had started as a small fishing village with an even smaller harbor access to the Sound. Located across from Point Defiance at the beginning of the Narrows, it was called Gig Harbor.

The economics of the town had changed from a fishing and boat building town to a tourist town, when the fishing died way down. Now most of the docks had pleasure boats and yachts tied up to them.

This man, Jonathan now would bet his life on, was born to an unknown father and a mother who for some reason could not care for him. Jonathan was pretty sure now who his half-brother might be, because he too had lived in this same town at the time of his birth. Check mate. New game.

# 2

The next morning the bedroom part of the jet turned back into an office. Joe and Jennifer Cornish did a double take at the six boarding the plane. Their clothes, hairdos, and hair color were all completely different. Joe Cornish just smiled and nodded his approval. Wheels were up at 8AM as planned.

Tony, James, and the blondes, who were now redheads, and Nicolus and Nickolaea were continuing their business planning. Joe and Jennifer were talking with Jack who was not quite sure yet that forgiveness for Tony was okay without bloodshed.

The reverend had just gotten back into the U.S. in time to leave again for Ensenada, Mexico, on the Pacific, to give a speech at a church school there about rescuing young girls. Then he was planning to visit the Seabeck safe house. Joe and Jennifer Cornish had plans to visit the shut-down Seattle club with Tony and crew and see first-hand how they operated. Then they were going to visit the Seabeck safe house, also.

Later, after landing at Boeing Field in Seattle, the Joe Cornish express was pulled into a hanger so the personnel deplaning would not be on undue display. An SUV limo was waiting and they drove by the club on the way to Karl's Boathouse. After a superb lunch, they all drove back to the empty club. After a tour and lots of questions, Joe Cornish began to understand the basic workings of the club: how drugs were received and then sold to the patrons, how the customers hooked up with the girls, and other ways money was made at the club.

Tony led them into the kitchen last. As soon as they were all in the kitchen, Jack trotted to the walk-in freezer and opened the door. All the food was still there and still frozen. Jack glanced at his former boss and then at Joe Cornish.

"Does Seabeck have a freezer big enough for this stuff?" Jack asked.

"Yes," Joe Cornish walked to the freezer door and looked in. "Yes, I believe they do. Let's call and make sure." Joe Cornish dialed Joe whom he had left to guard the Seabeck facility while they were out of the country.

"Joe."

"I like Mustangs, how about you?"

"I'm a Charger kind of guy, in cars and in football."

"Greetings, Joe. I trust all are in good health?"

"Yes, sir. Where are you calling from?"

"At the present time, I am at the open door of the walk-in freezer in the recently shut down club in Seattle."

"Really?" Joe responded, heading for the safe house kitchen.

"Oh yes, really. I always tell the exact truth; and Joe, it is full with no mouths to feed."

"Well, let me just...here, in anticipation of your next question, I am opening the door of our walk-in freezer and...yes, this one has about three quarters of its room available."

"Perfect. The reverend will be flying up tomorrow and driving out to visit you all. We will be yachting over to the Seabeck dock tomorrow, also. A refrigerated truck...," Joe Cornish raised his eyebrows at Jack. Jack nodded in the affirmative, "will be arriving at your location tonight with the contents of this freezer. What do you say you all cook us a nice dinner at Seabeck tomorrow evening?"

"Consider it done, boss. Give the trucker the code word 'molasses' to use just in case."

"Will do," Joe Cornish ended the call. Before he could address Jack, Jack was on his phone. He dialed and waited a moment.

"Charlie! Hey, how the hell are you? ...yeah, it's me...oh I've been on a little vacation... yeah, tell me about it. But no worries, listen... yeah I know they're watching the place, I got it covered, but I need a refrigerated truck to haul away the contents of the freezer...uh, no not the van, but the little truck should do... well, Charlie, I'm talking right now while I'm here, and I'll ride with you to the destination....Uh, a hundred, hundred twenty five miles, something like that...you got it...Okay, I'll be here; thanks, man. I'm going to pay you well...bye."

"Excellent, thank you, Jack. Joe and everyone will be there. He said to use the code word 'molasses' when you get there, but he doesn't know you're riding along." He handed Jack five hundred dollars, and then stopped, "You don't know how to get there."

"Seabeck? Yeah, I do. Over the Narrows Bridge, stay on the freeway until the Newberry Hill exit. Left up the hill to the T. Right and along the water to the general store. I'll call Gretchen if I get lost."

"Jack, you're a pleasure to do business with," Joe Cornish was delighted.

Then Tony offered, "Hey, maybe part of the time this club could be a safe house."

Jennifer caught on, "Wow, what a turn around. A negative into a positive!"

"Just like me," Tony was thinking now. "Hey, the kitchen and lounge area we turn into a restaurant. We could make living quarters for me and my bride-to-be, on site living areas for the four bodyguards/cooks/business partners-whatever, and a safe house which has access to the indoor pool. The other rooms we turn into hotel rooms. Tony's Inn. How does that sound?"

"With a secret back entrance for covert operatives, FBI workers, and other select visitors," Joe Cornish didn't want to be left out.

"You bet. Our secret handshake will be to rub your tummy and ask, 'Are you hungry?'" Everyone laughed. Tony was quickly changing into a nice guy.

As the laughing died out, Jack and Tony's eyes locked. Things got quiet fast. Jennifer looked at her husband, but he was sitting still with an even look on his face, not offering anything. Tony looked down at the floor and became serious. Then he raised his head and eyed Jack again. "Kid…I wouldn't blame you, or try to stop you for that matter, if you put a bullet between my eyes right now."

Jack unlocked his eyes and looked down, shaking his head. After a moment he said, "Tony…I guess…I just needed to hear you say that." Everybody began breathing again.

# 3

About six hours before Joe got the refrigerated truck heads up, Kitsap County Deputy Sheriff Sharon Madison pulled up to the safe house in Seabeck and got out. Joe met her at the door and wanted to give her a hug, much like combat veterans do when they see each other. She looked like she had the same idea but refrained because she was in uniform and on duty.

After greeting Joe and asking how everyone was, she asked for Tom. Joe and Deputy Madison walked back to the cafeteria where lunch was being prepared and there was Tom interviewing one of the girls. He excused himself when he saw Joe and the deputy and came over to them.

"Deputy, how much fun were you able to have yesterday afternoon?" Tom got right to the point.

She laughed and filled in the guys on her bridge episode and then said to Tom, "My sister-in-law works for the Coast Guard in Seattle. I called her when the boats cleared the bridge and mentioned the three boats heading her way with one riding low in the water. As a Deputy Sheriff, I was very interested in what was in them. She took my bait and ran with it. I asked her to send me the raw report of the stop and search and I got it this morning." Tom's eyes were getting bigger as she spoke. "Would you like to see it?"

"Good Lord, yes please!" Tom's mouth was trying to keep up with his brain. She handed a file to him and he took it like it was a cup of perfect coffee filled to the brim. He sat down at the nearest table and devoured it. Ten minutes of silence later, he handed it back and asked, "Can I use this in my story?"

"Yes, you can. You know how to be discreet. A little publicity on how dumb the bad guys are can't hurt." Tom thanked the deputy and excused himself. He wasn't seen for the rest of the day.

Meanwhile Joe introduced Deputy Sharon Madison to Kandee, PC, Janae, Gretchen, Joni, and the staff. The staff asked her to give an impromptu speech to the girls after lunch, and she heartily agreed. It ended up taking the major part of the afternoon. A short speech turned into a long talk, with the girls asking all kinds of personal questions about Sharon. Everyone involved had a meaningful time, including PC, who was furiously taking notes for Tom.

Tom wanted to finish his story of Jason Everett Samuelson. He would connect with Joe Cornish when they got in, to go over the story.

Joe and Kandee wanted time alone. Joe informed Gretchen a refrigerated truck full of food was coming in and asked her to meet it and make sure it was legit. He told her the code word, and said that he was going to take Kandee down to dinner at Bobbi's if she would take care of the truck. Of course Gretchen agreed, and with the support of Jeff and Janae, shooed Joe and Kandee out the door.

Joe and Kandee walked down the hill to Bobbi's and noticed all the boats on the way. After finding the most out of the way table, they sat down and stared at each other with no embarrassment whatsoever. When the waitress interrupted them, they ordered coffee and dinner.

Before the waitress came back, Joe took Kandee's hands and said softly enough that only she could hear it, "If indeed I did come back to life, the reason I did would be for me to father a son. This is what will fulfill my life even above my work. Kandee, I can't be happier than to have you for my wife and for you to be the mother of any children we might have."

Kandee recognized that tone of voice from her past. She had had many men want to take her to bed, but her Kent, a name that she still referred to him as in her mind, was so different from them. His sincerity and loving kindness for her and her feelings cemented her desire to make him happy, and a happy father as well. She ate up his love like dessert, and wanted as much as she could get. She thought it was so cute that he believed he might have seen her in heaven.

"So, I just want to make sure... are you feeling the same way, and are you okay with our wedding on the boat? We can redo the wedding if you like."

"Oh Kent, how is it that you love me so dearly?" Kandee's heart and mind were about to overflow. "Joe, you're the dearest man I've ever met. The only thing I would redo is to meet you way earlier in my life. To me you are a reward, one that I don't deserve. It thrills me to be your wife, and I will be the best mother anyone could imagine. I'll make sure our children know they have the best father in all the world."

When their order came, they both ate and began thinking and talking about their future together.

*

After the SUV limo wound its way down to Shilshole Marina, and the passengers walked down the dock to the yacht, Tony's eyes widened. Finally his wondering bubbled over through his mouth, "How do you fund all this stuff? You got to be stealing something somewhere."

Joe Cornish had been waiting for this question, "It's all legally and legitimately funded. The main ingredient: hard work. The old saying, 'crime doesn't pay' is correct. It always ends up with punishment sooner or later. Working with the law and under the law has no limits. You can earn all the money you want with hard work, and spend it however you want as long as all the laws concerning income are taken care of. If you're legal, your desire and intellect and willingness to work hard are your only limits. In other words, you are the only limit you have."

"You know, I've never lived without looking over my shoulder, knowing I'd be shot, blown up, or tortured to death unless I did that to others first." Tony was not being nostalgic. He was awakening to the fact that he had gotten out of that lifestyle alive because he had been given a chance to become new, and he had taken it. It was still new to him to think that he had crossed over to a new way of living.

As Tony, James and their two redheads boarded the yacht, with Nicolus and Nickolaea following, Joe and Jennifer Cornish felt like they had accomplished something. But they didn't feel like celebrating. They felt like doing more. Joe had told Jennifer that sometimes evil had a soft underbelly and when you are on a roll, you might as well keep going until you get stopped by something or someone. Jennifer liked that idea. So, on the yacht that night, docked in Shilshole Marina, plans were conceived by Joe and Jennifer Cornish that were slightly different than normal because Jennifer's input was welcomed, and Joe recognized its value.

# 4

The night on the yacht passed peacefully after a tour and a delightful dinner. Morning saw the two redheads and their beaus cavorting in the yacht's pool. This time they were appropriately appareled.

After breakfast, Joe and Jennifer Cornish left together to go to Joe's office in downtown Seattle. Tony's crew were to stay aboard and enjoy a day of sight-seeing because Joe wanted them to see the Seabeck facility that evening. He told the pilot to take the yacht south under the Narrows Bridge and then, on the way back, dock at Anthony's in Gig Harbor for lunch. Joe and Jennifer would drive down and meet them there.

As Joe and Jennifer opened the door and entered his office, the pane of glass with the etching rattled. To Joe it felt like home. Jennifer walked in slowly and eyed everything. She had known and loved Joe Cornish a long time. Now she was part of his life and seeing each and every part of his office was like meeting his family. Some things would tell all about Joe. Other things would speak of his likes and dislikes. Was he a neat man? Was he a slob where he lived but disciplined in his mind? Were there past girlfriends? She took her time looking and drank it all in. Joe was busy at his desk.

*

Charlie had brought a crew with him to load the frozen food. When he had paid them and dismissed them, he and Jack headed south out of Seattle. They traveled down I-5 to Tacoma and then took the Highway 16 exit just past the Tacoma Dome. They passed Cheney Stadium, home to the Seattle Mariners' triple A farm team, and out across the Narrows Bridge. They continued, leaving Pierce County and entering Kitsap County. They pulled off at the first Port Orchard exit just long enough to grab a bite at Dairy Queen and gas up at the 76 station, then continued up Highway 16. As the road went through Gorst at the head of the bay between Port Orchard and Bremerton, it turned into Highway 3. About ten minutes later they took the first Silverdale exit. But instead of turning right, down toward the water and the town, they went left, up Newberry Hill. At the Chevron Station the road came to a T. They went right, down the hill to Hood Canal, then along the water, crossing over Little Beef Creek and then over Big Beef Creek and on down to the town of Seabeck. Just past town they saw the fire station and then the safe house on the left and pulled in up to the sidewalk by the main entrance. A woman came out of the building and up to the driver's window.

"Can I help you?"

Charlie said, "Well, I got a truck load of food and the password is 'molasses'."

Jack then leaned over toward the open window and said, "Wow, you're cute."

"Jack!!!" Gretchen began bouncing up and down and ran around to the other side of the truck and into Jack's arms. They pretty much talked and enjoyed themselves the rest of the evening, alone.

Joe and Kandee said good night early, too. Jeff and Janae supervised the unloading and inventorying of the food, and planned a menu for the following evening. PC was helping Tom get his story written. The staff went over things for the next day with the girls. It was going to be a big day with VIP visitors.

One guy with a very good reputation, one guy with a very bad reputation, and one guy with a very smart reputation.

Wow! America, the land of opportunity.

As morning dawned, everyone awoke rested and ready. After breakfast, chores and cleaning began. A skit, to be put on by the girls was practiced, and dinner was being prepared. Kitsap County Deputy Sheriff Sharon Madison had also been invited, and a wonderful evening was anticipated by everyone.

# 5

The yacht left Shilshole and went south on the west side of Vashon Island, down through Colvos Passage. It sailed past the entrance to Gig Harbor and entered the Narrows. Under the old Narrows Bridge they went, and the new Narrows Bridge, side by side. One was built in the 1940's, the other built in the 2000's. They did a big U-turn between Point Fosdick and Fox Island and headed back under the bridges over the Narrows. They then turned left into the entrance to Gig Harbor. Once through the narrow entrance, it broadened into a many docked harbor. Anthony's restaurant was at the far end.

A little marina and a nice dock jutted out from the old Shoreline restaurant. Anthony's had bought it out about ten years before when they increased their number of waterfront restaurants around the Sound. The docking was slow and precise and watched by all the indoor and outdoor dining customers. Included in these were Joe and Jennifer Cornish who had finished their business in Seattle and had driven down to Gig Harbor in pleasant late morning traffic. Joe Cornish had given the hostess a one hundred dollar bill and requested a table for ten in the lounge, and an escort to meet the party on the incoming yacht and bring them to their table.

Taylor, the young hostess, got one of the waiters to cover for her at the reception desk, and went down the dock to meet the yacht herself. She took a small basket in which long stemmed red roses lay. As she met the party coming off the yacht, she handed a rose to each of the gentlemen. They in turn gave them to their ladies. Taylor welcomed the three couples to Gig Harbor, then led them into the restaurant and down the stairs to the lounge overlooking the harbor.

As they descended the stairs, they were met by Joe and Jennifer Cornish. Joe took over hosting duties at that point and seated everyone. He, of course, sat with his back to the view so as to see the entrance to the lounge. While they all exchanged greetings, Joe Cornish noticed a man enter the lounge and pause, briefly look around, then sit at a table for two across the room from them. The man sat so he could see them and kept glancing their way. There was something about the man, Joe Cornish noticed, that was familiar, as if he had met him before. As their drinks were brought and light conversation ensued about the voyage that morning, Joe Cornish saw the man give the cocktail waitress a note and point at their table.

The waitress disappeared and then a moment later approached Joe and Jennifer and their party with two bottles of champagne, and a note which she handed to Joe with the compliments of the man across the way. Joe took the note and thanked the waitress, then looked over at the man. The man nodded his head slightly, then turned his attention to his drink. Joe Cornish opened the note and read, 'May I have a moment of your time? Thank you.'

Joe Cornish only had his ankle holster .38 on him, but at least he had that. He whispered to Jennifer to hold the fort and rose to walk over to the man. As Joe rose, so did the man. He strolled with drink in hand to the windows where there was a place to stand and look at the view; the man projected a relaxed friendly stance. Joe approached him and the man turned from the view as Joe closed the distance.

Nicolus, who sat at the other end of the table from Joe Cornish, but on the same side, was watching every move the stranger made. He did not recognize this man.

"Thank you, Agent Cornish, for visiting with me. I only have a favor to ask of you," the man was self-assured and polite.

Joe Cornish decided to return the politeness, "You have the advantage over me, sir."

"Forgive me. You know me as Jonathan. I have requested your assistance on analyzing operatives in the past, and I consider your judgment of men to be excellent."

The name instantly brought recognition. Joe knew the man as some sort of publisher of combat-ready newsletters, or the like. Joe Cornish extended his hand, "I'm pleased to actually meet you, Jonathan. Please call me Joe." Joe Cornish looked for any telltale signs of concealed weapons as the man extended his hand. The two men looked each other in the eye as they shook hands and Joe saw the familiarity in the man's face again.

"I must say your face is familiar to me and I don't know why, if we have never met."

"Thank you, Joe. I am glad it is because I believe you might know a person that I would very much like to meet."

Nicolus relaxed a bit, if it was possible for Nicolus to relax, as he watched the demeanor of the two men. As the table's lunch orders were being taken, Jennifer glanced at Nicolus down at the other end of the table and was comforted by his attention to her husband. Just then a couple entered the lounge and Nicolus went on alert again breathing in through his nose. They sat down and talked excitedly, apparently just customers.

"May I ask who I might remind you of?" asked Jonathan.

"I'm trying to recall who you remind me of, but so far I can't. What is the name of the person you are hoping to meet?"

"I do not know his name. In fact the only clue I have is that, as with me, his parents lived in this town we are in right now when he was born. Perhaps a couple years younger than myself. So you see, if I remind you of someone, that would be very encouraging to me."

Then Joe Cornish lit up, "You remind me of Joe, one of my operatives!" He paused just staring at Jonathan. Then he said, "Would you please join us?" and gestured to the table. Then he continued as they walked the short distance, "We will be joining

Joe tonight. He is at the moment providing security at a safe house for me. I'd be very glad to introduce you both."

"Excellent. This is more than I had hoped for. Do you know Joe's last name?"

"I really don't know. Even his file uses the last name Smith, but I don't think it's accurate. His undercover code name is D. Charger."

At the table, Joe Cornish began introductions, "Friends, may I present Jonathan, a man I have a high regard for, but whom I had never personally met until he was nice enough to introduce himself just now. Jonathan, may I present my wife, Jennifer, and our friends," Jennifer stood and extended her hand. Jonathan took her hand gently and smiled. As Joe Cornish watched Jonathan acknowledge the rest of the party, he could see that Jonathan had the ability to quickly measure the caliber of people in the group. Jonathan joined them in a wonderfully prepared lunch with champagne. Then it was time to sail.

As the group rose to leave, the lovely and gracious Taylor arrived and offered to escort them to the dock. Joe Cornish liked the way she hadn't presented a bill, and he handed her five hundred dollars to cover lunch. As they walked to the entrance, Joe Cornish handed her one of his FBI business cards.

"Thank you, Taylor. Your hosting ability has impressed me. I would like to offer you employment. Would that be an option for you?" he was straight-forward, but polite.

Taylor thought quickly. She enjoyed being a hostess, but recognized that there was no room for advancement here; she would have to go back to school. She sensed an opportunity and didn't hesitate.

"Sir, my shift is just ending and I accept your offer," she hoped she didn't sound too anxious.

"Could you join us on the yacht and start immediately?" Joe Cornish calmly inquired.

"Yes, sir, I'll just get my things and be helpful however I can," Wow, this was exciting. Did she just get invited aboard a yacht as an employee?

After the eight, now ten, people boarded the yacht, the pilot eased away from the dock and motored slowly across the harbor to the Sound. The weather was actually lovely for this time of the year and the cruise north went smoothly. Joe Cornish whispered into Jennifer's ear and then said to Taylor, "If you would attend my wife, she will show you around and help make you comfortable."

"Thank you, sir," Taylor said with a sweet smile.

Jennifer showed Taylor around the boat and then they sat and sipped coffee just inside the dining area out of the wind. She gently told Taylor of their law enforcement background and current activities, including what the safe house was about, and the dinner tonight. Taylor couldn't believe her good fortune, but asked how she might fit in.

"When we get to the safe house, I'll introduce you to a gal named Janae. She'll tell you about her duties and help you learn what she knows, but I would be pleased to have you as my attendant while you learn the other things, too."

"I'd like that! Should I call you Mrs. Cornish?"

"No, darling. Call me Jennifer, please."

Meanwhile, Joe Cornish asked Jonathan to join him and Tony in his den. During the trip north past Seattle, up around the tip of the Kitsap Peninsula, and west into Hood Canal, the conversation was about their backgrounds and stories of their work for justice. The more they talked, Jonathan and Joe Cornish realized they could trust each other and revealed more about themselves and their operations. Tony just listened and could not believe the extent of what he was hearing. It seemed the breadth and length and depth of living with the law, not against it, was far more extensive than he had ever imagined. He was stunned at the revelations these two men were making. Joe Cornish had invited him to listen in just for that purpose. Joe knew most bad guys didn't understand the excitement and fulfilment that doing good afforded.

As they cruised through the open Hood Canal bridge, Joe Cornish called the safe house. "Hi Joe, how are things? ...wonderful ...mmm that sounds good ...very good. We are passing through the bridge and should be docking at Seabeck within the hour...fine, we'll see you dockside then. By the way Joe, I have a surprise for you," then Joe Cornish ended the call.

Joe also closed his phone. Hmmm, he knew he would never guess correctly one of Joe Cornish's surprises. Probably a Snickers Bar.

# 6

The reverend had finished his presentation in Ensenada, Mexico and drove to the border. After waiting in a backup for an hour and a half, he headed for the San Diego airport. He just barely caught his plane to Seattle. Touch down at Sea-Tac airport between Seattle and Tacoma was on time. The reverend rented another car and proceeded out to Seabeck. The farther he drove, the more definite he felt that something was wrong. He kept driving, not understanding what the problem was.

The problem was, one of the people at his talk was a spy for the boss of a prostitution ring. This boss was quite perturbed with the reverend and his accomplishments. It was time for the reverend to meet with an untimely death. He told one of his operatives to follow the reverend wherever he went and to take care of him any way possible. “Don’t come back till it’s done.” He was now following the reverend and looking for the right opportunity.

The sun had about an hour to go before setting behind the Olympic Mountains. As the reverend’s car approached Seabeck, he noticed the big yacht out at the far dock. He parked in front of the coffee shack, which was closed at this hour, and walked out to the yacht. The staff on the yacht told the reverend that everyone was up at the safe house and that he was expected there. As the reverend turned to go back to his car, the staff person called Nicolus. He had been instructed to protect the yacht and to call Nicolus with any odd circumstances. The reverend walking around on the dock alone was odd. As he spoke to Nicolus he mentioned that he saw a man at the beginning of the dock coming toward the reverend. They didn't seem to know each other. The staff person listened to Nicolus's instructions for a moment, then closed his phone and shouted out to the reverend to please come back. The reverend stopped and looked back and saw the man on the yacht gesturing for him to come back. So he turned and headed back to the yacht.

*

A few hours earlier, as the yacht maneuvered to the dock at Seabeck, Joe and Kandee were watching from a table at Bobbi's. They had each driven a staff van down to the dock to meet the group. They ambled out to the far dock and waited as the dock boys tied up the *Cascade Islander* A/B. Joe Cornish and Jennifer got off first, holding hands.

"Jennifer, may I introduce Joe and Kandee. Joe and Kandee may I present my wife, Jennifer," Kandee's hands went to her mouth, and with wide eyes and a squeal, she stepped up and hugged Jennifer.

Joe extended his hand and congratulated Joe Cornish. "Sir, this really is a surprise," then he extended his hand to Jennifer and said, "Jennifer, this is a real pleasure." Then Joe Cornish addressed Joe.

"Jennifer was the District Attorney in San Diego that we dealt with a couple of weeks ago. We've known each other for some time, and we were married before we went to South America. Let me introduce you to everyone else, because Jennifer was not the surprise I mentioned." Jonathan was standing at the rail staring at Joe, but let everyone else off first.

"Joe, this is Tony Aragapo, formerly known as Jason Everett Samuelson with his right hand man, James, and their brides-to-be."

Extending his hand, Tony said, "Joe it's a real pleasure meeting the guys and gals who work for this man." The two couples stepped onto the dock and made room. Joe was wide eyed; this was the big bad drug boss that was threatening Seattle and who knew how many other communities?

Then Joe Cornish spoke again, "Joe, this is Nicolus Aragapo and his wife, Nickolaea." The two men shook hands locking eyes and immediately Joe knew that Nicolus was security.

"My pleasure, Nicolus."

"As it is mine, also." Kandee and Nickolaea shook hands and smiled. Then Joe Cornish continued, "And Joe, I'd like you to meet your brother, Jonathan." He stepped aside and gestured with his arm to the railing where Jonathan was stepping onto the dock.

Joe heard what Joe Cornish had said and had opened his mouth to respond until he realized what he had heard. Joe just stopped and stared with his hand half way extended. Jonathan stepped toward him and offered his hand and said, "My name is Jonathan. I am extremely glad to meet you, Joe." The two shook hands and then Joe looked at Joe Cornish for some kind of explanation. Joe Cornish was silent and his smile was all he offered.

As Joe turned his gaze back to Jonathan, he noticed that there was a similarity in looks between them. Kandee took Joe's arm and said, "You two look a lot alike."

Then Jonathan spoke, "Joe I would like to talk more with you and Kandee at the first opportunity. Your boss has granted me his okay to take up a bit of your time."

"Have we met before?" Joe queried.

"Not that I am aware of, but my research suggests to me that we may have had the same mother." Joe was stunned. He stared at Jonathan, then at Joe Cornish, and then at Kandee. He did not know what to do or say.

Kandee came to his rescue and extended her hand and said, "Jonathan, we are excited to meet you, too. There's plenty of room up at the safe house to have a talk."

Then she added, looking at Joe, "He's a very handsome man, isn't he honey?" At this everyone laughed and the logjam was broken.

"Yes honey, he is. Jonathan, I'm...I still don't know what to say." Then patting him on the shoulder added, "But let's go talk." The group then headed up the dock and into the vans.

As they pulled into the safe house, a sheriff's car pulled in behind them and parked. As they got out, so did the female occupant of the sheriff's car. Joe and Kandee waved her over to them. She came and this time didn't shy away from hugging both Kandee and Joe.

Joe turned and announced to everyone, "Please, with a great deal of gratitude, it is my pleasure to introduce Kitsap County Deputy Sheriff Sharon Madison. Sharon basically saved all of our lives the other day." Deputy Sharon Madison was off duty and it showed. In her uniform she was all business however, she was not wearing her uniform tonight. She was dressed in a lovely maroon suit with her hair down, and a relaxed, friendly countenance.

As Joe was introducing her to each one, it was Jonathan's turn to be stunned. Did he hear right? This woman was a deputy sheriff? She must be, she was driving a sheriff's car. Her lovely blonde hair, her full feminine figure and perfectly fitting attire told anyone who happened to look at her that she was a stunningly beautiful woman. But a deputy sheriff, too? For Jonathan, this was too good to be true.

When Joe introduced him, Jonathan took her hand and quickly looked at her other hand and saw no wedding ring. Raising his eyes to hers, he spoke. "Ma'am, I'm very pleased to meet you, especially since my brother says you saved his life."

Sharon glanced at Joe and then back at Jonathan, "You guys look like brothers!" Kandee squealed again and took Jonathan's arm, then the group headed inside.

The next half hour was small talk, meeting the staff and some of the girls. Tony couldn't believe how young the girls looked. Had he really bought and used these young girls for his own profit? At seeing them, he assured himself again that he would work hard on the right side of the law as long as he drew breath.

Out of the corner of his eye, Tony noticed Nicolus answering his phone. Nicolus spoke into his phone and Tony recognized that look. Nicolus then closed his phone and glanced at Tony, then whispered into Nickolaea's ear. He then turned and addressed Joe Cornish.

"Sir, the reverend is at the yacht. I'll go escort him here."

"Thank you, Nicolus; would you like some company?"

"It's possible the reverend is hungry. I will handle it, but someone could follow me after a minute's delay for backup."

"I will do that, Nicolus. Go!" Joe Cornish tensed and whispered to Jennifer his intentions and for her to keep the party going. Then he left. Nicolus was taking one of the vans, so Joe Cornish walked.

Nicolus parked at the General Store and walked out onto the dock. He kept walking past Bobbi's, but noticed a man at the outdoor dining area, sitting alone at a table by the railing, facing the yacht. He kept walking, but smelled violence as he breathed through his nose. So far he could only see one point of danger. As he reached the yacht, he boarded and found the reverend, who instantly recognized and hugged him.

"Reverend, are you aware that you were being followed?"

"No, Nicolus, although I sensed something was wrong on my drive out from Sea-Tac."

"Okay, here's what we're going to do," Nicolus explained his plan, then called Joe Cornish and spoke to him. Then they left the yacht and together headed up the dock toward the restaurant.

Joe Cornish closed his phone and, having arrived at the General Store, eyed every car in the parking area. Then he ambled up the dock to the restaurant. He saw Nicolus and the reverend coming from the yacht, so he entered Bobbi's Café and approached the back of the man at the table close to the railing. The man did not notice him. His eyes were focused on the two men coming toward him. One he would kill, and the other also, if necessary. The man rose slowly. Nicolus and the reverend stared right back at the man, drawing his attention. As the man rose, Nicolus could see the gun in his hand, but the gun that did the talking was the one the man felt in the small of his back.

"Special Agent Joe Cornish, FBI. Please sit back down slowly and I will let you live." The man just froze. Joe spoke again, "Your life of crime has just ended. Your rehabilitation has just started. You won't be needing that gun. Place it on the table slowly." The man still did not respond. "If you try to take a shot, you will be dead before you see if your bullet hit its mark. It therefore would be of no value for you to try."

Nicolus stopped the reverend and stood in front of him. He saw Joe speaking to the man, but the man hadn't given up his gun. With their eyes locked, Nicolus carefully drew his gun and pointed it at the man. At this, the man's gun touched the table; he let go of it, and sat down. Nicolus moved in quickly, telling the reverend to stay right behind him.

Joe Cornish eyed Nicolus and then holstered his weapon. "Hands on your head, please," the man complied, and Joe Cornish cuffed him. With Nicolus's gun now only five or six feet away, Joe Cornish stood the man up and searched him. Another weapon, a knife, a wallet and keys were the only things of interest. Joe Cornish gathered them into a bag along with the gun on the table, then allowed the man's hands to drop to his front. He escorted him by the arm out of the café and to the van. They all got in and Nicolus drove them back to the safe house. On the way, Joe Cornish said with a smile,

"Reverend, what a delight to see you, and looking so healthy!"

"It's because I live right, Joe, and have the right friends,"

Joe Cornish smiled and nodded, as he took out and opened the wallet belonging to their prisoner. "Let's see who we have here."

"How about we fill his pockets with rocks and take him out to the middle of the canal?" Nicolus sounded serious and mean.

Joe Cornish perused the contents of the wallet, and then said, "Hmmm, this guy is a messenger sent to us to show us who our next target is," then to the man, "Sir, your ID says George Johnson. Is that your real name?"

"You have no idea what you're getting yourself into. Your best move is to release me right now," the man was mad and somewhat scared.

"In the next half hour, I'm going to decide if I'm going to talk to you more, or let Nicolus, here, deal with you."

"Yes, sir. I will be fast and thorough," Nicolus was playing along.

"In the meantime, let's go in and join the party. Nicolus, please escort this man inside and see to his security."

# 7

As soon as Joe Cornish whispered to his wife and then left, Jennifer announced the imminent arrival of the guest of honor. Everyone was given a glass of sparkling cider by the girls, who were having fun serving their guests. Tom had cornered Tony and James and was firing questions as fast as they were answered. PC had her hands full with the two redheads who were happy to unload what they had been through in the past month. PC was listening and scribbling. How two gals could talk so fast and at the same time, and the third understand what was being said, was beyond comprehension, Tom noticed, but PC was doing her job well. Janae was chatting with Taylor about what she had learned while working for Joe Cornish. Taylor drank it all in with fascination. Jeff, on the other hand, was fascinated with Taylor and, not knowing what to do, joined with Nickolaea in keeping an eye on everyone and everything.

Joe and Jonathan sat down to talk some more, with Kandee and Deputy Sharon listening. "The fact of our brotherly looks is all the reality we have. Everything else is circumstantial, but the circumstantial is quite impressive. We both lived in the same town when we were born, about two years apart. My mother was not married when I was born, and yours was newly married. It's our mother from which our resemblance comes. We were both adopted out with nobody having prior knowledge of our brotherhood except our mother, and she died in an accident a few years after your adoption. Your father moved away, and just continued on with his life. Only you know what happened in your growing up, and I know mine. The fact that we are living with similar values reflects our mother's influence, and only she knew why she could not care for us and adopted us out. With an analysis of our blood we could know for sure, and then go from there."

Joe slowly shook his head and said, "I've never had any brothers or sisters. I don't even know how to act toward you."

"Nor have I had siblings, but I think we can help each other based on what happened in the past, not on the importance of our performance toward each other. Our mother must have been an exceptional woman and passed her goodness on to us."

Joe thought and then concluded, "I would love to hear about you and your past, then." Joe was becoming excited and the reality of this was dawning on him.

"And I, you and yours," Jonathan took a deep breath as if he had finally caught what he had been chasing.

Then Kandee blurted out, "Hey, we want to listen in, too!" Joe eyed Kandee and smiled sweetly. Jonathan looked at Sharon who was staring at him, and then her stare changed to a gentle smile. With that one look, Jonathan's heart was captured. He had to remind himself to breathe again.

He said, "Perhaps we could sit down again after dinner?" Before anyone could answer, the door opened and Joe Cornish and the reverend entered. A cheer went up. As they greeted the crowd, Nicolus came in with his hand on the arm of a handcuffed man, standing slightly aside and behind them. The man was stunned at the crowd.

As the cheers subsided, Joe Cornish spoke, "Ladies and gentlemen, and all resident princesses, the Almighty has seen fit to deliver the reverend to us healthy and whole. By His power may our comings and goings always have similar results." Jennifer arrived at Joe's side with a sparkling cider for all. She included the man with Nicolus as if he was part of the family. Joe Cornish lifted his glass up to everyone and all followed suit. He toasted, "To the Almighty, who grants us life. May we enjoy His abundance as we live within His embrace." Everyone agreed and sipped. "Let's be seated and enjoy the dinner these young ladies have prepared for us."

Joe and Jennifer Cornish, the reverend, and the chief staff person sat at the head table. Joe Cornish whispered to Nicolus and he brought the man to a side table so he could witness the proceedings. Nickolaea joined them.

Joe and Jonathan sat with Kandee and Sharon between them. Tom and PC sat across from Joe and Kandee and tried to take it all in.

Tony, James and the redheads were seated at another table together with Jack, Gretchen, and Joni. Jeff just happened to sit next to Taylor who was sitting next to Janae.

The young ladies of the safe house sat at the rest of the tables while some of them served. The dinner progressed as dinners usually do, with the head table served first and done first. Presently, Joe Cornish rose and commanded everyone's attention with simply his smile.

"I've asked the reverend to speak to us about whatever he chooses to. I know his usual topic is striking a difference between right and wrong, between living with the law as opposed to living against it. It just so happens, we have a gentleman with us tonight, freshly caught out of a life of crime, and who is contemplating his own future. Or at least I'm contemplating his future since he is in my custody." Joe Cornish nodded to the man in the cuffs, then turned and said, "Reverend, if you would be so kind."

Everyone looked to the reverend and clapped. Deputy Sharon Madison looked over at the man in cuffs to see if she recognized him at all.

The reverend rose and began, "I want you all to realize that our dear friend Nicolus and our host, Joe Cornish, risked their lives not forty-five minutes ago, in my defense. Their ability, preparedness, and bravery has brought us to this point this evening. As we sit here, it is not hard to recognize the undeserved favor which the Almighty has bestowed on us. On some more recently than others."

Tony's heart stirred again just to think that he was free from his past life. All his desire was headed in one direction. He glanced at the man with Nicolus and thought of himself. The man had the look of a caged animal. Tony remembered the feeling. Suddenly he realized the man might recognize him.

"As recipients of such great favor, I estimate that most of us here, and eventually all of us, will dedicate what time and energy we have left to safe guard, propagate, and birth, a lifestyle commensurate with that said favor." The reverend went on in a speech that was inspiring and informative.

After half an hour of listening, dessert and coffee were served and the floor opened to anyone who wanted to say something. Tony stood up with determination and strode to the front.

"I address you tonight as friends, new friends. I know that the undeserved favor given to me is real. If I was given what I so justly deserve, I would be fitted with a noose, have a chair kicked out from under me, and experience the agony of being hanged." This caught everyone's attention, even the girls serving. "And then, I would come back to life and have that done over and over for each one of these girls present here." Now you could hear a pin drop. "Then a line would be forming around the block, as word got out." Laughter loosened the atmosphere. It seemed Tony was enjoying this, but was also close to tears.

He continued on, "I'm not sure I recognize the gentleman next to Nicolus, whose job it was to kill the reverend tonight or die trying. But I'm aware of the fact that he might recognize me. Nicolus would you ask him if he recognizes me?"

Nicolus leaned over and began to ask, but the man blurted out, "Yeah, I recognize you! We heard you were dead!" Nicolus squeezed his hand around the man's arm.

"You're right. I was dead. But now I'm alive again, and living! Do you understand living?" Now Tony left the front table and approached the table where Nicolus, Nickolaea and the man were sitting. "And I hope you're smart enough to realize the point you are at in your life. Take the opportunity to live, if it's offered to you, instead of blind loyalty to a boss that will kill you himself when he hears you failed at the job he gave you." The man stared at Tony, but said nothing. Then Tony bent over slightly and said to the man softly, "I'll give you a hand and keep an eye on you." Then Tony went over and sat down.

Deputy Sharon Madison whispered across Kandee to Joe, "Who is Tony?"

"He's the guy who called off the attack against us," Joe answered evenly.

Deputy Sharon's eyes widened and then narrowed, "What's happened to him?"

"We turned him. Well…Joe Cornish turned him." The deputy pondered this.

Meanwhile Jeff looked at the slice of pumpkin pie with a small dollop of whipped cream that was placed in front of him and then glanced at Taylor next to him. He then whispered to her, "Here," shoving his plate her way, "Do you like pumpkin pie?"

Taylor looked at him, "Sure, don't you?"

Jeff kept himself from being mesmerized by her loveliness by looking back down to his pie. "Only if it has lots of whipped cream."

Taylor looked at their two pieces of pie and then at Jeff and offered a slight smile, "Here," she said. "I don't do whipped cream."

Jeff watched her put her whipped cream on his pie and instantly fell in love with her. He looked up and into her eyes, "That was really nice of you." He said slowly, staring at her.

"Thank you, I'm glad you think so," she was staring back. "Are you a covert operative, too?"

"Yes," Jeff admitted. "I'm afraid I am."

"Wow. Janae's been telling me what she does. I'd like to hear your story sometime."

"I'd love to. We'll do it as soon as we can. Call me Jeff."

"I'm Taylor."

He wanted to say 'I love you' but instead said, "Okay, Taylor." Jeff ate all of his pie and whipped cream, and savored every bite.

One of the girls hopped up and ran to the front table. Standing next to the chief staff person she announced, "My name is Janis. We girls have a skit to put on for you." Applause erupted.

The skit was a takeoff on The Magnificent Seven. Janis and the other five girls from the Monterey Bay club, plus Janae, were the good guys. They got the girls from the Seattle club to be the bad guys with Jack and Gretchen as their leaders. The skit loosely followed the story line of the movie, only modern day. Everyone gave a standing ovation at the end. Then Janis brought up a lei made of paper flowers, one flower from each girl at the safe house with her first name on it, and placed it around the reverend's neck. He didn't know what to do, so just smiled, with tears running down his cheeks. The crowd stayed on their feet and clapped louder.

As things quieted down, the man in Nicolus's care stood up. His countenance had changed. "I need your help," he blurted out, "I'm a dead man unless someone helps me."

Tony spoke right up, "You got my help, son," and with James and Nicolus, he took the man into a side room. Joe Cornish took a deep breath and let it out slowly, once again thankful he could still breathe. But no one noticed.

Now the evening was about over so Joe Cornish stood and gestured with his arms for everyone to rise.

"Thank you, each one, for your participation tonight." Then he raised his arms with palms out like a pastor pronouncing the benediction and said, "May the Almighty find you in the palm of His hand, each time He looks your way. And may you find Him ever present, each time you look His way. Amen!"

Presently the girls began cleaning up as the guests were ushered into the old elementary school library. The group dispersed into smaller ones and the air was full: full of love, full of plans, full of changes in life's direction and revelations of the past, and full of joy from the Almighty, who never sleeps, always listens, and tends to smile now and then.

# 8

Deputy Sheriff Sharon Madison had listened with interest to Joe and Jonathan talking about their lives, but she realized that she needed to mingle. She smiled at Kandee and twirled her finger telling Kandee what she was doing. Deputy Sharon then met Joe Cornish and the reverend. She then said 'Hi' to the two redheads and made a point to remember their faces. Wandering into the kitchen she was momentarily mobbed by the girls doing dishes and cleanup. Then she wandered into the dormitory area and mingled with all the girls. She was in no hurry. She had tomorrow off.

After a good long while she ambled back into the library area and found Kandee, PC, Janae, Gretchen and Joni seated around a table playing Nertz. It was a solitaire-type game with as many decks of cards as there were people playing, and a wild free-for-all instead of taking turns. She watched for a few moments and then noticed Joe and Jonathan heading toward the excitement of the card game. Joe came up behind Kandee, but in Nertz one can't afford to have their concentration interrupted; there are just too many cards to keep track of, so Kandee ignored him. Deputy Sharon didn't ignore Jonathan's eyes. He moved around to her side of the table and they stepped back so they could hear each other talk.

"What a marvelous thing to find a brother after all this time," as soon as she said it, she realized it made Jonathan and Joe seem old, so she continued, “You really must have enjoyed listening to each other.”

Jonathan took a deep breath and said, “Yes, I’ve enjoyed this evening very much, including meeting you, Deputy.”

“When I’m out of uniform you can call me Sharon,” she started to blush just a little bit.

“Thank you, Sharon. I’m really very impressed with you, if I may say so. Kandee told me of your speech, and your informal talk with the girls the other night. Do you do things like that often?”

“Rarely, actually. Sometimes on my days off I will schedule a community meeting of some sort, or sometimes my bosses schedule something for me and my fellow deputies.”

“I see, and when is your next day off?” Jonathan was trying to be tactful because his feelings were colliding with his love for the woman of his past that he could never have.

“Tomorrow,” Sharon replied evenly.

“I imagine then, your schedule is full…tomorrow?” Jonathan carefully asked.

“Yes, it is. I’m going fishing.” She said it without any emotion.

Jonathan stared at her. “Fishing,” he said, sort of as a statement. His thought was of a big group of law enforcement people chartering a boat out of Westport on the Pacific Ocean, for a day of fishing and getting seasick. He could not comprehend why anyone would do that, much less where they would find the time.

“Yes. I have a boat docked at the Seabeck marina, and I go early in the morning out into the canal to see if I can catch my limit of salmon by noon.” Jonathan was just blinking his eyes with his mouth open, so she continued, “You’re not a fisherman?”

“Uh…not…of fish, uh…but I wouldn’t mind learning. Do you like fishing?”

Sharon broke into a slightly mischievous smile, “Yes,” she said slowly, “that’s why I’m going.” Now Jonathan really felt stupid.

The thought of being alone in a boat with this woman must be what planning a vacation is like. Jonathan was great at planning but short on vacationing, very short. He simply could not get his mind to imagine what tomorrow would be like if she invited him fishing. It would mean not working, and not working was not allowed, because, he reminded himself, his work reflected his love for the one dearest to his heart.

Sharon could see her mischief threw him off-kilter a bit, so she continued her thought, "but I must tell you, I'm a terrible teacher." Jonathan was about to tell her he didn't care if she was good or bad, but Sharon kept going. "I would tell you what to do, and then if you did it wrong I would get mad at you, and you would get mad at me for getting mad and..."

"I'd love to," Jonathan blurted out. Despite his maturity and commitment, he now found himself desperate not to lose this opportunity to see more of this woman.

Having been interrupted, Sharon wasn't sure what Jonathan had said. Had he said 'I love you' or 'I'd love to'? She wanted to know exactly what he had said. "What?" she blurted out, then realized it was a little more abrupt than she had meant it to be. Sharon Madison was much better at being a deputy sheriff than at being Sharon.

"I just said...would you like some company fishing tomorrow?"

"Well, I usually go alone...but I'd make an exception for you." Their eyes couldn't help but meet, and they both sort of gulped at the same time.

Suddenly, the card table erupted. Somebody had run out of cards and the game was over. Jonathan and Sharon's attention was diverted to the noise and laughter, but they both could feel how close they were standing to each other.

Kandee squealed because she had won, then stood, looked at Sharon and gave her a big hug.

Joe and Jonathan, on the other hand, looked each other in the eye and slowly embraced and held on. Seeing each other again even after a short recess brought back even stronger the amazement of being brothers. When they separated they each had tears in their eyes.

Sharon spoke first, "Jonathan is going fishing with me early in the morning till around noon. Care to make it a foursome?"

Kandee stepped right up, "Joe and I are sleeping in. How about a foursome for lunch at Bobbi's?" Joe raised his hands and eyebrows in a sort of surrender and smiled.

"Sounds good," Sharon said. "We can get twice as many fish with two people, so we've got to get started early. Jonathan, where are you sleeping tonight?"

"Uh..." Jonathon started to speak, but Joe jumped in.

"He'll be on the yacht tonight and I promise I'll have him up and ready by 5AM." Joe was confident.

"Perfect," Sharon replied. "I usually stop at Tammie's and grab coffee; what do you like?"

Jonathon thought, then spoke, "Black."

"Black? You just want black coffee?" It was Sharon's turn to not comprehend now.

"Yep!"

"Okay. I'm heading for bed. I've had the most wonderful time," Sharon announced. Kandee hugged her again and so did Joe.

Jonathan wanted to but offered his hand, "I'll be ready at 5 AM. Thank you Sharon, I've enjoyed meeting you!"

"Good night, Jonathan," Sharon Madison left after a few appropriate hugs and handshakes.

Joe patted his brother on the back and asked, "You don't get seasick do you?"

"I'm too lovesick to get seasick," he looked at Joe and they laughed and hugged.

The exodus was now on for the yacht. The reverend was staying at the safe house, as were Jack and Gretchen because Gretchen didn't want to leave Joni alone yet. Joe, Kandee, Tom and PC gathered their things, as did Jeff and Janae with Taylor in tow. Joe and Jennifer joined them and they all rode down together in a van.

Tony, James, the redheads, Nicolus and Nickolaea, with the former bad guy, rode together in the other van. That evening the yacht was full, but comfortably so.

# 9

At 5AM Jonathan was up and on the dock waiting. He had slept very little, but he was used to that. The clothes he had found in his closet fit okay, and even though the morning was a bit damp, he figured the wind breaker would be enough.

Jonathan could see the sheriff car parked across the road from the coffee shack and decided to walk that way. As he reached the road, Sharon was at the trunk of the car loading things onto a hand cart. Jonathan joined her.

"Good morning," he said before he got to her so as not to startle her.

"Hi. So, what did you mean last night when you said you fished, but not for fish?" Sharon had been thinking about it all night and figured they might as well dive into their relationship, as opposed to being unnaturally polite and slow. "Because, you probably already do know how to fish, even though not for fish."

Jonathan liked her early morning spunk. She must have had coffee before she left her house. He tried to perk up but needed coffee himself. He dove in and helped her load coolers, fishing gear, coats, water, and food. Jonathan contemplated the question, but said what came to mind, "Are you sure we're just staying out till noon?"

"Ha, ha. They train us to be prepared on the job, so I carry it into my free time, too. We might get enveloped in a fog bank and have to stay put out in the middle of the canal, for however long it takes for the fog to lift. It could take days," she pulled a small hibachi grill and some charcoal briquettes out of the trunk and put them onto the cart.

"In that case, I should have brought my pillow," Jonathan started smiling. Her early morning perkiness was so cute.

"Oh, I've got one onboard. We'd have to share, or take turns."

"So...do fish bite in the fog?"

She thought for a second and smiled up at him. Then she said slowly, "Fish always bite if you use the right bait..." then, back to normal, "Come on, I'll get the coffee and you head for the dock."

Jonathan pushed the cart and went one way, Sharon went the other. After a few minutes she caught up with him and led the way to her boat. It looked about twenty-four feet long and had a small cabin.

Mixing slurps of hot coffee with loading the gear onto the boat, kept them busy and working together towards getting underway. Their questions and answers as to where this goes and what to do with that, just helped their friendship develop. Sharon got the inboard engine going, then they sat side by side in the little pilot house as they left the dock and pulled out into the bay. It was about 5:30AM and the sunlight was still filtering through the trees on the hills of the eastern horizon. The wind was light, but with a bit of a chill the faster they went.

At the entrance to the bay they turned southwest out into the canal and traveled for ten minutes. They didn't say much, because of the roar of the boat, the wind rushing by, and so much to see. Both felt comfortable just being quiet together. Then Sharon stood up, looked both ways at the shoreline, and eased back on the throttle. She coasted the boat to almost a stop and said, "Okay, we're here."

Jonathan looked around as if searching for a sign saying 'fish' with an arrow pointing down. "How do you know we're here, and where is here?"

"Well, when you line up that house on that shoreline with that dock on the opposite shoreline, there is a deep hole out in the middle where the fish congregate and plan their day. We offer them some breakfast and go from there." Jonathan just stared at her and felt the strongest desire to kiss her, but she hopped up and said, "Come on, we've got fish to catch."

They went to the back of the boat and got the fishing gear ready as fishermen have been doing for eons. When the bait hit the water and the lines were paying out, it was time for patience.

Patience and skill usually result in success. They began to talk about that. Jonathan had experience in fishing for justice, and good results came from planning and skill and patience. This is what they were doing this morning. Did successful fishing produce patience and skill, or did patience and skill produce successful fishing? Who knew. They were both enjoying the time together.

As fish began to bite, they reeled them in. Some made it into the boat and some did not, but new bait was applied and the lines went down again. Caught fish were measured and weighed, and stowed in the cooler.

During breaks in the action they had coffee from a thermos and sandwiches Sharon had made. Bathroom breaks meant taking turns in the small cabin with a jar and emptying it overboard. As 11 AM came around they had caught their limits and stowed all the gear. Then Sharon said, "Time for sightseeing." She gunned the engine and headed farther south.

The sun was bright now and felt good. After ten minutes they slowed and turned into an estuary called Dewatto Bay on the east side of the canal. As they motored up the bay towards the mouth of Dewatto Creek, there was evidence of an abandoned building, but not a lot of other development.

"Back in the twenties, Hollywood types made this a popular bay. Many famous actors, actresses, and motion picture people visited here quite often. Then after a while it just fizzled and hasn't ever got back its former glory." They both looked at each other and burst out laughing. "Yeah, I moonlight as a tour guide."

"This is beautiful and remote. Makes me feel like an explorer," Jonathan was impressed.

Then it was time to head back and Sharon offered the steering wheel to Jonathan. The ride back was a more relaxed time than he could remember experiencing. Now he began fearing what would happen when they got back. He didn't want to leave her side. Yet they both had lives to live wholly without regard to one another. He decided to be serious and speak his heart.

"Sharon, I've known you less than twenty-four hours, but I've come to enjoy being around you more than I've said. I'm afraid of what to do when we get back. What if we never see each other again because of work? I tend to travel some, and am in charge of overseeing people. Your work is important to you as is your career, and you're good at it, and..." his eyes were looking off to the shore across the water as he spoke, but now he looked at her.

He pulled back the throttle and stopped the boat so they could talk while looking into each other's eyes. Soon they sealed their talk with a light kiss on the lips and both felt more at peace. It was time to head back to the dock.

After passing by the yacht and waving to those on deck, they docked and unloaded. Jonathan helped load the gear into the trunk again. She gave him his fish and then she was gone, and he brought his fish back to the yacht.

"How was fishing?"

Joe met Jonathan as he came to the yacht. Jonathan held up his three fish, and smiled, "I caught everything I wanted."

Joe smiled and decided not to ask any more. "Are we still having lunch together?"

"Sharon had some unexpected things to do, so she asked me to apologize for her...and..." Joe looked up as Jonathan paused, "I've got a hug from her for both of you." Joe opened up his arms to accept a hug and Kandee was by his side a second later and got the same.

"So what do we do with these?" Jonathan asked lifting up the fish again.

"Lunch," Joe Cornish said as he walked up, "We have them for lunch and then set sail."

# 10

As breakfast on the yacht finished, Joe Cornish invited Tony, James, Nicolus and the new guy into his den. They debriefed the man and got a lot of new information from him. They outlined his life living with the law instead of against it, and Tony offered to employ him and help him out. He said his real name was Alexander and he was on loan from the east coast to a west coast affiliate who majored in laundering money and bribing law enforcement with money and girls.

Joe Cornish considered him a very important catch. Now they had a source that knew the inside of the organization, and could possibly go undercover in the future. It fit in nicely with Jennifer's idea of exposing corrupt law enforcement. Ideas and plans were popping.

Later, after a delicious lunch of fresh salmon, Joe Cornish invited Joe and Jonathan into the den. He poured each a glass of wine and then sat back in his favorite chair.

"Jonathan, your brother is a huge help to me in capturing bad guys red-handed and then offering them a change of life instead of prison or death. These newly turned bad guys open the way to more of the same with the things they know, and it progresses with planning and execution. You've told me a little about what you do, and I know it's more than producing a newsletter."

Jonathan took a long sip of wine and looked at his goblet as he swallowed. He then glanced at Joe Cornish and at his brother Joe, and decided he might never be in better company again. So he began to tell his story. An hour later the wine bottle was empty, and a bathroom break was needed, and both Joes' respect for Jonathan had skyrocketed.

As a second hour progressed, Joe Cornish realized how similar their operations were. After some questions, Joe Cornish passed out cigars for their enjoyment. They thought about things and spoke their minds as three men who have similar visions.

At one point Jonathan said, "One thing I'd like to do before I die is find out all I can about our mother. What was it about her that inspired in us a need to see justice done, even though we grew up separately?"

Joe continued the thought, "We are quite sure we have no other younger siblings. Are we just as sure we have no older ones than you?"

Jonathan was stunned. He had never considered that there might be a brother or sister older than he. And what about their two operations, was there reason to combine or cooperate or just comingle information, or what?

The bottom line for Joe Cornish was, now that Joe had found a brother doing similar work as he, what did Joe want to do? Keep working with him, start working with his brother, or combine the two? Maybe Joe just wanted to stop and have a family of his own. After more deliberations of intense interest to all three men, Joe Cornish brought the meeting to a halt because he wanted to set sail.

The reverend came down to the yacht to see everybody off. Jack, Gretchen, and Joni boarded the yacht. Tony, James, and the redheads were instructed to drive Alexander in his car back to Seattle and set up shop at the old club.

When all were ready, the reverend blessed their voyage and returned to the safe house. Much work needed to be done getting each girl used to the new life of being a girl again and making contact with parents or relatives.

Just before leaving, Joe, Jennifer, and Joe took a quick trip to solid land once more. Joe and Jennifer said good bye to Bobbi and thanked her for her help and support of the safe house. They bought two wild blackberry pies and paid for them with a one hundred dollar bill, saying, "Keep the change," with a big smile. Joe trotted over to Tammie's and ordered his favorite drink and handed her a note from his brother for Deputy Sharon Madison, next time she dropped in. He also paid with a one hundred dollar bill and said, "Keep the change," with a smile. Then back on board, they set sail for Seattle. Shilshole Marina to be exact.

*

Tom and PC were aboard the yacht but hardly anyone saw them on the trip back to Seattle. They were trying to get the story down from their notes. So much had happened and was happening that they were frantically trying to keep up. Tom's boss had ended his opposition and had taken to calling whenever he had a chance, to ask what they needed. Tom said his wife was invaluable and wanted her on salary. The boss agreed and asked what else he could do for them. Tom had said, "Peace and quiet!" and then hung up. The story about the raid in Seattle had followed the Jason Everett Samuelson story. The raid story was followed by the aborted attack on the safe house. Now they were trying to put together a much larger story on the reverend's work including many of the girls' experiences.

The Seattle Times was being spotlighted because of Tom's stories and all the major newspapers in the nation were reprinting them in their papers. Tom's boss had hit up the Board of Directors of the Times for a significant raise for Tom. He liked hard working employees and was willing to go to bat for them. Tom had gotten an open invitation to Good Morning America, but wasn't interested. He wanted a Pulitzer Prize, not to have his face recognized wherever he went. Maybe he'd send PC.

As the yacht came around the top of the Kitsap Peninsula and turned south toward Seattle, he made himself take a break and went to hunt down Jonathan. It might be his last chance to interview him. Finding him on the deck in the sun, Tom asked for a short interview. Jonathan was pleased to do it, but wasn't as candid with him as with his brother and Joe Cornish. Jonathan made sure Tom got the spelling of his newsletter right, and told the story of researching and finding his brother. Then, off the record, he told Tom he had been a part of many operations like the ones Tom was reporting on, and would like to put them all in a book sometime. He would welcome Tom's help. Tom said yes of course, and Jonathan said it would be a big book. There were over one hundred stories to tell and more underway. Tom was very pleased and wrapped up the interview as they were pulling into Shilshole Marina.

Back in their cabin Tom and PC gathered all their paperwork, packed their clothes and things, and called for a cab to meet them at the main entrance to the Marina. They both wanted to get to PC's house where they would be more comfortable and interrupted by only important things. As the yacht docked, Tom and PC asked Joe and Kandee to come with them, but they said they had plans to disappear to where nobody knew them for a week.

"Then we'll be knocking on your door with hat in hand because we have no place of our own yet."

"Sounds good, send us a post card," the four exchanged long hugs, and Tom and PC were gone.

Joe and Kandee found Joe and Jennifer and told them where they were off to for a week. The four exchanged hugs. Joe Cornish asked for a moment and disappeared into his den. He returned with a bottle of his favorite merlot and a handful of one hundred dollar bills which he put into Joe's pocket as he handed the wine to Kandee. Then Joe and Kandee were gone.

Jonathan had said his good byes also and waved to everyone and accompanied Joe and Kandee to the entrance of the marina.

Then Joe and Jennifer found Nicolus and Nickolaea and asked if they could spare the time to have dinner with them and they left together. That left Jack and Gretchen. They gave Jeff and Janae long hugs and left with Joni for the club. Jennifer had given Taylor some money with which to go shopping for clothes. Taylor looked at Jeff and Janae. Janae wasn't jumping in so Jeff said he'd be glad to accompany her if she wished. Taylor said, "Yes, thank you," and caught a wink from Janae. Jeff and Taylor were gone.

Janae thought for a moment. If her calculations were right, she was holding the fort along with the yacht's crew. She decided to take stock of her life and make blueberry muffins.

After a few relaxing hours, Joe and Jennifer Cornish, Nicolus and Nickolaea, returned from their early dinner and went into Joe's den. Joe and Jennifer had expressed their appreciation for all their help and wisdom. Joe handed Nicolus five thousand dollars for them to use in getting a place to live or furnishings if they lived at the club.

Finally, they told Nickolaea they would see to her immigration paperwork and proceed with getting her citizenship on a fast track because of her usefulness to the law enforcement community. Then they exchanged long hugs. Jennifer could sense Nickolaea getting used to this hug thing especially from another woman. Then Nicolus and Nickolaea were on their way.

Joe fetched a bottle of merlot and two goblets and took Jennifer by the hand to the back of the yacht where they sat alone, in the sun. They reminisced about the past month and all that had happened, yet they couldn't keep themselves from discussing the plans they were making for the future, and how they would affect the growing group of those who they began referring to, between themselves, as their family.

# Part Three

## 1

When news of the demise of Jason Everett Samuelson and his right hand man in a fiery explosion got out, it quickly flooded the criminal world. All the lower level bosses in Samuelson's organization figured it was their chance to become the big bad boss. The squabbling and infighting that immediately began caused chaos in the distribution of drugs, the buying and selling of girls, and the smooth running operation of the clubs and bars. Usually the meanest guy, who did the meanest things, like kill off the competition, ended up on top, but Matty knew differently. Matty knew how to become the head boss and stay head boss. He knew because he knew what nobody else knew: Jason Everett Samuelson was not dead.

Years ago, Samuelson had recognized Matty's violent nature and put him in charge of his enforcement wing. Assassinations, kidnappings, torture, warnings--Matty was good at organization and ruthlessness. He was perfect for the job of Boss, and now the leadership had been handed to him. The fact that nobody else knew didn't matter. The plans he had in mind would be flawless. He knew what he was doing and how to go about it with stealth. He wouldn't become the Boss, he already was - except no one knew it yet. Matty would kidnap someone important to Samuelson and then trade for him. He would keep Samuelson in a prison of Matty's own making and rule the organization under Samuelson's blessing. Simple plans were the best. Easy-to-carry-out ruthlessness was what worked, and what Matty was known for. Important people knew his fingerprint or trademark on a job. People like Samuelson. He would recognize Matty's hand right away. The only thing Matty hadn't figured out yet was where Samuelson was, but the link to him had something to do with that Seabeck safe house, and he would start there.

Matty sent a 'husband/wife' team to Seabeck. They played tourist, had coffee at the coffee shack, spent time in the General Store, and at the café behind the store. They happened to be sitting at a table at Bobbi's when they witnessed an arrest being made of a customer. Richard and Rachael not only recognized the guy as a member of a rival gang, but recognized Samuelson's bodyguard as one of those doing the arresting. That didn't make sense to them, but Nicolus was the one guy they did not want to tangle with. They minded their own business and continued to watch, frequenting Bobbi's for every meal. They were driving a pickup with a camper on it to fit their disguise and have a place to stay.

Being at Bobbi's paid off, because they saw Samuelson coming and going from the big yacht out at the end of the marina. Their job was to pick from his acquaintances an easy person to kidnap and follow them to a location where they could carry out the job with a minimum of fuss. When Nicolus walked Samuelson and a small group out to their car, Richard and Rachael figured they were leaving. Good. They didn't need to keep track of them. Samuelson would come voluntarily if they did their job right. As they continued to watch, Nicolus went back to the yacht. They saw a few more people come and go, then the yacht started up and left the dock.

Richard and Rachael got up and paid their bill. They walked hand in hand taking in the sights as they headed toward the camper. They quickly headed for Seattle. In two hours they were at the Shilshole Marina main entrance.

They watched as more and more people got off the yacht and exited the main gate. Finally, a young couple came out and got into a taxi. Richard and Rachael realized they would be an easy target and followed the taxi.

Half an hour later the taxi pulled into Northgate Mall. The camper followed and pulled into an outer parking slot. Richard and Rachael followed the couple into the mall, and shadowed them for a while. They seemed to be skipping the bigger stores and stopping at the boutiques.

Jeff was enjoying being with Taylor. She was gorgeous and he couldn't keep his eyes off her. He liked the way she walked and talked, her sunny personality, and she seemed to like having him around. Clothes shopping wasn't something Jeff enjoyed, but when Taylor agreed to have him come along, he knew it was going to one of the best days of his life. He had to keep reminding himself that he was there to protect Taylor, and he would do that first and foremost.

Jennifer had told Taylor to get some expensive business suits as well as some casual things, underwear and accessories, and a couple of coats - one lightweight and one for warmth. Then, of course, she needed shoes. They went to store after store trying on many things. Taylor would try something on and then come out and ask Jeff what he thought. He had no idea what to say so he just went with his heart. "Gorgeous," or "wow," or "now that looks great on you." He never said anything negative because she was lovely to look at no matter what she wore. Taylor would buy one thing here and another there. She seemed to know what she was looking for, but for some reason wanted Jeff's opinion. He hoped she was catching on to the fact that he was head over heels in love with her, without him acting too juvenile about it. After a few hours they had accumulated an armful of packages for Jeff to carry, so they rested on some seating surrounding a planter with flowers in the middle of the mall. Jeff noticed the mall was well taken care of and clean.

A couple much like themselves sat down just a short distance away. They had boxes and bags, also. The gal looked over at Taylor, smiled and said, "Isn't this fun?"

"Yes it is, especially having someone to carry everything."

The guy looked at Jeff and sort of shrugged his shoulders and eyebrows, but with a smile. Jeff raised his eyebrows, too, and nodded with an easy smile.

"Well, it's time for lunch. Have you guys eaten?" The female half of the other couple was not shy and sort of reminded Jeff of PC.

"No, we haven't and I'm hungry. How about you, Jeff?" Taylor was being her polite, conversational self.

"Yes, I'm hungry," Jeff was experiencing Taylor's impromptu world, and loving it.

"Hey, join us!..." the gal blurted out. Then caught herself, "Whoops, I'm being pushy…sorry." Taylor smiled and just waved away the apology with her arm. "My name is Rachael and this is Richard. We are on our honeymoon and we haven't talked to anyone we know for three days now. Can you believe it?"

Now Jeff and Taylor were staring and smiling broadly. "Oh, congratulations, how wonderful! You both look so happy," Taylor was sincere.

"Thank you so much. Are you guys married?" Rachael asked.

Jeff blurted out, "No, no, we're not married." Taylor and Jeff looked at each other, sort of embarrassed.

Then Richard said, "Sounds like no, not yet. Am I right?"

Now they <u>were</u> embarrassed and didn't know where to look. They ended up looking at each other again, with a look of serious affection that they had not expressed to each other before.

Rachael came to their rescue. "Listen, we're in a camper out in the parking lot. We've brought lots of food and haven't hardly touched it. How would you like to join us for lunch at our place?" She made 'our place' sound like it was plush. Smiling and gracious with the right amount of need for outside conversation, they convinced Jeff and Taylor to join them for lunch.

As they stood and grabbed their purchases Rachael said, "Come on, we'll fill you in on what <u>not</u> to do on your honeymoon." Everybody laughed and headed for the exit.

As they approached the camper, Jeff noticed it had Washington State plates with tabs due in three months. He was impressed; it was big, sitting on a dually two-seat diesel Ford pickup. Lots of money here, he thought. Richard opened the rear door of the pickup and said, "Here, put your things in here for now." Jeff and Taylor did, and then Richard locked it again. Then they went to the back and, unlocking the camper door, all went in. It was very neat looking with not a lot of clutter.

"My mom told me to always keep my nest clean. That way the man of the house will always be proud to invite someone over."

"She's got a smart mom," Richard quipped.

"Wow, this is cozy and fun looking," Taylor said, looking around. Jeff also thought, boy wouldn't this be fun.

"Please sit and relax and let us enjoy your company. You're not in a hurry are you?" Rachael was a perfect hostess.

"No...we've got a couple of hours," Taylor said looking at Jeff. Jeff nodded.

"Sooo...we were engaged six months and couldn't stand it any longer. We had agreed to stay out of bed together till after we were married and it was hard, sooo...just last week...it was a big wedding, but my folks could afford it." She was making sandwiches and talking at the same time, "Oh, are sandwiches okay? We've got lots of fixings. Honey, would you pour something to drink?"

Richard opened the small fridge, "Uh...we've got juice already opened or bottled beer?" He looked questioningly at Jeff and Taylor.

Jeff thought to himself, no alcohol, I'm on duty, "I'll have juice."

"Me, too," Taylor added.

Richard poured three juices and opened a beer for himself. Holding up the beer, he toasted, "To new friends, who are willing to listen to newlyweds." Everyone took a good drink because they had been shopping all day. Except Rachael, she didn't touch her juice. She was making sandwiches, and talking.

"Well, we've had so much fun the last few days..." Jeff noticed right away the juice tasted funny, "and not all of it was spent in bed..." Everyone laughed. Taylor began feeling dizzy and looked at Jeff. "...but shopping is never boring so we..." Now Jeff started to feel dizzy and looked at Taylor. Right away he saw her eyes not focusing. Jeff suddenly looked at Richard who was staring at them. "...just shopped until we almost dropped..." Jeff's hand went for his phone in his pocket. Pulling it out he pushed the speed dial for Joe Cornish. It was the last conscious thing he did. Taylor reached out for Jeff as she lost consciousness also, and they collapsed onto each other.

"Yes?" Richard heard Jeff's phone say as he picked it up and shut it off. Richard and Rachael put the food away, made the table into a bed, and laid the two on it. They tied their hands and feet and tied a rope across them above and below their waists to keep them from rolling off. Then they got out and poured the contents of the glasses and the container of juice onto the beauty bark outside their camper. They then locked the door, hopped into the pickup, and headed for the freeway. They caught the freeway south and were gone.

# 2

Joe and Jennifer Cornish were relaxing and thinking about the future as Joe's phone rang. He noticed Jeff's name and answered. All he heard was background noise and then it was disconnected. He looked down at his phone and saw that the call had ended. He looked at Jennifer who was tidying up things and she asked, "Was that them? They should be heading back by now."

"It was Jeff's phone, but he hung up as soon as I answered it," Joe said.

"Oh. Probably low battery, I'll call Taylor." She punched in her number but it went right to recording. "Huh, hers is shut off. Must have forgotten to turn it back on after shopping." Then Joe punched in Jeff's number and it went right to voice mail.

"Jeff dialed me and now his phone is off? Something is wrong," Joe Cornish quickly dialed Tony. He answered right away. "Tony, something's not right. We might be under attack again; be very careful," Joe announced.

"What do you mean? What's up?"

Joe filled Tony in on the phone call from Jeff. "Have you heard from him or Taylor?"

"No, what do you want us to do?"

"Proceed to the club on high alert. Get inside, lock up and stay there, but be ready if I call back with instructions. Let me know if you hear from Jeff or Taylor. And will you alert Nicolus and Nickolaea of our situation? We have to assume something's happened to Jeff and Taylor, and any one of us could be next."

Joe Cornish ended the call and then yelled, "Janae! Call over to the reverend at the safe house and find out if everything is normal. If so, ask them to practice the lock down drill. Tell the reverend that Joe Cornish thinks the safe house might be hungry."

Jennifer came close and took Joe's arm. He calmly instructed her, "Call Tom and PC. Tell them what's up and to continue home, but to lock up when they get there and lay low till they hear back from us." Jennifer went right into action. Joe dialed Joe and Kandee.

"Yes?"

"Joe, I think we might be under attack. How far are you?"

"A few miles north of Seattle; we stopped at Kandee's mom's. What's going on?"

"Jeff called, but his phone disconnected as soon as I answered. Taylor's is off also, and nobody's heard from them. I'm alerting everyone and I'm going to have them paged through the Northgate Mall security. Joe, my gut says someone went after our newest link, and Jeff probably had his eyes on her more than anything else."

"What do you want us to do?"

"Let your brother know what's going on and see if he has any ideas. Meanwhile get yourselves turned around and stop in at that mall. Check back with me when you get there."

"Gotcha," Joe answered, but Joe Cornish had already ended the call.

Jennifer then asked, "What next?"

"Could you call the taxi company and see where they got dropped off?"

"I'm on it."

Then Joe Cornish called Tony again.

"Yes, sir?"

"Tony, are you all safe?"

"Yes, sir, we're already up at the club. Anything from Jeff and Taylor?"

"No. Do you think Alexander is leveling with us or could he be stringing us along, finding our weak point and passing it on?"

"No way. I'd bet my miserable life on it. He's being legit. That's my call."

"Okay, then tell him our situation and see if he has any clues."

"Yes, sir. Consider it done."

"Call me if you get anything," Joe Cornish ended the call. He and Jennifer sat together in the dining area thinking, and saying a prayer.

*

Tony called for a huddle. James, the redheads, Alexander, Jack, Gretchen and Joni all sat with him. Tony explained what he knew about the disappearance of Jeff and Taylor. He asked if anyone had a clue.

Alexander shrugged with his hands, "Not a clue from my end. I could make a few calls, but then they'd ask what I'm doing. But I volunteer for the attack-back team. I'm all in."

"Yeah, you're going to be valuable to us soon. Just lay low till the heat over your disappearance dies down. Anyone else?"

Gretchen started thinking out loud, "If they've been kidnapped, that is a big deal...but *they* are not. I mean, not for an information squeeze anyway. They'd only be valuable as bait in a trade...Tony, no offense, but this sounds like something you'd do." Gretchen was saying what she thought, but trying to be careful, too.

Tony thought for a minute, "None taken. But you're right." He looked at James. James was staring back with a look of terror. "What?" Tony asked James.

"She's right." It didn't take two seconds for Tony to realize what James was thinking, "Matty!" they both said it at the same time.

Tony and James got up, "Jack, will you take charge of defending this place? James and I got to think and call Joe Cornish."

Jack responded, "You're in safe hands. Alexander, come with me."

Gretchen took the girls upstairs and put them in a room with a view, "Keep peeking out that window and call me on my phone if you see anyone approaching the club." Then she went down to join Jack.

Tony and James went into Jack's old office, "That damn Matty; he's trying to take over."

"Everyone's trying to take over," James said and continued, "but Matty's got the inside track. He knows you're alive."

"You're right. I called him to abort the attack on the safe house. I better call Nicolus." Tony dug out his phone.

"Nicolus... we're thinking Matty's doing this... kidnapping those two kids and trading for me, or for my head on a platter... Yeah, he's the only one who knows I'm alive. Where would he hang out up here besides the club if he was running this? ...Okay, why don't you head that way and see what you can see... Thanks, bye."

Next Tony called Joe Cornish, "Remember the guy I called to call off the attack on the safe house?...It's possible he's behind this...Yeah, either a trade or evidence of my death...well, I sent Nicolus to check out where he might be hanging out if he's up here. I'll let you know if he sees anything...Okay, bye." Tony's temperature began to rise.

# 3

Richard and Rachael made it to Kent before they heard rumblings in the back. At the warehouse they eyed the big door but realized the camper was too tall to get in. They parked and unlocked the back. Richard untied Jeff and Taylor, who were still groggy, while Rachael put tape over their mouths. Then they escorted them out of the camper, into the warehouse and closed the big doors. Inside was a specially built sound-proof room about twenty feet by twenty feet. Richard and Rachael shuffled them into the room. Inside was a wheelchair-accessible, fully contained port-a-potty. The room had TV and radio, a kitchen with fridge and microwave, and a double bed. Two solar tubes extended from the ceiling up through the warehouse roof providing natural light. Two chairs and a table finished the decor.

Jeff and Taylor were woozy, but Jeff was awake enough to think. They were being held against their will for some reason and it was his job to free them. The door closed behind them, and Richard and Rachael sat them down and carefully took the tape off their mouths.

"I've got to use the bathroom," Taylor was desperate.

Rachael smiled and was reassuring, "I know you do, give me your hands." Rachael untied her and helped her into the port-a-potty, and closed the door. When Taylor was done it was Jeff's turn, and then they all sat down to talk.

"Look, you guys," Rachael began, "you're a sweet couple. We are not going to harm you. We were hired to detain you and care for you while you're with us. There's no reason we can't be friends and have fun together while you stay here. Look, we don't know why or how long you're going to be here, but we're responsible for you and it's our job to protect you. If anybody tries to hurt you, we will stop them. Okay?!" Rachael was trying hard to gain their confidence back. "So you guys make yourselves at home. We are going out for some food and we'll be back before you know it. There's bottled water in the fridge. Drink lots and it will help flush out your bodies. We'll be back in a while," Richard and Rachael left abruptly, locking them in.

Jeff and Taylor checked their pockets and found them empty. Standing in the center of the room they looked around at the room, then at each other. Taylor stepped close and wrapped her arms around Jeff. He lowered his nose into her soft brown hair as he held her, "We'll be alright, I promise."

*

Richard and Rachael locked the warehouse and drove the camper a quarter of a mile away, and parked it in the back row of a parking lot in front of a large corporate warehouse. After they emptied the camper and pickup, they wiped them down to erase any fingerprints. They loaded their gear into the Chrysler 300 with California license plates parked next to them. Leaving the pickup and camper behind, they drove away in the 300. Richard drove and Rachael dialed their boss in San Diego.

"Boss, we're done. The packages are secure in the warehouse. We're heading south," Rachael knew better than to remind Matty to pay them.

"Good work," Matty paused, "I'm going to transfer five grand into your bank account in San Diego. That's not bad for a week's work, huh?"

"Perfect, sir," Rachael rolled her eyes at Richard, "Call us anytime."

After she hung up she took a deep breath, "That cheap bastard. We're done. Let's head home."

*

Nicolus and Nickolaea drove south of Seattle into the Kent Valley. The farmland there had mostly been turned into industrial parks with row upon row of warehouses. Not just big ones, but smaller ones with an attached office and a big door that vehicles could go into and be out of sight. A person could almost get lost in the maze of warehouses and roads.

Nicolus had worked with Matty before out of a certain warehouse in this area. They drove carefully, and slowly approached the one Nicolus remembered. No cars were parked outside. Nicolus drove on by and stopped at the office door of the next warehouse. He got out and went to the door, but instead of going in, he walked over to the office door of the warehouse Matty had used before. The sign on the office door said Johnson Communications. That was a different name from what he remembered. He saw nothing through the window, so he tried the door and it opened. He stepped inside but the office was empty. He tried the door into the warehouse area and looked in. Empty. Nicolus retreated and got back into the car with Nickolaea. He shook his head and said, "Wrong one. No telling if he moved to another unit, or even another site. The only solid thing we have got to go on is, if he did kidnap them, he has to hide them somewhere."

Nicolus drove out to the main road and went down the street a ways. He circled back into the maze area. After a minute, Nicolus pulled over and stopped. He adjusted his rear view mirror to focus on a pickup truck and camper.

"What do you see, Nicolus?" Nickolaea wanted to help. So she looked forward and around as Nicolus looked backwards.

Slowly Nicolus spoke, "I think... I might have seen a camper and truck like that one out at Seabeck." He reached for his phone and dialed Joe Cornish.

"Yes?"

"Picture the parking lot in Seabeck when you backed me up and we arrested Alexander. Do you remember seeing a large pickup with a camper there?" There was a pause as Joe Cornish thought back.

"Yes, Nicolus, there was. The truck was...big...two seats, and dark colored. It was a dually with a big camper...white and blue," Joe Cornish spoke slowly as he remembered.

"Very good. I have the vehicle you have described in my rear view mirror, parked at a warehouse in Kent."

Joe Cornish thought for a moment, "Can you set up surveillance and see if anyone comes and goes and if so, where to?"

"Yes, sir, we can do that. We will keep you informed."

After taking turns watching through the night, the camper and pickup were still there and there had been no visitors. By eight o'clock the parking lot had almost filled up with cars as people arrived for work. Nicolus got out and walked the fifty yards to where the camper was parked. He looked in the pickup and saw nothing, then went to the back of the camper and knocked on the door. No answer. So, slipping on a set of latex gloves, he picked the lock in broad daylight, not caring who might see. Opening the camper he stepped in. Nothing. He searched for any clue of identity. Nothing. He was about to leave, when he stopped and checked the cupboard under the sink. There he found a garbage sack with a plastic bottle and three cups. The bottle said apple juice. He sniffed it. Wrong smell. He picked up each plastic cup and sniffed. Wrong smell. Nicolus found a plastic grocery bag, put the bottle and cups in it and left the camper, closing the door. Returning to the car, he dialed Joe Cornish.

"Yes?"

"No activity at the camper, so I entered it. It was clean except for an apple juice bottle and three cups; they smelled of a drug. I'm guessing it was used to incapacitate Jeff and Taylor. I've got the evidence in a sack in case you want to check them for fingerprints."

"Excellent job, Nicolus. Go directly to the Federal Building in downtown Seattle. I'll have an agent meet you at the main entrance. Give the evidence to him." Joe Cornish ended the call after giving Nicolus precise directions. Then he called his FBI office.

# 4

Jeff and Taylor were trying to figure out what was happening and what would happen next. They had found and made coffee and were sitting at the table.

"Okay. Richard and Rachael sucked us in, drugged us, and put us in this room to just wait. So that means we are kidnapped and are being held for some reason. Whoever it is wants something from either Tony or Joe Cornish and will trade us for it. Richard and Rachael are just supposed to take care of us."

"Yeah, they seemed nice. I liked them," Taylor was feeling better.

"Yeah, they were good. Good actors. We like who they acted to be, but not who they are. They're bad people. We should cooperate with them, but if ordered to, they would kill us."

"Oh, Jeff, I'm scared. What do we do?"

"There are a number of things we can do. First, we think, and don't panic. Then we assess our surroundings, looking for clues to our whereabouts and to who is doing this. Then, if we find something the kidnappers have overlooked, we exploit it without their knowledge and gain an advantage or even escape," Jeff's training was kicking in.

They looked at the room again as they sat. Only one door. No windows. Air and heat were pumped in and out, but there was no ductwork to crawl through. Then they eyed the two solar tubes. Not big enough to crawl through, but they brought sunlight from the roof into the room.

Jeff was thinking out loud, "If we could undo this end of the solar tube and poke something up the tube and break the part on the roof, we could stick something out the top like a flag saying 'send help'."

"Oh, my gosh! That's a great idea! What do we need?"

Looking around as he talked, Jeff continued, "We'll need a couple or more broom handle type things, tape, paper and something to write with."

Right away Taylor went for her purse. She pulled out a pencil, a pen, and some lipstick. Also, some band aids. The band aids gave her an idea, "I'm going to look for a first aid kit," she said excitedly.

"Good. Yeah, maybe there's some tape in it." Jeff found a mop and a broom, "Oh, where did they put the tape they took off our mouths?" Jeff found a garbage basket under the sink and the wadded up tape was there. "Here we go, this will help," getting down on his knees, Jeff looked behind the basket and found a fire extinguisher. He brought it out and put it and the tape on the table.

"Oh, yes," Taylor bounced up and opened the door to the port-a-potty. On the door was attached a first aid kit. She took it and put it on the table.

"Good," Jeff said, "Now, paper or something to write on and use as a flag." Then he said, "Oh!" he unbuttoned his shirt and took it off. He pulled his white undershirt off and put his shirt back on.

Taylor just stared, nodding in understanding, then asked, "What if Richard and Rachael or someone else comes back and sees all this stuff we're putting together?"

Taylor had a point so Jeff thought for a moment, "Well, since we don't know when they'll be back, we can't let that stop us. We have to do what we can, with smarts, until we get stopped or succeed. I remember Joe Cornish saying that more than once."

There was a pole lamp by the bed. Jeff looked it over and unscrewed the base. "Okay, let's un-scrunch the tape from our mouths and see if we can tape together the mop, the broom and the pole from the lamp," in a few minutes they had a pole almost fifteen feet long taped together.

Next, Jeff stood on a chair and inspected the solar tube, "See if there's a table knife in the drawer."

Taylor looked, "Only two spoons and a can opener."

"Hand me one of the spoons," Jeff used the handle of the spoon and pried the metal rim around the tube away from the ceiling. It was sort of spring-loaded to stay attached to the ceiling. He carefully undid it and the textured glass pane came down with it. He looked up the tube into the glaring light. It looked about the same length as their pole. Then Jeff said, "Look around for something hard or sharp to tape to the end of the pole. We've got to break the plastic dome on the top of the tube."

"Okay," they both looked around and found nothing.

"The spoon might do it, but I don't think taping it to the pole will hold it strongly enough."

"Let's try anyway."

So Jeff took the light pole end of the pole and started to tape the spoon to it, "Wait a minute. The other end has threads on it, doesn't it?"

"What do you mean, 'thread'?" Taylor was thinking sewing.

"Okay," Jeff laid the pole across the table. He un-taped the joint between the broom and the lamp pole, turned the lamp pole around, and taped it back up. Then he grabbed the lamp pole base and screwed it back on to the end of the pole. It was solid, and heavy enough to hold up the lamp, and it fit up the tube with about an inch to spare on each side. Jeff then grabbed a chair and, putting it under the solar tube, stood up on it. "Okay, Taylor, hand me the pole."

"Okay…here…Jeff, please be careful," the tension was rising for Taylor. Jeff eased the base up the tube and kept feeding until the lamp pole, the broom and most of the mop had gone up. Then the end hit something.

"Okay!" Jeff took a good hold of the sponge mop end and shoved the pole hard up the tube. It hit solid resistance, but held together. Jeff slowly lowered it again and then jammed it up again. After six tries the pole was getting wiggly, but the resistance at the top sounded like it was cracking. Jeff lowered the pole and handed it to Taylor.

"Let's re-tape and make it stronger."

"We still have some first aid tape," Taylor was getting anxious. They were getting close, but the door could open any minute, because they couldn't hear outside the room. "Jeff, what if they catch us doing this?"

"They might, and we'll deal with that when it happens, but we can't anticipate what we can't control. So we have to keep going in a forward direction until something or someone stops us."

Those words, echoing in his head, were from Joe Cornish, and Jeff was glad for them.

They re-taped the joints of the pole, then Jeff got back up onto the chair. The pole went back up the tube and Jeff rammed it another six times. On the seventh, a few pieces of plastic came down the tube. Three more rams and the base of the lamp had broken through. Some of the plastic dome came down the tube in jagged pieces, and some went out onto the gently sloping roof. Jeff quickly withdrew the pole, handed it to Taylor and got down off the chair.

"Okay. First things first. I'll clean this mess up, you take my shirt and write SOS in big red letters on each side with your lipstick."

"Okay.... Do you think we'll get caught?" Taylor asked, excited and scared.

"Nope, we're not going to get caught."

"How do you know?"

"Cuz we're the good guys," Jeff looked at her and smiled. He cleaned up the mess of dust and plastic and put it down the port-a-potty. Then he unscrewed the lamp base and set it back where it belonged, "How's it going?"

"I've just about got it," she had to hold Jeff's shirt against the table with her tummy and hold the top with her hand in order to draw the letters with the lipstick. When she was through she handed it to Jeff.

"Super! Now..." Jeff tied a knot in one sleeve of the shirt and stuck the pole up the other sleeve till the pole crossed the width of the shirt inside and stopped at the knot. Then he stretched the lower sleeve down the pole and taped it to the pole, tight. It looked like a flag.

"What if there's no wind? I'm sorry Jeff, I keep thinking of what could go wrong," Taylor was near tears. Only the next few minutes would tell if they would be tears of terror or tears of joy.

"No, that's okay. We've got to think of all the angles, good or bad. You're great," he stopped and looked at her. "We're doing great and we're doing it together. It's sort of fun, right?"

Jeff was existing on the words of Joe Cornish, and it was working.

"Sort of, but I'm scared. I'm sure glad you're here."

"Me, too. I love you," he just blurted it out and there it was. Jeff had tried hard not to say what he had been feeling ever since he first laid eyes on Taylor, but it just bubbled out.

"I love you, too, Jeff," now Taylor was smiling with tears in her eyes.

"Oh! Hey, where is that first aid kit?" Jeff asked. Taylor got it for him. It said 'car first aid kit' on it. "Yes!" Jeff opened it and at the very bottom, under everything else, was a folded banner about a foot square. It was red with white letters and said, 'SEND HELP', on both sides. "Here, this will help," he taped the banner to the end of the shirt. "Okay, let's try this."

Now he got back onto the chair. Taylor fed him the pole and he gently pushed it up the tube. He reached his arm as far up the tube as he could and with strips of tape, secured the sponge end of the mop to the inside of the tube. It angled across the tube, but that worked. He made sure the bottom was tight to the tube and then let go. "There must be some wind, I can feel it fluttering some."

"Alright!" Taylor had her hands over her mouth and made a little jump.

"Okay, hand me the glass pane and the metal ring," Taylor did and Jeff carefully put the bottom of the solar tube back together.

"Okay, let's put away everything where we found it, and make the place look like nothing happened." They worked together and then looked around. When they caught each other's eyes, Taylor jumped into Jeff's arms.

"Come on. Let's lay in bed like we're scared and don't know what to do." Taylor burst out with a half cry, half laugh, "Okay, that won't be hard."

They laid on top of the covers, clothes on, but Jeff put his arms around Taylor. She snuggled close. They stayed silent for a few minutes. Wow. They had finished and gotten away with it, and no one interrupted them. Their breathing and their heartbeats began to relax. Without realizing it, they both drifted off to sleep.

# 5

The club was locked down. The three girls were upstairs keeping a look out. Tony, James, Alexander, Jack, and Gretchen were huddled, talking. They were armed.

"I've got to control my temper on this one," Tony was saying. "I can't tell Matty what I want to say to him. If he wants to trade those kids for me and I make him mad, he'll kill them right in front of me before he kills me."

James was hanging his head. "We've got to be in charge of negotiations. We've got to change his offer even before he offers it. We've got to give him more than he bargained for or expected."

Tony jumped in, "...and convince him he has got to get rid of those kids."

James again, "Kidnapping is a federal rap; he doesn't want that."

Tony again, "How about we offer you and me and the girls. He'll like that. We hide guns on the girls. They won't search them. Then when things get dicey, the girls act scared and jump into our arms. We grab the guns and give Matty what he deserves," just then Tony's phone rang and everybody froze. Tony looked at his phone, then answered, "Yes, sir."

"Tony, has anyone contacted you yet?"

"No, not yet. I was just going to call Matty and see what he's got in mind."

"Listen, Nicolus has a line on Jeff and Taylor. He thinks they're in the Kent Valley. Maybe in a warehouse. He's looking, so we need time. But might as well call your Matty and make sure he's the one who is doing this. But stall. If he wants a trade right away, tell him okay, but you have to be careful because the FBI is tailing you. Also, send Jack and Gretchen down to the Kent Valley to help Nicolus and Nickolaea, if you can spare them."

"Yeah, no problem."

"Okay, let me talk to Gretchen a minute," Tony gave the phone to Gretchen.

"Yeah," she said.

"Is Tony hanging together?"

"Yeah, I like the way it looks."

"Okay, I asked Tony to send you and Jack down to the Kent Valley to help Nicolus and Nickolaea. They think they have a line on the kids there."

"Okay, gotcha," Joe Cornish ended the call. Gretchen handed the phone back to Tony. "Tony, the last thing Joe Cornish said was, 'Tell Tony, no matter what, I've got his back,' Just keep him posted."

"Okay. Hey, I love that guy. He wants you and Jack to hook up with Nicolus and Nickolaea. Jack, you got keys for a ride?"

"Yes, I got my Magnum around back," Gretchen and Jack got up and left.

"Okay, James, dial up Matty," James did. It started ringing. James handed it to Tony.

"Yeah?"

"Matty! Tell me what the hell you're doing," Tony was almost conversational.

"I'm taking over. News is out that my boss is dead, so I'm in charge now. Only, I know you're still alive."

"Matty, have you got those two kids?"

"Sure I've got them. And you're not going to like what I'm going to do to them unless you give me what I want."

"Matty, listen. I'm out. I'm going to take my money and live. You can take over, I don't care. But kidnapping is a federal offense.

You don't need that. Let them go. They're undercover operatives, their boss won't let them tell anyone. You'll be clean if you let them go. James, and the girls and I, we'll meet you. Just say where."

"You listen. I'm talking now, and I'm only going to say it once. I want you and Nicolus. You two are the only ones I'm afraid of. You two meet me. Put James in his stall. When I get you and Nicolus in my hands, we decide who lives and who dies. You two die, the kids get let go; you two want to live, the kids die, and I do it slow, right in front of you. That way you know who's in charge."

"Matty, the FBI is following me. If you want me to bring them, I'll be right over. Come on, if you're going to be in charge, you have got to think ahead," Tony heard a loud chop over the phone.

"Listen, you fat bastard. I got a big cleaver and a chopping block. You get to where I say without anyone tailing you, because in one hour I'm going to start chopping. And I'm kinda looking forward to it. I haven't had that much fun in a while."

"Matty, nice try. You're trying to make me explode. I'm not going to run around like my head's cut off, trying to lose the FBI. You go ahead and have your fun. But, if you get your butt over to the club, we let you in. You hold all the cards Matty. We have an undercover exit here just like San Diego. You and me leave and go get Nicolus. We talk, convince you that we're out, and we take custody of the kids. You take over in my place with no FBI, no federal rap, and no mess. Think, Matty, nobody dies, therefore nobody has a murder charge wrapped around their neck. No kidnapping charge. You'll be free to go on about your business. Don't complicate this, Matty. The easiest thing to do in this whole scenario is to walk away, free of trouble. Live free, not dogged by troubles because you're afraid of Nicolus and me. Hell, Matty, we'll help you. But I mean help you get free, not help you entangle yourself more. I'm not living in a mess I caused any more, I'm going to live free," silence. Then the phone call ended.

Tony was left without an answer. He looked up at James.

"What does that mean? Is he on his way over, or killing the kids as we speak?" Tony didn't know what to think.

James was thinking out loud. "Matty's a hothead, but he's smart. He knows how to choose his battles," James paused, trying to make sense of the situation. After a moment he continued, "You just handed him a couple of simple ways out. If I know Matty, he'll take one of them, but not on your terms. My money says he just leaves, but doesn't tell you. He wants to hurt you so he keeps you hanging, not knowing what's happening, but he disappears and goes on defense, in case all your freedom talk is just BS, and you're really coming after him." James finished and looked up at Tony. Tony was staring at the wall.

"Okay..., Okay..., we can't control what Matty is going to do, so... we got to find those kids. Call Nicolus. Tell him he's got to find them fast. Ask what we can do to help," James dialed his phone.

*

Jack and Gretchen pulled into a coffee shop across from a warehouse management office. They spotted Nicolus and Nickolaea and stopped next to their car. They spoke through rolled down windows.

Nicolus held up a handful of papers and said, "I just got a list of warehouse renters who are based in California. Here, you take half and check them out. We'll check these others. If you see anything, call us. We'll do the same. Be careful," so off they went--two navigators, two drivers.

After an hour of driving around looking for addresses, walking into offices, making up stories as to why they were there while they looked around, they were about halfway through their papers. As Nicolus approached the next address, Nickolaea saw something and pointed to the roof. Half the roof slanted toward them, the other half slanted away. Just over the ridge line was the top of a banner or flag that looked other than professional, not like the 'One month free if you rent me' banners that were all over the place. Nicolus stopped and they looked up at it.

"What is that?" Nickolaea asked, "There are letters on it."

Nicolus pulled up to the entrance closest to what they were looking at. He got out and tried the door. Locked. He climbed up on top of the car roof and hoisted himself up onto the warehouse roof. Having a better view up there, he first looked around the whole area, then called down to Nickolaea.

"Call Jack and Gretchen. Tell them to come here," Nickolaea nodded. Nicolus walked up to the ridge line and looked over the other side. A solar tube top had been broken out and a handmade flag was poking out. He walked to it. Holding it out, he read it. Then digging his phone out, he called Nickolaea.

"This is it. Keep looking around. We might be sitting ducks."

"Be careful."

Nicolus looked down the tube and listened. Nothing. He took the pole of the flag and banged it against the tube a few times.

Inside, Jeff froze. The combination of fear and excitement had overtaken them and they had slept through the night. He and Taylor were still lying in bed. He wasn't sure what it was, but something had caught his attention. He listened quietly. Then he heard the banging again, and then heard his name being called. He jumped up, waking up Taylor.

"What's wrong?" she cried.

"I hear something," he went to the tube and looked up.

"Jeff!"

"Yes! Yes, we're in here! Nicolus?"

"Yes, what's your situation?"

"We are locked in this soundproof room. We're fine, just can't get out."

"Okay, sit tight. We're coming," Nicolus headed back to the edge of the roof, hopped down to the top of the car and to the ground.

"Got them. They're inside, keep watch," Nickolaea pulled her gun and stood outside the car, gun behind her. When a car pulled up, she readied herself to shoot, then relaxed again. It was Gretchen and Jack.

They all joined Nicolus at the office door. After a moment, Nicolus successfully picked the lock. They carefully stepped inside and closed the door. Nicolus motioned everybody to crouch down as he turned on the light. The small office was empty and the door into the warehouse was blocked open. As they rose and entered, they saw no one.

"Jack, stay here with Nickolaea and keep watch," he motioned for Gretchen to follow him. They went over to the door of the soundproof room.

"Look for wires, in case it's booby-trapped," seeing none after a thorough look, Nicolus rapped on the door three times. A second later three raps came from the inside. Nicolus focused his attention on the door latch and lock. He took a pen light from his pocket. The light did not reveal anything out of the ordinary inside the lock. Nicolus then applied the tools and his know-how and unlocked the door. He eased the door open until his eyes met Jeff's. He pushed the door open all the way and Taylor saw Gretchen and flew into her arms.

Nicolus stepped into the room and looked around. When he was satisfied, he put his hand on Jeff's shoulder and they went out. Joining Jack and Nickolaea, they checked to see if the coast was clear. Nicolus put Jeff and Taylor in with Jack and Gretchen, and instructed them to head for the yacht. Jack drove while Gretchen called Joe Cornish and filled him in. Nicolus and Nickolaea drove around the block and parked a little ways away to see if anyone would show up.

When in position, he called Tony, "The kids are safe and on their way to the yacht with Jack and Gretchen. We are watching the warehouse where they were kept in case anyone shows up. So far we have seen no one."

"Great work, Nicolus. I talked to Matty. He threatened you and I, but when I called his bluff, he hung up. James thinks he just bailed and left town. It sounds like maybe that's what happened. Would you stay another half hour just in case he shows, and then come here to the club? I want to hear all about it."

"Okay, see you in about an hour."

When Jeff and Taylor got back to the yacht, they showered and dressed and joined the Cornishes, Janae, Jack, and Gretchen for a seafood dinner with wine and chocolate cake. They leisurely talked out their episode and Joe Cornish asked questions until they all felt fully informed. Everyone was notified of the successful end to the kidnapping, and that night everyone slept soundly. Jeff and Taylor kissed each other good night before they went to their respective rooms.

# 6

Having heard of the successful conclusion to the kidnapping of Jeff and Taylor, Joe and Kandee turned back to their original course: away from everything and everyone for a week alone. Joe's new-found brother, Jonathan, had disappeared without telling anyone how to find him; however, to Joe he had given a phone number that would reach him or someone who knew how to reach him. Joe and Kandee had memorized that number. Now as they were driving, Joe looked at Kandee and said, "Try dialing that number. See if Jonathan answers."

"Okay," Kandee dug out her phone. "I was thinking the same thing. If we have time off, it would be fun to find out more about Jonathan," she dialed the number.

"Joe?"

"Hi, Jonathan. Joe's driving so I dialed. How are you?" Kandee was being Kandee.

"I'm wonderful. Tell me you're the same."

"Yes, we are and the thing with Jeff and Taylor ended in the best way possible."

"I'm so glad. Nobody hurt?"

"Nope. So we wanted to tell you that, and ask you a question."

"Thank you. And the answer to your question is 'yes'."

Kandee looked at Joe. "Jonathan says the answer to our question is 'yes'."

Joe kept driving but said loudly, "Jonathan, you don't even know what the question is."

Jonathan heard it and replied as Kandee pushed the speaker button, "My dear little brother, we are just now learning what other brothers have known for a long time. When brothers call each other, there are only two things they want. One is time together to do this, that, or the other thing. The other one is money. My answer is yes to either, or both."

Joe just smiled, shook his head, and kept driving. Then he said, "Both sounds good to me. Joe Cornish agreed to give us a week off. Kandee and I both thought of you. If your answer is still yes, what do we do?"

"Well, you're northbound on I-5, just past Exit 182. Keep going and take Exit 186 onto Airport Road. Call me back when you get to Paine Field."

"How do you know where we are?" Kandee had to ask.

"I'm just tracing your call to me back to you. Pretty cool, huh?"

"Yeah, I didn't know you could do that," she said.

"Oh yeah, all older brothers can do that."

Joe laughed out loud and said, "We'll call you back." When the directions brought them to Paine Field, Kandee started to dial Jonathan back.

"Hang on, gorgeous. Let's drive around a bit and see if we can find him, if he's here."

"But he'll know we are here."

"Not if we don't dial him up," they drove into the airport complex, and past rows of hangars housing private jets. When they came to the end of the complex, they turned around, and just got a glimpse of a corporate jet in front of the hangar on the runway side. Suddenly their phone rang.

"Hello?" Kandee said.

"Hi! You found my jet! Pull up to the office door and come on in."

"But how do you know where we are? We didn't dial you."

"Because I'm looking right at you," Kandee looked up and pointed to the office door of the last hangar. As Joe headed for it, they both saw the door open as Jonathan stepped outside and waved. Joe parked and they got out.

"Come on in, it's just about time to fly away," Jonathan was upbeat.

"Where are we going?" Kandee asked with a growing smile.

Jonathan was delighted that his little brother had Kandee for his wife. "Well, we'll let you girls figure that out," Jonathan smiled and held the door as they entered.

"What do you mean, 'us girls…'eeeeee!" she screamed with delight as she saw the answer to her question. Kitsap County Deputy Sheriff Sharon Madison was standing in the office, out of uniform, and in a gorgeous summer dress.

The girls ran into each other's arms. Joe and Jonathan just smiled and gazed at them, and at each other, thinking they were truly blessed.

"We didn't know you would be here!" Kandee blurted out.

"And we weren't expecting you. This is divine!" Sharon gushed with delight.

Jonathan jumped in, "It sure is divine. Divine Providence. We need a couple witnesses and I couldn't have picked better ones myself."

Then Joe, "Witnesses are only needed in marriage and in court cases. By the way, what was in that note you had me leave with Tammie at Seabeck?"

"Just a simple question."

"To which I said, 'yes'." Sharon interjected.

"Eeeeeee…" the girls were hugging again. It was the only thing that kept Kandee from screaming more.

"Well, what are brothers for?" Joe quipped.

Then Jonathan continued the thought, "Bachelor party partners. Come on, let's go party, little brother!"

"Oh, no you don't," Sharon warned, "I'm not letting you out of my sight, and I got my cuffs in my purse if I need them."

"Oh boy, I'm really going to have to cut back on my lifestyle," Jonathan said, teasingly.

Sharon moved right into Jonathan's face, "On the contrary, you're going to have to wine and dine me. I'm high maintenance."

Jonathan wrapped his arms around Sharon and held her, "Friends, I am in love over my head."

Kandee jumped into Joe's arms and he held her close. "That makes two of us, brother," the two couples just held each other for a few long, delightful minutes. Then Joe's phone rang.

Joe Cornish was serious, but not at all desperate, "Joe, sorry to butt in on your time off. If you happen to run into your brother or hear from him, tell him I have some plans I'd like to go over with him. Is that possible?"

"Yes. I think he said he would be out of touch for a while, but when he gets back, I'll tell him."

"Thanks, Joe…what…oh, please give Kandee a big hug from Jennifer and I," Joe Cornish ended the call.

"What was that about?" Jonathan wanted to know.

"Can't tell you until we get back, so let's go."

"Yes, excellent idea. Let's load up into the jet."

The jet was very comfortable and they all got situated nicely. It taxied down to the end of the runway and lined up for takeoff.

"Hold on everybody!" Jonathan was smiling as he said this. They were all buckled in, so Joe thought maybe Jonathan was uncomfortable flying and tried to cover it with a smile. Then the pilot found the gas pedal, because the jet screamed down the runway and lifted steeply up into the atmosphere faster and more powerfully than any commercial flight he had ever been on. Heck, it pinned him to his seat harder than any ride at the county fair! As they leveled off Joe exclaimed, "Wow!"

"Told ya!"

"Yeah, I think I'll start believing you from now on. Can we do that again?" Kandee reached over and punched Joe in the arm.

"Don't let the pilot hear you say that. He'll start doing barrel rolls and fly upside down," Jonathan quipped.

"Really? Where did you find him?" Now Joe was taking Jonathan seriously.

"Retired Air Force. F-15 fighter pilot."

# 7

Janae Halvorson was versatile. Even though she was one of the youngest operatives Joe Cornish had ever recruited, she had been excellent at whatever task she was given, whether it was secretarial, or maid duties on the yacht, or an occasional covert operation. Plus, she had another important quality that she was just born with: she did not stand out in a crowd. She blended in with any situation and could act in any way needed at any time. She was perfect for intelligence and covert operations work, and Joe Cornish wanted to keep her interested.

That was why, after a week or so of things settling down, he called Janae into his den on the yacht to join he and Jennifer. As Janae closed the door after herself and sat down, she began to wonder if she was going to get fired or something.

"Janae, you are more important to us and to what we are doing than we can accurately say. I have taken your abilities into account and concocted a plan for which you are perfectly suited," Janae's tension eased and she started to get excited.

Joe Cornish continued, "We would like to go over this plan with you. Would that be alright?"

"Sure."

"Okay, great. Since we've been married, Jennifer has increased my scope, just by telling me some of the ideas on her mind. One idea in particular has me excited and we have been doing some planning on it. It's in the realm of politics. Does politics scare you?"

"A little, yeah."

"Well, good. It should. It scares me, also, and yet I think it is an arena that could benefit from our abilities. Have you ever heard of a United States Senator named William Williamsford?"

"Yes, I've heard the name. A bit of an unusual name."

"Indeed, and he is a bit of an unusual man. Jennifer has, in the past, been privy to information about some of his dealings which are not commonly known. Since he is a Senator from the State of California, Jennifer has had the opportunity to assess his performance more than I. We would like to approach him with the offer of your help, which we are sure he would greatly benefit from."

"Uh... I'm not sure I'm following you. Is he a good guy or a bad guy?"

"An excellent question, Janae, which goes directly to the point, as we are not sure of the answer to that question ourselves. He seems to have the trappings of a selfish, rich, ambitious politician as per normal. Yet Jennifer has received information that says maybe the opposite is true."

"A Batman type of guy?"

Joe Cornish chuckled at this, thinking of himself.

"Possibly. If this is correct, we would offer you as a liaison in his employ to covertly help him with the projects he has in mind. If he turns out to be a bad guy, you would be in a position to find that out. Perhaps a dangerous assignment for you, Janae, but we know of no one who would be better qualified for it."

"Hmm... sounds kind of exciting. What about family?"

Jennifer tackled this one, slowly. "Believe it or not...he is a widower...with two preteen children, girls... How's that for a job for a man who has a hobby as a U.S. Senator."

"Whoa..."

"We would like to insert you into his employment as a nanny, or maid, or cook's helper, or secretary, or public relations person. Someone who would not necessarily be noticed, but who could notice everything."

"Have you figured out a way to do that yet?"

"Actually yes, we think so. We have an undercover operative in touch with him in the capacity of a business consultant. We have convinced him that he needs one person to oversee all the people who do those jobs I mentioned, so he only needs to talk to one person in order to address any part of his home life. Our operative will search high and low for the right person and then recommend you."

Janae was increasingly more interested, "What if he says 'no' to hiring me?"

"He has already said 'yes'."

Now her jaw dropped and her eyebrows raised, "He's already agreed to hire me, without meeting me or interviewing me?"

"Yes, that is correct. One of the reasons we thought you were perfect for the job," Joe and Jennifer Cornish smiled at each other.

"Wow, your operative must be very convincing. What is the time frame?"

"Well, he wanted you last week, but you were busy. He's hoping for tomorrow, so we thought it was time to fill you in. He knows he's getting the best, so he's willing to wait. So, what do you think? Interested?"

"Ah…well, let's see. Run the household for a rich, single U.S. Senator…or not. Hmm?" Janae was using both hands to weigh the situation, but with a definite smile on her face.

# 8

To anyone watching over the next few weeks, the former Seattle club turned into a restaurant and an inn. This was supervised by Tony, with James and the two redheads helping. Alexander and Joni took a liking to each other and were being groomed to be the overseers of the food and hotel facilities. Tony had his private investigations office on the site as well as living quarters for everyone. He and James had not flipped a coin yet, but no complaints were heard from the redheads, as long as things were prospering. They traded beds when asked and it was okay with them, as long as they were well taken care of.

Tony's knowledge of his own former drug distribution network and those of rival gangs provided valuable information for Joe Cornish. Nicolus and Nickolaea were Tony's undercover operatives in his investigations, and their excellence spoke of better things for them in the future.

Jack and Gretchen had been asked by Joe Cornish to spearhead operations in Anchorage, Alaska. The greater Anchorage area was the southern end of the oil pipeline, as well as the northern end of the drug pipeline, and the politics that took both of these pipelines into consideration had not had bright sunlight shone on it for far too long. Joe Cornish had been investigating this area for quite a while and now it was time to initiate events. Some would enjoy the bright light and some would crawl under the rocks. A catalyst was always helpful in those situations.

*

For Tom and PC, life was pleasant. They were relaxing at her home and putting out a story every week.

The story of the reverend's work, rescuing and rehabilitating young girls from a life of forced drug addiction and prostitution, was very popular and increased dramatically the sales of newspapers on the day it came out. Tom's boss put the stories in the Tuesday paper as it was the lowest circulation day of all seven. Tuesday quickly became second only to the Sunday paper in sales volume. The paper's general manager noticed this right away and gave Tom's boss a raise since increased sales in a generally decreasing newspaper sales and circulation world was a big thing.

Tom and PC's stories seemed to have a positive rippling effect on anyone involved. Even the donations to the reverend's causes sky-rocketed, because everyone wanted to feel involved in rescuing young girls from harm's way. And so it was, after a few weeks, having written down a month's worth of stories, Tom and PC met with Joe and Jennifer Cornish on the yacht for lunch one day.

"Your stories are very good, Tom. I must say you are an excellent writer," Joe Cornish was pleased with the content. "Most of the truth, but not all, and a slant that makes the bad guys look inept."

"Thank you, sir. I think what you're witnessing is the profound inspiration a woman from the nursing profession can have on a journalist, when the two are in close proximity with each other." Tom knew now how to avoid a kick in the leg.

"I'm sure PC is the secret ingredient to your successful writing," Joe Cornish began, but Jennifer continued, "and we want to provide you with more subject matter. Are you interested in traveling again?"

"Yes. Yes of course," Tom and PC both said, "What do you have in mind?"

"Well now," Joe continued, "We are sending Janae south to California alone, to infiltrate an interesting situation down there. I would like to send one or both of you along to help, until she gets comfortable in her new job down there."

"Also," Jennifer continued, "we're sending Jack and Gretchen up to Anchorage, Alaska, to do precisely the same thing. We would like one or both of you to go along with them, also."

"I feel a splitting headache coming on," Tom jested. He received a kick in the leg for his efforts.

"This could be fun," PC jumped in, "A brief week apart would make us grow fonder."

"Yeah, you'd probably dump me as soon as I let you out of my sight," Tom was poking fun.

"Well, I have been thinking about that, now that you mention it," PC quipped.

"Okay," Tom again, turning serious, looking at Joe and Jennifer. "PC could accompany Janae south, and I could accompany Jack and Gretchen north for the beginning phases of the operations, and we'd get first hand info for twice as many stories as otherwise."

"This is precisely what we were wanting to propose. How long would you need to prepare yourselves for separate assignments?" Joe Cornish asked.

"Well...after getting a little more information...we'd just have to pack accordingly and...whatever your timetable is."

"Very good. Would flights out of Seattle tomorrow morning be agreeable?"

Tom and PC looked at each other questioningly, "Yes, yes that would work," they both said. Since their whirlwind romance and marriage, they had not been apart and both excitement and apprehension flooded their hearts.

"Anything for a story," PC offered semiseriously and Tom marveled at her bravery and yet obvious love for him.

"Well then, for dessert, why don't we break up and have PC join Jennifer in our cabin, and Tom, you join me in the den. We will fill you both in on your respective roles in these operations."

An hour after these separate disclosures began, they ended to everyone's satisfaction. Tom and PC left for home to pack and say goodbye with a night of early merriment and wonderful slumber.

The next morning they were at Boeing Field loading their gear onto separate small jets and were almost in tears. After a quick kiss and embrace, Tom went over the basic guidelines for note taking and noticing things that were not normal. PC replaced her nagging uneasiness with the anticipation of the upcoming adventure with Janae, whom she had become very fond of.

Janae and PC boarded their jet and sat together, PC with pad and pen. Janae began telling what she knew would happen when they arrived in the San Francisco area and how they might have to improvise. To PC this was an adventure. To Janae it was serious business. It was her first operation alone and away from base, and she was glad to have PC even only as a check in. The thing that was troubling Janae was the inability to not focus on the fact that her employer was rich, single, and probably handsome.

Tom boarded with Jack and Gretchen and noticed immediately that he was a little taller than Jack. A measure that men always take when a woman is in their presence. It mattered very little to Tom in this case as he saw a uniqueness in Jack and Gretchen and their ability to work, operate, and live as a couple.

As soon as they got seated, Tom opened up with a question, "Why do you two work so well together? It is obvious to me that there is some ingredient in you two that makes an impact when you're together working. PC and I are just learning how to work together, and…there is something unique with you guys."

Jack and Gretchen both smiled at Tom and at each other. Gretchen let Jack begin, "Tom, there was a life and death desperateness in the situation that caused us to work together. I witnessed the quickness and finality of death right in front of my own eyes. It left me with only one job: survival. We had to join forces without any time to learn how. We were under a literal death threat if we were not successful. We learned quickly what to discard in terms of bad feelings, or jealousies, or envies in order to survive, but that refining of our lives was so intense, that what remained was good and profitable and benefits us today. Joe Cornish bought out my debt to death, and eventually Tony was claimed by the same wisdom and cunning."

Gretchen just beamed. She had made the right decision to have Jack. This former young gangster had become wise through hardship. He was smart enough to recognize a good honest break when it was handed to him, and he had taken it. With her help, of course.

Tom nodded and reflected on how hard circumstances sometimes lead to strong men and women. Now Jack and Gretchen were taking on a political environment that had been left alone to grow without any compass to keep it headed in the right direction. This was going to make one hell of a story.

# 9

When the jet attained cruising altitude, Jonathan turned to Kandee and Sharon. "Okay girls, where to for a small but worldwide affecting wedding? Hawaii, Rio, Niagara Falls, the southern tip of Chile? You pick."

Sharon started out, "My parents were missionaries in China when I was little, and I remember China. I begged my dad to let us walk on the Great Wall of China. We did when I was about six years old. I remember how I felt walking along that wall. I felt powerful, I felt important, because only important people could be on that wall back when they built it. The people on that wall protected China. They patrolled along it and warned the Emperor when danger was approaching. They were the first defense against evil. They could be brave and stand on the wall and stop evil, or be cowards and accept bribes from the enemy. I guess my life sort of took on some meaning when I was six. I wanted to be brave like the men and women who patrolled those walls and kept vigilant watch."

Sharon stopped to catch her breath and dab her tears. Nobody else spoke, so she continued, "My parents were imprisoned for a while for their beliefs and luckily we, my brother and I, were sent back to the U.S. and stayed with our mom's sister till they were released. I remember feeling so strongly that I would have been able to save my parents from imprisonment if only I was like one of the brave ones that protected that wall. I was only about eight when we were separated, but I remember those feelings so vividly; I could have rescued them if someone had given me the chance."

Sharon stopped and looked at Jonathan who had tears in his eyes, too. Then she finished, "Jonathan, you're giving me the chance, as your wife, to do that--to be brave, and to do things with you that are way beyond what I was doing as a deputy sheriff, which had quite a bit of adventure in itself." Everybody smiled. "As silly as it seems, on that wall is where I would choose to be married to you."

Nobody spoke. All four had tears running down their cheeks. What do you say when somebody speaks the most important thing in their life to you?

Then Jonathan stood, reached down and picked up Sharon's hand and lifted it to his lips. He kissed her with his tears dripping onto both of their hands. She smiled at him through her own tears as he moved forward and stepped into the pilot's compartment. A moment later, before Jonathan even got back to his seat, Rocko, the retired F-15 fighter pilot, had the corporate jet turning to the west, out over the wide blue expanse of ocean, that roared louder than the jet engines if one would only listen.

*

Mr. and Mrs. Nicolus Aragapo were being as silent as the grave. They were out of sight, but not out of earshot of a drug transaction between two gangs, each brandishing automatic weapons. Nicolus saw in his mind, from the sounds that he heard, two suitcases of drugs and two suitcases of money. The weight and value were about the same and was what the deliberations were all about. When all was agreeable, they all went their separate ways. Guns, drugs and people one way, and guns, money, and people the other way. Nicolus then shut off his recording equipment and came out of hiding. He and Nickolaea dusted the room for fingerprints and got a lot of them. When they were done they reported back to the old club and laid out the evidence for Tony.

"Ah, perfect," Tony said after listening, "Okay, we'll send the prints to Joe Cornish for him to analyze through the FBI. This should be enough to snag the top guy out of each gang and give them a chance at life instead of death." Tony glanced at Nicolus and sensed something wrong. "What's up?"

"I can't get Matty out of my mind. He's got to be planning something. He doesn't just give up and go away. I'd like to go down incognito and find out what's going on. The trouble is, everybody knows me by sight down there."

"Yeah, that's good thinking Nicolus. How could we do that?"

"Obviously, to be successful, we'd have to send someone that no one knows. The trouble is, that person wouldn't know who the people down there are either and wouldn't know if they were blown until it was too late."

"Yeah,... I got an idea!" Tony said. Nicolus looked up at him, "Let's send someone they might recognize but would never think of as a source of trouble. Someone who could walk right into the midst of them and find out what we need to find out and come back with no trouble either way."

Nicolus raised both hands palms up like nothing was coming to him.

"Ha, ha, ha. This is perfect! If you can't figure out what I'm thinking, Matty sure as hell won't. Come on, let's talk to James."

James was by the indoor pool, watching the redheads frolic. Tony, Nicolus, and Nickolaea pulled up chairs and sat in a circle with him. James dropped his reading material and looked at everyone, "What the hell's going on?" Everyone had a serious look on his or her face and James felt like he was being charged with having his hand in the cookie jar, or something.

Then Tony busted out laughing, and everyone joined him.

"What the hell's going on?!" James asked the same question, but this time the tone was different. It was like everyone was playing a practical joke, and he was the only one out of the loop.

"James, I got a brilliant idea, and nobody can figure it out yet. So let me try it out on you."

"Okay, but I think I need a drink," James picked up his glass from off the floor and held it up in the air. When the guard at the door saw it, James gestured that they all needed something to drink. The guard caught on and left.

"Okay. We're going to send a team down to see what Matty's up to. This team will be recognized by everyone down there and will be able to recognize everyone there, also. They'll walk in, get all the info we need, and leave again without a hint of trouble. Who's the team?"

James heard the question, thought it through, and slowly turned his head and looked into the pool. He stared at the two redheads and then back at Tony.

"Yeah!! Bingo. James, we speak the same language." Tony loved it, "We send the girls, by themselves."

Nicolus and Nickolaea looked at the girls. Now everyone was looking at the girls. The girls suddenly stopped, saw everyone looking their way and quickly checked their swimsuits for some wardrobe malfunction. Tony laughed again and waved the two over to the group. Nickolaea hopped up and handed them towels as they climbed out of the pool.

Tony leaned back and put his hands behind his head, "How would you two like to go down to sunny San Diego for a week and do some shopping and some other things for me? And when you get back, James and I will flip a coin and you girls are getting married."

"Eeeeeee..." they both screamed and yelled and jumped into the arms of Tony and James.

"I think this may mean the answer is 'yes', to all the above."

James added, "Who's going to flip the coin?"

The rest of the afternoon was taken up with consultations and what not between Tony, James, and the two redheads. Tony made sure the seriousness of the job was understood. The girls remembered who Matty was and saw no problem at all. It would be fun.

The next morning Nicolus and Nickolaea took the redheads to Sea-Tac airport and saw them off to San Diego on a commercial flight.

Nicolus felt better that a loose end was attempting to be tied. He drove out of the airport and across the street into the parking lot of 13 Coins Restaurant. They went in for an early lunch and some serious talk. After ordering, Nicolus gazed into Nickolaea's eyes and said, "You've come with me thousands of miles away from your home, served my boss with me as your father asked you to, and have excelled at everything you've done. How can I thank you?"

Nickolaea never hesitated to speak what was on her heart or mind, "I'm fearful for my father. There is so much corruption there. It will be harder for him to survive, the older he gets. To bring him here, to live with us, would be more thanks than I deserve."

The food came and was served, but all Nicolus could do was be amazed. All this woman of his wanted was the welfare of the ones she loved. If he lived in pain and suffering the rest of his years, he would not be able to sufficiently pay back what he owed God Almighty for allowing this woman to be part of his life. He would plan and fulfill her wish.

Later that afternoon, while Nickolaea was swimming laps, Nicolus visited with Tony and James in their office.

"I would like to try to bring Rolando here. Nickolaea is fearful for his life in Paraguay. Someone else will simply have him eliminated in order to take his place of influence and power." Nicolus was straightforward.

"Rolando is a good man. I'd do anything to help him," Tony said as his thoughts went back to Paraguay. "Let's make some plans."

James, Tony, and Nicolus spent the afternoon talking and planning, and when dinner time arrived they did not want to stop. Tony ordered dinner for four, and Nicolus went and brought Nickolaea to join them. Tony spoke of his profound respect for her father and also for her and her service to him. They shared the plans they had made so far with Nickolaea and she was humbled with gratitude. A trip to Paraguay was in the plans and Tony wanted to be part of it.

# 10

The staff at the Seabeck safe house noticed right away that one of the girls acted older than she was. Janis was almost fifteen and was a beautiful young woman. The psychological scars from her former life should have been more profound, but Janis was upbeat and didn't hold on to the past. She just naturally cared for all the other girls and they looked up to her.

In Kandee, PC, Janae, and Deputy Sharon, Janis saw older women who had accomplished something with their lives and she wanted what they had. She knew she could do a lot to help others if she could get out from under the things that had held her in their grip. Now she had her chance and she would take it.

Janis had no caring family to go back to; no one was looking for her. Her family was involved with drugs and crime as she grew up and she didn't want to go back to that. She had two older sisters but had no idea where they were or how to get in touch with them. They would not be glad to see her anyway. She would either be a bother to them or competition. They might know where her parents were, but Janis knew where her parents were--they were high or getting the means to get high. No way would she go back to that, not with older women around that she could look up to, who seemed to know right from wrong, and how to live that way.

Janis's dreams knew no bounds. Wow! To be Janis and also be a law enforcement person would be more than she could imagine, but Deputy Sharon had done it. To be Janis and be a nurse, helping real doctors, and helping sick people feel better because she had gotten an education...it had to be possible. Kandee and PC had done it. Or being like Janae, doing the dangerous work she did, helping people like herself, would be awesome. But she needed to belong somewhere. She needed family. She asked the staff if she could stay and help since she had nowhere to go, and the staff made an exception in her case. She helped them with the process of reconnecting the other girls to their loved ones and otherwise helped out however she could.

One day Janis noticed the dock boys working down at the Seabeck Bay docks, making money every day. Janis asked if she could work at the dock also to make some money, and she was given permission to work there for part of the day. And so it was that Janis met Robbie.

Robbie liked the idea of a gal working the docks with him and the other guys. There were always women on the boats that came in and a girl could work with them a lot better than he had been able to. He found out Janis was about the same age as he was and she was pretty. And not only pretty, but she liked to work. Janis learned how to work the docks faster than anyone Robbie had taught before. She had that knack of knowing what was needed next. She was also easy to work with, not like some girls.

Janis liked Robbie right away. He was smart and was not afraid of hard work. She was surprised that he treated her respectfully from the moment they met. Usually the men she had met in her past had treated her crudely when introduced to her. Around Robbie, she felt that she was being treated carefully because she was a woman, as if just being a woman made her special and important. She had always felt that being a woman was the problem and had fought against it, wanting to be different than she was, but Robbie made her feel like being a woman was a privilege, a lucky break, a positive to start out with. She had always felt comfortable with girls her own age or younger, but she had never felt that family feeling where men were involved. Her rescue and life at the safe house had begun a change in her.

A change that accepted men as family, not just as customers. Robbie was different, like a brother she had never had. She could feel him looking after her in a caring, helping way. She simply had not had that feeling with a man before.

Relating to a guy without the guy demanding physical attention right away was new to her. And she liked it. She secretly wondered if Robbie had ever kissed a girl before. She thought probably so, but with her he acted as if she was of royal blood and could not be had except by another of royal blood. Well, sooner or later he would find out she was used goods and he would change his mind about her. Or maybe he already knew, since she was from the safe house, but why then did he treat her so respectfully? She did not know the answer, but decided to enjoy it while it lasted.

Early one morning she got a scare. A group of men came onto the dock heading for a big boat to drink and fish all day. When they saw her they asked if she'd like to come with them. Right away she felt that trapped, scared feeling creep over her. That feeling of having to say yes, and that refusing was a no-no. She mustered her courage and said she had work to do, and headed straight for Robbie. He looked up as she came toward him, and saw that something had upset her. He took her by the hand and sat with her at a deck table at Bobbi's and asked if the men had been rude.

Tears started flowing, which was rare for Janis, "No, no, not really. They were just kidding, but it brought back those bad feelings that I grew up with. What scared me was how fast those feelings came back."

"Come on, I'll walk you back to the safe house. You need to talk to the counselors. My mom knows one of them. She says they're really good."

"Could we just sit here awhile? Would you just talk with me?"

"Sure," Robbie looked around and motioned one of the other dock boys over. "We're on break. Take over for us, okay?"

"Yeah, sure."

Robbie realized he was holding Janis's hand as they sat at the table and he carefully let go. Janis was wiping away tears and then looked at Robbie, "Why do you treat me so careful and nice?"

Robbie quickly searched for words that would answer the question without him having to reveal his innermost thoughts. "Janis, I only have a brother... and you're like a sister to me. So it's fun for me to help you learn, and the dock needs a girl down here. You should hear some of the things the ladies from the boats want me to do or go buy for them. I've been asked to put suntan lotion on them and to go buy a list of lady's things that embarrassed me so much that I just stay away from them anymore. I'm really glad you're around."

"Thank you, but I don't mean that," Janis paused. "Robbie, you can probably guess what my past involved, my being from the safe house. I've never been treated with respect by a man until this last week. I just don't understand why you would treat me respectfully when there is no reason to. I mean, I like it and all. But I just want you to know that there is nothing in me worth respecting and that I'll understand if you want to treat me differently. I'll still be your sister." She kind of smiled and looked at him again.

Now Robbie wasn't sure what to do. Most girls he knew at school demanded to be treated respectfully if you wanted any attention from them at all. Janis was saying that if he didn't treat her with respect, she'd understand and still be his friend. He liked the idea of having a girl treat him like a sister would treat him.

Robbie took a deep breath, "Janis, my mom is pretty smart. She's a banker in Silverdale. She told me a long time ago that everybody deserves my respect. Then a year ago, when I turned fourteen, she told me that women, and especially girls my age, not only deserved my respect, but that they needed it. She told me that if I treated girls with respect, they would grow up more healthy and become better mothers than if I treated them like I treat my guy friends. I always figured my mom knew what she was talking about and I've taken her advice. So when I treat you like you're special, it's not because of what did or did not happen in your life. It's because you are a woman. And I think you're cute. And you're different than the girls at my school. And I like you, the way you are, better than I like them, the way they are. And…" now Robbie felt lost. He didn't know what else to say. 'She probably thinks I'm a mama's boy,' he thought.

"Thank you, Robbie. That's the nicest thing a guy has ever… ever said to me. I really liked what you said, and it made me feel special. I've only got two sisters and they hate me. I'd love to have you for a brother and I'd like to be your sister. I'd sort of like to meet your mom sometime, too."

Robbie's heart flooded with relief. That was a close call. He reminded himself what a bad idea sharing his innermost feelings was. Thank God, that this girl just happened to understand what was inside of him. Most girls, and guys for that matter, would have laughed in his face. If he didn't really think that his mom knew what she was talking about, he would be just like them… just like them.

Janis was amazed. She hadn't known what a special feeling it was to have a boy talk from his heart and say what he really felt. It was uplifting and powerful. She figured someday Robbie would be someone important like Mr. Cornish or the reverend. If she could just be his sister for a while, she'd like it.

"Sure, my mom would like you, I'm sure," Robbie said. Janis perked up.

"Okay, I'm all better. Let's go back to work."

# 11

The yacht was Joe and Jennifer Cornish's home. Jeff and Taylor had taken on the duties of butler and maid to them as a continuing parade of people came and went, sometimes having lunch or dinner, sometimes staying overnight. They were enjoying working together and taking their new-found love slowly. They had not strayed too far from the yacht since their kidnapping experience. Even so, they kept busy and felt needed. Joe and Jennifer sometimes went on short trips and left them in charge.

It was on one of these occasions that Jeff woke up early one morning to the sound of knocking on the side of the boat. He went up to the deck, looked over the side and saw something swimming around in the water. It would submerge, then come up for air, and it was playing with something. Jeff recognized it was about at the level of Taylor's cabin and her room had a porthole above the water line and one below. He went back down the stairs and gently knocked on Taylor's door. She opened it right away.

"There's an otter outside my window!" she was trying to be quiet.

"Can you see it? How do you know it's an otter?" Jeff was excited. Part of the reason was that Taylor had a long T-shirt on and probably not much else.

"The underwater window has a small outside searchlight and you can see it underwater. It's playing with a herring," Taylor was excited, too. Jeff had taken time to put cutoffs on with a tank top.

They laid across the bed and peered out the underwater porthole that was at about bunk level. After watching the otter for a while, it swam off. They waited to see if it would return, but it didn't. Their gaze slowly turned toward each other.

Taylor smiled and looked dreamy, "Remember how we held onto each other in bed in that awful room, not knowing if we were going to live or die?"

"Yes, I remember. I'd like to do that again right here, right now."

"Me, too," they shifted to lengthwise on the bed, cuddled into each other's arms and fell asleep with the light on.

*

The two redheads were walking up the extendable ramp at the airport in San Diego. They were side by side and determined to have as much fun as humanly possible on this trip.

On the flight down they smiled, winked, teased, and flirted with as many men, married or not, as they could. Their summer San Diego attire had stood out as they boarded the plane in drizzly Seattle. They flaunted everything they had and thoroughly enjoyed it. Now they breezed through the airport, perfume following, and paid a young man with a cart to help them bring their luggage to a taxi. The cab brought them to the Sheraton, only a couple of blocks from the club where they knew they would find Matty. After getting settled into their room, they went down to the Sheraton's lounge just to check out what was going on. They had one drink and then took a leisurely stroll down to the main San Diego club that their future husbands used to own and run.

Millicent and Wallace were sisters only thirteen months apart. They looked enough alike so that people mistook them for twins. Not identical, but twins. They had always fed that thought by dressing the same and looking as much like each other as they could. When asked if they were twins, they always said yes. In their prostitution they always worked together. Whether one guy or two, they stayed together. They had their own fan club of men who desired their duo services, almost rivaling the young girls. Then the Boss and James had chosen them for their own, with a promise of marriage when they returned from this fact-finding mission. And they knew just where to get the facts.

Their stroll down the few blocks to the club was fun. Their summer dresses, tight fitting on top and flowing below, worked well with their frolicking cadence.

But Millie and Wallie weren't stupid. They enjoyed teasing men. But as every prostitute knows, if a guy asks you to marry him, you say 'yes', no matter how drunk he is, hound him to follow through, and deal with the consequences of what kind of guy he is later. If he's no good, you bug him until he divorces you and try the next guy. Sooner or later your prince will come.

Now that Millie and Wallie had snagged the king and his right hand man, life was good. It was so cute how guys think they are the ones that do the choosing.

*

The next commercial flight of consequence that landed in California, touched down in the San Francisco area. Janae and PC were attired in business suits and accessories. Even though they weren't trying to attract attention, men noticed them, also.

Janae had an appointment in two hours so they got their luggage, taxied to their hotel, and settled in. Janae was exhilarated. She was going to play the role of her life and she was sure she could do it. The appointment at 4PM was not to her liking. It should be in the morning, not when the person she was meeting was suffering from a long day.

The person in question was the Senator's Chief of Staff. In charge of all the Senator's affairs, she was very organized and knew what she liked and didn't like. What she liked was the business consultant who recommended Janae. He was charming, handsome, and relaxing to be around. Janae would fit in nicely no matter what she was like. She wanted to keep the relationship with the business consultant on the up-swing. What the Chief of Staff didn't know was that Janae knew that the business consultant was an agent, like herself.

The four o'clock appointment went well. The Chief of Staff, who compared all employees with herself, found Janae surprisingly competent and rather likeable. It was a plus for her dinner tonight with the business consultant. She could genuinely say she approved of his choice for the children's nanny. She would fit Janae into the growing family of Senator William J. Williamsford, one of the two Senators from the State of California.

Back at the hotel, PC jotted down notes and Janae checked in with Joe Cornish. The first phase was accomplished. Tomorrow Janae would move into the Senator's mansion, and PC would stay a couple more days at the hotel and stay in touch. They ordered room service and then got to bed early. Tomorrow would be a big day.

*

Millie and Wallie entered the club. They knew the hostess who greeted them and they breezed right by her. The lounge was their destination and they sat at a table and ordered. As they ate and drank, they kept watch. Every once in a while an acquaintance would stop and say 'hi', but they just acted normal and weren't interested in talking. Then they saw her enter the lounge. She was Matty's girl and they knew her well. When she saw them, she lit up and joined them, kissing and hugging. "Where have you guys been? Haven't seen you in a while. You two just disappeared."

"We've been busy reeling in some big fish," Millie started.

"Yeah and we're getting hitched next week," Wallie continued.

"And tonight is our bachelorette party and you're invited," Millie finished.

"Ohhhh, yesss!!" exclaimed Matty's girl. "When do we start? I'm ready." They got up and went to the bar. The bartender was new to Millie and Wallie. Millie handed him a one hundred dollar bill for their dinner and drinks and ordered three bottles of Tequila. When he brought them, Wallie leaned over the bar and caught a whiff of his cologne. "Want to join us?"

The young bartender swallowed hard, smiled, and went about his business. He had five hours left. The girls found a room decorated with life-size photos from the firemen's calendar. Each girl had her own bottle, and when Millie, and then Wallie, made a point of visiting the restroom, they emptied half their bottles down the drain and refilled with water. Matty's girl just drank freely.

They were having a marvelous time and after a while, Millie and Wallie steered the conversation to business, the club, and then Matty. The more Matty's girl drank the more she told Millie and Wallie things she knew she shouldn't. But this was a celebration and she was in good company. By the time the fun died down, the bottles were empty, and Matt's girl was passed out, Millie and Wallie had more than enough facts about Matty to report back with. They breezed through the club, out the door and up the street to their hotel. The evening was very pleasant out, but they needed to get to their room and crash. So they did.

# 12

The earth along the California coast was stressed out and tense. It was about to transfer that stress onto the people of California. The earth did this every once in a while and this morning it was time again, except nobody knew it.

Janae had arrived at the Senator's mansion, and was given a tour by an assistant to the Chief of Staff. Then she was ushered into the three-bedroom suite of the Senator's daughters who were ten and twelve years old.

When the assistant introduced Julie and Janet Williamsford to Janae, there was a mutual attraction between them. Janae could tell just by their looks and their polite demeanor, that these girls weren't rebellious, grown-up wannabes. They seemed sophisticated for their age, at least compared to their peers, and carried on a conversation without turning it to being about themselves. The girls spoke without getting in each other's way and seemed very pleasant. The assistant left the three alone to get acquainted.

The girls saw Janae's youth and beauty and recognized a certain strength and maturity that they liked. They showed Janae their rooms and their trophies from soccer, horseback riding, and swimming. One of the rooms in the suite was for Janae. Julie and Janet showed Janae her room and helped her with her luggage. The windows of the suite looked down at the large outdoor pool. The girls looked at Janae, "Did you bring a swimsuit?"

Janae nodded, "Somewhere in here."

Julie suggested they all go swimming before lunch. The two disappeared into their rooms to get their suits on. Janae dug hers out and put it on. She found a towel in her bathroom and met the girls in the living area of the suite as they emerged from their rooms. Janae noticed one of the walls was a huge bookcase, full of books. She would have to explore there. The three scampered down the hall, down the stairs, and out into the sunshine. They trotted toward the shallow end of the pool, tossing their towels on lounge chairs.

As the three huddled on the cement stairs at the farthest corner of the pool, their attention was drawn across the pool to a round umbrella table on the patio tucked into the L-shape of the house. There sat their father, having just arrived from Washington, D.C., talking to his Chief of Staff at the table.

"Daddy!!" the two girls shouted and waved excitedly. Janae focused on the Senator. The Senator stood and waved, but focused on Janae and her two piece swim suit.

As he opened his mouth to return the greeting, the earth chose to interrupt. It started with a slight shudder and then quickly grew in power past what anyone expected. A crack in the concrete patio started near the deep end of the pool and extended straight under the table at which their father stood. The house stood firm, but the extensive brickwork and tile roofing came loose in various places and showered the patio with debris of lethal proportions.

The girls' joy was interrupted by the shaking under their own feet. They fell into each-others' arms and into the pool. Janae corralled Julie and Janet and held them in her arms, squatting in the water at the shallow end of the pool. She lost sight of the Senator in all the debris and dust landing where he had been standing.

As the shaking continued, Janae looked up for falling objects, and covered the heads of the girls with her hands. They huddled closer in the water, but were far enough away from the house so as not to be hit by debris. The water splashed around them, but it felt like safety. As things finally settled down, an eerie silence reigned.

At the same time, further south in San Diego, things were worse. Freeways buckled and a tsunami hit the low-lying coastal areas. Millie and Wallie were enjoying a late breakfast in their room when the whole Sheraton began to sway. They held on to each other until it stopped. Then they just waited. The silence was soon interrupted by sirens near and far. Millie and Wallie stayed in their room for a couple of days, ordered meals in, and had the waiter restock their minibar.

Tony and James checked in with them when the cell phones started to work again, and they told the girls to stay put until the airport reopened and then get their little butts home. Instead, the sisters paid for a flight to Santa Fe, New Mexico, and visited with their parents to see if anything was new. No, nothing was new. Druggy parents. They left them some money and headed back to Seattle.

Back in San Francisco, PC rode out the earthquake in her hotel. When things calmed down she tried to call Janae, but couldn't get through, so she just waited. She looked out her window and began to write about what she saw.

Janae took her hands off the girls' heads and enveloped them in her arms. They were on their knees in the pool with the water up to their necks. They didn't want to move, it felt so safe. The dust was still settling closer to the house, and an occasional brick tumbled down. "Aftershock" was the word in Janae's mind and she was in no hurry to move out of the pool. However, her eyes focused on the pile of rubble where the Senator and his Chief of Staff had been. They were not in sight. Then she heard a soft moaning sound.

It was a call with coughing, over and over. Janae knew what needed to be done, so she began. Slipping out of the pool, she retrieved the towels and returned to Julie and Janet. Carefully and softly she beckoned with her arms and said, "Come girls." They quickly dried off and wrapped their towels around themselves. Janae, with a girl on each side, hand in hand, walked around the outside of the pool and approached the moaning, coughing call.

"Girls!" a low gravelly sound. "Girls." Janae stopped, looked up for any more falling objects, and then put the girls' hands together. Then she inched her way toward the pile of rubble and the sound. "Girls...girls..." then coughing. Janae reached down and pulled two brick chunks off the pile. She saw the back of a head. Two more chunks uncovered shoulders. The Senator was covered by rubble. Janae quickly removed more, until the major portion of his body was uncovered.

"Senator! Help is here. Lay still, lay still. It's okay now, help is here. Just lay still so I can check you."

"Girls..."

"Yes, Senator, your girls are safe. They are right here with you. They can see you. Lay still. Help is here. Your girls are fine. They are right here with you. Don't try to talk. Help is here now. You're going to be fine," Janae spoke slowly in a cadence. Even if the Senator couldn't understand her, her voice might be soothing to him. "Just lay still, Senator, help is here. Julie and Janet are here by your side. They can see you. Just lay still and let the help that is here do their job." Janae sounded like a mother calming her children. Janae felt his arms and legs as she spoke to see if there were any breaks. There were. He hadn't said anything since she spoke, so now she thought she should see if she could find a pulse.

"Is Daddy okay?" Julie was the brave one. Janet the smart one.

"Yes, girls, your dad is going to be fine. Talk to him like I was; he needs to hear your voices. It will comfort him." The girls took over the talking and Janae had found a pulse, but it was nothing to write home about. Probably internal injuries also, she thought. She took off her towel and laid it over the Senator from shoulders down. She looked up as sirens came closer. Standing up, she said,

"Girls, stay here; talk to your dad. I'm going out front to get the aid car guys."

"Wait! Wait...please!" a gravelly voice, with coughing. "Are you still here?

Janae knelt down by the Senator who had not moved his head, but could evidently talk. "Yes, I'm here," she said softly.

"Are you...the woman with my girls...at the end of the pool?" It was a long sentence for him to get out, so it took time. His breathing was labored.

"Yes, sir, I am. My name is Janae. I'm your daughters' new nanny. The three of us are okay and here with you. The aid car has arrived. I'm going out to lead them here to you. Your girls will stay..."

"Please... please don't go... Hear me please, Janae."

"Yes, sir, I'm right here. I'll stay. I'm listening to you."

"Girls...I'm sorry...your mother died...I could not save her... Now you might lose your father..." coughing, "Stay together and stick close to Janae...she will watch over you...Janae, I have hired you...will you watch over my Julie and my Janet while...I'm gone?"

"Yes, sir. I will do my job with pleasure, and we three will help you get better. You will soon tire of us, because we won't leave you alone."

The Senator let out a chuckle, but it turned into a cough and almost did him in. "Janae...my Chief of Staff?"

"She is buried, sir, not much hope," Janae took the edge of her towel that was covering him and wiped his face and mouth.

"Janae, I know who you are...and who sent you...In my safe, in my den..." coughing, "5,6,1,3,6,6,0,...Janae...my girls." He lapsed into unconsciousness. Janae checked his pulse. Still there.

"He's okay. I'm going to find help, girls. Stay with your dad." She got up and went out the gate, around the side of the house, stepping around rubble, and found the aid cars. The paramedics were entering the front door. She caught their attention and said, "The Senator is this way." They promptly followed her.

The Senator and his Chief of Staff were carefully removed from the debris. His weak pulse remained, but hers was gone. When the girls asked the paramedics about their dad, their guarded answer was optimistic. Janae comforted Julie and Janet as they followed the gurney to the aid car, and watched it leave.

Janae steered them into the kitchen via the front door, but they found out the electricity didn't work. "Does anyone know where to find a flashlight?"

"I do," Janet answered. She retrieved three flashlights from the pantry shelf.

Flashlights in hand, they walked upstairs to their bedroom suite and sat down for a talk. "What will happen to Daddy?" Julie asked.

"They will have him at the hospital until he's ready to come home. He is a United States Senator, which enables him to have the very best healthcare. Kings and Queens do not have better healthcare than your father will have."

"Will he die, Janae?" Julie spoke bravely.

"Your father is hurt quite badly. Yes, he could die, or he could live, but with a permanent disability. Or he could bounce back and be healthier and more energetic than ever."

"Janae, which do you think will happen?" Janet asked.

"I think he will almost die, then remember that God gave him two of the world's most beautiful, smart, and brave girls, and because he misses you so much, he'll become completely well again and grow old with you two providing him with grandchildren to adore almost as much as he does you."

Then Julie asked, "Do you want to know about our mother?"

Janae paused. She was taken aback momentarily, but she thought, the girls needed to talk, and about whatever they wished. So she responded positively and learned all about their mother. It was a wonderful time with laughing and crying. A story of cancer with bravery, encouragement, and love to the very end.

"The last thing our mother whispered to us was to find daddy a woman to marry that was almost as sweet and loving as she was," Janet had taken it seriously. "I think you would be perfect."

"Janet, that's so sweet. Our job is to help your daddy get well again. Then it's his job to find you two a new mother. One almost as good, like your mom said. And he will, because he loves you so much." Janae was getting saturated with emotion. "Tell you what. Let's have a quiet time and then just before dinner, we'll go in and see your dad before we go to your favorite restaurant. Okay?"

"Okay!" They went to their rooms.

Janae went into hers also and collapsed onto the bed. She put the pillow over her head and cried more than she had in a long time.

# 13

Rousing herself after just about slipping into a doze, Janae reminded herself who she was. She was a covert operative, not a heroine destined to save a family. Since the electricity was restored, she quickly showered and dressed and went to look for the den. She neither heard nor saw anyone. She remembered the location of the den from her earlier tour and knocked softly on the door. Trying the door, she found it unlocked and slipped inside. The open curtain at the window provided enough light to see. She closed the door and quietly stood inside. She heard nothing in the room or out in the hall, just distant sirens dealing with the major disaster outside.

Her eyes scanned the room. A safe? Where would a room like this have a safe? Her eyes landed on a safe. It was big and tall, standing along the far wall between windows. Moving lightly to it, she recognized it as a gun safe. This is not what the Senator meant, but she saw the keypad lock and punched the numbers the Senator had given her. 5,6,1,3,6,6,0. Nothing. It did not open. She turned her back to the gun safe and scanned the room again, her training keeping her from running to and fro searching for it. She noticed the desk, the many pictures, the curtains, walls of books, hardwood floor, huge area rug, one small round rug at the base of the bookcase wall. Now she moved. She stopped before the small rug and squatted down. It was attached to the floor, not just laying on it. She stood back up and eyed the wall of books. Was there one book in that whole wall that triggered a compartment holding the safe? She noticed a ladder at the side which rolled along the bookcase. Move the ladder, tip a book, too many things to try. Think!

She forced her eyes off the bookshelf and onto the rug. She squatted again in front of the rug, then raised her eyes to the bottom shelf, level with her eyes. Straight in front of her, she read a title, 'Open Me.' It was a big book and she hadn't heard of it before.

A slight smile came over Janae's face; men and their tricks. So she stepped onto the rug, reached for the book and tilted it back toward her so she could get a grip on it. Nothing happened except the book wouldn't come out, it just tilted. Logically then, she tilted the book back to its original position. She heard a click. Slowly the rug and the floor under her rotated ninety degrees, then stopped. Now what? She stepped off and the floor with the rug raised six inches and then tilted up to a forty-five degree angle. There under the floor was the safe.

Janae punched in the numbers and pulled open the safe. She quickly memorized the way the contents were arranged. Confident that she could tell next time if anything had been rearranged, she noticed a file with her name on it. She looked up and around the room from her crouch, then took the file and carefully leafed through it. Okay. The Senator did know about her. She replaced the file the way it had been, and closed the safe. As it clicked shut, the floor/rug mechanism replaced itself. Pretty cool. Making sure the room was the way it was when she found it, she turned and left.

In the kitchen, Janae found the assistant chief of staff sitting at the table staring at nothing. She moved closer.

"What's our situation?" she asked carefully.

The assistant looked up at her blankly and said, "Uh... the Senator is in the hospital... my boss is dead... I'm in charge, but I don't know what to do. You'll have to run this household. I've got to run the Senator." He was used to being a go-fer, not being in charge of things.

"No worries," Janae sounded confident. "I'll run the house. Is there an office with household files and ledgers, checkbooks and income statements?"

The now Chief of Staff looked at her. "Office? Yeah, down that hall." He pointed back the way she had come. "It's a den when he's home, your office when he's not." He was rubbing his eyes and his head. Janae could see she needed to encourage him.

"Thank you, sir. You'll do great; your boss knew you would do well if she had to leave." Having met the original Chief of Staff, Janae knew the opposite was true. The woman would never pick a person to rival her. "I'm going to take the girls to see their father. We'll be back after dinner."

"Yes, of course," he hadn't even heard her.

Janae went back to the girls and found them dressed nicely for the evening.

"Is there a household car?" Janae wasn't sure, but felt the girls would know.

"Let's take the Mustang!!!" both girls chimed.

"Lead the way. And what about keys?" Janae thought, hmmmm, Mustang?! The keys were in the den and the girls knew right where to find them. Janae decided to probe; what did the girls know? "Is there a safe in here?"

"Of course, silly," and they pointed to the gun safe. Janae nodded and then looked at the row of keys hanging on the wall and took the ones with the Mustang emblem on them. Then they went back to the kitchen, down another hall and into the garage. Wow! The garage had four stalls. First was a huge SUV, probably bullet proof. Second, a motorcycle with sidecar big enough for ten and twelve year olds. Third was a minivan, and in the fourth was a 1966 Mustang convertible, top down, deep red. Whoa.

"Okay, who wants to drive?"

"Me, me," both girls wanted to drive. "Daddy lets us drive all the time."

Janae realized they meant 'steer,' when they said 'drive.' "Is there a button for the garage door?" Janae looked around.

"I'll get it." Julie found and pushed the button. The garage door to the fourth stall opened on to a rubble strewn circular driveway.

Janae looked around again. "Okay, everyone man a snow shovel." There was a whole rack of them. Even though they were in good clothes, the three shoveled enough debris to get the car out and away from the rubble. Then they jumped into the Mustang. Janae started it up and it came to life with a throaty roar.

"Oh, Lord!" Janae prayed out loud. Would she be the envy of everyone! Especially the guys. Then, backing out and away from the house and into the fading sunshine, she drove down to the gate. "Oh, you've got to meet someone!" Janae said to the girls as she paused and called PC. "Meet us in front of the hotel in fifteen minutes. We're in a red Mustang." She found a cap on the passenger seat, put it on and pulled her hair through the slot in the back.

"Okay, who's 'we'?" PC asked, but Janae had already hung up. She wanted to drive.

Off they went, the girls in back. Janae was in heaven. She loved Mustangs, but this was incredible. A throaty sounding, dark red, '66 Mustang convertible! You didn't have to go fast to enjoy this.

As they got closer to town and the hotel, the rubble increased proportionate to aid cars, cleanup crews, fire engines with their fire marshals, all helping people and checking structural integrity with the greatest of professionalism.

Janae eased up to the curb across from the hotel and spotted her friend. PC jaywalked over to the Mustang and got in. "Wow! Want me to drive?" PC lit up everybody's day.

"Nope. Girls, this is my best friend, PC; she's a nurse. PC, this is Julie and Janet, my new best friends."

"Hi, hi."

"Wow, I heard you were supposed to be kids. You look like young ladies. Ohhh, isn't this fun?" PC's hair was flying wild. The girls were in braids. Julie reached forward and began to

French-braid PC's hair. "Wow, smart and handy, too!" Then she continued, "I'm sorry to hear about your dad. Are we going to visit him?"

"Yeah, Janae is driving us to the hospital and we're going to tell Daddy we love him." PC had to pause and get ahold of her emotions.

"Yeah, Janae's pretty cool isn't she?"

"Yes, she sure is. Hold still."

PC glanced at Janae and almost burst out laughing.

As they drove, they noticed the damage from the quake. Soon the hospital came into view and Janae turned down the ramp into the parking garage. They put the top up and locked the car.

In the elevator they pushed the first floor button. The doors opened to a lobby full of news reporters and cameramen. As they walked up to the information desk, the press recognized the girls and swarmed them. Janae corralled them and PC went into action. She whipped out her old nurse ID and bent over and asked the person at the information desk where the nurse's lounge was. The lady gave directions and PC took Janet's hand and Janae took Julie's, and they moved through the crowd, down the hall, around the corner, past the cafeteria and to a key padded door, which was unmarked. PC punched the code the lady gave her and they swept into the nurse's lounge away from the confusion. "Okay, sit down and I'll find out where he is," PC grabbed a white coat off the rack by the door and left. Janae and the girls looked around and saw a handful of nurses. They were staring at the girls. Then one jumped up and came over, "Oh my goodness, you are Senator Williamsford's girls aren't you? Well, just relax, we'll protect you. First things first--restroom over there." Both girls made a beeline.

"Hi, my name is Gloria," the nurse reached out her hand to Janae.

"Hi, I'm Janae; thank you for your help. My friend PC is a nurse from Tacoma, Washington and..." the door burst open and PC came in. "PC, this is Gloria."

"Hi Gloria! Did we lose the girls?"

"Restroom," Gloria pointed.

"Oh, thank you. You're sweet to help us. Their dad is in emergency, can we get there without going through the halls?"

"You bet. When you're ready I'll lead the way," Gloria finished up what she was doing. Janae took a couple of minutes to make a phone call. Then the four were ready to go. Gloria led them out and through the back hallway into the emergency room area. They paused and Gloria whispered into PC's ear.

Then Gloria went up to the handful of reporters outside the Senator's room and announced, "Ladies and gentlemen of the press. The Senator has a statement for you that I'm going to read. Shall we go out to the waiting area where there will be more room?" Gloria led them out after a glance back down the hall to the four girls.

The press gone, PC led the girls, followed by Janae, into their father's room. PC noticed the gravity of the situation right away and whispered to the girls, "He's sleeping, but whisper in his ear and see if he wakes up."

"Okay," Julie and Janet each took a different side of the bed and whispered, 'I love you, Daddy,' at the same time. The Senator's eyes fluttered and opened.

"Julie, Janet, you're here…are you alright?"

"Yes, Papa. We're here to make you well."

"And to make sure you're doing what the nurses tell you to do. They're nice."

"Well, I guess I…needed to hear that…I promise I will…Will you promise me something?"

"Yes, Papa."

"Anything."

"Remember after your Mama died…we remembered her saying…she'd always be with us…even if we couldn't see her?… Remember?"

"Yes, Papa."

"Yes, Papa."

"Well…the same goes with me…If I can't come home…or if I go see your Mama…we'll both always be with you even if you can't see or hear us."

"Yes, Papa."

"We'll remember."

The Senator looked toward the door and saw Janae. "I've picked someone to be your new mother…do you like her?"

The girls saw he was looking at Janae. "Yes, Papa. Yes, we like her. Should we call her 'mother'?"

"You can talk to her…about that…How did you like the… big rumble?"

"We were scared, but we hid with Janae in the pool."

"She kept us safe till it stopped."

"I bet she did…How can we ever thank her?"

"We let her drive the Mustang!" This made the Senator chuckle which led to coughing, which led PC to check the machines that were monitoring him. It took him a minute to catch his breath.

"Daddy, can people get married in a hospital bed?"

"Yes, Janet, but we won't…put Janae through that." Then, continuing in the same tone, but looking at Janae, "I've put some papers in my floor safe…in my den and if she signs them…she will have the right to be your mom." The girls looked at each other like they were just given a big bowl of ice cream. Then they all looked up at Janae.

Janae stood still with a smile. She knew if she responded at all, tears would start flowing. She tried to blink them away and then gave up. "We'll find those papers, won't we girls? Your dad's going to be just fine, but should we let him get some more rest?"

"Yes, get some rest, Daddy, Mommy says so."

"Yes, Daddy, both our mommies."

Janae opened the door and PC ushered the girls out, but held up Janae, and nodded to the Senator. Janae stayed for a moment. Outside, PC saw Gloria was still down the hall answering questions, so she brought the girls the other way and sat them down on chairs in the hallway by the stairs. After a few more minutes,

Janae joined them and they disappeared into the stairwell. The girls raced down the stairs while PC looked at Janae, "He did, didn't he?" Janae's eyes were glistening.

*

They stopped at the hotel first. PC went in to pack and check out. Then dinner. Not the Horse and Carriage, not Denny's, the girls wanted McDonald's.

"Let's drive through and eat out by the pool at home," Julie suggested. When their turn came, Julie leaned out to the machine and ordered for everyone. Half an hour later they pulled into the fourth stall and put the Mustang to bed. In the kitchen they arranged their meals on trays and each carried their tray to the pool. Oh, no table. A mere hiccup. They looked at each other and then just sat down on the edge of the pool, two on one side of the outer corner and two on the other side with their feet dangling in the water.

"I think Daddy loves you!" Janet said looking at Janae.

"Yes, Daddy loves you!" Janae answered.

"No, I mean you!" Janet began to smile, knowing this routine.

"Yeah, I mean you," Janae continued.

"No, Daddy loves me," Janet countered.

Janae ended the routine, "Yes he does, very much. Tell us about your dad." As the girls talked and ate, taking turns telling stories about their dad, Janae couldn't help but let her mind wander to what the Senator had told her. PC saw what she was doing, so kept the girls going by being excited and asking questions.

Janae had come close to his bedside when PC and the girls had left. Even though he was on death's doorstep, he had eyed her with puppy-like big brown eyes, "Janae…the recommendations about you were perfect…then…when I saw you at the end of the pool...with one of my girls on each side...I couldn't take my eyes off you. I was stunned...to think one guy...could find...the woman of his dreams...twice...in one lifetime. I didn't even notice the rumbling start...I thought it was my heart going crazy...then... with you and my girls in sight...I must have gotten hit on the head. I woke up with your voice...your comforting voice...in my ears. I figured I must be in heaven...then I heard my girls. Janae, you saved my life...But I started scheming...I could marry you... resign as Senator because of my health...and devote my life to my other work. But Janae...you're so young and perfect...with your whole life ahead of you...I have no right to even ask you...The trouble is...I'm dying...I beg you to sign those papers...and be my girl's guardian...until they are twenty-one...And then...if you could...keep an eye on them..." Then his eyes had closed. He was exhausted. She had taken his hand but felt no squeeze from him.

Janae was eating while she was thinking and listening as they all got done with their meals. A work crew must have come, because all the rubble between the pool and the house was gone. The Chief of Staff apparently had gotten under the patio table when the shaking started, but the table top was made of glass. The glass and brick rubble had killed her.

When is death expected? Actually, more often than not. A sudden death without notice is more rare. And unfair. People who suddenly face death should be able to say, 'Hey wait, freeze everything for a moment. I'm not ready to die yet. I need more time. I have important matters to tend to.' Janae paused in her thinking. Why didn't the Senator die, but the Chief of Staff did, two feet away from each other? Well, the table was the difference. She dove under it. He stood and waved at her. At his girls, and at her. That was the logical reason. But what if the Senator, because he was important, or maybe because he had important matters to attend to: his girls; had said, 'Hey wait, I can't die yet. I have to make sure somebody good takes care of my girls.'? Would

God allow him to live, or at least live until he attended to his responsibilities?

However it happened, the Senator was still alive, and had asked Janae to do just that very thing. He had fallen back to sleep from exhaustion before she could answer. She was not sure what her answer would be. Yet, how could she say no? Would the Senator die just after she would say yes, or just after she would tell him she signed the papers? Was he already dead? Or would he be fine like she told the girls he would be? Janae didn't know. It wasn't her job to know the future. It was her job to make the right decision as best she could. She refocused.

"Long day, huh, girls?" she said.

"Having Daddy almost die, and meeting you and PC all in one day is weird," Julie declared.

"Not weird. Really cool. And weird," Janet was more the thinker.

"Well, let's head for bed. There may be more aftershocks, but none as bad as the main quake this morning." They all got up and took their dishes and drinks back to the kitchen. Then worked together to tidy up the kitchen. Janae set the alarm that automatically locked all the doors in the big house. Then all four went through their bedtime routine and crawled into bed. PC slept with Janae in her king size bed. All four girls, unbeknownst to each other, had a talk with God before they went to sleep. And so it was, that God heard those four prayers, and in His gracious kindness, He answered them.

The next day, His answer was quite apparent.

# 14

Touchdown in Hawaii became a long wait for maintenance and refueling. The President of the United States and his family were vacationing there and all the islands were on alert. Joe, Kandee, Jonathan and Sharon drove to a beach house Jonathan somehow had access to while the pilot took care of business.

The house was big enough for the four and yet was cottage-like, on the beach, and airy. The breeze seemed to flow right through the house. They enjoyed a nice afternoon: a swim in the ocean, a catered dinner with music, candlelight, and sparkling cider. They all slept well.

Kandee woke first and pulled Joe up. They pulled on their suits, ran together down to the ocean and dove in. They enjoyed the water, then ran back to their bedroom soaking wet. They showered and dressed, then joined Jonathan and Sharon in the kitchen. The smell of waffles and fresh fruit being cut up led to breakfast and then a dash to the car.

The airport was busy, but the pilot had the jet ready at a hangar at one end of the airport. They left the runway and joined the cloudless blue sky, heading west toward Japan.

Halfway to Japan the pilot came on the intercom, "Sir, there's been an earthquake of some size on the west coast of the U.S. They say it was centered in California. Hawaii is on tsunami alert. Apparently a real possibility of damage there. Coastal California has seen damage." The four looked at each other. Their thoughts were of Seabeck, Shilshole, and their loved ones. Then, after a pause, the pilot, listening to news, continued, "As we speak... Hawaii is...experiencing a receding of the tide. Sir, the live observer I'm listening to has seen Air Force One take off...and a... an approximately five foot tsunami is hitting all the islands... Sir, if this is accurate, there won't be much left of the house that you all stayed at last night." They were all still looking at each other and listening. "Apparently the earthquake was felt in Hawaii, but it was only a minor event...The...tsunami...has hit and continues on toward the eastern coast of Asia. We may have a disaster on our hands when we land in Japan."

The next few days were unusual for everyone. As they landed in Japan, the government was in disaster relief mode. When they landed in China, there was no mention of the earthquake or tsunami at all. Their short stay there was beautiful and very special. Sharon contacted missionaries there that she had sent support to, and they accompanied the four to the Great Wall. The missionaries performed the ceremony; Jonathan and Sharon were married. They traveled a bit on the Great Wall and then spent the night with the missionaries. Jonathan and Sharon left them with kisses and hugs and a sizeable donation. The trip back was enjoyable and they spent two more days in Hawaii. Things had settled down by that time, and the weather was perfect.

The house they had stayed in was swamped, but still standing, so they stayed in the hotel chain, Coastal. Coastal Hawaii, Coastal San Diego, Coastal San Francisco, Coastal Seattle, any big city on a coast had a Coastal Hotel. They were luxury all the way. Then after breakfast on the third day, lift off. As they reached cruising altitude and seat belts were unfastened, Joe and Kandee just smiled at the newlyweds.

"By the way, am I permitted to know where the new home is going to be?" Joe asked.

"Of course. My ranch on the Big Horn River in Montana will be our home and base of operation. Since we are heading east as we speak, let's skip the west coast and land at the ranch. We'll give you the tour and I'll get caught up on business. Then we'll fly back to Seattle and touch base with your boss. You'll be a couple days past your week off, but when you tell him you're bringing me, he'll love the idea."

"Yeah, we're not tired of you two yet," Sharon teased.

Kandee leaned closer to Joe, grabbed his arm and said, "Ohhh, this is so much fun."

And so, the long flight was filled with questions and answers about the early years of two brothers who had only recently met. It was so very interesting to hear the stories of each brother, especially any remembrances of their real mother. They both wanted to find out all they could about her. Joe and Jonathan both had the same thought, that maybe Kandee and Sharon could work together on that research.

# 15

Millie and Wallie had wedding bells in their ears when their commercial flight landed at the Seattle-Tacoma International Airport. They hadn't told Tony and James about visiting their parents, nor had they told them when their flight was due in, so no one was waiting for them. No problem. They hired another kid with a cart and followed him out to the taxis. They moved to the third cab in line because its driver was a woman. The kid loaded their luggage and thanked them for the tip as Millie and Wallie climbed in the back and gave the driver the address.

"Take your time, we're not in a hurry," Millie said, and the lady driver ambled out into the drizzly Seattle traffic. Millie dug out her cell phone and called James, "We'll be home in two hours. Have dinner and champagne ready; we'll bring the guest speaker." That's all she said and James got busy.

The cab pulled over at a small downtown store front which exclusively sold used wedding dresses. Millie handed the cabbie a one hundred dollar bill and told her to wait. Then she changed her mind, "Come on in with us, we need someone to make decisions." The cabbie called in and announced she was on break, locked the cab, and followed the girls in.

Millie and Wallie waded through aisles and racks of wedding gowns and found their size. They picked each one off the rack and held it up. The cabbie would nod yes or no until they each had three or four to try on. Then the dressing room part started.

Millie and Wallie each tried on the gowns they had carried in, and then traded gowns. Each time they tried one on, they came out to see what the cabbie thought. This took forty-five minutes and was the most fun the lady cabbie had ever had in her career as a driver. When they left, each with a big box, the weather was starting to clear up.

Next stop, Capitol Hill, home of the oldest church in Seattle's history. They asked the cabbie to wait this time and both went into the church.

Assistant Pastor Julianna was in her cubbyhole of an office and jumped up with a hug and kiss and a huge smile for the two girls.

"Well, you two look excited. What in the world do you have going now, and how can I jump into the middle of it?"

"Thought you'd never ask!" Millie joked, then Wallie continued:

"We're getting married tonight and want you to do the honors."

Pastor Julianna thought for a moment and slowly turned serious, "Oh, no, no, I couldn't possibly. I've got a group of ten people coming in for counselling, and a funeral right after that tonight. I just can't disappear on a moment's notice just because the two prettiest ladies of the evening decide to go straight and get hitched. Who do you think I am? I've got a reputation to think of." She could only hold the serious look for about two seconds after she finished speaking. Then they all burst out laughing. Pastor Julianna had been one of those ladies herself, and always dropped everything when an acquaintance from the past needed help, or advice. "Let's go!" she grabbed her purse, coat, and prayer book.

*

Not too long ago, Jack had said "no" to going to Alaska. Too much on the downside: cold, mosquitoes, high living expenses. Gretchen had convinced him to try, but life changing events resulted in them never arriving.

Now, with his new mission in life, and a woman to go with him whom he adored, he didn't really care where he was sent. It was the first time in his life he had experienced a change of heart. He had changed his mind about many things after gaining new information or understanding the situation better. Assessing the facts sometimes makes changing one's mind a smart move. But having his heart changed, while he was just minding his own business, was a first.

He had lived his whole life in fear, afraid he was not good enough, and desperately trying to prove otherwise. His older brothers always reminded him of his inferiority simply because he was younger. His only recourse was making the people around him feel inferior, so he would look better, even if it was only in his own eyes. He hadn't even realized he was living that way, but he was living a life of survival, enslaved to the happenstances of life around him. Walking lightly sometimes, stomping other times, trying desperately to keep his nose above water. He slipped under to the darkness of addiction once and fought his way back. There was nothing there but confusion.

And then he got rescued.

Faced with a future of failure, and the price of failure--death, he was offered freedom. The freedom to turn his back on his way of life and allow himself to be embraced by something outside of himself, something good.

Freedom: having before him an unlimited amount of good things to accomplish and someone smarter than he leading the way. Plus, someone else to be beside him all the way, comforting, encouraging, and not reminding him of his past or present failures. Gretchen helped him keep his focus up and forward, and he loved her so. The leadership of Joe Cornish and the companionship of his wife took the place of his fears. As the wheels touched down in Anchorage, he was ready.

Alaska was a big, open place. So, the politicians had to have a big, open view, and base of support for reelection to be possible. There were not many besides Alaskans interested in Alaska. Even the FBI's presence in Juneau was smaller than the tourist bureau. Alaska had enough problems just surviving, let alone worrying about corruption. Just worry about staying warm in the winter and making money off of the tourists in the summer. Keeping the oil flowing and the drugs flowing, kept the money flowing.

So, in Alaska, there was an opportunity for good to be done.

The need for good was always there. Were there any evil hearts here who would change and allow good to come in? Just one heart changing from bad to good was more powerful than Jack could have imagined. He himself, not to mention Tony, his former boss, was living and experiencing doing good and a growing number of its blessings, wholly undeserved. They had simply said "yes" when the offer came.

One of the cases that had landed on the desk of the Office of Special Investigations for the FBI in Seattle, was the murder of a candidate for governor of the State of Alaska, some years back. It had never been solved, and no one seemed to care.

Usually the person who won the election would be a good suspect for the murder. But the new governor at the time went out of his way to try to solve the mystery. Now, years later, that governor was out of office and out of public life. It seemed to Joe Cornish that now was a good time to pick that former governor's mind. Enter Jack and Gretchen, with Tom in tow.

Not knowing the extent of their stay, Joe Cornish had rented a furnished house through the Vacation Rental By Owner website. This provided more privacy and security than a hotel and cost less over the long run.

A cab brought the three and their luggage to the house and they got things set up nicely. Then they went to dinner at a pancake house not too far away. That evening they went over again what they knew and what they wanted to find out.

It seemed that the candidate for governor that had been murdered was not all that transparent himself. The coroner's report citing an unnatural death was a 50/50 guess. He might have been accidentally killed. In fact, most of the facts seemed muddied, either by natural course, or by someone on purpose. Either the victim was a good guy who would expose corruption if elected, or, he was a bad guy disguised as a politician, murdered by another bad guy. Or, perhaps, as Joe Cornish theorized, his lack of transparency in his past proved he was somebody's undercover operative. The question: to what end, and did his death end the operation, or was it ongoing even now?

Joe Cornish wasn't necessarily interested in digging up the facts wherever they led. He was interested in proving his theory, and that the facts that mattered would point to something bigger. Perhaps they would point to a bigger plan which the operation was a part of. He was convinced that some of the so-called facts of the case were inserted to muddy or cover up the true facts.

Since the case was on his desk, nobody else was interested in it. So, he had toyed with it in the past few years, and lately had sensed that his "fishing expedition" might just catch the proverbial great white shark. Not good unless that's what you're fishing for, and are prepared to deal with it. For Joe Cornish, if something smelled fishy, even in Alaska, it needed to be exposed, or if not exposed, perhaps some good could be coaxed out of it.

Tom, as a journalist, was going to interview the former governor. No undercover work here. Just let his nose lead the way. There were a number of ways to go about this, and Joe Cornish trusted Tom to unearth anything valuable to the case. The main question: was the former governor hiding anything? If so, what was he hiding, why was he hiding it, and so on as investigations go. If he was not hiding anything, what did he know that he didn't realize he knew.

Usually, in a stubborn investigation, one small clue that was given no importance, ends up being the key to unlocking bigger things. It was like losing your car keys. They didn't disappear, they were right where you put or accidentally dropped them. You simply can't remember where that was. But after you stumble onto them, you remember how and why they got to that place that was out of the ordinary. Then, thinking back, it all makes sense.

Investigation was like that, like a puzzle. It took intense scrutiny. Some people enjoy puzzles. Others have a nose, almost a compulsion, to find that missing piece. Joe Cornish recognized that in Tom, because he had it in himself.

Jack and Gretchen's job was to check out the club scene in Anchorage. Having the knowledge they did, they could find out if the bad guy pipelines were working well or not. Were there tensions? Were drugs and prostitution, money laundering, and whatever else, running smoothly? Was there a big evil plan out there that was slowly growing and everyone wanted to be in on it before the next guy was?

The desire for more seemed to drive good or bad. The fact that the sky was the limit if you worked hard and obeyed all the laws was a draw for good. The sky was the limit also for breaking the laws, except the penalty for being caught was steep. The time and expense of hiding what you were doing, or of defending yourself if caught, negated any upside in the long run. Crime paid, but the chance of it all being taken away was high. On the other hand, there was no law against doing good. Figure out how to do good, obey all the laws pertinent to what you are doing and to the making of money, and become wealthy. If you get caught? You get a book written about you instead of being thrown in jail. But, some people just had to go through the process to understand it.

It was time for bed. Tom, Jack, and Gretchen would start work tomorrow.

# 16

California was recovering nicely from the earthquake. They had all gone through it before. Janae woke early after a good night's sleep and had no idea if there had been aftershocks throughout the night or not. PC wasn't on the other side of the bed, so she must be up, maybe making breakfast. Janae got herself ready for the day, and within half an hour, peeked into the kitchen. PC motioned her in and was setting pancakes and scrambled eggs with cheese in front of Julie and Janet. PC saw Janae trying to focus on the TV and held up two fingers.

"Two aftershocks last night. Nothing serious. How about some breakfast?"

"Mmmm, smells good," then, to the two girls, Janae said, "Good morning, young ladies."

"PC woke us up early because there is news about Daddy on the TV," Janae raised her eyebrows and looked at PC.

But Janet took over, "They say recovery and rehabilitation and therapy will take a long time so Daddy stepped down as Senator so the business of the State of California, as represented in Washington, D.C. by him, would not be hindered." Everyone looked at Janet.

PC chimed in, "She must take after her dad," she pointed to her head.

But Janet wasn't through, "Daddy made a deal that he would step down if the person he wanted would fill out his term."

Janae perked up and got serious at the same time, "Did they say who he chose?"

Julie's turn, "Yes, some lady named Emily J. Halverson. Daddy called her a close aide. Do you know her, Janae? We can't remember her."

Janae reached out for the kitchen island where they were eating and sat down heavily on a stool. Her mouth hung open and her eyes stared straight forward, as if someone had shot a gun and she wasn't sure if she had been hit or not.

PC's hand went to her mouth as she saw Janae's reaction. "Oh, my God!" Janae covered her mouth with both hands almost as a reaction to seeing PC do it. The girls were diving into breakfast and didn't really notice the shockwave registering on Janae's face. PC walked around behind Janae and put her arms around her. Janae was visibly comforted by PC's embrace and looked at the girls and then at her own plate in front of her. She reached down and started to eat.

"You need some coffee," PC said and went into action.

Not knowing what to say, Janae found the act of eating and chewing, using her mouth for something other than talking, gave her brain time to reset and start functioning again. It was a wonderful reprieve for about ten seconds and then her phone rang. She dug it out and answered out of habit.

"Is this Emily J. Halverson?" the familiar voice from Seattle was soothing.

"Yes, sir, I'm afraid it is. Can I come home now?" Janae asked.

Joe Cornish laughed out loud and heartily. "My dear, I will not leave you stranded. Jennifer is on the way to the airport as we speak. She will be your Chief of Staff and work right with you on everything. Did I mention Jennifer is a lawyer?"

"Oh, thank you, thank you," Now Janae had to fight crying. She told herself she would wait until Jennifer was there and gave her a hug. Then she would cry.

"My dear, it's amazing how we try our best and sometimes we fail, and sometimes we succeed beyond our imaginations.

I'm at your service night and day. Jennifer is very excited; you might have to calm her down. But she's good, very good. Tell PC to contact Tom, they can decide what to do. I'd love for PC to stay connected with you and Jennifer, but if Tom needs her up in Anchorage, it's fine. They can decide. We're all rooting for you, Janae!"

"Thank you, sir. The sound of your voice was the comfort I needed." Joe Cornish had hung up. Janae touched her phone and slipped it into her pocket. PC put a mug of coffee down in front of her. Janae smiled up at PC and PC had to put her hand over her mouth again just to keep from giggling.

"Jennifer's on the way down. And Joe Cornish wants you to check in with Tom. He prefers you here, but if Tom needs you in Anchorage, that takes precedent."

"Thank God for Jennifer," PC said.

The two girls had slowed their eating and were listening to the conversation.

"Who's Jennifer?" Julie asked.

Janae thought for a moment and answered, "She's older than we are, and smarter than all of us put together, and she's on her way here to help us."

"To help us with Daddy's rehabilitation?" Janet this time.

Janae was still thinking, "Girls, you and me and PC are going to be very busy helping your daddy get better, and with another important job that Jennifer is already very good at."

"What's that job?" Julie asked.

"Well, I'm going to give you a hint. Okay?" Janae was trying to go slowly.

"Okay, hint number one, go ahead," Janet liked this.

"Okay, hint number one. Janae is actually my middle name," Janae could see after a few seconds another hint was in order.

"What's your first name?" Julie asked.

"Well," Janae said slowly, "the first letter of my first name is E."

"E.J." Julie said, "Did everyone call you EJ?"

"Wait a minute," Janet said, "what is the first letter of your last name?" PC had both hands over her mouth now and was shaking her head in amazement.

"H," Janae said sort of weakly. Nobody said anything for about five seconds. Then Janet spoke again, slowly and softly as if what she was saying couldn't actually be true.

"Are you...Emily J. Halverson?"

Janae just slowly nodded her head and smiled. Janet looked at Julie, their eyes widened.

"You mean...Daddy wants you to take over for him in Washington, D.C.?" Janet asked, still slowly, wanting confirmation.

There it was. Janae had to be very careful. She could see on the girls' faces the feeling of being abandoned by another mother figure. "Well, I think we should go talk to him about that, don't you? If it's okay with you two, I think the four of us, plus Jennifer, would make a great team. We could work, play, and live together. That's what I would like. How about you?"

"Me, too."

"Me, too," and they all had a group hug.

Then a moment later, "Well, team, we've got work to do. Let's get ready to go see your dad!"

"Alright, can we take the Mustang again?"

"Yeah, and let's have lunch at McDonald's again." The girls ran off to get ready.

PC and Janae just looked at each other thinking 'oh, to be ten and twelve again.' They went and got ready and then stopped at the den. Janae found a briefcase and put all the pertinent papers from the safe in it. Then, to the garage where they piled into the Mustang. With PC driving this time, Janae sat in the passenger seat and carefully looked through the paperwork, making sure it didn't fly out of the car.

When they got to the hospital, they took a side door, down a back hall to the nurse's lounge. Gloria was there and led them to the Senator's room. She stepped ahead and shooed the reporters out and down the other hall saying the Senator needed rest. Then the four girls went in.

The Senator was awake and sitting up in his bed. He had a confident smile on his face. When the four entered his room, Julie and Janet ran to each side. Janae stood at the foot of the bed and PC stayed at the door guarding the way.

"My girls are here! Where have you been? I haven't seen you in so long!"

"Daddy, we were here yesterday!"

"Yeah, Daddy, you look lots better."

"Did you pray? I'll bet you prayed a big long prayer and God said to Himself 'I'm going to have to make their Daddy better. They just can't get along without him.'"

"Oh, Daddy, He heard our prayers!" they both hugged their Daddy.

"Did you pray, Daddy?" Janet asked.

The Senator held them and looked full at Janae, "I sure did."

"Daddy, guess what. We have something important to tell you," Julie spoke and then looked at Janet.

"Okay. Go ahead, I'm listening," the Senator chuckled to himself. This was a phrase he was used to using as a Senator.

Janet began, "First of all, you're not going to believe this. However, the lady you picked to take your place as Senator is Janae. Daddy, her real name is Emily J. Halverson! Isn't that a cool name?"

"I think it's a very cool name," now Janae and the Senator were staring at each other.

PC jumped in, "Who wants ice cream bars down in the cafeteria?"

"I do!"

"I do!"

"I do!" the Senator said raising his hand. "Will you bring me back one? Don't let the nurse see you!"

"Daddy, PC is a nurse!" Julie said as both girls took PC's hands. "We'll be back!"

"Don't go anywhere, and don't die," Janet was leaving instructions.

"I promise, I'll be good. Can I talk with Janae while you're gone?"

"Okay, but no secrets."

"Yeah, we're a family, no secrets!"

"Ten-four. I hear you loud and clear."

PC took the girls and left. Janae pulled up a chair next to the bed.

"Your boss called me early this morning. He filled me in on who he is and who you are. I filled him in on what I have been doing when not doing senator stuff. It seems we have a mutual acquaintance in a man I only know as Jonathan. We talked about some possible scenarios about how your involvement in my life might further his, yours, and my ideas about life." Then the Senator paused and very slowly and gently said, "What would you like me to call you?"

"Please, just call me Janae. My dad's name was Jay, and my mom's name was Renae, so they combined it for my middle name. My great grandmother's name was Emily, but Mom and Dad liked the name they made up, so I've always been Janae."

"I love your name, too. I'm not sure of all I said yesterday. I think I begged you to sign the papers in the safe and keep watch over my girls. I wasn't sure I was going to make it through the night. Since I feel much better, I ..." he paused, so Janae interrupted.

"You were very eloquent. You spoke of when you first saw me with the girls in the pool. You were deeply moved and fell in love with me, then realized I was too young to waste my life as your wife. Then you begged me to be their guardian and fell asleep from exhaustion. I wasn't sure you would make it either."

"I bet I'm at least fifteen years older than you."

"I'd take that bet. I'm twenty-five."

"Oh, I think I lost. I'm thirty-seven."

"Pay up!"

"Oh, if I could sail out of this room with you, we'd go to my favorite spot for lunch."

"Where's that?"

"Oh, it's a secret. I'd have to show you."

"The girls said we're a family. No secrets."

"That means you…signed those papers, or…"

"Those papers would make me their guardian upon your death or complete disability. You might have to draw up some others."

"Janae, I can't think of anything I'd like more than to have you be my wife."

"I kind of like the idea, too. I couldn't imagine a better scenario for me. But there's got to be women you know who would be smarter and more capable. I bet you've met some foreign women that are perfect and speak with an exotic foreign accent. And probably rich and high up in society and politics."

The Senator's smile grew into a laugh as Janae was building her case of someone better for him. "Yes, Janae, I've met some women just like that. Some have visited at our home in the past, when Jeanie was alive. The girls hated them. So did Jeanie. And I was fearfully slipping into the 'Sound of Music' where my only hope, if Jeanie died, was an older, more sophisticated woman to replace my 'I Dream of Jeanie.'"

Now Janae smiled and laughed, "You do have sweet girls. I told them, my boss's wife was coming down to help with your senator stuff and that Jennifer, PC, and me and the girls would make a great team working, playing, and living together.

"You said that?"

"Yes. When they found out that the person you chose to replace you was me, I could see their hearts start to crash, as if they were losing another mother. So I told them, no matter what, we'd be a team."

Now the Senator just stared at Janae. She thought maybe he wasn't saying anything because his emotions might spill out if he tried to. He so dearly loved those girls. So Janae continued, "So, I'm in your life from now on. If you ask me to marry you I can't imagine saying no. But I can imagine quite easily being the girls' nanny and your little-sister-type, who adores her older brother. By the way, do you want me to continue calling you 'Senator,' Senator?"

"Oh yes. I must insist. That's all my wife called me, even in bed."

They both burst out laughing. And then they both knew what their future held.

He reached out and took her hand in his. "I'd like very much for you to call me Jay."

"Jay's my father's name."

"Yes, I remember you said that. Jay is my middle name. Jeanie started calling me Jay because she didn't like William or Bill. She's the only one who has ever called me that. I'd love for you to, also."

"Okay, I will."

"Do you mean 'I will' or 'I do?'"

"I will and I do!"

Then PC and the girls burst in through the door.

# 17

When Robbie got home that night he was tired. He had a wad of cash in his pocket, but second most valuable to him was the time he had spent talking with and helping Janis. He enjoyed that, and he didn't know why. So he decided it was time for a talk with his mom again.

Robbie's mom was cooking dinner, so he sauntered in and helped. "Mom, I talked with a girl named Janis today. She asked if she could help at the docks a few days ago. I said sure, we needed a girl to help out."

"Well, that was very gentlemanly of you, Robbie. Does Janis live around here?"

"She lives at the girls rehab center, but I wasn't uncomfortable around her like I am with most of the girls at school."

"Oh, how interesting. Tell me more," Robbie's mom was all ears.

"Well, the girls at school won't have anything to do with you unless you treat them like a princess. But Janis, she didn't understand why I treated her respectfully, like you taught me. She said most guys don't treat her that way."

"Uh huh. What else did she say?" Now Robbie's mom stopped peeling the potatoes.

"Well, we talked about ourselves a little. She's only got sisters, and I only have a brother. She said she would like to have a brother to be a sister to, and I said I'd like to have a sister my own age.

Then we went back to work. Mom, how come I wasn't afraid to talk to her and I am with other girls?"

"Well, there's a good answer to that question, Robbie," his mom quickly tried to organize her thoughts. "God has given you the ability to recognize who would be a true friend and who would be a shallow friend. It's alright to have lots of friends, but true friends are a gift."

"How do you know it's from God? And what if she could only be a true friend for a short while?"

"God gives that ability to everyone, but not everyone looks at it as being valuable. True friends are a gift whether for a short time or a long time."

After a moment went by, Robbie said, "I told Janis that I treated her the way I did because you had told me to treat girls my own age that way. She said she would like to meet you sometime."

"Well, that's wonderful, Robbie. I'd like that very much. Do you think a Saturday afternoon or a Sunday afternoon would work? Why don't you just line it up. Those are my best days. I could come down to the docks and we could sit at Bobbi's and have lemonade or something."

During the rest of the week, Robbie and Janis touched base frequently and worked together sometimes. They decided Robbie could cover for Janis Saturday afternoon so she could talk with his mom at Bobbi's.

Meanwhile, Robbie's mom had called the gal she knew on staff at the rehab center and they met for lunch in Silverdale one day.

"Janis is way more mature than other girls her age. Apparently she mothered the other underage girls before they all got rescued. She doesn't talk about herself much or her past at all. She's basically an optimist. I can't imagine what she's been through, but if a guy could get around that, he'd have a gem for a friend or whatever."

"She has no family?"

"Not that want her around, or that could help. Janis would end up helping them. Which is not a bad idea, but it's not what she needs right now. She has asked to stay and help the staff at the rehab center and work the docks, also. She's a hard worker, doesn't complain, helps out without directions, and yet follows directions well. And she's cute! There's nothing not to like. Except what's in her past."

"Thank you so much. Robbie works with her and sees her sort of like a sister he never had. I'm going to meet her and have some lemonade with her this weekend. Pray for us!"

"Sure thing. Count on it, Rebecca!"

*

Saturday afternoon, Robbie's mother sat down at Bobbi's out on the deck. Robbie and Janis walked over and Robbie did the introductions.

"Mom, this is my friend, Janis. Janis, this is my mom, Rebecca." Then he went back to work.

Robbie's mom stood up and extended her hand, "Hi Janis, I'm very glad to meet you. Would you like to sit with me a bit and have some lemonade?"

"Yes, thank you, Rebecca. I feel like calling you 'Mom,' because that's what Robbie always calls you. Forgive me if I slip up."

"Oh, that's really sweet, Janis. I don't mind in the least if you call me 'Mom.' In fact," Rebecca suddenly swallowed hard, "Robbie probably hasn't told you, but he had a sister who died very young," now she could feel tears coming and it surprised her, "and I've always thought it would be nice to have a young lady call me 'Mom.'"

The waitress brought lemonade and Rebecca took a big sip. "Well, Janis, Robbie's talked with me about you a few times. He says you are a hard worker and a smart girl, and you're easy to be friends with. And I can't help but notice how pretty you are. Any idea what you'd like to do in your life, with all those things going for you?"

Janis just stared at Robbie's mom as she took a drink of lemonade. Rebecca saw her eyes filling and she thought to herself, 'Oh no, what did I do now?!' Janis wasn't responding so she said, "Sweetheart, I'm sorry. Did my question bring up bad memories?"

"Yeah, sort of, but I don't mind. The men I used to work for made me work hard. That's how I learned that. And in order to survive I had to be smart. I've never been friends with a guy my own age before, but I'd like to be Robbie's friend. Only men have told me I'm pretty. I've never had a woman tell me I'm pretty. I always figured that was because it wasn't true."

"Oh, sweetheart, of course you're pretty. You are gorgeous." Now tears were flowing down both of their faces and they both went for another sip of lemonade. Then it was Janis's turn.

"Could I ask you a question?"

"Yes, Janis, you may. You may ask me anything, anytime you want. That's what moms are for."

Janis blinked back tears and composed herself. "Thanks, Mom." Then she smiled because it felt so good to call Rebecca 'Mom.' "Before I...left home, my mom and dad were always around even though they were not very nice people. I was just wondering what happened to Robbie's father?"

"Oh..." 'and I thought this was going to be light and easy,' Rebecca thought to herself. "Well,...after Robbie's little brother, Glen, was born, their father, my husband, just didn't come home one night. He called the next morning from California and said he had fallen in love with someone down there and was sorry for the inconvenience. The divorce was all handled through lawyers. We never even saw him again. Still haven't to this day."

"Does Robbie remember him?"

"Robbie does, Glen doesn't," Rebecca hadn't thought about Richard in years.

"Have you...fallen in love with someone new, since then?" Janis was trying to be gentle, but she was intensely interested.

Rebecca smiled and inside shook her head in amazement, "If I answer that, can we keep it a secret between us?" Janis smiled and nodded, so Rebecca continued. "Yes, I have, but the person I've fallen in love with doesn't know it."

"Why?" Janis just naturally asked.

'Oh my God, why is this so hard?,' Rebecca thought. "Good question, Janis. Good question. Well...he doesn't know because...I haven't told him."

"Why?" For Janis it was uncharted territory. For Rebecca, it was a constant question in her mind.

"Because it wouldn't be proper if I did. He's...married...at the moment and...I would want him to say something to me first... and he's just honorable enough to not even hint at anything...He's the pastor of our church and his wife has cancer...and I hope and pray she gets well soon."

Now Janis didn't know what to say. She was amazed at the wisdom and fortitude of older women. Would she ever have that patience to do things the right way? "I don't know how to pray, but if I did, I would help you pray."

"Oh, Janis, yes. It would be so nice to have someone praying with me. It's not hard at all. I just remember God's promises and tell Him I believe Him, and leave the timing in His hands."

"I'd like to try that. What has He promised?"

'Oh Lord, out of the mouth of babes,' Rebecca thought.

"Janis, the biggest one is that since He has forgiven our sins and misdeeds, He has promised not to bring them to His mind ever again. So even though we still mess up, it's comforting to know our mess ups don't make Him uncomfortable anymore. That brings peace to my heart."

"Next is His power. He is so powerful, He has promised to love us no matter what. And there is nothing that can come our way that is more powerful than His love. That brings joy to my heart."

"Next, His wisdom and understanding. He has promised not to withhold that from us. So whether we feel like it or not, whatever He has, is ours." Now Rebecca laughed. "I sound like I'm preaching! Sorry."

Janis was all attentive, "I like it. I've never heard that before. Does God really exist?"

"Yeah, He does. He really does. And you wouldn't believe how much He loves you, and is pleased with you."

"Wow, that's hard to believe, but I believe you. If I work hard, doing good things instead of bad, I bet I can get Him to love me more and he would be even more pleased with me!"

Rebecca was going to say something to the contrary, but just smiled and reached for Janis's hands, "Here, let's pray right now. You pray what I pray. Dearest God in heaven...thank you for forgiving my sins...thank you for guiding me...providing for me...and bringing me as close to you as Jesus is...thank you for doing everything needed for Naomi to be cancer free...and for comforting her husband...and thank you for giving me a prayer partner... Amen.

They opened their eyes and just smiled at each other. "Does Robbie know how to pray?" Janis asked.

"Uh...yes, Robbie knows how to pray."

"Do you think Robbie would let me be a prayer partner with him also?"

"Uh...just ask him. See what he says."

"Okay," Janis got up. "I'd better get back to work. Thank you for letting me talk with you and ask you questions." She started to leave, then turned and said, "I really enjoyed meeting you, and thank you for letting me call you 'Mom.' You don't know how much that means to me." Then she was gone down the dock.

Rebecca sat for a while longer. She didn't know whether to laugh, cry, or order something stronger to drink. She was amazed that God would rescue a girl like Janis, and provide her with a staff of good people to help her, and at the same time give herself a daughter to relate to. What in the world would happen next? Naomi would probably be healed! Oh, Lord...

# 18

When Millie and Wallie pulled up to the old Seattle club, the taxi driver hopped out and put their boxes, bags, and luggage on the curb. She hugged Millie and Wallie and wished them good luck, and shook hands with Pastor Julianna, just because. As a cabbie, it was one of her better days.

Tony and James opened the door, welcomed the girls, and brought their things inside. Pastor Julianna did not recognize Tony and James, but did recognize the old club. She had been there before.

As soon as they entered, they smelled dinner. James had planned everything, Alexander and Joni had made sure it happened, and Tony was ready to eat. He had arranged for Joe Cornish to join them and his guest breezed in the door as everyone was being seated. With eight at the table, Tony figured introductions were in order.

"Millie, would you be so kind as to introduce your friend and, as you said on the phone, 'guest speaker'?"

Millie stood and introduced, "This is Pastor Julianna. She is one of Wallie's and my most trusted friends. She is here to marry Tony and I and James and Wallie tonight." Brashly but sweetly, turning to them she asked, "Would after dinner work for you two?"

Tony and James both sat with their mouths open like they had just opened their wallets and found nothing in them. Tony recovered first, "Yes, of course it will. I invited Joe Cornish here so he could flip the coin."

"Oh, we've already decided. I've got you. Wallie gets James."

Joe Cornish was absolutely enjoying this. Tony and James were stunned once more, and Alexander and Joni were looking at each other. Tony mustered himself and stood up, "Well then, before I go on with proper introductions, I have a question for Pastor Julianna."

Pastor Julianna perked up and said, "Please," nodding her head.

"Is pastoring the same as lawyering in that there is a pastor/client relationship where things are kept quiet?"

Pastor Julianna's answer was serious, "Sir, most of the people I counsel and help are or were addicts, prostitutes, and worse. I see it as an honorable responsibility to keep private the things that they share with me."

"Excellent. Pastor, we are delighted to have you here tonight. I'd like to continue introductions starting with myself. I was a topless club owner, a drug dealer, a pimp, a murderer, and an all-around terrible guy who has been convinced to turn my life around completely, and am in the custody of Joe Cornish. James here is my business partner. We are in the business of running a restaurant and hotel, and a private eye service now. Joe Cornish is FBI and has given me a second chance at life as long as I remain in his custody. Alexander is a former gangster from a rival drug dealer, and he has turned his life around, also. His friend Joni used to work at this club, and now works at the restaurant and hotel here in a different capacity."

Alexander raised his hand and stood with Joni when Tony nodded to them. "We'd like to be married tonight, too."

Then Joe Cornish raised his hand and stood to speak after a nod from Tony. "Well, I have been at numerous dinner parties, but none where over 50% of the attendees were about to get married. I could not think of another place that I'd rather be than right here tonight." Joe raised his glass, "To six special people. All the best, forever." They all stood, drank, and sat down.

Then Tony motioned for dinner to be served. During the light conversation, with Millie and Wallie talking animatedly about the earthquake, Pastor Julianna and Joe Cornish kept glancing at each other from across the table. Finally they smiled as their eyes met. Wallie noticed this right away and as the one who usually got trouble started announced, "Okay, we've got a secret going on over here," and pointed to Joe Cornish and Pastor Julianna. Joe Cornish held his tongue and his smile, and just beamed as everyone looked at him. Tony could see something was up, and that Joe was not trying to hide anything, so he jumped in, "Well, the blessings of true confession are their own reward."

Pastor Julianna smiled and looked down. She picked up a grape from her plate and tossed it at Wallie. Wallie screamed good naturedly and picked up her fork with a scoop of potato on it and took aim. Millie, being in the middle of the two, caught Wallie's wrist and said, "Hang on, hang on now. Celebrations are for after the vows!"

Pastor Julianna raised her hand, "My apologies. I do believe I recognize the gentleman from the FBI from many years ago. As I remember, you arrested me and interrogated me."

Joe Cornish laughed in recognition, "Okay, I knew I'd seen you before, and was trying to remember where. You were..."

Pastor Julianna continued, "An accomplice at a bank robbery. At fifteen, you lectured me before dropping charges and letting me go. You said working on the side of the law pays better, and I always remembered that, although it was years before I understood what you meant and took your advice."

"Ah..." Joe Cornish couldn't resist, "advice has a way of slowly aging," and he lifted his glass.

Pastor Julianna jumped in, "And becoming more valuable. It seems that, over time, the benefits of good decisions outlast the drawbacks of bad decisions. You all here are taking advantage of that, and I salute you." She stood and raised her glass. Everyone joined her.

After a slow and delightful dinner, ice cream and coffee were served as wedding cake had not been planned for. Then they moved into the indoor pool area and a grand entrance was made by Joni in her best outfit, and Millie and Wallie in their wedding gowns. They joined their men and Pastor Julianna, and Joe Cornish stepped up and heard their vows.

Then Pastor Julianna spoke. Among other things, she mentioned the delights of the freedom to do good. "Sin," she said, "has been arrested and convicted and incarcerated. If you want to entertain your sins and rehabilitate them, you have to go to jail to do it. And no one likes jail. Better to live out your freedom than to risk incarceration again. God has set us free, let's enjoy it." Her talk ended with a pronouncement of husband and wife, three times.

During dinner, James had excused himself long enough to make a phone call. Nicolus and Nickolaea were on a stake out. He asked them to come back and stop at a grocery store and bring back the largest cake available.

Just as the ceremony ended, Nicolus and Nickolaea pushed open the pool room door and entered with a cart holding a big cake. All the newlyweds' names were on it. Pastor Julianna whipped out a camera and started taking pictures.

After more pictures and signing papers, Wallie sauntered over to the cake, got three pieces and handed one to each bride. Then the trouble started. They walked up to their new hubbies and mashed the cake into their faces. The girls then ran around to the other side of the pool and undid their dresses. The gowns fell to the floor. The three brides had their swimsuits on underneath and into the pool they went. The three grooms stood trying to wipe cake and icing off of themselves and became targets for splashes. Not knowing what to do, soaked, messed with cake, and under attack, they emptied their pockets of valuables, kicked off their shoes, and dove in.

Nicolus and Nickolaea backed some chairs up to the wall as far from the pool as possible and sat down. Joe Cornish saw this wise move and joined them. He motioned for Pastor Julianna to join them, but she was walking around the pool taking pictures. She had never witnessed a more fun-filled wedding.

By and by the celebration died down and Tony, soaking wet in his clothes, with a towel around his neck, asked Joe Cornish if he would like to spend the night and be in on debriefing the girls in the morning. The reason for their trip south had been serious business. He accepted the invitation, but also offered to drive Pastor Julianna home, and she accepted.

As the FBI agent drove the pastor home, they talked of mutual interests. The City of Seattle and its condition, being one. They agreed to an occasional comparing of notes.

The next morning Joe Cornish was up early with Tony. They had time to talk together about rescuing Rolando, Nickolaea's father. This took on increasing importance as Paraguay had been in the news recently. The world economy was causing unrest, unrest was causing instability. Instability gave headaches to the government, run by a military junta. Asuncion was the capital and the location of the problems and the solutions. Thus the flashpoint.

Rolando was military and it was soon time for him to take the money he had amassed and say good bye to Paraguay.

Nickolaea had written to him as soon as they had left Paraguay, informing her father that she and Nicolus were indeed alive. Recently, she had written again and said they wanted him to join them in the U.S. She had mailed the letters to a post office box in Asuncion which only she and her father knew of.

Thus the operation to save Rolando, conceived in the hearts of Nicolus and Nickolaea, and encouraged by Tony and James, was birthed with the help of Joe Cornish, and his ability to plan, finance, and execute with sustained success, the right thing in any given situation.

After breakfast, Joe Cornish, Tony, James, Nicolus and Nickolaea, sat down with Millie and Wallie and listened to their account of their trip south to get intel on Matty.

"We went in and found Matty's girl. We told her we were getting married and it was time to celebrate," Millie started.

Wallie continued, "We cut our booze with water and got her good and drunk. Then she told us everrything."

Then Millie again, "Matty's scared. He can't sleep. She said he is scared of Nicolus. He thinks Tony has sent Nicolus to kill him because Matty knows Tony is alive. She's worried about him." Then she looked at Tony, "You should talk with him and bring him here to start new. And please bring his girl, too. She's miserable."

Tony got an earful and looked at Joe Cornish, who nodded his head and lifted both arms palms up in a 'whatever' gesture. So Tony wrapped it up. "Okay, let's do some thinking and planning. You girls go shopping or something. Well done, by the way."

"Yes," Joe Cornish chimed in, "Well done, girls."

After an hour they arrived at what seemed to be the best plan.

Joe Cornish would travel to San Francisco and spend a few days with his wife. James and Wallie would go south to San Diego and make contact with Matty, or at least his girl. If a meeting could be arranged, Joe Cornish would go down and offer life to Matty. At the same time, Nicolus and Nickolaea would go to Paraguay and bring back her father.

As much as Tony wanted to go both ways, he and Millie would stay in Seattle monitoring both trips. They needed to be ready to supply help in either place if results were disastrous, or better than expected. Someone had to stay at the base and be in charge.

The group finalized the details, and because each operation was important, no one wanted to dawdle. Flights were arranged for the next morning. Joe Cornish called Jennifer in San Francisco and told her his arrival time. He asked her to tell PC she might as well fly up to Anchorage to visit with Tom. Then Joe Cornish left for the yacht to pack and put Jeff and Taylor in charge of his base of operations while he was gone.

The next morning Nicolus and Nickolaea rode with James and Wallie to Sea-Tac airport. The first couple boarded a big jet for a long trip to Rio De Janeiro, Brazil. The second couple boarded a smaller jet to San Diego. Joe Cornish boarded his private jet at Boeing Field and two hours later landed in San Francisco in a fog that was trying to burn off.

# 19

After visiting Senator William J. Williamsford in the hospital, Janae, his secretly agreed bride-to-be, Julie and Janet, his ten and twelve year old girls, and PC, the best of friends, made a beeline in the Mustang to the airport. Jennifer Cornish was coming in and they were going to meet her. Halfway there they realized they didn't have room for her and her gear in the Mustang, so they detoured back to the mansion and traded the Mustang for the minivan. When they arrived at the airport, they parked and connected with Jennifer at baggage claim. Each grabbed a bag from Jennifer as she pulled them off the line and then they found some seats along the wall and sat down.

As Jennifer caught her breath, Janae introduced her, "Julie and Janet Williamsford, this is our teammate, Jennifer Cornish."

Julie and Janet stood and extended their hands and shook with Jennifer. "We're glad you're here," Julie started.

"Yes, we are. Janae says you're smarter than all of us put together," Janet continued.

"Well, I'm delighted to meet you two young ladies," Jennifer said shaking their hands. "I think I'm going to like being on your team."

"Oh, you will. We have to help Daddy get well and help him do his job," Julie commented.

Then Janet, "Daddy has picked Janae to fill in for him and Janae told us she needs you to be her right hand man."

Julie interjected, "And we have a secret."

"Oh, I love secrets," Jennifer said, "is it a team secret, so you can tell me?"

Janet continued, "Oh, yes, we can't wait to tell you. Daddy loves Janae and wants her to be our mom! Isn't that the coolest thing?"

"Well, it sure is!" Jennifer caught Janae's eye. "Would you two stay here with PC and guard my luggage while Janae shows me where the restroom is?"

Julie stood back up at attention, "Yes, ma'am, we will."

Jennifer took Janae by the hand and patted PC on the shoulder as they headed for the restroom. Even though it was crowded they went to a corner of the lounge area and Jennifer wrapped Janae up in her arms. Janae let loose crying and laughing and letting her emotions do whatever they wanted. Moments later she collected herself and lifted her eyes to Jennifer.

Jennifer spoke first, "Things always happen fast when politics are involved. We'll get through this and end up leading the way. Has he proposed?"

Janae nodded her head feeling tears again, but caught herself. "Yes, and I said 'yes'. That's as far as we got."

"Okay, good. Let's get home and get settled, and then go talk to him again." So they did just that.

*

While the Senator-to-be and her Chief of Staff left for the hospital, PC and the girls stayed at the mansion to change two adjoining rooms into an office for Janae and one for Jennifer. With the help of a hand truck they found in the garage, PC, Julie, and Janet had fun moving what they didn't want in the offices out into the hall. Then they scavenged what furniture they wanted from other rooms in the house. It was like redecorating. Desks, wall dividers, file cabinets, lamps, sofas, chairs, coffee tables, pictures, and rugs were gathered and arranged into an ideal office for the new Senator's team.

Jennifer had a briefcase with her as she and Janae approached the Senator's room in the hospital. There was only one person visiting with him as they went in and he left as they came in and sat down. Jennifer followed the person to the door and put the sleeping sign out and closed the door. Janae had moved to the Senator's bedside and they were holding hands, "Jay, this is Jennifer Cornish. I suggest her as our new Chief of Staff."

"Jennifer, last time I heard, you were the District Attorney from San Diego."

"Yes, sir, and I remember we met briefly at a victory party of yours, a couple of elections ago."

"Ah, yes, I do believe I remember."

"I have recently been rescued from my prosecuting duties to enjoy a short stint at uninterrupted marital bliss by a gentleman from the FBI."

"Ah, indeed. Congratulations to you both. I've talked with him recently and I consider him a man about whom most people know only a fraction in regards to what he has accomplished."

Jennifer paused a moment, thinking, "Yes…you are exactly right. And, may I say, he has heard the same about you."

The Senator lifted his hand up with Janae's hand in it and glanced at her and then back at Jennifer. "I have successfully hidden from most people's view the things I have accomplished in a covert type of way. These things of course, have benefitted people, not hurt them. Well, not most of them anyway. I admit to knowing of your husband's adventures to an extent perhaps larger than you think. For instance, I know of his interdiction into Paraguay and the bringing to a fiery justice the gangster and drug lord, Jason Everett Samuelson."

Jennifer paused and then said, "You would be happy to know then, sir, that Jason Everett Samuelson is still alive and living under his real name in the custody of my husband. He is now prospering under the law, not working against it."

The Senator's mouth dropped open. Janae squeezed his hand and smiled. Jennifer continued, "We also have a covert operation in Anchorage where political corruption seems to be the norm. Our intention is to offer life to whoever wants it and turn over to the law enforcement community those who don't."

Now the Senator took a deep breath and smiled at Janae, "My dearest Janae, I do believe you've made an excellent choice for our Chief of Staff."

They then spoke about Janae becoming the senator, the Senator doing his side work as he recuperated, and Jennifer being Janae's Chief of Staff and the former Senator's confidant. The arrangement seemed to please everyone involved. After a couple of hours the former senator needed sleep, so Jennifer and Janae headed home. On the way, Jennifer got a call from Joe Cornish announcing his visit the next day. They arrived home to find their offices, and a bedroom for Jennifer, ready for them.

*

The visit of Joe Cornish the next day was important. When the girls met him at the airport, PC had just enough time to give him a hug, and then she was off to Anchorage, and Tom. Jennifer introduced the Senator's daughters to her husband, then the five went to visit the Senator, who was now out of ICU and into his own room. After a visit of half an hour, Janae took the girls to the cafeteria for lunch. Joe and Jennifer Cornish then had a chance to talk seriously with the Senator.

Joe Cornish admitted to manipulating the situation to get Janae into the Senator's employ so he could find out what was going on, whether on the side of good or bad. The Senator related how he had fallen in love with Janae when he saw her sheltering his two daughters as the quake hit. The rest seemed logical, and the three spoke of the future.

The more they talked they realized how they could combine their efforts and accomplish more than working separately. Joe Cornish had emphasized turning bad guys and rescuing people who were being used against their will. The addition of Jennifer and her influence had changed their emphasis to include political corruption. Now the opportunity had been given them to actually operate in the political arena, and the prospect of doing as much good as possible through the office of a Senator of the United States, seemed unbelievable.

Joe Cornish had always said, "If you are on a roll, keep going till you get stopped." The power of doing good seemed to create its own inroads into crime, into corruption, and now into power. He now began to realize why a connection with Jonathan was so important. The wider range and scope of Senatorial power and influence would take tremendous skill and organization which Jonathan already had in place. William Williamsford, Jonathan, Joe and Jennifer all seeing eye to eye on things, would multiply the amount of good that could be accomplished.

The sky really was the limit when doing good was the goal. It was as if the Almighty was generating a wave of His work and they were just riding it.

# 20

The pilot announced that Rio De Janeiro was sunny and about seventy degrees. They would be landing in approximately five hours. Nicolus and Nickolaea snuggled together in their seats, snoozing after talking and planning the first part of the flight. Their plan was simple. Meet Rolando in Rio and fly back to the U.S.

Meanwhile, Rolando was being very careful. The political wind was changing direction and he was counting the days to his vacation. He had told Rodriguez and the people under him that he was going on vacation, but while he was gone there was a lot to be done. He lined up all kinds of work for everyone to do. They would be so busy trying to get their work done before he got back that they would take his delay as a godsend. By the time everyone realized he wasn't coming back he would be long gone. Just one more day to be vigilant, keeping the appearance of power, no matter what was happening with the junta.

After receiving news from Nickolaea of their escape from the ranch, he was elated. Then when she wrote again inviting him to live with her, it intrigued him. Since then, with the government getting shakier, he had calmly and slowly taken his money out of the banks and filled suitcases, keeping them in his office. Also, he had drawn up papers, giving to Rodriguez all his holdings in Paraguay.

*

Rodriguez was weighing his dinner engagement with Rolando. It was the only time he would have the opportunity to do what he had not yet decided to do. His father-in-law was close to the men in the junta who wanted to reform the government of Paraguay. With the change of power coming, Rodriguez's father-in-law had to have enough power already in his hands to be an asset to the new junta that would be formed. He told Rodriguez that if he loved his wife and wanted good for her, he had to have holdings and wealth in order for their family to be seen as an asset. He must murder his boss, Rolando, and take over what he had amassed. Only then, if everyone did their part, could their family be included in the ruling class of new leadership.

Rodriguez had respected and admired Rolando and served him faithfully, but that was how things were done in life, at least in Paraguay. Faithfully serve a master, heaping up his assets until it was time to take that master out of the picture before somebody else did. This was difficult because Rolando was, for the most part, an honorable man. Rodriguez's father-in-law wasn't. Both of them knew that the new government would just be a variation of the old, yet he loved his wife, and life had a habit of going on. So tonight after dinner he would take Rolando to a secluded place and end Rolando's life, somehow.

As Rodriguez entered the restaurant that evening, Rolando smiled and gestured him over to a booth. There they sat, as close to a father and son as a boss and an employee could be. Rodriguez was having eruptions in his conscience. He could not look Rolando in the eye and imagine how he could murder him. Yet, it had to be done. If he had someone else do it he would be susceptible to blackmail. For his wife, he would do it. It would only be a few minutes of agony for a lifetime of privilege.

Rolando had ordered for the both of them. He knew what Rodriguez liked and they were served within minutes of being seated. This dinner was the last chance to be together before Rolando left on his vacation. They ate and talked of their past and how Rodriguez was the son that Rolando had lost. Rodriguez felt less and less courage to do what he had to do, but he could not stop now.

Finally, after dessert, Rodriguez asked Rolando to come with him to see a new home he was thinking of buying for the wife he loved, if he could spare half an hour. Rolando said he would take the time, and be pleased to give his advice.

Rolando was enjoying their time together because he knew he would never see Rodriguez again. So, before leaving the restaurant, he had a few items for Rodriguez to sign. Rolando put his briefcase on the table and took out a stack of papers. He turned them around and placed them in front of Rodriguez.

Looking at them, he recognized sales agreements, so he read them more carefully. Rodriguez went through each page of the pile and could not believe what he was reading. He looked up at Rolando across the table and saw his fatherly smile. Then Rodriguez saw his salvation. He stared at Rolando and said, "You are not coming back."

"No, my son. Nickolaea has made a place for me and I will be with her."

"Nickolaea?" Rodriguez thought she was dead.

"Yes, she is alive. You will never see me again, nor will I see Paraguay again. I leave you all my holdings because you have been a son to me. I will pray for your health and safety each morning when I wake, my dear son."

Now, Rodriguez was close to tears, thinking of what he had planned. Wealth and power were being given to him freely, as opposed to him murdering to get it. He began signing the papers as something to do to help keep his emotions in check. What should he do now? The honorable thing to do in this case would be to kill himself, but he knew he was not as honorable as he led others to believe.

When he had signed the papers, he looked up at his employer who had mentored him, and Rodriguez drank in the loving expression of a father who delighted in doing good to his son.

"I will drop these off at my lawyer's office in the morning. He will process them and you should be able to take possession in a few days. All my love, Rodriguez, and best of luck. When you remember me, remember me as a friend."

Rolando rose to his feet and extended his hand to Rodriguez. It was over that fast, no need for the pretense of showing the house. He shook Rolando's hand and could not think of what to say, "Thank you, sir. God bless you." It sounded good, but he knew it was phony. He walked out of the restaurant that he would own in a few days, and into a privileged life. Now his wife would be pleased.

*

Rolando went back to his office and bunked down there for the night. In the morning he loaded four big suitcases and one travel bag into the Jeep wagon he had in the office's garage. It was fueled, tuned, and with good tires, was ready for the eight hundred mile journey to Rio. He left by 5 AM and proceeded to the lawyer's office. Rolando gave him the signed papers and fifty thousand dollars. It was his way of saying thank you and good bye. Then he was on the road, and it felt wonderful. He drove east into Brazil and across the mountainous area rather than down by the sea. Even though he took the long way, rather than the scenic route, he arrived in Rio a day before Nickolaea's plane was due.

Entering the busy city, Rolando parked in an underground garage for the Rio Hilton. He paid a bellboy to cart his bags up to the front desk while he checked in, and from there to his room on the nineteenth floor. Rolando never let the bags out of his sight.

He had cut all ties with Paraguay, all in an honorable way. Now he would bless his daughter and be blessed by her and her husband. He ordered room service for dinner, and for breakfast next morning, and slept better than he thought he would.

Turning on the TV during his breakfast, Paraguay was all over the news. There had been an early morning coup. Half the junta was dead. The other half was planning reforms and touted themselves as saviors. Suddenly, there was Rodriguez, standing behind one of the new leaders, all sitting at a table like nothing had happened. Rolando looked closer and recognized the seated one as Rodriguez's father-in-law. Well, more power to him. Rolando loosened his tie and unbuttoned his collar button even though he had just finished dressing as breakfast had come. He wondered how close he had come to being hung or shot? Silly thought. Rodriguez would have protected him.

After a while his phone rang. Nickolaea had landed. He told her to come to him and gave her his room number at the Hilton. And so, Rolando, Nickolaea and Nicolus had lunch together on the nineteenth floor of the Rio Hilton. Then, they put their plan into action.

Knowing they couldn't get all that cash out of the country by plane, they loaded it all back into the Jeep, then drove down to the branch of the Bank of Brazil by the waterfront. Rolando went in and deposited one suitcase, about one million dollars. Then the three went boat shopping.

After about an hour they settled on an ocean-going yacht for eight hundred thousand dollars. Rolando went with the business manager of the yacht sales company back to the bank. For another fifty thousand dollars it would be fueled, provisioned, and ready to sail that evening. A young female pilot and two crew were thrown in for the duration of the maiden cruise. With the transaction completed, Rolando and Nicolus transferred the contents of the Jeep onto the yacht and locked the luggage in the stateroom.

As the yacht was being outfitted, the business manager took them to dinner. Rolando gave him the keys to the Jeep, along with the title, and thanked him for his help. The business manager thanked them for their business and said he would be happy to assist them in the future.

And so it was that a yacht called the *Princess Knight*, sailed out of Rio De Janeiro, northeast around the bump of Brazil, then northwest past the mouth of the Amazon River, and up into the Caribbean. Their destination was Seattle, but once through the Panama Canal, they took their time and enjoyed the scenery, the weather, and each other.

# 21

When it was finally time to leave Montana, the ranch up the Big Horn River Valley belonging to Jonathan and Sharon had become the home of Joe and Kandee, also. They had stayed a week longer than planned because Joe Cornish had inserted into his plans a quick trip to California. He had called back with two addendums. One, he had to stay longer than expected and two, the reasons for meeting with Jonathan when he got back had become measurably more important.

Joe and Kandee had enjoyed the first few days at the ranch. The tour, the animals, the view, the sky, the ranch had a lot going for it. It had a guest house for their use, horse-back riding, a big outdoor pool and smaller indoor pool, the Big Horn River on one side and U.S. Government land on the other. With fishing, hunting and endless trails, Kandee was out of her element, but what was not to like? Joe liked it all, right away, as if it was built for him.

Jonathan and Sharon invited them to make it their home, but Joe had a concern. "Being a guest is one thing, but I'm not sure I can pay the rent."

Jonathan answered, "I inherited this place from my father. It's paid for. The ranch operation makes a profit. Your value to me over and above being my brother, is you being a liaison with Joe Cornish for me. I will probably be owing you."

Then Joe's phone rang and it was Joe Cornish again, asking if the four of them could possibly meet with him and Jennifer in San

Francisco in two days. Getting the okay from Jonathan, the two Joes settled on a time and place to meet.

Kandee and Sharon looked at each other and said, "Let's go horseback riding."

*

James and Wallie landed in San Diego and didn't notice how hot it was until they followed their luggage out the door to a taxi. Wallie told the cabbie to go to the same hotel she and Millie had stayed in not too many days before. At the hotel she asked for the same room, but it was taken. James stepped in and asked for a room he had in mind, and somehow it was available. When the young man helping them with their luggage opened the door for them, the very pleasant smell of fresh flowers greeted them. Wallie walked in and she knew it had to be the wrong room. The suite was three times as big as the one she and Millie had last week. She walked all the way across the room to the balcony and looked out before she turned around, expecting the young man to apologize for the mistake. Instead, James was handing him some money and closing the door.

Wallie stared at him, "James...what are we doing here?" she honestly didn't know.

"We're in San Diego on a covert operation. We're in this room because I wanted to tell you and show you that I love you. I have secretly loved you for a long time, Wallie."

Her mouth dropped open, "You mean me and Millie."

"I like you and Millie a lot, but I'm especially in love with you, Wallace. You two work so hard at being the same, but I see the difference and love the difference. Wallie, I have wanted you specifically for my wife for a long time." James was being James, smart, gentle, truthful, and with very little emotion.

"Wh... wh... why didn't you say something a long time ago?" Wallie asked, mainly because she didn't know what else to say.

"Because you two are inseparable and I figured you would marry together, too. When Tony told me to pick two girls to take with us to South America, you and Millie were the only ones I had in mind. It fit into my long range plans perfectly. Sometimes love ages wonderfully, like wine. Sometimes love needs to be sewn up quick. For me, the timing was perfect. How about you? Do you mind being married to me?" James honestly wanted to know.

Wallie couldn't believe her ears. She had never heard James speak like that before, nor had she ever had any man ask her about how she felt. Seeing the love in his eyes, she slipped into his arms and let the tears come. She had had a hard life and men had loved her hard, but kindness in love was so unexpected. Was it okay to respond without fear and steeliness to a man's love? She had never done it before. James held her and massaged her back gently. Her eyes were wide, staring at the floor length mirror on the back of the door. Yes, it really was her, in a man's arms and listening to tender words. It really *was* her. She held on even tighter. She would never betray or let this man down. He had been in love with her for a long time, before she ever knew it, and she had thought *she* had chosen *him*. This was all new to her.

Later that afternoon the two headed for the club.

*

Matty stayed drunk pretty much all the time. It was his only relief from the fear that gripped him. Nicolus was out there somewhere waiting for the right time to get him, torture him, and finally kill him. Matty could not control Nicolus, or when he would strike. He could not contain the fear, or control the circumstances.

Rage was his outlet. The people who worked with and for him felt the lash of his anger constantly.

Even his girl. She had about had it. When she saw James and Wallie walk into the club and sit down, she froze and eyed them. They seemed to not be in a hurry, ordering from the waitress, and enjoying themselves. Wallie was smiling.

Matty had gotten up late, quickly taken care of business, and was now in his office, well on his way to his hiding place. Matty's girl, knowing this, approached James and Wallie in a way that only Wallie could see her. When she caught Wallie's eye, she sat down at a vacant table two tables behind James's back. Wallie kept her expression the same but spoke softly to James, "Matty's girl just sat down behind you. I'm going to get up like I'm going to the lady's room. Don't let on that you know. I'll touch base with her."

James nodded and smiled up at Wallie as she rose and excused herself. She winked and nodded toward the lady's room when she went by Matty's girl, and after a moment she rose and followed. Just as soon as they got into the lady's room they entered a stall and closed the door. Each stood with one foot on the floor and one foot on the seat.

"Wallie! What is James doing here? Please don't let him kill Matty! Where's Millie? Can you get me out of here and take me someplace where Matty won't find me? Is Nicolus here, too?"

"Hey, hey, hey, calm down, sweetheart. It's me. Do you think I'd let anyone hurt you!? Hush now and listen." They were whispering, but it was busy and the racket was too loud for anyone to hear them. "James and I are the only ones here; we're married. We're here to offer Matty a deal, and you've got to be the messenger."

"No way! He's crazy! He's scared and drunk most of the day. He thinks Nicolus is around every corner and going to kill him slowly. I can hardly talk to him!"

"Okay, okay, hush now," Wallie spoke slowly, with confidence, "We're ladies and we are going to make this happen. Do you love him? If he went straight, would you marry him?"

"Wallie, I'm telling you, it won't work!"

Wallie took the girl's face in her hands and looked into her eyes. "Do..you..love him?"

Now tears started, "Yes. I love him. But I don't think he will change."

"You know what? James told me he has dearly loved me for a long time. Just because I didn't know it, it didn't stop him from loving me. He just waited for the right time. Millie and the old boss are married and we've all gone straight. We turned the Seattle club into a restaurant and hotel! Plus, Millie and Tony, and James and I are owners of a private eye business. No drugs, no clubs, and no violence. We're living with the law now, and prospering. Wouldn't you like to do that with Matty?"

"Well... yeah. Sure...of course. But who would tell Matty?"

"You will."

"No way, he'll beat me till I'm dead."

"No. He won't," Wallie was being strong for her, "I've got a plan. Now listen."

*

James was getting a bit nervous. The waitress brought dinner and wine, so he had something to do. He tried not to look around too much, but in just acting normal he had to look up once in a while. When he did, he noticed people he vaguely recognized. Nobody was staring at him and he didn't catch anybody's eye. After what seemed like way too long, Wallie came back and sat down. Her crafty little smile, James had seen it many times before and loved it, meant she was up to something. "Big plans hatched in small places?" he asked.

Wallie smiled broadly, "This is going to work. Let's just enjoy dinner and later she'll bring Matty to our hotel room."

"Probably armed to the teeth."

"I think the proper description is 'disarmed'. We women are good at it."

*

Matty's gal knocked softly on his office door and walked in. Matty was at his desk with his head in his hands and a bottle nearby. He lifted his head enough to see it wasn't Nicolus and then asked, "What do you want?"

"I want *you*."

"Well, get in line. Behind Nicolus."

She moved behind him and began massaging his shoulders, "I've got something I want to say to you in the realm of good news, and the only time I get your full attention is when I'm on top of you." She reached down and took his hand, "For the next half hour, you're mine." She pulled him up and into the small bedroom off of the office. As soon as she started to undress, he did, too. In a minute she had him just where she wanted him.

"Matty, do you love me?"

"Of course…of course I love you."

"I'm going to leave San Diego. Now do you love me?"

"What?...What are you talking about?" Matty was only half listening.

"I talked to Wallie; remember her?"

"Millie and Wallie you mean?...Of course I remember them."

"Wallie and Millie married James and Tony. They've all gone straight, along with Nicolus, in a deal with the FBI. Live under the law and no prosecution for past crimes."

"Baby…you're not making sense. But I'm crazy about you! You know what we should do…?"

"Shut up, Matty. I'm talking, you're listening. You and me are walking away from a life of breaking the law and we're going to live free from prosecution. No more fear. I've found a way out, Matty, and I'm taking it. And, I'm taking you with me, if you love me."

"I love you, baby…I love you…you crazy girl….But what you're talking about, it's got to be a trap."

"Yeah, Matty, a trap. Peace instead of fear. No one after you. Free to earn money the right way instead of the wrong way. The sky's the limit in doing good. I'm going for it and you're coming with me, if you love me."

"Baby,…this is crazy, you're crazy,…I mean I'm crazy, about you…What do we have to do?"

"We'll get dressed and go over to James and Wallie's hotel room."

"Right now?"

"Right now. You know James, he's not a fighter. He'll explain more."

"This will never work. I'm in over my head. Too many people looking for me."

"I'm going to try it, big boy, and you're coming with me!"

Matty was still half drunk but tired of being afraid. It was way too good to be true, but he was going to die soon anyway, one way or another. The thought of being with this woman and being at peace was a long shot, but at this point he had nothing to lose, "Okay, girl. Let's go look death in the eye. Maybe you are meant for something better; I'll just tag along."

It was seven o'clock in the evening when Matty, led by his girl, walked across the hotel lobby to the elevator and up to Wallie and James's floor. They had walked from the club, and the nearer they got to the hotel, the slower Matty walked. She was practically holding him up as they found and knocked on the right door.

They had stayed together all afternoon and she had kept him from drinking more. He was jittery from the fear of the unknown, as well as a lack of booze. Now he was starting to shake and needed a drink, bad. Matty was sure he was looking at a bullet between the eyes when the door opened, or a knock on the head from behind. But what the hell, might as well go out in style, and this was the nicest hotel in town.

The door opened. "Cindy! And Matty! I'm so glad you both came! Matty, you remember me, don't you?" Wallie was effervescent. She hugged Cindy, and then Matty, too. He just stood in the doorway expecting a knife in the back along with the hug. When Wallie let go, she tugged on his arm and drew him in enough for her to close the door.

Now Matty just stared. This wasn't a hotel room. It must be the bridal suite or penthouse or something. Cindy grabbed him and followed Wallie into the living area. James was sitting down on the couch with a mug in his hand. The smell of dinner hit Matty and suddenly he was starving. As they stayed standing, James rose and poured a second mug of black coffee, came over and handed it to Matty. He took it as James was saying, "Matty, welcome. The girls arranged a dinner for us, so let's eat. I'm hungry. How about you?"

Matty looked around as he took a sip of coffee. Then he looked at James. James didn't look nervous or scared. He looked hungry, "Yeah, I'll sit down with you."

James moved to the dining table loaded with food and pulled out Wallie's chair for her. Then they both sat down. Cindy and Matty walked slowly over and Cindy stood at her chair until Matty caught on and pulled out her chair for her.

"I hope you like lasagna, salad and garlic bread, Matty, because that's all we have." James knew it was Matty's favorite.

"Can I eat in peace without someone putting a bullet in me in between bites?" Matty asked seriously, looking at James.

"Yeah, you can. I give you my word." James said, just as seriously.

The girls served their guys and then themselves, and carried on a light conversation while Matty devoured his food as if someone might take it away before he got done. When James finished his dinner, he got up and went into the kitchen area. Matty's eyes followed him. When James came back in, Matty had stopped mid-mouthful and looked him over. James was carrying a chocolate cake and a carton of ice cream.

"Boy, I got to say, you really know how to feed a guy his last meal." The food was slowly starting to sober Matty up. After a big hunk of cake and ice cream, Matty pushed back his chair and looked around, "What's with the fancy room?"

"It's a honeymoon room for Wallie and I," James knew he had to keep things simple.

"Yeah, congratulations. I heard you got married."

"Thank you, Matty. Things are changing." James said, trying to lead him.

"What do you mean, 'things are changing'? And what are you doing here, James? What I mean is, what am I doing here in your honeymoon room?"

"Matty, the Boss and I got offered a sweet deal. So...we took it."

Matty looked around the suite and up at the high ceilings and lifted his palms, "What...you run a hotel now?"

"Yeah, actually we do," Wallie chimed in as she brought a silver service in from the kitchen area, and poured everyone a fresh cup of coffee.

James continued, "An FBI guy was good enough to show us the evidence that would put us away for good. He offered us a clean slate if we would put ourselves in his custody and begin to work <u>with</u> the law instead of against it."

"Good for you."

"It is. We turned the Seattle club into a hotel and restaurant, and we run a private eye business, too. Nicolus works for us."

"Yeah. I can imagine what Nicolus does for you."

"We want you to work for us, too."

"What?"

"The Boss, me, and Nicolus want you to work with us. That's why I'm here."

"I thought you said you were going straight," Matty sipped his coffee, trying to think.

"We're all smart guys, we proved that doing illegal stuff. Now we are using our smarts for doing good stuff."

"You're trying to trap me!"

"Yeah. Prison for life, or freedom. Working for good, and making as much money as you want. That's the trap."

Matty held the mug up to his mouth, sniffed and sipped the coffee. He shifted his eyes from James, to Wallie, and then turned to Cindy, his girl.

Cindy steeled herself, but said in a tender voice, "I'm going up to Seattle with James and Wallie, and I'm damn well not going to leave you here without me."

Matty swallowed hard, not sure what was happening inside him. "You should! I'm a murderer, I use people, I scare little girls into doing what they don't want to do. I take people's freedom away by selling them drugs. I ruin people's lives!"

"All the more reason for us to take this once-in-a-lifetime offer; to get free and stay free," Cindy was hiding her emotions and staring Matty in the eyes. "You and me, Matty; you think I've been your girl for five years because I don't love you?"

Now Matty was losing it. The pride and hardness of doing things his way was hard to give up, but they were right. Prison or death was just around the corner, he knew that. He took another sip of coffee and then put the mug down. He just sat and looked at his hands. Then he raised his eyes and looked straight at James.

James expected more questions, but none came, so he started closing the deal, "We leave here tomorrow morning, then drive to the airport where we meet with the FBI guy. Instead of your worst enemies, Tony, Nicolus, and I will be your best friends. You've got my word on that." James offered his hand.

Matty pursed his lips, dropped his eyes to James's hand, and then glanced at Cindy. She met his eyes with a strong, confident look, but a tear escaped and ran down her cheek. He shook his head slightly. Damn, he loved this woman. Matty reached out and slowly shook hands with James, but kept looking at Cindy. Her hands went to her mouth and both eyes gave way. She bounced up and sat on Matty's lap, wrapped her arms around him, and would not let go.

"From this point on we stick together. You and Cindy stay here tonight in our guest room. We'll leave at 5 AM, go to your office at the club while it's closed, you take care of business quickly, and we leave. For good. You probably have to make a few calls tonight. Tell them you're on vacation until you get back. That will give us some time to get settled in Seattle before the shooting begins down here once they figure out you're gone."

Matty tried to dig for his phone, "Baby, I got to make a call." Cindy got up and swung her leg over his lap and sat back down straddling him. He just got his phone out of his pocket before she had him wrapped up even tighter.

Wallie leaned over against James and he put his arm around her. They both just marveled at the power of good trumping what seemed like overwhelming odds on the bad side.

Matty made his calls with Cindy wrapped around him. She just would not let go. He finally stood up and scooped her into his arms and looked at Wallie. She pointed to a door, and in Matty's girl went, carried by her new man.

# 22

Sometime during the night, Cindy finally let go.

At 4 AM Matty woke up and heard Cindy in the shower. Throwing off the sheet and sitting up on the side of the bed was a big mistake. The momentary lull in blood flow made him dizzy and his hands went to his head. He needed a drink. He reached for the bottle on the bedside table, but there was no bottle. He fumbled for the lamp and turned it on. Whoa! Way too much light! After a moment he opened his eyes and squinted around. Where was he? Then he remembered. Last night. A major change in his life. Fear gripped him. What had he said and done?

He remembered he was as good as dead. He rubbed the sides of his head. That's right! He and Cindy were going to disappear today and never look back. Even after the way he had treated her the last two weeks, she still wanted him. He wasn't sure what to do.

He felt like he was hung over. Well, duh, of course he was hung over, after two weeks of drinking. He needed a drink. NO. He did not need a drink. He needed Cindy. Cindy helped him in so many ways, he realized. He dropped his hands into his lap and looked at them. Then he remembered more: friends, support. Okay, he needed a job to do, something that he could focus on. Something so big and important, that he would forget how he felt. Wait a minute. Freedom! He was going to be completely free from his past actions, and he needed to jump on this. He had to focus on living free and doing good instead of slipping backwards! Now,

Matty got excited. He stumbled into the bathroom and after a minute he was in the shower with Cindy.

Cindy heard him come in and use the bathroom. She got ready for him, but when he got in, he started babbling. Freedom, new start, he was thanking her, couldn't have done it without her, thank you. So she got done, kissed him and got out so he could shower. 'Wow! That was different; he's changed already,' she mused.

By 4:45AM they were dressed and joined James and Wallie. The four went down to the lobby where the coffee bar was just opening. At 5:05AM they walked out, coffee in hand, and down the sidewalk to the club. Matty unlocked the door, disarmed the alarms, and everyone went in.

When they entered Matty's office, he got a suitcase out of the closet and went to his safe. The safe was full of money. After he filled the suitcase he wrote a quick note and left it in the safe with the remaining money. Then he busied himself with other things around the office. By 5:45AM he was done. Cindy had gone to their bedroom and packed some clothes for them. At 6AM they were at the door. Matty set the alarms, they all went out, and he locked the door. They walked back to the hotel, up to their rooms and James and Wallie got their things. By 7AM they were entering a taxi and heading for the airport.

As the cab pulled away from the hotel, Matty looked at the suitcase on his lap and then at James, "Are we taking a commercial flight?"

"No," James understood Matty's concern, "the guy we are meeting at the airport has his own jet."

As they got out of downtown and onto the freeway, a cop pulled in behind them and flipped on his lights. The taxi driver pulled right over and stopped the car. Matty looked behind them and then at the driver with a scowl, "What did you do?"

"Hey, I got no beef with you, man," that's all the driver said. He opened the door, got out and went back to the cop car. Matty was wide eyed, "Hey, something's wrong." When he saw the taxi driver get into the back seat of the cop car, he yelled, "Damn!" and stepped over into the driver's seat. Looking in the rear view mirror, he saw a cop and another man exiting the patrol car.

"What's wrong, Matty?" James growled.

"Get down! Bend low!" was all Matty said. He put the taxi in gear and tromped on the gas pedal. Then the back window shattered. The taxi fishtailed out into traffic, got into the fast lane and up to a hundred miles per hour before Matty had to slow for morning rush hour traffic.

"What the hell was that?" James and the girls were covered with glass. Matty was driving but had to think, too. He didn't have time to answer questions at the moment. He veered hard right and took the next exit. He headed down some side streets and pulled over under a huge maple tree covering the whole street.

Taking a deep breath, he explained, "What the cabbie said when he got out was just wrong, and the cop was probably a guy we own. The other guy that got out of the cop car was an assassin from Louisiana! I know, because I've used him before. He didn't care if I recognized him, so he was going to plug all of us right there! Somebody hired him to get me and he must have been following me for days, waiting for the right time." He turned around and looked at Cindy, "Baby, you literally saved my life by talking me into this. We all very easily could be dead right now." Both girls put their hands over their mouths.

"Yeah, and <u>you</u> just saved <u>us</u>. Now what?" James felt trapped now. He dug out his phone.

"I got to think for a minute," Mattie said. He was silent for a bit, then, "What time is it?"

"Seven forty-five," Wallie said as James put his phone to his ear.

"Okay. We're going to be okay," Matty said it and everyone needed to hear it. He started driving again.

James was talking into his phone, "...Yeah, and Matty thinks he can get us out of it. But the four of us just missed making a deposit in Fairlawn Cemetery... Okay...I'll ask,...Matty, what's your plan?"

"We're getting another car. Can't stay in this taxi."

James spoke into the phone again, "First we switch vehicles."

*

Joe Cornish got the plan from James and then described how to get to the safe house up the coast that he had used the last time he was down there. James was acquainted with the area and understood the directions. Then Joe Cornish called Tony. He filled Tony in and asked if Nicolus was anywhere near San Diego.

"Yeah, I talked to him. They were going to refuel and restock in San Diego last night. They're probably just leaving."

"Okay, good. Ask Nicolus to go slowly and expect a smaller boat with James, Wallie, Matty and his girl to rendezvous with him. Then head north fast. They might have a tail."

"Yes, sir. Keep me posted," Joe Cornish had already hung up.

*

Matty drove on residential streets until he found the right street leading up to the main business drag. Before he got to the stop light, he ducked into the back side of a big Chevy dealership. The mechanic's bay door was just about all the way up and Matty drove the taxi with the busted-out back window right in and up to the front bay and nosed it in, like it was being worked on. All the mechanics just stared.

"Everybody out and grab all your things! We're not coming back to this car." Everybody did what they were told. "Follow me," they went through the 'employees only' door to reach the waiting room. Matty pointed to seats. He had his briefcase with him.

The salesman that rapidly approached Matty turned white.

"I've got to see your boss right now," Matty was bigger than life.

"Uh...yes, sir...uh, he's in a meeting...and I'm not supposed to..."

"No, he's not. He's talking to me in his office...You know who I am; go tell him I'm waiting."

"Yes, sir...I'm happy to, sir. Please step into his office and..."

"GO!"

Matty went into the owner's office and hardly had time to turn around.

The owner of the dealership ran in, "Matty...I owe you...what do you need?"

"Vince," Matty put the suitcase on the desk and opened it, "I'm buying a SUV with tinted windows from you right now. How's fifty grand sound?" He pulled that much cash out and shut the suitcase.

"Matty, you've got the pick of any of my cars, no money needed; you know that." Matty stacked the money on the desk and just looked at Vince.

"Uh...the only SUV with tinted, all ready to go, is the one I drive."

"I know. Is it gassed up?"

"Yeah... sure..."

"Toss me the keys."

Vince tossed him the keys, then took a step closer and whispered, "Matty, my car is yours, no money..."

Matty stepped toward Vince, "Vince, you've been a good guy to me. The taxi in the first bay is hot; shots were fired. Do whatever you do to make it disappear. Your car was stolen, and you can't remember when you saw me last, if the cops ask." Matty held out his hand.

Vince just stared at him, remembering what shaking hands with Matty meant. You were dead if you broke your word. He slowly reached out and shook Matty's hand, "Be good, my friend."

Matty walked past Vince and then stopped, turned, looked at him and said, "You might not believe this, Vince, but that's my plan." Then he left. Motioning the other three to follow, he went out the dealership's front door and straight to Vince's SUV.

All loaded up, Matty drove the SUV out the driveway and onto the main street. Down a ways he took the entrance to the freeway. He had never seen so many cop cars going both ways. He kept it at the speed limit and headed for the ocean. No one in the car had spoken more than a word or two. As he turned up the coast highway, he turned on the radio.

The local radio station had interrupted the national talk show in progress with breaking news: "...this bizarre story had its beginning on the freeway about 7:20 this morning. When the police pulled over a speeding taxi, the taxi driver got out and ran back toward the police car. The police then came under gunfire from the occupants of the taxi, and it sped away. Police returned fire and shattered the back window of the taxi. Police determined it was best not to pursue the taxi because of potential danger to the public. However, we have just confirmed that the taxi has been found. Apparently a mechanic from Vince Caldera Chevrolet, in San Diego, found the taxi inside the service repair garage when he opened up this morning. The owner then reported to police that as he arrived at work he was approached by a lone gunman who demanded his car. The police now have an all-points-bulletin out for a black, tinted Tahoe, with a personal plate reading SELL ME. If you see this car you are asked to call 911..."

Matty turned the radio down, "James, how far?"

"A couple more miles on the water side. Look for Coral Cliffs; it should be gated."

Five minutes later Matty asked, "Okay, here it is. What's the code?"

James gave him the code. Matty nosed up to the gate and punched the code onto the keypad. The gate began to open slowly. The fifteen seconds it took to open seemed like fifteen minutes because the back of the car was less than twenty feet from traffic, and his plate SELL ME, was noticeable to any and all who looked.

Finally, they drove through and the gate began to close. Four houses down on the left was the address, and as they pulled into the driveway a man had pulled a car out of the garage and he motioned Matty to drive right in. The garage door quickly closed behind them. Matty turned off the engine. In the silence they all breathed a sigh of relief.

"Okay. We've got to keep moving. Let's get out and get all our gear into the house." Matty knew the tenacity of the man in the police car.

Inside the house, the man from outside exchanged car keys with Matty and pointed to a woman on the couch, "She is your driver and pilot. Load your gear into the car outside quickly." The woman got up and helped with the gear and she, plus the four, squeezed into the smaller car. As they backed out onto the road down to the community dock, they heard a siren getting louder.

The lady drove and spoke, "Okay, here they come. Somebody must have seen you at the gate and called it in. Steady now, we are not in a hurry. We're not the car they are looking for." The cops were now at the gate and it was opening. "They didn't see us back out, so will assume we came through the gate, also. Everybody relax."

They drove slowly down past the expensive houses and toward the dock. Two police cars came through the gate. The first came right toward them but continued around them down to the dock. The other one was going slowly and stopping at each driveway. More sirens could be heard and Matty didn't like this go-slow-act-cool routine. As they neared the dock parking area, the cop car came back toward them. His window was rolled down and he motioned her to stop. The lady driver had insisted that Wallie ride up front with her, and now Matty saw why. The cop might have his picture. She rolled down her window and stopped.

"Morning, ma'am. A black SUV was reported to have entered this community, probably about the time you did. Did you see it?"

"Oh yes, sir. It came in behind us and went right around us and down here like he was in a hurry."

The cop automatically turned and looked the parking lot over again and asked, "Do you see it now?"

"Oh no, sir, it came right back up and I waved, but I guess he didn't see me."

The cop furrowed his brow, "What do you mean, he didn't see you? Why did you wave?"

"Because I saw his back license plate when he first went by. It was Mr. Caldera! We bought this car from him and I recognized his SELL ME plates. He drove us to lunch in it the day we bought our car, while it was getting detailed. Instead of waiting in the waiting room, he took us out to lunch. I really thought that was..."

"Ma'am!!" The cop interrupted, "Did you see where he went?"

"Well, officer, back out the gate... like he had turned down the wrong road, you know."

"North or south?"

"Uh...well, I was looking through my rear view mirror. He went through the gate...but I don't think he had a blinker on. I'm sorry officer, I'm not sure which way..."

"Thank you, ma'am," the officer sped off. She sat for a second and then proceeded to park as close to the dock as possible.

"Geez, you're good, lady," Matty exclaimed.

"Yeah," Wallie added, "Do you work for Joe Cornish, too?"

"Who's Joe Cornish?" Matty asked before the lady could answer.

James answered, "Joe Cornish is the FBI guy that we work for and he was going to meet us at the airport. This was plan B. You'll meet him in Seattle. Good guys don't come any better, Matty."

*

The lady driver turned off the car and said, "Okay, we all calmly get out, get our gear and calmly walk down to the dock and onto the boat. We want to look like tourists, not in any hurry. People might be watching and we don't want them to report people with luggage running down the dock."

The four followed her example and casually walked toward the boat, talking and pointing and looking around. When they were all aboard, Cindy said, "We made it!"

The lady driver/pilot said, "Not yet. A cop car just pulled into the dock parking area again and two men have gotten out. Get below while I start the engine." They moved below quickly as she hopped out to untie the mooring lines.

Matty looked out the small porthole toward the cop car. "Damn!" he blurted out, "Get down and stay quiet. It's him! The same cop that pulled us over and the other guy. Me dead means big bucks to him. He is a Louisiana bayou guy; he can smell me."

The two occupants of the police car trotted down the dock and yelled, "Hey, lady, what are you doing?"

"'Morning officer, how can I help you?"

They reached her and held out a picture of Matty. "Have you seen this guy this morning?"

She looked at the picture, "No, sir, I have not seen that man."

"May I see your ID please?" The cop was polite, while the other man was looking all around.

The lady pilot dug out her wallet and showed her driver's license and her professional pilot's ID. "I'm a professional pilot and I'm taking this boat into San Diego to pick up its owners. They've just gotten back from Mexico and instead of sitting in traffic, they are sitting in a lounge on the waterfront waiting for me to pick them up and bring them back here." Both men looked around.

"Damn," Matty whispered this time, "I'm not going to get rid of this guy. James, you packing?"

"Yes."

"Me, too. Girls, go out there and proposition those guys. Ask them if they want a quick freebee. Lead them down here. Have them come in first."

Cindy and Wallie shifted gears fast. They hadn't forgotten anything. Out they went, up onto the dock, giggling.

Cindy started, "Hey, who are you guys? Mmm. We do cops free, right Sally?"

"Yeah, Suzie, especially cute ones," they walked right up and took the men's arms.

Cindy looked at the pilot, with a scowl, "We're going to wait a little right here, honey. We're going to show San Diego's finest a little respect."

The officer looked at the pilot, "Hey, I thought you said..."

Cindy broke in, "Come on, handsome, you're mine," he allowed himself to be interrupted and drawn toward the boat.

Wallie grabbed the other guy's arm, but he jerked his arm away, and pulled out his gun. He grabbed Wallie's arm and pointed the gun square in the pilot's face, "I'm searching the boat, and we're all going aboard. You're driving. Move!" The pilot had managed to get the lines untied and now the boat was drifting slightly. Cindy had Matty's words in mind and had kept moving. She got onto the boat, pulling the cop with her, and pushed him down the few steps saying out loud, "Onto the bed, big boy!"

Following what was going on topside, Matty and James carefully moved to each side of the door in the small lower cabin of the boat. Guns drawn and waiting, Matty heard the demands from outside. The next second, the cop half stumbled down the steps, having been assisted by a big push from behind by Cindy. He landed on his hands and knees on the bed. As Matty and James moved to him, they felt the boat list as the other three stepped across the foot or so of water and onto the boat. Matty grabbed the cop's hand and held it pinned to the bed, while James unsnapped the officer's gun and confiscated it. With his other hand, Matty poked his gun up under the cop's jaw and whispered, "Your one chance to live is here, now. One sound from you and I pull the trigger." He rolled the cop to a sitting position, then James and he returned to the sides of the door.

Seeing Matty nod to her in the cop's direction, Cindy launched herself onto the cop, pushed him onto his back on the bed, and started kissing him. The bayou bad guy had a handful of Wallie's hair and was pushing her ahead of him down the steps. Wallie saw Cindy and the cop on the bed, and James and Matty out of the corner of her eyes. When the boat lurched forward as it got underway, she fell back and, with a little added pressure, pushed the bad guy back onto the steps. He had to let go of either Wallie's hair, or his gun.

Feeling set free, Wallie scrambled up and dove onto the bed with Cindy and the cop. The bayou bad guy quickly recovered and managed to mutter, "You stupid little slut," he reached out his gun and aimed at the two girls.

In the half second it took Matty to move his aim from the cop on the bed to the stairwell, he heard a shot, but the sound that registered in Matty's brain, a small sharp crack of gunfire, didn't match the size of the gun barrel he could see. Before Matty pulled the trigger enough to fire his gun, the bayou bad guy stumbled down into the room and onto the floor in a heap. Matty's training caused his gun barrel to rise but his gun still fired, up into the ceiling. The much louder noise stunned everyone in the small room.

Matty and James both looked around the corner and up the steps. They saw the lady pilot with a very small hand gun pointed up and a determined, professional look on her face. She spoke softly into the silence, "Sorry, buddy. Bad guys don't get to pull guns on my boat." Then she disappeared up to the pilot house and slowed the boat. Matty looked at James and then down at the bayou bad guy. A small hole at the base of his skull was starting to ooze blood. Matty holstered his gun, dug his handkerchief from his back pocket and held it against the wound. He felt the neck with his other hand for a pulse, but there was none.

"Girls, are you okay?" They had their faces in the cop's accidental embrace, and started to get up at Matty's voice, "Go topside with James." James holstered his gun and handed the policeman's gun to Matty and led the way upstairs. With one hand still pressing the wound, just wanting to stem the size of the mess, he eyed the cop, "You going to give me any trouble?"

"No, sir. I've got no beef with you. I was afraid he'd kill me if I refused to help him."

"Cuff yourself."

"Sir, I've got to use the bathroom."

"Cuff yourself in front," Matty said, pointing to the door of the tiny toilet.

As the cop dug out his handcuffs and applied them to himself, he started to babble, "Sir, you know me, I'm on your payroll. Just tell me..."

Matty interrupted, "Son, do you want to stay on my payroll?"

"Yes, sir...yes, sir... I do, sir."

"I'm walking away from my past. I'm going straight. I've been set free to live on the good side of the law. You can come with me now, or go back to being a dirty cop, with the bad guys gunning for each other because of the power vacuum. Choose now." The cop stumbled over the body and into the toilet, just barely able to close the door behind him and yet turn around and undo his pants without falling over.

Matty climbed the steps and Cindy was into his arms, tears flowing. He saw James and Wallie in the same condition, so he held Cindy for a whole minute. Then he sat her down next to Wallie and James and went up to the pilot house. The lady pilot was using binoculars, looking behind them towards the dock.

"Anything?"

"No, but we'd better get out of here. All they've got to do is call his radio and not get an answer, and half a dozen cops will show up. They know exactly where that car is."

"Okay, head for the horizon. Once we get out of the sight of land, head north. We're supposed to meet up with a yacht somewhere."

"Yes, I have the co-ordinates. It will be a one way trip unless the yacht gives us gas."

"Interesting. That might just fit into our plans."

# 23

Joe Cornish was in San Francisco visiting his wife, Jennifer, and the others. He planned to go to San Diego if James and Wallie were successful in lining up a meeting with Matty. When James called and informed him that Matty had already made a decision, and that he and his girl were spending the night with them, Joe Cornish asked that the four meet him at the San Diego airport so he could question Matty himself.

When the second call came, and he realized Matty, James and the girls were under attack, he cancelled his flight south and went right into protection mode. He lined up the rendezvous out in the ocean, and made sure Nicolus knew the four were being dogged by an assassin.

When the next phone call from James described the narrow escape, the dead assassin, and a cop wanting to come with them, Joe Cornish moved the phone away from his ear and looked at it. What in the world would happen next?

James then said that Matty had an idea, so Joe Cornish told James to put the lady pilot on, followed by Matty.

The lady pilot explained the situation to him and that it was she who had killed the assassin. Joe Cornish told her "Well done" and then asked for Matty.

"Matty, my name is Joe Cornish. I'm afraid that all the excitement which you folks are encountering is my fault; but I applaud the decision you've made."

"Yeah, Cindy and I would be dead right now if you guys hadn't extended an offer of freedom. Listen, the cop wants to disappear with us because he's dirty. His patrol car is at the dock so they'll connect this boat with his disappearance. The assassin needs to disappear because he's dead. The boat's only got enough gas to rendezvous with Nicolus. So we've got three strikes against us. I'm thinking we ought to meet Nicolus's yacht, tow this boat farther out, and sink it with the dead guy aboard. The cop was on my payroll, so I'll have him work with me. What I mean is, I want to take you up on your offer."

"Matty, your thinking is excellent, and your decision is the right one. Congratulations. Make it happen like you said, and put James on, please." Matty handed the phone back to James and Joe Cornish congratulated him on his good work, and told James he thought Matty's plan was sound. James agreed and promised to keep Joe Cornish posted.

An hour later, ten miles off shore, Nicolus and Matty shook hands. They had both worked for Tony outside the law, then when Tony changed they became adversaries. Now they were working together again, this time on the side of good.

Much had changed, yet some things remained the same. Nickolaea hugged Wallie and Cindy, and then introduced her father, Rolando. James introduced the cop, and asked if anyone wanted to see the dead guy. The lady pilot went up to the pilot house and found another lady pilot who told her to go get a good night's sleep. Matty's plan worked perfectly and the evidence of how they escaped sank to the bottom of the ocean.

Freedom was breaking out. It was causing inroads into long closed-off areas.

# 24

When the flight from Montana landed in San Francisco, Joe and Jennifer Cornish met them with a limo and they all rode together back to the Senator's mansion. Jonathan, Sharon, Joe, and Kandee, sat at the kitchen table with Joe and Jennifer Cornish, and Janae. They all got caught up with each other and had some lunch and spoke lightly of the future.

Joe and Jennifer then retired for the afternoon to her office for planning and making contact with Nicolus on the ocean, Tony at the club, and Jack and Gretchen up north. The other two couples decided to enjoy the pool for the afternoon while Janet and Julie practiced soccer.

Janae had gotten the girls into the habit of getting up early for horse-back riding, swimming, or practicing soccer. The mansion had a half court for basketball that the girls used for soccer practice. They kicked the ball off the three walls and took turns at kicking it back. It was like hand ball with feet.

Another thing Janae had begun was cooking lessons for the girls. They had a cook at the mansion, but Janae and the girls volunteered to make dinner for everyone. They put up a menu for the evening and all three did the cooking.

The menu tonight was good old-fashioned home-made cheeseburgers with macaroni and cheese and green beans. This was standard fare in many homes across the country, but a seldom had treat at the mansion. They included sautéed onions and real cheese, dill and sweet pickles, tomatoes, lettuce, mayo or home-made thousand island dressing, ketchup, or BBQ sauce. And for dessert? Home-made chocolate/peanut butter milkshakes.

The evening meal was delicious and nutritious, especially if you were trying to gain weight. For everyone present over the age of twelve, it took a little longer to digest. Joe and Jennifer Cornish walked laps around the swimming pool for an hour after dinner.

Senator Williamsford and Janae had arranged for his recovery to continue at the mansion. Workmen were not only continuing repairs from the earthquake, but were also adding to the Senator's master suite the equipment needed to keep him alive and getting better. He was going to be transferred from the hospital to the mansion the next day.

The atmosphere at the mansion was expectant, from the hired help who knew their boss was coming home, to Joe and Jennifer Cornish and the visiting adults who had plans and strategies to consider with the Senator. The girls expected their daddy to need their help and encouragement as he healed up. Janae had told them they were their dad's two most important assets, and they intended not only to figure out what that meant, but to do it. That night everything seemed ready and everyone went to bed with a prayer of thanksgiving for the return of the Senator.

The next morning, Joe and Jennifer Cornish walked more laps while Janae and the girls swam. Jonathan, Sharon, Joe and Kandee took the Mustang for a drive around the neighborhood.

After breakfast the call came that the Senator was on his way. He arrived in an ambulance, but was sitting in a wheelchair with all his attachments and IV's surrounding him. First in the order of business was a hug from his two girls. This was followed by a kiss on the cheek from Janae. Then the family, the paramedics, the Senator in his wheel chair, along with all the contraptions, wound their way through the mansion to his master suite. The Senator refused to lay in his bed, but eyed the new electric cart/wheelchair, a gift from Joe Cornish, which would allow him to move from room to room with all his attachments. The seat even reclined. He pointed to it and the paramedics helped him change his address from wheelchair to super wheelchair.

Short audiences were then held with the Senator by all from gardener to senator-to-be. After an morning of greetings, Janae and the girls came in again to help him recline and get situated for a nap. Janae gave him a real kiss and he quickly fell asleep with a smile on his face. The danger was past, but his recovery was going to be slow.

Janae was at peace even though she was faced with more responsibility than any of the others. She was a covert operative who was in place when the Senator's extra-curricular activities were revealed. Within 24 hours she went from new nanny to bride-to-be and mother-to-be of two preteen girls. And then, if that wasn't enough, she was named by the Senator as his replacement as one of California's two senators in the U.S. Congress. Her peace came from knowing somebody planned the basics of this operation and was with her in the carrying out of all her new jobs and responsibilities.

Over the next week, Jay and Janae grew closer in love and appreciation for each other. Julie and Janet woke each morning remembering their daddy was home. They flew into his bedroom and woke him up.

Jennifer had sessions with the Senator. He helped her become familiar with the responsibilities of a United States Senator. As Chief of Staff, she would have her hands on the reins of a powerful office.

The Senate's job in Washington, D.C. was to slow things down. The House of Representatives had five times as many members as the Senate. They were elected by the people every two years. In order to get reelected as a representative, they had to either bring home federal dollars to their district, or be very good at representing what those who elected them wanted. Seldom did both happen. Things could go from fast paced to crazy if enough representatives would agree on one thing. And they held the purse strings. No new money was spent by the federal government unless the House had something to do with it. But the Senate had to give their stamp of approval before it was sent on to the

President of the United States for his approval or veto. Thus, the senators, who were elected every six years, had for a long time seen it as their job to slow things down, so the country would not blow itself apart with partisan fights or individual power grabs.

There was also time for Joe Cornish, Jonathan, Joe and the Senator to get to know each other better, and imagine a world where their kind of operations had beneficial results. It was possible to change a culture from bad to good, but good had to lead the way, not just point the way. And if enough people participated, dreams had a funny way of acting. They came true once in a while.

After a week, Jonathan, Sharon, Joe and Kandee left for Montana. Jonathan had catching up to do. Before leaving, they all had shaken hands in agreement with Joe, Jennifer and the Senator regarding keeping each other informed of the Senate deliberations in which Janae would participate. Their goal was to promote the advancement of good rather than allowing the slide into corruption and greed that was sometimes the case in government bureaucracies.

The men who had led the executive branch since George Washington on April 30, 1789 had been good and bad, smart and dumb, detail oriented and summary oriented, rich and poor, liberal and conservative, understanding and greedy. The Presidency of the United States was what it was, and did not actually matter in the long run, except for in the arena of checks and balances. Most of the men of the presidency did not understand this. The men of the Senate did. They were the power and they knew it. Fifty states and one hundred men, with some occasional women thrown in, kept the country together in a slow growing, crock-pot-like cooking process that by 2026 would amount to 250 years of contained growth--well on its way to the record of empirical stability held by the Roman Empire of somewhere between 500 and 800 years, depending on which historian one adhered to. Not counting China, of course, which everyone agreed was not included in Western culture.

New senators had all this explained to them in their orientation. The continuation of the country was job one. Representing the people of their state was job two. The politics of Senatorial tenure, who held power inside the Senate all down through the years, had taken some strange twists and turns.

Senator William J. Williamsford had been tutored by his father as to the real job of a senator. After serving as a senator for two terms, his father had accepted the ambassadorship to England. Jay, therefore, had lived for ten years, from age 5 to 15, in London. He had received quite an education during those years both in academics and culture.

He had visited London with his wife and girls twice in the year when the girls were four and six. Jay remembered how England had affected him at that age, and wanted their girls to enjoy the same sights and feelings.

Senatorial seniority was another aspect of consideration. Jay was in his second term with three years to go. There were Senators with less time in the saddle than he had. Janae would inherit his tenure and he was sure that wouldn't sit well with some. Also, there were six women in the Senate. Janae would be expected to caucus with them more often than not. She would be a new female Senator with tenure. This was an odd set of circumstances, that Jay, Janae, Joe and Jennifer would use to promote the advancement of good.

Part of the grooming of Janae to be a working Senator when she arrived for her first day on the job was for Jennifer and Janae to make a tourist trip to Washington, D.C. They would see the Senate offices and Chambers, Jay's house, and other sights that would help her be more comfortable with her surroundings as one of the elite of the nation.

Joe Cornish also recommended a few books on Senate history for Janae to read. Having a working understanding of the history of what you are involved in, affords a better chance of good decision making.

Most important of all was the schedule for the next session of the Senate. Jay had gotten inside information which listed the items to be debated and voted on. The sequence was important.

This would give Jay, Janae, and Jennifer, plus Joe Cornish and Jonathan, a basis for planning and carrying forth an agenda for good in a world where compromise reigned.

The good guys were saddling up.

# 25

Life in Alaska was a little bit different than life in other places, but human nature and the relationships between people were basically the same.

Jack and Gretchen had visited four of the night spots in and around Anchorage both in the afternoon and in the late night/early morning. Over two days they took in the ambiance of two clubs in the afternoon and two different ones at night. Then the next day, they switched so they could see what all four were doing at both times.

It was fun to not be in charge. They could just relax and see how someone else ran things. Knowing how they had run things in Seattle, they were able to see under the veneer and notice what was not supposed to be noticed. They saw differences, but nothing huge or so different that it would cause them to want to look deeper. So they planned to meet with Tom at noon on the fourth day of work to compare how things were going.

The third day they slept in and tidied up the house, did laundry, and did some meal planning and shopping. PC was due to fly in on the evening of the fourth day and they knew she would be a big help with cooking and such. It didn't take long before eating out lost its glamor.

Tom launched his part of the Alaska investigation the morning after they arrived. He found the former governor's huge house and knocked on the front door. It was quite a palace for Alaska.

The former governor was swimming laps in his indoor pool before a late breakfast. Tom was ushered into the pool area and watched as the governor finished his laps. He was actually glad to have some company, so he invited Tom to join him for breakfast.

Tom knew the questions he planned to ask did not deserve this kind of polite treatment, but he decided to partake anyway and get thrown out afterwards. So, as the former governor of Alaska and the Seattle journalist sat down and ate breakfast, introductions and small talk quickly turned to serious questions, as was the journalist's way.

"Governor, I'm writing a story on the election several years ago that saw two important things happen. One, you were elected governor, and two, one of the candidates in the primary died under suspicious circumstances. How are those two things related?"

The former governor stopped chewing at the abruptness of the question, and then continued as he recognized that journalistic nose that he had become used to dealing with in the past. It had just been a while.

"Son, time seems to scab over troubled spots and that's the natural way they get healed." Tom started to respond, but the former governor held up his hand. He had more to say, but it wasn't going to interrupt his breakfast. During the swallowing of his latest bite and the arranging on his fork of his next, he continued, "Now, if there is something infectious under the surface, it will show itself eventually and then it will be dealt with." Out of respect, Tom slowed himself and said nothing. After another bite and some coffee the wisdom continued, "So either you've found some infection, or you're just picking at a scab because you've got nothing else to stick your nose into." He took another big bite and looked up at Tom as if to say 'go ahead, what are you waiting for?'

"Sir, the person who is paying my expenses has a theory. He is mostly interested in proving his theory, not necessarily in digging out the truth, unless they just happen to coincide. My questions are meant to extend this purpose, not to hurt or embarrass you. My employer knows you went out of your way to solve this puzzle, but thinks only you have the answers to questions not even you had thought to ask."

It was an intriguing answer from the young journalist, the former governor thought as he munched, "I have answers... that I don't know I have, to questions I hadn't thought to ask... Hmmmm." At this, the former governor pushed back his plate and pulled his coffee closer. He sat back and pulled out, filled, and lit his pipe, then said, "Go ahead, son, ask your first question."

"Sir, the investigation focused on the death of the candidate, the location where it happened, what the evidence showed, and where it led. We want to focus on before the death. What kind of man was the candidate? Was he careful with what he said or gregarious? Was he a mudslinger or an idea pusher? What do you remember about him that did not fit into the overall facts of the case?" Tom didn't want to be too focused, but wanted to draw out into the open what the former governor knew.

Now the former governor puffed and thought, "Well Tom, you'll have to give me some time. You're right. I haven't given that part a lot of thought. Actually, I do remember one thing. Before the candidate died I remember thinking that it would probably get down to him and I in the general election, and I had to bury the thought that deep down I knew he was a better man for the job than I."

Okay, bingo, Tom thought. This was what he was looking for, "Excellent, sir. Very good. Now what was it, his personality, or his intellect, or his experience? How did you know he was the better man?"

"Please, Tom, call me Roger," Roger looked up from Tom to the maid bringing fresh coffee and took the quick break, as she poured, to think back. "Well, you know, we all check out our competition, as best we can. This guy had no family that we could find, yet he acted like he did. I mean, he wasn't a loner like you might expect." Roger picked up his cup, smelled the hot aroma and then blew on it and sipped. "He was not crude or rude or a mudslinger. My handlers told me to start hitting him hard with mud, but I held off. I figured I could do it in the run up to the general election if I needed to." Tom just about jumped in but held himself back. "I do remember the one time I spoke to him. There were five of us involved in a debate and afterwards we shook hands. I said something like, 'May the best man win,' and he said, 'Time will tell good from bad, right from wrong.' That was the only time I talked with him and I remember not really knowing what he meant by that."

Bingo again. Tom was furiously writing but projecting calm interest, and perhaps a bit of marvel at the wisdom of the former governor. After some more conversation, Tom said, "Sir, uh... Roger, I'm so glad you were available today. This is precisely what I was hoping to hear. Can you remember any other tidbits or things you admired about him?"

"Well, he didn't seem to be concerned about money, like he was well funded...Oh, another thing I remember. He wasn't a longtime resident of Alaska, and I wondered why he was running for governor of Alaska and not Texas, or California, or Florida, or some important state. I mean, I think he could have. I wondered what drew him to Alaska." The former governor was staring across the pool out the steamy window to the lightly falling snow outside. "A man has to have a reason for living in Alaska...I know I didn't want to move up here when I did. But, it kind of grows on you and I'd never want to leave now."

"Roger, you've touched on a very basic question. Why was he in Alaska? I think the answer to that question might unlock this mystery and help solve this investigation. Sir, would it be too much to ask if you would accompany me to the accident site? We could take my car."

"Uh...sure. That wouldn't be a problem. But let's do it tomorrow and I can drive. I do have some appointments today. Would you mind?"

"That works for me, sir. What time shall I come back tomorrow?" Tom rose as he spoke.

"Oh, uh...would eleven o'clock work for you? I think it would be just about right for me."

"That will be fine. Thank you, sir, very much." Tom extended his hand and they shook genuinely. The maid appeared and escorted Tom to the door. She was an older woman, but younger than the former governor.

When Tom drove out the open gate with high hedges on each side, it was snowing. He had checked the weather forecast last night and it said low chance of snow. However, this was Alaska, and the whole state, the people, and yes, the weather, too, seemed to do pretty much whatever they wanted. Tom had rented an all-wheel drive car so he wasn't worried. What did worry, or at least interest him, was how the former governor was spending the rest of his day.

*

The rest of Tom's day was taken up at the local newspaper office, going through their archives. He sifted through as many of the articles on the candidate as he could, from when he first announced his intentions to run for governor until the articles about him petered out after his death. One unusual thing he found was that the candidate had visited Nome, Alaska on the western coast across from Russia. The town had given him a rousing welcome, a key to the city, and a 90% vote in a straw poll. Tom's thought was: why would they like him so much unless he had been there before or made a good impression through business, or philanthropy, or some sort of promise for the future. Tom's best shot at finding the answer to that was to visit Nome like the candidate had. Who knew why politicians did what they did, but it was out of the ordinary, so Tom noticed. He called the airport and purchased a ticket for tomorrow afternoon with a return flight the next day.

After a couple of hours of searching the archives, Tom decided to pay for a copy of all the articles with the candidate's name in it. He went to the front counter and looked for help. A young office worker got up and walked to the counter to help him. After the fashion of Alaskan weather, she gave him a somewhat frosty greeting.

"Hi. My name is Tom. I'm from the Seattle Times. I would like to buy copies of the articles from your paper that have the name Len Lancaster in them. As far back as possible and up to the present." Tom smiled and was pleasant.

The gal sighed and produced a fake smile, "Hi, my name is Tina. That information is on micro-fiche for public viewing. It will take you all day and into tomorrow if you want to make copies. They are one dollar apiece."

Tom produced a look that said he had learned a valuable lesson and was very appreciative for it. Tina reminded him of Claire, back in the Seattle office and he knew just how to handle her. "Oh my gosh, Tina, I'm glad you waited on me." Tom leaned in closer and lowered his voice, "I'm on an expense account, so you and I can both make this easy on ourselves and have my boss pay the bill." He slipped a fifty dollar bill to her and looked into her eyes, "Why don't you push the right buttons on the computer and then get your coat. I'm buying you and me a late lunch and we'll establish a liaison between our two papers."

Tina's eyes softened at the gentleness of Tom's answer. She took the fifty, looked at the clock, then back at Tom, "I'll get that information started, sir, and be right back." Tina spent about thirty seconds at her computer and then whispered to the other girl in the office. The other girl broke into a smile, glanced at Tom, and nodded her head. Tina grabbed her coat and purse and came around the counter.

Tom gestured with his hand toward the door and said as she took the lead, "Since I'm new up here, you'll have to choose a place for lunch."

# 26

With two pilots, two former enemies, three guys who were enjoying the time, and three gals who felt they had the world by the tail, the yacht's cruise north along the California coast was uneventful.

The cop only had his uniform to wear so he felt like he stuck out more than he actually did. At breakfast the next morning, James sat down and tried to comfort him.

"Listen, Archie, your life is going through a big change. A life of fear and shame is being replaced by freedom and peace. Just relax and let the process happen." Archie took a deep breath and looked at James.

"Thank you, sir. That helps. I've...been using off and on for about a year and now...I'm afraid..."

"Yeah, I hear you. Drink lots of water and take aspirin. It will pass. You've got a boat full of friends here." James noticed Nicolus taking a phone call. "You've chosen the right path, just hang in there." Nicolus bounced up and went up to the pilot house. James followed.

The pilot handed Nicolus the binoculars and James looked behind them in the direction Nicolus was looking. Boats. Lots of them.

"Push it," Nicolus instructed the pilot. She did, and the water erupted behind the yacht. But James saw something out of the corner of his eye, in front of the boat. The water was erupting in front of them, and alongside, also. James opened his mouth to speak, just as a jolt shuddered through the whole yacht.

Nicolus dropped his hand with the binoculars and spit out, "What the hell...?" James grabbed on to the wall of the pilot house and happened to see the answer. He put his hand on Nicolus's shoulder and said,

"Whales! Whales, Nicolus!"

The yacht had swayed sideways like a skyscraper in an earthquake. Nicolus looked all around them at the water, "Good God Almighty!" he said. The water around them was filled with whales surfacing and spouting and diving.

"Slow back down!" he yelled. The pilot lady agreed and adjusted the speed. Now everyone on board had finished the short trip from panic to amazement and stood by the rails to watch the pod of humpback whales surrounding them. They seemed to be minding their own business, migrating north along with the yacht.

Nicolus eased a bit, realizing all those boats were probably whale watchers, not law enforcement or bad guys headed for them.

"Okay, let's act normal and enjoy the sights like we are whale watchers, also," his booming voice alerted everyone below and all took his advice. To James he said, "We have to keep an eye on all these boats. One could be bad guys coming after us disguised as tourists."

James passed the word on to Matty, Rolando, and the cop. Nicolus went down and unlocked the safe and retrieved everyone's hand guns and passed them out. He gave the cop's gun to Matty.

Archie saw what was happening and said to Matty, "Give me my gun. I'm on your side."

Matty looked at him with a sort of fatherly expression, "Don't worry. If we have need of them, I'll be giving you your gun."

*

The day played out. A group of whales and a group of boats, and the yacht steadily moving north through them. The yacht had sustained no visible, or so far invisible, damage from the bumping of the whale. The same could not be readily ascertained about the whale.

James called Tony and filled him in on the situation. Tony was at the old club in Seattle, being the base of operations for them, for Alaska, and for San Francisco. He didn't like it much, but was noticing that one guy, getting input from all the operations, got an overall picture that the individual operations did not have. This was important because it gave him wisdom which he had not been looking for, as opposed to power he had formerly worked hard to acquire. 'Hmmm,' he thought, 'this freedom thing was blossoming in more ways than I could have imagined.'

As dusk descended over the ocean, the boats were all headed back to port. The whales had moved to the ocean side of the yacht. Peace returned to this ocean-going family, and to the temporary ocean-going family who were all sitting down to dinner. James, Wallie, Matty, Cindy, Nicolus, Nickolaea, and Rolando who was just enjoying everything and everyone, Archie the cop, and the pilot lady, were being served by the two attendants, who, with the other pilot lady, came with the purchase of the yacht in Rio De Janeiro, and were attending to their duties.

Dinner was enjoyed by all with an increasing amount of stories told by Rolando as he became more acquainted with these new friends. His hard to understand English was fun to listen to. His tales of Paraguay, which were close to unbelievable, had a hint of nostalgia to them, and if not home-sickness, then perhaps just a bit of a fever for the land of his birth.

After dessert and coffee everyone wandered off to bed. With the radar clear and the other pilot lady taking over, Nicolus left instructions for him to be called at the slightest sign of anything out of the ordinary. After one last look around with the binoculars, he collected all the hand guns again and locked them in the safe. Then he took Nickolaea's hand and closed the cabin door behind them. The steady sound of the engine and the ocean air were wonderful sleep inducers.

Overnight they would leave California waters and continue up the beautiful and rugged Oregon Coast. The warm weather and the calm of the ocean would be deteriorating as dawn approached.

*

The late lunch between the two newspaper kids from Seattle and Anchorage was a little flirty, a little bit of business, and a lot of enjoyment. They were each getting something they knew they didn't deserve. She, a fantastic lunch she couldn't afford, with a handsome guy nobody else knew. She enjoyed showing him off to those she recognized. He, the information he needed without working for it, and some lone female companionship that was delightful in that it reminded him of how soon PC would be back in his arms.

When they returned to her office and she gathered his information, Tom extended his hand and smiled, "Thanks, Tina. That was fun."

She gave Tom a flirty smile and placed her hand in his, "You know where to find me." She had put her phone number on the top sheet of the information.

When Tom got back to the house he loaded the information disc Tina had made for him into his computer. It started at the beginning of Len Lancaster's visits to Alaska. Tom realized Len's visits to outlying communities in Alaska began before his candidacy for governor. Tom muddled through, writing tidbits of interesting information down in his notes until his mind's focus began to wander. It was bed time; today was big, tomorrow would be bigger.

In the morning he went through some more articles until it was time to leave for the former governor's house. He packed an overnight bag so he could go straight to the airport afterward.

Tom pulled into the open gated driveway right at eleven o'clock. The former governor was outside the garage warming up his SUV. Tom pulled up alongside and got out.

"Good morning, Tom. Hop in," Roger offered with a smile. Tom did and off they went. They headed southeast around the inlet and onto the Kenai Peninsula, then after a while turned off the main road toward a small town by the water called Hope, Alaska. They drove through the sparsely populated town and continued past vacation-style chalets. Roger pulled into the driveway of one of them and they got out.

Roger opened the front door of his summer cabin and commenced building a fire in the wood stove. As the warmth began to affect the room, Roger found a bottle of Merlot and poured a glass of wine for each of them. Tom was starting to get restless, but decided to wait Roger out. Sitting down in an easy chair in front of the fire with his wine and his pipe going, he began, "I was right here, smoking and drinking a toast to my success, when I heard the news that Len Lancaster had died. I couldn't believe it. The old saying, 'The good, they die young,' kept going through my mind."

Roger took a sip and then got up and poked the fire with one of the tools standing on the floor next to the stove, with his pipe held tightly between his teeth. "My victory seemed more assured, but the feeling of the loss of a friend was strong, and I wasn't sure why. We hadn't been friends."

Roger was back in his chair with his wine, staring into the fire, "The accident happened about five miles further down the main road out there. It was dark and his car hit a moose walking across the road. It happens all the time. Those damn moose need lights on them. Len died, the moose died, but the driver of the car lived. The problem was, the autopsy put the time of death at odds with the time of the accident." Tom looked up at Roger with an inspired question. Roger saw it and continued, "Yeah, me, too. When I heard of the discrepancy I called the county animal disposal office and asked some questions. It turns out the veterinarians do an autopsy of sorts on most road kill to look for disease or anything unusual, and the time of death for the moose was at odds, also."

Tom's jaw was dropping as his mind tried to add this all up. Roger continued after another sip, "The driver's side air bag deployed but the passenger side, where Len rode, didn't. Just a malfunction that nobody could have anticipated. A car drove up minutes later and stopped. Len either wasn't wearing his seatbelt or it malfunctioned, too, and he went through the windshield and actually followed the moose off the side of the car to the ground. A full grown moose's legs are so long they are usually broken and the body hits the windshield and breaks the moose's neck. If it's a direct hit the antlers hang over the side of the car and drag the body off to the side before the car stops. Len's body went with it. It wasn't pretty or easily identifiable."

"But, they were sure it was Len's body?" Tom interjected; his nose was twitching.

Roger looked at him, "Yes...the DNA matched...so they said." Now Roger was thinking back, "...but he had no relatives...so nobody made a big deal of whether it was him or not..." Roger looked at Tom with eyebrows raised. Tom returned an equally puzzled look. Both were engaging in "what if" scenarios and neither knew what to do with them.

Tom was now staring into the fire, "If it wasn't Len Lancaster in that accident, we just blew this investigation wide open." He looked over at Roger.

Roger looked from Tom over to the fire again. He said slowly, "The coroner's office was in an old building. It had a fire in the first year of my governorship. Most everything was lost." They both slowly turned toward each other. Then each finished their wine in one gulp.

"Tom from Seattle, I hope your employer has some deep pockets."

"Yes, he does. And a damn good nose for things that don't add up."

On the ride back to town they talked about what they should do. Tom comforted the older man by saying that his employer would take the reins on this, but would keep the former governor up to speed on what was happening. Back at the house, Tom thanked the former governor for his valuable help. Roger and Tom parted as new lifelong friends who had birthed something together that was important to the whole state of Alaska. And who knew, maybe to the whole country.

# 27

The country didn't know it, but its capital was experiencing a whirlwind tour by its newest senator-to-be. Janae and Jennifer were both giddy like school girls and savvy like operatives noticing everything about their new assignment. What they did not know was that they were being watched by a special unit of the D.C. Police. What the D.C. Police special unit didn't know was that they were being watched by a guy named Jim who worked for a different agency. Joe Cornish had made a call.

*

Tom drove to the airport and found his puddle jumper, which seated ten, including pilot and co-pilot. It was the one flight per day to Nome and two seats were empty. A young boy of part native Alaskan descent and his parents were, Tom learned, returning after a visit to a pediatrician in Anchorage. The boy didn't look well. Otherwise, two businessmen of probably Chinese descent, talking between themselves, rounded out the passengers.

Landing in Nome was an experience. The runway looked like solid snow. The pilots, doing this each day, brought the plane down safely. At the buildings they helped the passengers with their luggage. They seemed to know the small boy well.

Tom checked into the Nome Inn and warmed up by a small wood stove in his room, which was already going. Apparently it was the only heat source because he didn't see a thermostat control for heating. The thermometer outside the window said thirty-two degrees. The slight wind outside had made it feel like thirty-two below zero, but what did Tom know? He was from Seattle.

What Tom did know was exploding in his mind. He sat at the small desk and wrote out his thoughts regarding his interview and trip with the former governor. He stopped to add another chunk of wood to the fire and wondered where the wood came from since he didn't see any trees as he looked out the window. Probably flown in like everything else.

That night Tom went to the biggest restaurant/lounge in Nome. He took his time listening and looking around while he ate. More than half the patrons were Asian. Not only that, most of the scantily clad ladies, who took men by the hand and disappeared upstairs, were Asian. For some reason he thought Chinese. There was a group of obvious workmen huddling together on one side of the room drinking their paychecks. Tom sauntered from the bar over to a table near them. He sipped his beer and wrote on his note pad.

"Hey, who the hell are you?" one of the workers had noticed Tom and was loud, but not meaning to be rude.

Tom looked up and then stood, "Oh, I'm a businessman from Seattle. My boss told me to come up here and find out what Nome needs more of or doesn't have."

"Hell, tell him we need some blondes and red-heads. These Chinese are all the same. We need some different flavors."

Bingo, Tom said under his breath. "How about the food and drink?"

Another guy yelled, "We need a Mexican restaurant here. We got Chinese, and we got plain American. We need Mexican; and where the hell is McDonald's when you need them?"

A different one yelled with raised bottle, "The booze is good, though." Everyone cheered and raised their bottles or glasses and drank.

As Tom sat back down, a lovely Asian woman, very nicely dressed, sat down across the table from him. She brought with her a whiff of perfume and another bottle of what he was drinking. She greeted him with a big smile. Tom took her to be the manager, or owner. He stood and said, "Ma'am, I'm Tom, from Seattle." She extended her hand so Tom shook hands.

"If I may suggest, we could use more workers. Workers who know how to work hard, and play hard." She was dripping with an invitation to adventure.

Tom sat back down, "What does the work involve?"

"The runway is being tripled in length and doubled in width, and the airport buildings are being added on to. The port is being increased and dredged, and new housing and business buildings are going up. Also, a road is being pushed through to the Anchorage area. We need workers; lots of them. Pass the word on, if you have connections." She noticed two of the workers arguing so she rose to leave, "You're cute. Save me a dance later." She calmly walked over and inserted her body between the two potential fighters. That cooled them down right away. As she took both their hands and led them toward the stairway, she nodded to two girls and they followed.

Tom packed up his little bingo game and headed back to his room, a winner. Nome had the feeling of the wild west and he didn't want to step in any trouble. The only other thing he wanted to check out was the local police department. He would do that in the morning. He stuffed the stove full of wood and closed down the dampers. He'd be asleep before the toasty feeling left, and still have coals to add wood to in the morning. This was kind of fun, though he missed PC. She would love this.

Early in the morning, the fire took off again as Tom opened the dampers and threw wood in. No coffee pot. He dressed and went down to the continental breakfast. After loading up a plate full of food and pouring a large cup of coffee, he returned to his room.

A morning call to Joe Cornish proved timely. He said he was thinking about Tom and was about to call him. Tom filled him in and Joe Cornish thought for a moment.

"I'll find an operative who speaks Chinese and likes to work hard and play careful. Good work, Tom."

"Have you talked to PC by chance?" Joe Cornish had already hung up. Oh well, PC was due in tomorrow afternoon. Man, he couldn't wait. This spy stuff had temptations galore. He needed PC's expert assistance in more ways than one.

After breakfast Tom walked to the city offices and asked what kind of government services were in Nome. He was told that the police chief was appointed by the town council, and the sheriff was elected. In last year's election the police chief was elected as sheriff, also. He was Chinese.

Tom's afternoon flight back to Anchorage was uneventful, except the copilot was cracking jokes all the way. The pilots were the same ones who flew him there. Obviously they stayed overnight and flipped a coin as to who would do the flying on the way back and who could drink.

After landing, Tom drove back to the house and continued the process of writing down his experiences and going through more news articles. That evening Jack and Gretchen went out to a movie and Tom watched one at the house. They really didn't want to leave the house unattended, especially with the increasing amount of information they were accumulating.

Tom had the feeling that Alaska was the wild west covered by a layer of snow, and anything could happen if someone wanted it to. What did Alaskan's want that they could be tempted into giving up something else for? Only one thing came to Tom's mind: prosperity. What would they give up that would be valuable to someone else? Again only one thing came to Tom's mind: freedom. The promise of prosperity for the giving up of freedom was an old story that started in the earliest history of mankind.

That trade-off never worked out for the benefit of the ones who did the sacrificing. Tyranny, dictatorship, communism, socialism, whatever it was called, was riches and freedom for a few at the expense of freedom and self-rule for the many.

Tom chose to watch the movie, 'Red Dawn,' the first one, made in the late seventies before he was born. The movie gave him an idea. He went to sleep thinking about it.

By morning Tom was writing again, but this time it was a scenario he couldn't get out of his head. After writing the gist of it down, Tom went back to the computer and looked for the best photograph of Len Lancaster. Then he enlarged and copied it. By the time noon came, he was ready for the meeting with Jack and Gretchen.

They all sat at the kitchen table with chips and salsa dip, and bottles of hard cider. Jack then dialed Joe Cornish who had asked to be included via speaker phone in the discussion of what each had found out. With Joe Cornish listening, Jack asked Gretchen to go first.

"From my perspective the night life up here held no surprises. Drugs, girls, normal stuff. The girls are a larger percent Asian, and the drugs more expensive than in Seattle. The girls I was able to engage were making money, and okay with the way things were being managed. The drugs they used were 'safe,' that is, consistent in purity and availability. Whoever runs these clubs up here knows what they are doing. They like stability and are willing to pay for keeping things that way. Some of these Alaska boys are big, and come to town only once a month or so. I can't imagine what these girls go through sometimes, but it goes with the job. I did not find an underlying opportunity that was being talked about or planned for in any of the clubs."

"Okay, very good, Gretchen. Jack?" Joe Cornish was listening with great interest even though he was still in San Francisco.

"There seems to be a mild building boom in the state. A larger percentage of the guys frequenting the clubs are construction workers. They exchange news of jobs in different towns, what they pay, and what living and working conditions are like. Booze, drugs, and girls are important. Some workers are actually from the lower forty-eight and are sending money home to family while they work up here. A construction boom and a labor shortage favors them. Like Gretchen, no underlying huge opportunity that everyone is talking about. Just a mild boom in building: commercial, industrial, and housing. The workers are happy, Boss."

"Okay, very good, Jack. You both did excellent even though nothing stood out. Things seem to be running smoothly in Alaska. Tom, how about you? Fill us in on everything you've found out, even the things you've talked to me about already."

"Sir, I took time to visit Nome because Len Lancaster visited there before and after he announced his candidacy for governor. Nome has a building boom going that is exploding. The whole town is expanding. Airport, runways, the port, public buildings, housing, everything. I told the hostess at the lounge I visited that I was sent by a businessman from Seattle to see what Nome needed. She was not shy in telling me that they need men to work hard and play hard. I got the idea there was no limit to the amount of workers they could use. The workers want more variety in girls. Ninety percent of the girls are Asian and are busy. The booze and drugs are plentiful, but one guy demanded a Mexican restaurant. The Chinese are expanding their presence in Nome. The police chief and the elected sheriff are the same guy, and he is Chinese. Nome had the flavor of the wild west and my question was, what is coming that the building boom is preparing for? And were Len Lancaster's visits more than political?"

"Excellent, Tom, and excellent questions."

"Sir, I have something bigger than all that."

"Good, Tom, keep going."

"I met with the former governor. He's a good guy. In talking things through, he and I came to the conclusion that whether Len Lancaster died from the accident or was killed was not the right question to ask. The better question would be, where is

Len Lancaster today? I think he is alive, and finding him would be paramount." There was a pause from the speaker phone and from the kitchen.

"Okay, Tom…you've got a whopper hooked. Can you reel him in with some facts?" Tom had not informed Joe Cornish about this.

"The findings of the autopsies on the body of the man and the moose both suggested a time of death other than that of the time of the accident."

"Somebody did an autopsy on the moose?" Jack blurted out.

"It's routine up here. But nobody cared and no relatives were involved. The DNA matched Len Lancaster, but that could have been planted and lied about without consequence if law enforcement had been paid off. That leaves a staged accident resulting in the death of a political candidate where the question was accidental death or murder. That question was never answered, so the case faded away. As did Len Lancaster. I think that was the plan. A high profile death was needed so everyone knew he was dead. What was he involved in that he would need to be dead and out of the picture to accomplish? I think Len Lancaster is in China, either as a subversive working for China planning long range exploitation of Alaska, or as a double agent who is monitoring a Chinese move against Alaska, and is being run by…who?"

"Uh…that is quite a leap, Tom. Do you have a few stepping stones for us?" Joe Cornish didn't know whether to be wildly excited or what.

"I've got two so far, sir. Len Lancaster took Chinese as a foreign language in high school and college. And two, the building that housed the evidence of the death, including the autopsy findings, burned down within a year of the election which the former governor won. Sir, I think he is the only one who has the information we need who has any credibility. I was thinking of taking a life insurance policy out on him."

There was a noticeable pause from Joe Cornish, "Wow… okay,…those would be stepping stones…any other hunches?"

Joe Cornish was actually stunned, but he never let anyone know when that happened.

"Only speculation, from where the circumstances seem to lead. China, with all of its people, needs room to expand. The only route available to them for expansion would be north. They could go through or around Mongolia, which is rich in natural resources, ignore North Korea, then annex eastern Siberia, which at its eastern-most end is only seventy miles from Alaska, across the narrow Bering Strait. Russia did it once before; they used to own Alaska."

"An army the size of China's could hold Alaska. If the construction was already in place to accommodate the Chinese Army, and the invasion was a surprise attack, the U.S. would have to respond. The Chinese, after securing Alaska, would offer the U.S. a compromise that would please no one, but would avoid war. Possibly something that included the reduction of the U. S. national debt to China, which has to be addressed anyway. The U.S. would never sell Alaska to China, but if forced to deal with a take-over, the U.S. would probably consider a compromise to avoid hostilities. The U.S. administration and the U.S. Congress would have a big decision to make no matter which party was in charge. Have we got any operatives in Washington, D.C.?" Tom stopped to catch his breath. He grabbed his bottle of hard cider. An even longer pause was happening.

"Tom...uh...Jack and Gretchen, are you getting this?"

Jack and Gretchen were both stunned and staring at Tom, "Yes, sir," Gretchen inserted, "We...are...this is very interesting and, excuse the understatement, it's world changing."

Joe Cornish's mind was trying to catch up with his excitement, "Okay, boys and girls. Once again a small push into the underbelly of bad-guy-dom results in clues, the importance of which can't readily be measured. Uh...again, well done to you all. Tom...I don't seem to have the words to address your speculation and its potential import. Please...please just keep going and...let me know if you need anything. And yes, I gave PC a hug at the airport this morning. She should be arriving this afternoon. By the way, did you hear that Senator William J. Williamsford, senator from California, has stepped down due to health reasons and appointed Emily J. Halvorson as his replacement for the remaining three years of his term?"

Tom squinted at the question. "Who is Emily J. Halvorson?"

"You're on a roll, Tom. You'll probably figure it out by the time I hang up."

Tom suddenly put two and two together, "Surely you don't mean Janae?" Joe Cornish had already hung up.

Tom, Jack, and Gretchen just looked at each other, and then all three grabbed for their hard cider at the same time.

# 28

That afternoon Tom drove to the airport. PC, of course, looked as cute as ever and less plump. They fell into each other's arms on a waiting bench on the side of the busy hallway. They basically just held onto each other not wanting to make a spectacle. After about five minutes, Tom dug out his phone and called Jack.

"Hey, I got PC. We can't wait, so we're getting a hotel and we'll be back at the house in about twenty hours," Jack understood.

So, they got up, retrieved the luggage, and found an old brick five-story apartment building that had been converted into a plush hotel with only twelve suites. They picked one on the top floor.

They spent their afternoon and evening about the same as when they first met. Loving, talking, sharing about what had happened during their week or so apart, and then loving some more and ordering room service. They collapsed into a wonderful sleep and slept in until breakfast came with a knock on the door. Oh, the wonders of preordered room service. Check-out was at noon, so they took their time showering after breakfast and then headed for the safe house in a lightly falling snow with the sunlight trying to filter through.

That evening the four dined together and talked about what was next on their agenda. Tom acquainted PC with the disc of articles to search through and what to note as she did. He planned to visit more small towns where Len Lancaster had visited. Jack and Gretchen were going to interview as many politicians, business managers and owners, and even church leaders, as possible just to get an overall flavor of what was going on underneath the veneer that was Alaska. Their job was to build a case regarding whether or not to continue with Tom's speculations. PC would man the safe house, cook, clean, and keep Tom in love with her while he was experiencing all the temptations this spying job brought with it.

*

From San Francisco, Joe Cornish arranged the rental of a slip at Shilshole Marina for Rolando's yacht, the *Princess Knight*. It had turned east into the Strait of Juan De Fuca from the ocean and was half a day from Seattle. He was mindful of the people aboard the *Princess Knight* and their potential value to his operation, so he arranged for three men in a power boat with necessary armament to intercept the yacht and ride shotgun until it arrived at its berth. Joe Cornish informed Tony, who called Nicolus, who saw them coming just as he received the call.

As the yacht slowly made its way toward Puget Sound, Rolando was stunned at the rugged beauty of this huge scenic waterway dotted with islands, and surrounded by mountains and trees. Yet, the land had evidence of civilization, from summer cabins to large cities. He was amazed at the light drizzle and the fog which shrouded many of the hilltops. Rolando was not used to this type of weather. The sun was still shining, it was just on the opposite side of the clouds covering Puget Sound. This area would be his home, with his daughter close by, for the remainder of his years.

Matty was antsy to get his feet on solid ground. He sat Archie down and said, "Stay close to me. Be aware of our surroundings and be my bodyguard for now. When we meet Tony, he'll put us to work."

Tony and Millie were planning a welcome home dinner party at the club for the occupants of the yacht. There would be ten from the *Princess Knight*, Jeff and Taylor from the *Cascade Islander A/B*, and four from the club. An invitation was also extended to Pastor Julianna.

Tony had hired a transit bus to transport the ten and their belongings to the old club. At the club they were all given rooms and some time to shower, change, and relax before the celebratory dinner. Matty and Cindy shook hands with Tony, who exclaimed how damn glad he was that they were all on the same side again. Jeff and Taylor called and asked what they could bring. Millie asked if they could swing by and pick up Pastor Julianna. Of course they were glad to, and got directions.

As dinner time approached and everyone wandered into the dining area, Tony began seating them. He and Millie were at one end of the large rectangular table, James and Wallie at the other end. On the side between Millie and Wallie, sat Nicolus, Nickolaea, and Rolando. Then Taylor, Jeff and Pastor Julianna. On the other side between Tony and James, sat Matty and Cindy, Archie the cop, the two pilot ladies, and Alexander and Joni.

When everyone was happily seated, sparkling cider was set in front of them. Tony stood back up and raised his goblet, "Ladies and gentlemen, I welcome you to Tony's Inn, and to our lovely city of Seattle. Most of us here have had a dramatic change of direction in our lives in the past days, weeks, and months. This change is due to the cunning and courage of the man I would like to toast tonight. Joe Cornish. May the Almighty protect him as he continues to charge into the world of bad-guy-dom and offer life or death to people like us. May we conduct ourselves in a manner worthy of his respect."

Everyone drank and dinner was served. Tony asked Pastor Julianna to say a word of grace over the meal, which she was glad to do. During dinner, Wallie whispered to Pastor Julianna. She looked down at Millie, Millie looked over at Cindy and Cindy, seeing Millie looking her way, glanced down at Wallie. Wallie was smiling at her and wiggling her ring finger and pointing to Pastor Julianna. When Cindy moved her gaze to Pastor Julianna, she saw a broad grin and caught the hint. Then Wallie and Cindy excused themselves for five minutes to use the ladies room. When they returned, Cindy was all smiles. Matty looked at her and asked what was up. "You and me," was all she said.

After a wonderful dinner, they all moved to the pool area. Wallie whispered to Tony and then disappeared with Cindy again. Everyone sat on chairs along the wall and a big cake was pushed in on a cart. Matty looked at the cake and leaned over to Archie, "Geez, looks like someone's getting married." Archie was just taking it all in, so different were the last few days for him. Then Tony rose and got everyone's attention.

"It's quickly becoming a tradition at Tony's Inn to have at least one wedding at these special dinners. Tonight we are favored with tradition again. I direct your attention to the door across the pool." As he pointed, the door opened and Wallie stepped out wearing a lovely full-length dress. A moment later Cindy stood by her side adorned in a beautiful wedding gown on loan from Wallie.

Everyone stood up, and with wide eyes Matty looked at Cindy. She was gorgeous, with her hair up and everything perfect. His chest started to tighten. "You crazy girl," Matty muttered as Tony walked toward him. Tony took Matty's arm and said, "Come on, I'll help you through this."

The four met at the end of the pool where Pastor Julianna stood ready.

Pastor Julianna, with Matty's approval, led the couple in vows of commitment to one another. She encouraged them as they started a new life together and blessed them in prayer. Matty and Cindy were married in a moment of serious demeanor. Then the four walked over to the cake.

James looked at Nicolus and they both began to shake their heads. The formality of the cake cutting ceased when Cindy took her piece and mashed it into Matty's face. She and Wallie then ran around to the other side of the pool, unzipped each other's dresses and let them drop to the floor. Clad in two piece swim suits, they jumped into the pool and headed toward the men. To Tony's surprise, Millie dropped her evening dress revealing a swim suit, too, and joined the girls in the pool.

"Oh boy, here we go again. Come on, Matty!" Tony and James began unloading their pockets and removing their shoes and socks. They looked at Matty, "You're going to get all wet, anyway."

Sure enough, the girls started splashing the guys and into the pool went Tony, James, and Matty. Archie, the dirty cop, shook his head and leaned over to Rolando next to him and said, "Boy, did I make the right decision." Rolando didn't quite understand him, but he was enjoying the merriment anyway.

*

The evening slowly melted away and Jeff and Taylor enjoyed being together with friends. Pastor Julianna caught their eyes and they all got ready to leave. Giving hugs all around and appropriate thanks, they offered to take the two lady pilots back to the dock with them. The five left, and on the way to Pastor Julianna's home, Jeff and Taylor broached the subject of marriage with her.

"Let's get together and talk about this. Would you like that?" Pastor Julianna asked. Before dropping her off, they had an appointment all made. Jeff and Taylor returned to Shilshole Marina, and safely saw the lady pilots to their yacht. The whole evening was orchestrated by Almighty God, through one of His adopted sons who wasn't a pastor or a clergyman, but a man who decided to do good and invited others to go along with him on the journey.

# 29

Anchorage, the following week, brought no surprises. Tom knew how to take note of the small steps forward and trust they would add up sooner or later. When the big steps came, good, but he didn't despise the small ones. Jack and Gretchen met with a lot of people in business, politics, and government. They kept a record of who they visited and interviewed, and an outline of their questions and answers. They were all looking for something significant that they could pass on to Joe Cornish, but for now they were in the midst of the investigation, gutting it out, not yet realizing which small details meant something, and which ones didn't.

In the meantime, Joe Cornish had made two decisions. It was time to leave San Francisco, and it was time to show Jonathan what cards he was holding and see which ones he held. He would pick up Jennifer and Janae at the airport, spend one night at the mansion, and then fly to Montana for some frank discussions. Joe Cornish called Joe and asked for some guidance.

"Joe, I have some serious items to talk about with you and Jonathan, and I need to ask Jonathan some direct questions about his operations. I was wondering, would your place in Montana be the best place to discuss sensitive subjects?"

"Yes, please come whenever you can. He is flying in tomorrow night from Singapore. I'll arrange for a time and place for a talk."

Then Joe Cornish went in to see the Senator. He was with his girls in his master bedroom suite which doubled as his office, planning his wedding with Janae. As Joe Cornish entered the Senator said, "Girls, give me and Mr. Cornish about a half hour and then bring us each a sandwich." They jumped up and gave Joe Cornish a hug, then left for the kitchen. Joe Cornish and Jay exchanged pleasantries and then got serious.

"Jay, on the subject of Alaska, what does the Senate have scheduled for discussion, and what dealings do you personally have up there?"

The California senator looked at Joe Cornish. He was healed up enough to know that if he shared his secrets with someone else, he'd be subject to that person's judgment. Yet Joe Cornish had proved to be an exceptional man. Jay ventured in carefully, "As for the Senate, there is a rumor that someone is introducing a bill to sell mineral rights on federal land in Alaska to the Chinese. That's about the strangest proposal that has come before the Senate in a while. I personally have two men in Alaska looking into it."

Now it was Joe Cornish's turn to decide how truthful to be. He liked the senator, so he asked carefully, "Why do you have two guys working in Alaska?"

The Senator pursed his lips and then continued, "I told them to try to find out who is funding the drive to sell the mineral rights and who all is involved."

"Jay, you're looking into this. Is that because you think this bill might grow legs and have a chance to pass?"

The Senator tilted his head back and grabbed hold of the control panel of his super-wheelchair. He put it in motion and traveled around the room, ending up at the window overlooking the outdoor pool. Joe Cornish joined him.

The Senator stared out the window and spoke softly, "Nothing passes through the Senate of the United States without the okay of a few senior senators. Those people control the Senate leaders. It doesn't matter how outlandish a bill is, if it has their approval, it will pass." Then he slowed even more, "If that rumored bill passes, we're in trouble."

Joe Cornish squatted down beside the Senator, "Jay, I'm kind of in the dark here. Why would we be in trouble?"

The Senator paused to gather his thoughts, "Joe, the owners of the underground mineral rights have a legal voice in the use of the land on the surface. Foreign corporations, and in some cases foreign countries, own real estate in the U.S., but never the mineral rights under the real estate except for on rural farms or ranches. If a foreign entity at odds with us, whether China, Russia, or an Islamic Fundamentalist state, should gain the legal rights to our underground mineral rights, they would have legal rights to partial control of what happens above ground, also. It would be a foot in the door that we couldn't close, and a way to conquer us without a shot being fired."

"What possible gain would men in the Senate acquire that would make it worth their while to facilitate our enemies in this regard?"

"Joe, you know that answer as well as I do: a share in the power of a new order, which eventually would come. Our country is already bankrupt, we simply don't recognize it publicly. If someone got scared enough, they would switch allegiance to a stronger player and use their power to facilitate the takeover."

Now Joe Cornish was stunned. He had never been in the way of a tsunami before, but he suddenly felt the panic of being in the path of something that had already been put into motion, and could not be stopped. He breathed deeply and let it out slowly, "Jay, we've got to stop this before it begins."

The Senator looked at Joe Cornish, "That would be nice. I'm just not sure the beginning hasn't already passed us by. This type of thing is like a chess game. It takes time to arrange your pieces in the right places, but once they are in place, checkmate will come no matter what. Joe, why are you questioning me in this matter? Do you have some insight into these things?"

Joe Cornish was immediately candid, "Jay, one of my guys visited Nome. It is tripling its airport, building a brand new port and remaking or adding to everything. He thinks someone is preparing to take over Alaska, and deal with the consequences later."

The Senator rested his chin in his hand, then glanced over at Joe Cornish, "We have some work to do."

Joe Cornish slowly nodded, "I'm traveling to Montana to talk to Jonathan again. I'd take you with me if I thought it wouldn't kill you."

"You'd better go without me. I've got to keep an eye out here. If my network produces anything, I'll keep in touch with you. I trust you to do the same, and Jonathan, also. This thing could be bigger than any one of us is aware of. And it might be coming faster than we think."

Another deep breath, "Okay, I'll be back in three or four days." Joe Cornish turned and walked toward the door.

"Joe!" the Senator yelled over his shoulder. Joe Cornish stopped and looked back, "Thank you for introducing Janae into my life."

Joe Cornish stared at the Senator until he got his super-wheelchair turned around to face him. Then he just broke into a broad smile and nodded, then turned and left.

*

Joe Cornish went to his room and dialed Jennifer, "When are you landing? ...Okay, I'll pick you both up ...Want to go with me to Montana? ...As soon as we drop off Janae back here ...Okay, see you tonight."

Joe Cornish then called Jack and Gretchen, "Jack, I've got some new information. Find out what the Alaskan legislature has in the way of a bill to make legal the selling of mineral rights to foreigners, or some variation of that idea; ...right...okay, I'll be in Montana for four days. Be good."

Then he called Tony, "Tony, I'm leaving San Francisco and flying to Montana, but I want to stop in Seattle and personally update you and everyone there. Would an 8 AM breakfast meeting work for you?"

"Yes, sir. I'd be glad to arrange that. See you in the morning," Tony replied.

Then Joe Cornish buried himself in his thoughts for a few minutes. He had begun to consider what direction to take when he had heard Tom's ideas a week ago. He now decided it was past time for action. He called the safe house in San Diego, "George, I want to initiate a move of all our assets from Southern California to Seattle. Tony's Inn will accommodate everyone until other arrangements can be made. If you could catch a flight up overnight, I need you at a breakfast meeting at 8 AM at Tony's... Thank you, George. Good flying."

Then Joe Cornish began packing: clothing, paperwork, everything he and Jennifer had brought. As it came closer to time to go to the airport and get Jennifer and Janae, Joe Cornish called Jeff.

"Jeff, give me a summary of the yacht and our general profile in Shilshole."

"Sir, everything is as it should be, with the addition of Rolando's yacht. We are holding the fort here and she's ready to sail at a moment's notice."

"Excellent, Jeff. Jennifer and I are coming up for breakfast at Tony's, 8 AM tomorrow morning. I'd like you and Taylor there. Could you both pack a week's worth of things for Jennifer and I, and also for the both of you? That is, if you two would like to come with us to visit Joe and Kandee in Montana. Bring everything with you to breakfast."

"Yes, sir. Consider it done. See you in the morning at Tony's."

Then Joe Cornish called a limo service and arranged to be picked up in half an hour at the Senator's mansion. He made two trips down to the front entryway, lining his luggage up along the wall to wait for his arrival back from the airport. When the limo came, not one second was wasted.

During the trip to the airport, Joe Cornish called the pilot of his jet and informed him of his need to be in Seattle for an 8 AM meeting. The pilot told him he would begin preparations immediately, and that wheels up would have to be at 6 AM in order to get him to Seattle and to his meeting on time. Joe thanked him and then called his FBI Seattle Office for an update on things there. After his secretary updated him, he asked her to begin a computer account labeled Alaska Rescue. He needed her to book one hundred random flights from Seattle to Anchorage over the next two weeks. This was all under the unsolved case of the Alaskan candidate's death.

The limo waited while Joe Cornish went into the airport to retrieve his wife and Janae. They briefly embraced, but Joe Cornish kept them moving with one gal on each arm. The limo driver helped load the luggage and away they went back to the mansion.

"Janae, we're leaving for at least a week. Are you comfortable being alone with the Senator and his girls?"

"Yes, sir, in fact I'm uncomfortable now when I'm not around them. Is there anything I should know?"

"Well, the investigation in Alaska is looming large. The repercussions might be worldwide. The focus will be on the administration and the Congress of the United States. My dear, you and my dear Jennifer might be the only obstacles between bad guy success and bad guy defeat. I'm sure you girls can handle it."

"Oh, no problem. I thought maybe something important was going on," Janae was looking at Jennifer with a smile.

"Well," Joe Cornish broke into a smile, "I think Jay and the girls have been planning your wedding."

"I know, I've been on the phone with them a lot. Joe and Jennifer, they really are becoming my family. I'm not sure how I could be happier. I owe you two a great deal of thanks," Joe and Jennifer just beamed.

At the mansion they unloaded Janae's luggage and then loaded their belongings in the hallway. Then the three went to greet the girls and the Senator. Janae was enveloped in the love of a father and two girls who were overjoyed with the prospect of adding a fourth member to their family. Joe and Jennifer were sent off with kisses and hugs.

At the airport Joe Cornish directed the driver to the hangar housing his jet. The driver was handsomely paid and the pilot was not surprised to see them.

"We'll just spend the night on board. Just pretend we're not here," Joe Cornish had the utmost confidence that the pilot would have the plane ready without making a sound.

"Oh..." Jennifer said, "the old 'room-behind-the-office-in-the-back-of-the-plane-that-turns-into-a-bedroom' trick. I think I fell for that once before."

"Yes, and you fell so beautifully that time, I thought I would try it again."

"As usual, your planning is impeccable."

"Yes, and this Alaska thing is going to take every bit of expertise we can muster, with help from Jonathan and the Senator."

And so, for the rest of the night they got caught up with news and other things that even old married couples do occasionally. And they enjoyed themselves immensely.

# 30

The fog was rolling in, lending the Golden Gate Bridge the illusion of floating in the clouds. It was 5 AM and Joe and Jennifer Cornish were up, dressed, and had their bed made. The coffee pot was brewing and the pilot had the engines humming. Joe Cornish told the pilot he could take off whenever he was ready to, so by 5:20 AM they were in the air. They left the fog and rose into the sunny blue sky.

The hour and a half flying time revealed the beauty of the northern west coast of the United States. The Cascade Range showcased one mountain in northern California, one mountain in northern Oregon, and four mountains in Washington State, not to mention numerous lower peaks. As Puget Sound and Seattle came into view, the rugged mountain range on the Olympic Peninsula sparkled brilliantly to the west. The Olympic Mountains broke up the storms coming in from the Pacific Ocean, while the Cascade Range walled Puget Sound on the east and squeezed most of the rain out of the clouds before they got into eastern Washington. The huge valley between the ranges, made up of streams, rivers and bays, islands and peninsulas, farmlands and forestlands, cities and highways, was mostly green and mostly wet. That explains why one of the country's best writer/philosophers of yesteryear had quipped, "The mildest winter I have ever spent, was summer on Puget Sound."

The view from the air made Joe Cornish nostalgic. If a foreign entity was going to force itself on Alaska, then British Columbia and Washington State might fall like dominoes. No. He would not let that happen. He would see, even if that attempt was inevitable, that it would fail.

*

Jennifer could see the look in Joe's eyes as they began the descent into Seattle. The two talked of the year ahead--a year of separation. Jennifer would be in California and Washington, D.C. as Chief of Staff to Janae who would be completing Jay's term as one of California's two senators. Joe would be directing a herd of assets, directing them to where they would do the most good. Joe was an exceptional planner and his ability to execute those plans was not far behind.

As they were landing, Joe Cornish called one of his men who guarded the yacht and dock area at Shilshole. He explained that Jeff and Taylor would be with them out of state for a week, so he and his men would have responsibility for his yacht and the two on either side, as well.

Then Joe Cornish called Tony and mentioned that he had invited George from San Diego and Jeff and Taylor to have breakfast also, and they all might show up early. Tony replied, "We're ready, Boss. Come as soon as you can."

Next he called his FBI office again. He knew it was early; he only wanted to leave a message.

"Hi, Carla. George from San Diego is visiting. I'm sending him to you this afternoon so you can help him book flights from San Diego to Seattle for him and his men. George is a good man, Carla. Make sure he gets whatever he needs. Thanks."

Then he looked over at Jennifer, "will you try to get ahold of your cousin, Jim? I want to know what he knows about the current operations his organization has going in Alaska. Are they aware of what we are aware of?" She nodded.

Then he called for a taxi to meet them at the hangar at Boeing Field. The weather at touchdown was dry, with the sun peeking through the patchy overcast. Joe Cornish left instructions with the pilot to be ready for a noon flight to Montana. When their taxi came, Joe and Jennifer exited the plane and entered their ride. Off they went to Tony's Inn, each with a cell phone to their ear.

"Tony, we're on the ground and heading your way. I want to talk to you alone first, and then meet Matty. Can you arrange that?"

"Yes, sir. We're ready and waiting for you."

Then Joe Cornish called Joe in Montana, "Joe, our plan is to leave Seattle at noon, which will get us to you around three, your time. That will give us some time together with you and Kandee before Jonathan touches down. Am I right? By the way, we're bringing Jeff and Taylor with us."

"Sounds perfect. We'll schedule dinner at five and some dessert for later with Jonathan and Sharon. What else can I do?"

"Buy some warm clothes!" Joe Cornish hung up. Jennifer did, too.

"I had to leave a message," she said. They both looked at each other and smiled. It meant Jim was busy, and that was a bit of optimism for Joe Cornish.

*

As the taxi pulled up to the curb of the old club, Joe and Jennifer noticed a new sign: Tony's Inn. Another cab was in front of them and George from San Diego was getting out of it. Joe Cornish paid for both cabs and greeted George. His left hand held on to Jennifer and his right shook hands with George.

George recognized Jennifer as Joe Cornish introduced her. She didn't recognize George. Then Tony came out the front door of the Inn and embraced Joe and Jennifer in one big bear hug. Joe introduced Tony to George. George recognized Tony. Tony didn't recognize George.

Behind Tony came Jeff and Taylor, already there. James, Wallie, and Millie rounded out the welcoming committee. Soon there was a family reunion of sorts on the sidewalk in front of Tony's Inn. So Tony announced, "Come on. Everyone inside, breakfast's cooking."

Joe Cornish handed Jennifer off to Taylor and Jeff and followed Tony into his office. James, Wallie, and Millie tended to the guests and saw them into the dining area for glasses of orange juice.

Joe Cornish walked straight to the biggest window. He took a deep breath and let it out slowly. Tony followed him in. Joe turned and met Tony's eyes, "I need your help more than you or I could have imagined. In this next year, I want you to consider yourself free to call me with questions, answers, advice or needs, whenever you deem it necessary. I need you to be my base of operations here in this building. Someone besides me has to be aware of everything that I have going. I want that to be you. I want you to upgrade this facility with the latest electronics for communications, defense, and intel. We need electronics that don't depend on any outside source, and communications that cannot be taken out in the first phases of an attack. Defense, meaning this facility will be the fort that holds back the enemy's offense. A conventional attack or a missile attack will not compromise this fort and its importance. Covert intel will have its base and main reporting here, with many agents sent out into the field from this location. The field is north of here--Alaska, Canada, and northern Washington State. I will be mostly in the field, but will be in touch daily. Your expertise in this endeavor will make or break my plans. You will be the strongest link, and the one the enemy will come after the hardest. Our best asset is surprise. We are new to this game that has already been put into play. We will stay covert as long as we can while we plan and execute our play. Tony, I'm budgeting ten million dollars for upgrading this facility."

Tony's jaw dropped, "Our enemy must mean serious business."

"Tony, I don't want to be caught underestimating the enemy's resolve or ability. I am so very pleased to have you here working with me. Let's go have breakfast. I've got more to tell."

"Let me get Matty first."

"Oh, yes. Thank you, Tony."

Tony went to the door and motioned Matty in. Joe Cornish extended his hand and introduced himself.

"Matty, from our brief conversations, I am relieved and glad to have you on our side. I've lined up Tony with more work than he can handle. I hope you can be a huge help to him on my payroll. If all this is going too fast and you need time to catch up with all that has happened, I can make that happen. Congratulations, by the way. I heard you have recently gotten married."

"Sir, meeting you is my pleasure. I would like to take my bride away for a few days, but I'm in all the way. Please sign me up for the toughest job you need done."

Joe Cornish was impressed, "Tony…I like your friends. Matty, how does a Montana ranch for a few days sound? I happen to be going there myself when breakfast is over, with my bride, Jeff and Taylor. Would you and your bride care to join us?"

Matty looked at Tony who was nodding his head. "Yes, thank you. We'll be ready when you are." Matty opened the door and went looking for Cindy.

Tony and Joe followed and joined in the conversations in progress as everyone was sitting down around the big rectangular table.

Joe Cornish asked for permission and led the group in thanks to Almighty God for the food and the pleasures of the extended family they all comprised. He asked for God's continued care and providence in their lives. Then breakfast was served.

After about two bites, Joe Cornish stood up, "Please enjoy this delicious breakfast as I make some announcements. What I have to say might scare you, so I want you to keep one thing constantly on your mind. We are all on the winning side!" Joe Cornish let that sink in as he slowly engaged his coffee cup.

Then he continued, "I am so glad I have you all on my team. Your expertise in the coming year, as we work in the arena of the Almighty's undeserved favor, will see a victorious conclusion to a war that has begun and is continuing under everyone's radar, in a controlled and steady march toward changing the ownership of some of the fifty states comprising the United States of America."

Tony glanced at the remote electronics pad by his plate to make sure the recording gear was getting this. In the near future, the United States could have less than fifty states?

"We have intel that suggests our enemy's strength is time, organization and daring. Those three factors used in a controlled and steady march cannot be stopped, and will result in a worldwide change of land ownership that will unbalance the economic status quo. The super-power status of the United States will be diminished and the attacking entity will gain that sole distinction."

"We do not have a play against their time, their organization, or against their daring. We are in a chess game where one player has its pieces almost perfectly placed so checkmate will come quickly and with unseen finality. Our play will be to disrupt the controlled steadiness of their offense. It's like a football game where one team has a relentless offense and a solid defense. The only chance to avoid defeat is to cause that team to make a mistake or two that can quickly be exploited. Good organization, and exceptional daring on their part cannot stop mistakes from happening. They can only minimize the consequences. Our exploitation and advance planning of those mistakes will stop the juggernaut."

Joe Cornish noticed Tony pouring him fresh hot coffee, so he paused to partake. Then he continued, "Ladies and gentlemen of the underdog team, I give you this pledge: We will not lose this game."

Joe lifted up his cup and so did everyone else. They all drank coffee to the idea that an underdog team can and has won, on any given day or in any game, no matter what the odds are. It happens every once in a while, and Joe Cornish knew this was one of those times. His courage was based on the knowledge that good is greater than bad, if only a person would believe it and proceed accordingly.

Now Joe Cornish shifted into second gear, "Tony is going to upgrade this facility to the status of a fort." He looked at Tony. "I'd like to quarter agents here in the rooms of your Inn as they come and go from assignments." Tony nodded. Then Joe Cornish looked at George, "George, I want you to move all our assets in Southern California to here, with the idea that our men and women will be sent north on missions. I know some have families and can't come. Just do what comes effortlessly. I'm not twisting any arms. And speaking of arms, George, add all our armaments from down south to Tony's cache here."

Then Joe Cornish looked at Nicolus. "Nicolus, my plan is to send you and Nickolaea, and Rolando if he wants to go with you, up to Anchorage on Rolando's yacht. I need you as a rover to oversee agents up there, including protection for Tom, PC, Jack and Gretchen. We have a house rented indefinitely up there and that would be your base, unless you are more comfortable on the yacht, or find something else. I will stay in touch with you, but you stay in touch with Tony, too. If this is agreeable to you and if Tony can spare you, you could leave whenever you like. In fact, pick a marina in Anchorage and rent two slips. I'm thinking I'll be up there enough to have my yacht there, also."

"Yes, sir. We can leave today. Sir, when I look for the enemy, who do I look for?" Nicolus wanted to be sure of details. Recognizing the enemy was top of the list.

"The enemy could employ a variety of people, but our intel says it's the Chinese who are running things. Check with Tom when you get up there. If Tom's speculation is correct, he knows more than I do."

"Also, Nicolus, let me address the other side of that question: our assets and allies up there. Alaska is the flashpoint. We're checking with Jennifer's cousin, Jim. His organization may or may not be aware of what we are aware of, and they might have agents there you might run into, also. As far as I know, the FBI guys up there know nothing. Senator William Williamsford has two men working in Alaska that I know of. Also, I'm leaving for Montana when I leave here this morning. I am going to have a 'lay your cards on the table' talk with Jonathan. I'm almost sure he is involved up in Alaska and he might have assets in China already in place. By the way, the way this plot was uncovered was through investigating an unsolved death many years ago of a political candidate. Tom thinks this man is still alive and in China helping them, or is a double agent for us keeping tabs on them. I'm thinking he is one of Jonathan's men or perhaps one of Jim's guys, or maybe he really is dead. I'm not sure yet. Tom faxed his picture, so I have copies of it. If we could find this guy, a lot of questions would be answered."

Nickolaea had her hand on Nicolus's leg as they sat at the table. She could feel Nicolus's body fill up with excitement and desire to do good and add to the Joe Cornish underdog express.

Joe Cornish went on to encourage Alexander and Joni to enjoy hosting the men and women transitioning through Tony's Inn. Their kindness and attentiveness would be important to people who were being sent into harm's way up north.

Everyone seemed to have an abundance of work to do and it was work that produced good results. Good itself produced the work, and everyone had the feeling they were on the right side.

Joe Cornish ended breakfast with a history lesson. "The history of war across this world of ours follows a pattern: organization based on good planning wins the war, whether waged by good people or bad. The side bringing justice to the conflict rather than tyranny, has an intangible favor about them, that through hard work and time, prevails. We are on the side of justice. God keep each one of us until we see each other again."

The breakfast meeting was a success. Everyone got the direction they were to go in and Joe Cornish provided the access to funding that would mobilize the various aspects of his army.

*

Joe and Jennifer gathered Matty and Cindy and loaded them into the SUV which Jeff and Taylor brought from the marina. Their drive to Boeing Field took twenty minutes in a drizzling rain.

With the six people and their luggage on board the jet entered Pacific Northwest airspace and headed east over the Cascade Mountains. The travelers went across the rolling hills of eastern Washington and into Idaho, up over the Rocky Mountains, and down the other side into central Montana. Though they descended towards Billings, Montana, they landed at the ranch up in the hills above the Big Horn River. The sun was shining as they touched down.

Joe and Kandee drove out to the hangar in a small bus; they hopped out and warmly greeted everyone, as Joe Cornish introduced Matty and Cindy. Once they arrived at the ranch house, they were shown to their quarters. Kandee then invited Cindy to go see the horses and maybe take a ride.

After they were settled, Joe motioned for the men to join him in the library of the ranch house. Everyone helped himself to something to drink from the refrigerator and sat in a semi-circle facing a huge fireplace.

Joe Cornish spoke first as he was expected to do, "Joe, I don't know what you know about what's going on in Alaska, so let me brief you. Forgive me if I assume you don't know something you do."

"You are forgiven. Now please continue, because I don't know what you are talking about," Joe replied honestly.

"I sent Jack, Gretchen, and Tom to Alaska to try to get somewhere on a case regarding the unsolved death of a political candidate that's been on my desk. I've been playing with it off and on for years. I had a hunch, so I sent them up. Their speculations, based on what they found, point to China annexing eastern Russia and crossing over to take Alaska. Then, having secured Alaska, they would bargain with the U.S. using the national debt to China to get an agreement for legal transfer of the ownership of Alaska. Either way, if an agreement is reached or not, they would use the Hitler tactic of breaking the agreement and moving into British Columbia and down into Washington State, forcing further agreements and breaking them as soon as they are inked. The U.S. would not wage war on their own territory, as many of its own people would be in harm's way, either accidentally or on purpose. The Chinese Army has enough men and resources to keep going as far and as long as they want."

Joe held up his hand. He was surprised to have this kind of speculation from Joe Cornish. "Whoa, ...does this story carry any proof?"

Joe Cornish sighed, "No, Joe, it doesn't. But if someone yells 'tsunami', I'm going to move, not wait till I see it myself. If this scenario is coming, it will not be able to be stopped unless a plan and an operation is already in place and active when the first warning comes. I am playing this like this speculation is the first warning. I hope to God I'm wrong. But if the first warning is here and I'm still blinking my eyes, we're behind already. And I refuse to be behind. That's why we're here."

Joe was nodding his head, seeing the situation more clearly.

Joe Cornish continued, "My sense is, Jonathan either knows something about all this but doesn't know he knows it. Or, he knows more about it than me, the U.S. Government, and maybe the Chinese, too. I need to find out what he knows and put it together with what I know, then work together with him and Senator Williamsford to go on offense covertly. That's where you come in."

"Okay, what's my job?" Joe was one of Joe Cornish's first picks when he needed people to stand with him in a fight where the odds were long.

"I need you to handle Canada. With Jonathan's okay, I want to send you and Kandee to Vancouver, British Columbia, to meet with my counterpart at the Royal Canadian Mounted Police, William Buckingham. Bill loves to stir up a hornet's nest if the cause is right. I want you to keep on the Canadians until every piece of armament bigger than a peashooter is along their western border." Joe Cornish pulled out a file from his briefcase and gave it to Joe.

Joe nodded and took the file, his homework.

Next Joe Cornish addressed Jeff, "Jeff, you and Taylor will pretty much work with Jennifer and I when we are together. When it's time for Jennifer to leave, I want her to have Taylor with her. Jeff, I'd like you to go with her, too. I'll be swamped here and she will be, too, in Washington, D.C. I'm asking you to guard her, Taylor, and Janae with your life. You be the guy who looks around while they are focusing on their jobs." Joe Cornish handed Jeff an even bigger file than Joe had.

Jeff took it and realized Joe Cornish had not given him this kind of responsibility before.

"I want you to meet with Jennifer's cousin, Jim; he's in an intelligence agency, I think. He'll be keeping an eye on you all, too."

Now, Joe Cornish looked at Matty, "Matty, you and Cindy's job over the next few days is to kick back and relax. But while you do that, I want you to help me think. I need to put operatives in Alaska. There is a construction boom so many of them can go in as workers. The cop you brought with you…tell me his name again."

"Archie. He was a San Diego Police Department cop, and dirty. He was on my payroll," Matty explained.

"Okay. You know him. Could we put him in the Anchorage or even the Nome police department? He worked both sides for you; could he handle himself as a cop yet be our eyes and ears? This would be huge for us."

Matty thought and quickly warmed to the idea, "Yeah. Yeah, he could. He was smart enough to bail and come with me. Now, you give him an important job to do, that no one else can do, a job for good, and he will excel in it."

"Good. Will you talk to him about it? I'll see what can be done about placement up there."

"What else?" Matty wanted to go to work and accomplish something.

"I'll be thinking about that this week. You think about it, too. This first phase is gathering intel, so we need a lot of undercover people looking and listening. Matty, if this thing ever becomes a reality, and we find ourselves in the middle of an armed aggression, the skills that gave you a reputation in the bad guy community will be a big asset to us. Only this time, there will be no guilt or shame. You will be doing it for good, not evil. You used to hurt and kill good guys for your boss's benefit. Could you hurt or kill bad guys for the benefit of our country?"

A slow smile crept across Matty's face. He had always hardened himself to the atrocities he had done in the past. They had earned him respect and honor amongst the people he had looked up to. But to torture or kill bad guys who were killers themselves in order to advance civilization instead of undermine it, was a thought he had never had before. "Yes, sir. I can."

Joe Cornish saw the change. It was the first time in conversations with Matty that he had called him "sir". In the bad guy world, respect came from performance. In the good guy world, respect came as someone stood up for an idea--an idea that helped people be free, not enslave them for someone else's benefit. Working for good brought its own reward of respect and honor without effort. Joe Cornish loved it, "Very good, Matty. Keep thinking along these lines as you enjoy some relaxation. Talk to me anytime, ...questions, ideas, advice."

Joe Cornish then looked at the wall clock, "An hour before dinner. I'm going to take a nap."

Joe headed for the kitchen and dining area to oversee preparations. Matty and Jeff took a walk around the ranch to get the taste of Montana.

As Joe Cornish laid his head down on the pillow in his room, he thought of the revelations he might get from meeting with Jonathan tonight. The peace in his mind and the joy in his heart allowed him to fall asleep very soon after.

# Part Four

## 1

When Joe Cornish opened his eyes, his wife was hovering over him. Jennifer Cornish had come into their room at the Montana ranch and quietly sat on the bed. She had bent over and brushed her brown hair across his face. His eyes opened to her smile which told him how happy she was. She bent over again, nibbled on his earlobe and whispered, "Dinner is ready."

Joe Cornish quickly recovered from his short nap and remembered the importance of his visit to Jonathan's ranch up in the mountains above the Big Horn River. The world was about to have the shock of the century and he figured Jonathan might know more about it than he did.

In the past twenty-four hours, Joe Cornish had rallied his cadre of covert operatives and bad guys turned good guys (as long as they stayed in his custody), toward the field of battle, Alaska. The aggressor in this situation seemed to be the Chinese. He was readying his troops without any proof of his speculations. Jonathan, he was sure, would fill in some of the blanks with real time intel and an up to date history of what was going on.

He rose up off the bed and into his wife's arms. Five minutes later they were entering the dining area of the ranch house. Waiting for them were Joe, his best operative, and Kandee, his wife, Matty and Cindy, his latest bad guy turned good guy acquisitions, and Jeff and Taylor, his and Jennifer's attendants. The eight enjoyed their dinner and each other's company.

Joe and Kandee told of their trip with Jonathan and Sharon to the Great Wall of China, where they witnessed the two giving themselves to each other in marriage. Jonathan and Sharon were the newest newlyweds, but now Joe and Kandee were informed of Matty's and Cindy's marriage only a few days ago. They all slowly turned and looked at Jeff and Taylor who were slightly blushing. Jeff explained, "We have an appointment to talk with Pastor Julianna when we get back." Taylor held up a finger with an engagement ring on it. Whoops and hollers erupted. Joe Cornish raised his glass of merlot and nodded at them with a smile, "The very, very best to you two dearly loved ones." Before a tear had a chance to escape from his eye, they all heard the increasing sound of a business jet coming down for a landing on the ranch runway. Jonathan and Sharon were back from a trip to Singapore.

Joe and Kandee, had recently been invited to call his brother's ranch their home also. He stood and invited all to the library for dessert with Jonathan and Sharon. As they all took seats in the cozy room, in walked the arriving couple with hugs and kisses for everyone. When Jonathan and Sharon came to Matty and Cindy, they expressed their delight in meeting them and told them how glad they were to have them there. They were invited to stay as long as they could.

Cindy was on the verge of tears to have people treat her so nicely. Not two weeks ago, Matty was a bad guy assassin who was himself a target, and so full of fear that he basically stayed drunk all the time. Cindy was a prostitute who had been Matty's girl for five years. She had been at the very end of her rope when her friends, James and Wallie, had come to her rescue with a weird offer for them both. Change from bad to good. Skip prison or indictment and join the ranks of do-gooders. These do-gooders, however, were serious and sincere, and the most loving people she had ever met.

Cindy thanked Sharon as best she could. Sharon had recently resigned as a deputy sheriff of Kitsap County, Washington State, to marry Jonathan and help him plan, organize, and run his covert forty-man army. Doing good was not a hobby or sideline for these people, it was serious business.

Joe Cornish, who was in charge of Special Investigations for the FBI Seattle Office, and had past ties with the CIA, sat down on a sofa and lead a prayer of thanks to the Almighty for the favor He was showing him through these dear and valuable friends. Jennifer poured two mugs of coffee and sat down beside her husband. She would soon be on her way to Washington, D.C. as Chief of Staff to the newly appointed senator, Emily J. Halvorson. Janae, as they knew her, was one of their operatives and soon to be wife of widower William J. Williamsford, one of California's two senators. He was recovering from injuries he had received during an earthquake and had appointed Janae to fill out his remaining three years in the Senate of the United States. Good works were just waiting to be done and Joe and Jennifer loved it.

As all were seated, dessert was served. Presently, Jonathan stood and raised his mug of coffee. Chatting stopped and he said, "May we always be at least one step ahead of the bad guys," they all agreed and took sips.

Joe Cornish marveled at Jonathan's choice of words. Perhaps he did know about this Alaska/Chinese business and was a step ahead of them.

After dessert and a pleasant time together, Jonathan's eyes met Joe Cornish's and they rose to go somewhere to talk. At the door they both gestured for the other men to come with them. The girls would find something to do, Sharon would see to that. The five walked to the front door and out into the dusky evening, and strolled up the runway to the hangar. The jet Jonathan had just arrived in and the one Joe Cornish and the rest had come in earlier that day, sat side by side. They entered Joe's jet since Jonathan's was still being cleaned. They sat back with a glass of wine in comfortable seats facing each other. Now was the time to put all their cards on the table.

Joe Cornish went first, "Jonathan, I want you to know what I've found out, and I'd like to know what you know. I recently sent

Tom, Jack, and Gretchen, who you know, to Alaska to check into a hunch I had on some leads to a very old unsolved case involving the death of Len Lancaster, a political candidate for governor of Alaska many years ago. In following leads they became aware of a possible move of aggression by the Chinese Army into Eastern Russia, Alaska and on down through British Columbia and into Washington State, if left unstopped. Senator Williamsford said he knows of a bill coming up for debate this year that would facilitate that kind of change of ownership of U.S. property to foreign powers. He sees it as inevitable. I see it as a first warning of a political tsunami, and am actively getting all my assets ready to defend us, and/or attack an aggressive force."

Continuing, Joe Cornish said, "Please tell me you know all about this, and you've got it all under control, and it's okay for me to go back to my Seattle Office where the glass pane in the door rattles when I go in and out."

Jonathan smiled, got up, filled his wine glass, then settled into his seat again. The jet was plugged into the hangar power source and was comfortably warm in the increasingly chilly night.

"Len Lancaster was the first man I recruited after my father died and I inherited his forty man army. Len was smart, but his biggest asset was his ability to speak Chinese and at least understand the different dialects. I deemed this as vital in view of China's economic growth. We planned and executed Len's death so he could effectively serve in my army without strings from his past life getting in the way. He had not married and had few relatives. He was perfect. He still is perfect."

"Len is now undercover in China as a missionary, and has been since his 'death.' When Sharon and I were married last month in China, with Joe and Kandee as witnesses, we stayed with missionary friends of Sharon's. They did the honors at our wedding. When I mentioned Len's missionary name, they said they had heard of him. I said I knew him, so we all got together one night. I had a chance to talk with him that night and he confirmed many of the messages he had been sending with increasingly urgent warnings."

Jonathan paused and looked at his brother, Joe, whose jaw had dropped at this revelation since he had been present that evening. Jonathan smiled at him and continued, "I was able that night to confirm with him that he is not ready to come in. He wants to stay and be a watchman for us as the Chinese attempt their expansion. Since our first message about this plan, five years ago, we've inserted ten operatives into Chinese society and government."

"Two years ago, the son of the chairman of the Communist party in China died. We actually recruited him, faked his death, and he runs all our operatives in China from our office in Oakland, California."

"This idea of expansion through Russia and into Alaska was a pet idea of Mao's. After his death in 1976, it waned. Not until the turn of the century did we get a hint that an expansionist theme was resurrecting as part of the freeing up of the economy. We know there are generals in the Chinese army who mean to bring this about. They're just waiting till their man gets into power, but even if he doesn't, they will still make their move. Len recruited a woman who is a prostitute for one of the generals. Through her he has a direct line into their plans."

Joe Cornish raised his hand, "Are the Chinese funding the construction in Nome and other towns in Alaska?"

"Yes and no. The government funds the army. The army is funding the construction of ports, airports, barracks, and such in various towns in eastern Russia and Alaska, but the money can't be traced back to the Chinese government. The government, of course, knows, but is using the army as camouflage. The army doesn't care. They have the strength, the men, the armaments, and the desire. They are going to do this, and Len Lancaster can only tell us when. He can't stop them.

Joe Cornish raised his hand again, "What is Len's motivation to stay undercover so long? What is in it for him?"

"Sharon's parents were missionaries in China. They were imprisoned for a while when she was young. Len Lancaster's parents were also missionaries, and were imprisoned at the same time. One of the generals who is hot to go into Alaska was prison administrator where his parents were held. They were brutally killed, and he personally had a hand in it. If that general doesn't die of natural causes, his death will be caused by Len Lancaster's hands around his neck, squeezing the life out of him. That is why he is doing this. He can't be bought and he won't quit."

Joe Cornish raised his hand again, "Do we have names and pictures of the generals who are going to execute this expansion?"

Before Jonathan could answer, Joe shot his hand up, "Whoa... something's missing. The photo of Len Lancaster in the file you gave me does not resemble the man that I remember meeting one night in China." Joe had the photo out and handed it to Jonathan to see.

Jonathan sort of smiled. "Yeah, we had his appearance altered some, and he's older now."

Joe Cornish jumped in, "Okay, I'll let everyone know the picture I sent out is not accurate. Do you have a recent picture?"

"No, I..." Jonathan replied, then stopped himself and looked at Joe. "Kandee was taking pictures of us at the wedding and during our stay with Sharon's friends. She might..."

Joe whipped out his phone and had Kandee on the line in less than five seconds. "Hey gorgeous, there is something important on those pictures of the wedding in China and the trip. Can we go through them? ...Okay. Thanks, sweetheart."

Then Jonathan continued, "Yes, we have pictures and names of the generals involved. They are important. If we take out the leader, we shortcut the war." Jonathan looked at Joe. Something was still wrong, "Brother, you've got something; speak."

Joe was looking at the file picture of Len Lancaster and remembering the man he had casually met on that evening in China, "Yeah, something doesn't add up, but I don't know what it is."

Joe Cornish recognized the intuition that was working in Joe. He had seen that look before. He didn't say anything, knowing that Joe was processing.

Jonathan spoke, "Well, the only importance of having a picture of Len Lancaster is so we can recognize him if he wants to come in or meet some place."

Joe looked at Joe Cornish with a serious look. Their eyes locked. Joe Cornish just waited.

Joe then spoke slowly, "I...didn't..." he shook his head, obviously trying to put words to his thoughts. "I didn't like the guy," he finally got it out. Joe looked up at Joe Cornish and then at Jonathan.

Joe Cornish knew something important when he heard it.

Jonathan looked at his brother, "What do you mean?"

Joe tried to clarify his feelings. "I don't know. Len Lancaster and the guy I casually met in China are not the same guy."

Jonathan just stared at him.

Joe Cornish knew something monumental was breaking. He dug out his phone and dialed Anchorage, "Tom, have you and PC finished going through those articles about Len Lancaster? ...Excellent. I need you to put your notes together and give me an in-depth profile on everything about him, especially small details. Tom, your work on this is proving timely and vital. I'm sending my jet tomorrow to pick you and PC up. Come here to Montana and present your findings to us ....Perfect. Thank you, Tom," Joe Cornish hung up and looked at Jeff.

"Jeff, I'd like you to ride up tomorrow on the jet and just acquaint yourself with the house and things up there. I'll want a report on your observations on our base there and Anchorage in general. See how Jack and Gretchen are doing, too."

Matty jumped in, "Sir, the next few days will be great for Cindy--women to be around and beautiful surroundings, but I'll be going nuts by tomorrow. I need to be back in the game. I hate sitting on the sidelines. I could help Jeff check out Alaska. That is, I'm willing to. Very willing."

Joe Cornish smiled and loved Matty all the more. He looked at Jeff. No problem there. "Yes, Matty. I would appreciate your insight, too. Go ahead."

Jonathan still felt like he was being left behind, "Okay, I'm not sure where we are going with this, but should we go look at Kandee's pictures?"

Joe Cornish nodded his head, "Yes. Let's rejoin the girls."

# 2

Tony was busy. He had a ten million dollar line of credit and needed to put it to work ASAP. He had Millie, James, and Wallie in his office, talking.

"Joe Cornish mentioned a defense for this facility that could stop a missile. That would mean one of those Gatling guns that shoot so many bullets at an incoming missile that it destroys it in the air before it hits its target."

James countered, "Yeah, how much does that cost?"

Tony continued, "Yeah. Find out. What else?"

Archie, the dirty cop, was keeping an eye out in the lobby while Alexander and Joni were overseeing the operation of Tony's Inn. A gentleman walked in the front door without luggage, looked around, and ambled up to the front desk.

Alexander addressed him, "Sir, may I help you?"

"Yes, thank you," the man was impeccably dressed, like a professor of English at a college or something. He had that harmless look. "I'm looking for a former classmate of mine. He had always said he'd be glad to help me out with my research if I needed him. I talked with him the other day and he was eager to meet with me and gave me this address. Matty said to just walk in and ask for him. Am I at the right place?"

Alexander stared at him. Then said, "Matty…yes…yes, you are in the right place. Let me go find him. Please sit down over here. Joni, could you bring this gentleman some coffee? Thanks, honey. I won't be long."

Alexander walked toward Tony's office. He glanced at Archie and pulled his finger across his throat and then kept going. To Archie that meant be on alert. Alexander knocked softly and entered. Tony looked up and asked, "What's up?"

Alexander was turning white, "There's a guy out front, just walked in, wants to see Matty. He acted like he didn't recognize me, but I think I've seen him before. He's bad news and good at it."

Tony stood, opened his drawer and got out five handguns. He gave one to everyone in the room, "Is Archie armed?"

"Yes, he is," Alexander was telling himself to breathe.

"Okay. I'll probably recognize him, too, and he me. This is what we'll do. Alexander go back out, whisper to Archie to check outside. See what kind of back up this guy has. Tell the guy Matty is on his way. I'll walk out and we'll see what he does. Girls, go to the back entrance and make sure it's secure. Lead with your gun. James, sit at my desk. If he plays along, I'll tell him Matty's in here. I'll open the door for him and then get behind him. Something's bound to happen by then. Okay, let's go."

Alexander went back to the lobby, connected with Archie, then sat down across from the professor. Joni had brought coffee and was talking with him.

"Matty's on his way. He wasn't sure what I was talking about, but you know Matty. His head could be anywhere. Tell me about your research." Alexander could hear the door opening behind him and watched as the professor's expression changed. His eyes widened as Tony came up. Alexander had his hand in his jacket pocket on a gun.

"Henry. It's been a while. What's up?" Tony recognized him and called him by his real name. As the professor rose, his hand went to unbutton his jacket button.

Tony stood behind Alexander and aimed a gun at the visitor's head. "Easy, Henry, you don't need to unbutton your jacket. Just relax and talk to me," Alexander stayed seated so as not to get in the line of fire where the man could use him as a shield. Archie was positioned at the front door. Joni followed Alexander's example and stayed put.

"Henry, surely you recognize me. What? Do I look like a ghost or something?"

"Jason...you're supposed to be dead," the professor was a bit shocked.

"Yeah, Henry, and I can't have you tell everyone that I'm not, can I? Let's go talk in my office."

"Jason, you know me; we've worked together before. This is just business. I've got no beef with you. You want to live without anybody knowing about it? I'm good with that."

"Easy, Henry. Let Alexander take your guns so we can talk. We're just going to talk."

The professor held out his arms and Alexander reached out and unbuttoned his jacket. He reached in and took the gun from the shoulder holster, checked down his leg and took the ankle gun out. He put them on the chair behind him and reached around back of the man and took a gun from his back waistband. Something was also hooked to the back of the shoulder holster straps, "He's got something in the small of his back."

"Henry, if you don't mind," Tony was still leveling the gun right at the professor's head, but far enough away that he wasn't vulnerable to a quick attack before he could fire. Alexander collected the three guns and backed off. Joni moved with him. The professor carefully took off his jacket and slowly took off his shoulder holster. The back had a sheath with two long double-bladed knives. The professor let them drop to the floor.

"Henry ...are you going to make me ask if that's all?" Tony asked.

The professor smiled and lifted his hands up and said, "You've got me."

"Okay," Tony said. "Let's go into my office. I've got an inn to run here, you know. I'm sure Matty will be glad to see you."

The professor turned serious, "Jason, if Matty knows I came for him, he'll kill me with his bare hands, if you let him."

"Henry, I give you my word. I won't let Matty kill you. I'll keep that particular pleasure for myself. Now relax and do what I say and you'll be fine. We're heading for that door over there. You first."

The professor moved slowly. He did not want to go in and face Matty unarmed. At the door he stopped, "Jason, don't let Matty kill me!"

"Easy, Henry, just walk through the door. What? My word means nothing to you anymore?" Being a bad guy was still easy for Tony. He was a little bit surprised.

The professor turned the knob and pushed the door open all the way, telling him no one was behind it. He saw Matty sitting at the desk. But it wasn't Matty, it was...James, Jason's sidekick. Henry froze, but Tony pushed him on into the room. Henry quickly glanced all around but saw no one. He knew he could not beat Matty in a fair fight. But he had other options if he could just see Matty coming.

Tony closed the door. He pointed to a chair by the desk where James was seated and motioned for Henry to sit. Henry put his hands down and deftly unbuckled his belt as he sat down.

"James."

"Henry."

Tony stood behind Henry. He laid the barrel of the gun on Henry's shoulder aimed at the base of his neck, "Henry, I'm going straight. I'm on the side of law enforcement now. James and Matty are with me. I don't mean to threaten you, but I'm only going to say this once. Come work with me and James and Matty and Nicolus. You remember Nicolus don't you?"

A physical shudder went through Henry's body. He couldn't help it. He was more afraid of Nicolus than of Matty.

"We're working together with an FBI guy for good instead of bad. You can join us without ever looking back, or I'll let you go and you can go back to all the good times and good friends you've got. Except you'll have to go back without Matty. What will your boss say then?"

Henry's hands were resting on his lap close to his belt. He would stand up, slip his belt off, losing the leather cover. The flexible blade would flick across James's throat and then back to Tony whose gun aim would be off as he rose up. Okay, on the count of three. One,...

The door opened and Nicolus walked in and went straight up to Tony. He motioned Tony back and put a knife blade right against Henry's throat, "James, please back away." Nicolus asked and James bounced out of the chair at the desk and moved over to Tony. "Okay, Henry, make your play."

"Nicolus, we disarmed him. He's clean."

"No, sir. I remember Henry. He has a belt with a flexible blade in it." Nicolus grabbed the back of Henry's shirt and pushed him over so his chest laid on his knees, his hands caught between them. "Now, we are going to stand up, Henry, and I'm going to start sawing my way into your jugular vein, just so you know my intentions. Pull the belt and drop it to the floor. Move too fast, and I plunge my knife into your voice box. Move too slow, and the jugular will already be cut."

Nicolus' knife was already drawing blood as he lifted Henry to a standing position. Henry drew his belt through the loops and flung it away from himself. Nicolus had him up against himself with an arm around his forehead. Henry's throat was bleeding but he said, "Okay, okay, I'm clean, I give up. Jason, help me! Please, don't kill me. I want to live. I'll do anything!"

Nicolus did not loosen his grip, but eased up on the knife, "Unbutton your pants and let them drop." Henry did. His pants landed on the floor around his ankles. "Unbutton your shirt and take it off." Nicolus still had him around the head and again applied pressure to his throat. Henry opened his shirt and let it fall. Now he was in his underwear.

Suddenly Tony could see something under his undershirt, "He's transmitting! James, go check the girls." Tony raised his voice. "Alexander!" Alexander burst in. "We might be under attack. You and Archie take the front."

"Nicolus," Nickolaea's calm, low voice told Nicolus she was there.

"Nickolaea, come around in front of us. Bend down and take off this man's shoes and pants."

Nickolaea carefully did and tossed his shoes over toward Tony. She slipped his pants over his feet, but something was in his pants. She reached in and retrieved two knives sewn into the inside of his pants. Tony just stared as he picked up Henry's shoes.

"Be careful, the heels have explosives in them," Now Nicolus addressed Nickolaea again. "Take one of the knives and cut down the length of his undershirt."

Nickolaea did and peeled off the undershirt. The wires and a little transmitter were taped to his body. Nickolaea pulled the tape and the wires off. On the back of the transmitter was taped a razor blade. She handed the thing to Tony.

"For the love of God, Henry. You lied to me twice about being clean. I'm done with you. I can't trust you."

Now Henry was standing in his socks and undershorts.

Nicolus continued, "We're not done yet," Nicolus still had him by the head with the knife to his throat. The nick was still bleeding and trickling onto Henry's chest. Nicolus nodded to Nickolaea and she wiggled his shorts down from around his waist, to his ankles. He was obviously reacting to Nickolaea being so close to him, but underneath, taped to the inside of his upper leg was a small caliber gun. She took care of business and tossed the small gun to Tony. He was wide-eyed. Nicolus had saved his life again.

Nickolaea then picked up one leg and took off a sock. His ankle was wrapped. Under the wrap was a small knife. Nickolaea took the other sock off and stood back.

"Your chance at freedom is gone, Henry. What will it be, a slow death or prison?" Nicolus whispered loudly.

"Let me join you," Nicolus eased his grip to let Henry make his play. Henry's legs buckled and he dropped out of Nicolus's arm. He grabbed Nicolus's knife hand, twisting it enough to slash Nicolus's arm. Nickolaea plunged the knife she had into Henry's leg, making him lose his balance. Then Nickolaea pulled the knife out of Henry's leg and plunged it into his back. She pulled it out again and rolled Henry onto his back. Nickolaea struck hard, pinning Henry's hand to the floor through his palm with her knife. Then she reached for the knife Nicolus had dropped, and stretched out Henry's other hand and did the same.

Henry lay on his back, both hands pinned to the floor. His right lung was filling with blood and his left leg was bleeding. His eyes were glassy. Nickolaea reached for the other knife from Henry's pants, and turned his head to the side. She plunged the knife into the man's temple. Then she got up and attended to her husband.

# 3

The five men were walking back to the ranch house when Joe Cornish took a phone call from Tony. He quit walking as Tony began describing the attempted attack. The others stopped, too, and gathered around him. Joe Cornish put the call on speaker phone as Tony went through the whole tale. When Tony threw in the fact that Henry was after Matty, Matty yelled into the phone, "Save him for me! I'll take care of him. Don't trust him!"

Tony explained, "Sorry. Nickolaea killed him. She stabbed him five times with three different knives. Nicolus saved all our lives and got stabbed in the arm for his efforts. Matty, he had a wire and transmitter taped to himself. We checked outside; no one around. Does that ring a bell with you?"

"Yes, damn it. Henry carries an explosive device with him. Probably in his shoe. He always has a partner. If Henry is killed, the partner waits till cops and firemen or medics come, and then he blows them up, too. Henry gets his revenge even if he's dead."

"Oh, for the love of God! I'll call you back," Tony hung up. All five could imagine what scrambling was happening now back at Tony's Inn.

Matty reminisced, "That Henry, he always had the last laugh, always. Even after his death he had revenge planned. Shoot! Give me that damn phone again!"

Joe Cornish handed the phone to Matty. He dialed Tony back.

"What?"

"Tony, check to see if he left a coat or umbrella anywhere, anything he walked in with, briefcase, pipe in his mouth, hat. They all got explosives in them. There also are explosives in the car he drove, and he probably planted them around the outside of the building. But don't call the cops or firemen. His partner is just waiting for those types to show. His explosives aren't complicated or booby trapped, there's just lots of them so one or two won't get found."

"Okay, thanks Matty," Tony hung up.

"Who is this guy?" Joe Cornish asked.

Matty answered, "Just a Texas guy who loved to plan and have the last laugh. I've used him before. He's effective and deadly. Shoot! I forgot. He's probably got explosives in his behind! They got to get rid of the body, too."

Joe Cornish handed Matty the phone again.

*

The girls inside the ranch house had chocolate chip cookies and hot cider ready. The five men came in all with a scared, wondering look about them.

Sharon noticed right away, "What's wrong, honey?"

"Nothing here. An attack at Seattle. Everyone's okay. Just a weird set of circumstances. Something smells good." Everybody helped themselves.

Kandee had the pictures spread all over the table. Sharon started explaining where they all were taken. Joe quickly searched and found two from the night the visiting missionary was there and he looked closely at them. Then he got out his file picture of Len Lancaster again. The guys were all focusing on Joe. Finally he said, "I don't know. I just remember not liking the guy I met that night, that's all."

Joe Cornish posed a question to Jonathan, "Jonathan, was there ever a time after Len Lancaster was in place in China that he disappeared or didn't check in when he was supposed to?"

Jonathan was thinking, "Yeah..., yeah, actually there was. Uh...about five years after he was in place, he dropped off our radar for six months. When he showed up again he was apologetic. Said he fell in love with a girl and they ran away for a while. It made sense. He's been good ever since."

"No changes since then?"

"Not that I've noticed," But Joe Cornish could see Jonathan was thinking. After some more discussion and enjoying themselves over dessert, Joe Cornish spoke again.

"Okay, how about we meet again after breakfast in the morning? Girls, can you possibly do without us between breakfast and lunch?"

Jennifer answered for the girls, "Kandee, Cindy, and Taylor are going horseback riding. Sharon and I would like to sit in, if we may."

"Very good, we could use your input. Jonathan, you have our sincere thanks for a wonderful day. It's my bed time. Goodnight one and all," Joe Cornish shook hands with Jonathan as he spoke, grabbed Jennifer's hand and off to bed they went. Planning, and prayers were their nighttime routine. Before midnight all were in bed, and the Montana "Big Sky" night did its thing, whether anyone noticed it or not.

*

As the sun was peeking over the eastern horizon, Joe Cornish was already up, walking, thinking, planning, and making phone calls as needed. After breakfast, Jeff and Matty boarded the jet and headed for Alaska. While Kandee, Cindy, and Taylor went riding, Joe and Jennifer Cornish, Jonathan, Sharon, and Joe sat down to talk.

Jonathan started, "Okay, I think we left off on the thought that Len Lancaster could have been compromised during his absence. If that's true, either he got bought off and became a double agent against us, or Len could be languishing in a prison somewhere and a look-alike in his place. How do we find out?"

Joe Cornish entered the conversation, "I'd like to get Tom's report on Len Lancaster first. I think it might shed some light. Our intel from China is either good or not good. If it's not good, the result of the deception would be a faster incursion into Alaska, not a delayed one. If that's the case, we won't be ready for them. They will gain a foothold in Nome, and shortly afterward control the whole state. We must plan even if our plans become obsolete. The question is this: How can we disrupt an organized and well-planned-out invasion enough to make them vulnerable? That's what we have to find out."

The five looked at each other. Joe decided to jump in, "The Chinese are smart. Hitler was bold and aggressive, but what if the Chinese are smart enough to have the invasion be a non-event?"

Sharon was having a similar thought so she said, "Yeah. Keep going with that thought."

So Joe did, "Well, if they own Nome, they could ship in war supplies as business or construction stuff and truck it all across the state. Nobody would know it was anything but business. They could..."

Sharon finished his thought, "...already be doing it."

Now the look on all five faces became more serious. Joe Cornish reached for his phone. He dialed the jet.

"Jeff, put me on speaker phone so Matty can hear. Matty, see if armaments are already being shipped into Nome and distributed across Alaska disguised as business or construction supplies, or something other than war supplies. This thing might have already started and we aren't seeing it. Jeff, tell Jack and Gretchen I'm sending Nicolus up on his father-in-law's yacht. I'm going to load it with weapons for the base house. You help them get the stuff to the house and get it ready for an attack. Stay there until I send Tom back," Joe Cornish hung up, then dialed Tony.

"Tony, have Nicolus load the yacht with any and all armaments you have. We need to prepare the base house in Anchorage for an attack. You'll be getting resupplied from George in southern California. Can you catch Nicolus before he leaves?"

"Yes, sir. We're on it," Tony knew what to do.

Joe Cornish ended the call and spoke, "My God, we are just sitting here speculating, and while we speculate, this thing could already be done and in place," he spoke what everyone was thinking.

Now Jennifer had a thought, "The press. They can't have the whole press in their pocket. Publicity would force their hand before they were ready, assuming they're not ready yet. That could slow them down and make them vulnerable."

"Okay, excellent," Joe Cornish grabbed his phone again. "Tom, stay up there, and send PC and Gretchen down here with the information on Len Lancaster. Jeff and Matty are in the air, headed your way already. Help Matty see if the invasion has already started under cover of business or construction supplies. If that's the case, start work on a story that includes all your speculation and if we find evidence, we'll run the story as our first offensive play. If it works, we'll keep running with it until they shut the press down. That will get worldwide attention. Know any press people up there?"

"Yes, sir, I believe I do. I'm on it," Joe Cornish hung up. Tom was sort of happy to get PC out of Alaska even though he would miss her terribly. If this thing began, flights might get cancelled, permanently. Now what was that girl's name at the Anchorage newspaper?

Joe Cornish was as pleased as could be with the caliber of critical thinking his group had produced. He decided to throw in a light touch, "Well, at the rate we're going, we might have this solved and the world saved by lunchtime."

# 4

"Okay," Jonathan said, sort of to get the floor. Everyone had chuckled at the optimistic comment of Joe Cornish and took advantage of the break to use the bathroom and refill their coffee cups. "When we get this intel from Alaska, if it somehow leans toward Len Lancaster being held somewhere with an imposter in his place, I want to have the ball already rolling."

"Yes," Sharon said. She was on the same wave length.

Jonathan wasn't sure what Sharon had in mind, but he kept going, "I have ten other people in China. I'll put them on alert and put together an extraction plan so they will be ready at a moment's notice in case we locate him."

Sharon added to it, "And I'll go visit my missionary friends again. I can trust them and we'll find out from a different angle what we can. Remember, I speak Chinese."

Jonathan looked at her like someone had just stolen his favorite toy, "You can't go alone..."

"I'll bring Kandee with me."

Now Joe had the same feeling as Jonathan.

Jonathan continued, "I'll go with you; we stick together."

"Honey, if China is the aggressor, and you are in China stopping them, they would concentrate on catching you. You'd be worth one hundred Len Lancaster's to them. They'd use you as part of the bargaining to gain legal ownership of Alaska." Sharon was smart, serious, and ready to do her part. It was the sheriff in her.

Joe tried to help his brother, carefully, "I need Kandee in Canada."

"Then I'll bring Jennifer."

Joe Cornish entered the debate, cautiously, "Jennifer will be swamped in California and Washington, D.C."

"Then I'll bring Gretchen, or Cindy, or Taylor. See, it's best if I just go alone. I'll be covert with a good cover. I just got married there, now I'm back visiting my dear missionary friends. If they check my past, they'll find my folks were missionaries in China when I was young and lived there for years. I'm just visiting the beautiful country I grew up in. We visited and got married on the Wall. This really is a great cover." Now Sharon was starting to smile, "I'm shocked you three didn't think of this first."

Joe and Jennifer Cornish just smiled at each other. Jonathan rolled his eyes and turned to Joe, who had that 'I surrender' look.

"Well," Jonathan said, "there goes the honeymoon period."

"Yeah," Joe added, "you should have married down, not up."

Then all five laughed out loud, knowing how perfect Jonathan and Sharon were for each other and how in love they were.

A few moments later, Joe Cornish turned serious again, "Okay, let's summarize. We are going to find out if this invasion has already started. If it has, we will attack through the press as a first shot."

"As fast as we can, we are placing covert operatives in as many areas of Alaska and China as possible for intel and ultimately action."

"We are planning for assassinations of the leaders of the Chinese Army if indeed it becomes a full-on aggressive violent invasion."

"Also, we will work with the opposition in the Senate of the United States to oppose the okay of foreign powers to own mineral rights on Federal Lands. And we will help the opposition in the Alaska Legislature to oppose the same ideas."

"We are building a defensive stance in Seattle and Anchorage capable of standing and being a strong foothold in the face of an attack."

"Also, we are going to find out what the current status of Len Lancaster is and deal with it accordingly."

"And while we are at it, how did this guy, Henry, know how and where to find Matty, and who hired him? Because I think we should send a message back to whoever hired him."

Everyone was wide-eyed and looking at Joe Cornish. He paused for some coffee.

Hot out of the pot, the perfect amount of creamer, stirred, just the right color. Mmm. Joe Cornish carefully lifted the mug to see what was on the outside. Hmm? The mug had a picture of two Asian children huddled together, and said 'Pray for Mongolia.' As he lowered the mug, he turned his gaze to Jonathan.

# 5

Len Lancaster's altered appearance had made him look more Asian than American. It had served him well as a covert operative. At least for five years anyway. Then it had caused the train wreck in his life.

Her name was Qui Ling, and she was something else. Her humbleness, her soft beauty, and her intelligence, got him. Len had loved and admired women in his past, but never had he fallen in love. He fell hard.

Qui Ling had grown up under the tutelage of her father. He was Chinese Army Intelligence. She had been trained as an Army Intelligence operative and was assigned the job of compromising enemies of the state. She had performed with excellence, despite a yearning for freedom which she kept secret from her father. When she was introduced into the life of one of China's enemies, she saw a chance for freedom. And even more secretly than that, she fell in love. Secrets carried a death penalty in China.

Qui Ling was tasked with seducing a Chinese/American missionary and causing him to run away with her. She did this quite successfully to the pleasure of her father. Her mark was interrogated until a look-alike was confident he could be Len Lancaster. When the imposter showed up again, he claimed to have fallen in love with the woman Len Lancaster had been seen with. Now the relationship was over and he was back, full of apologies.

Qui Ling was reassigned, but bided her time until the real Len Lancaster could free himself and meet her at a prearranged place on a Thursday at noon. Each Thursday she showed up and finally, one Thursday he did, too. He had bided his time as a good prisoner, and when his oversight relaxed, he successfully made his move. When they finally met up again, Qui Ling had given birth, to his child. She was the cutest little Asian/American girl. Len Lancaster had named her Rogette, after a man he had admired.

The three had escaped China, but moved slowly with a low profile. They headed northwest dressed as peasants and finally crossed into Mongolia. Len Lancaster knew his only route back to the west was through a free country. Mongolia had shed Communism only fifteen or so years earlier and was experimenting with democracy. With the right paperwork they could fly out of Mongolia.

Traveling on horseback with a tent, they arrived safely in the inland country. Once in Mongolia they quickened their pace and secured rides up to Ulaanbaatar, the capital city. There they rented an apartment and lived as middle class workers even though Len had plenty of money. Len Lancaster began looking around the city to see if there was anyone he knew, maybe someone from the forty-man army, or maybe a CIA agent. He was looking for someone he could reveal himself to and possibly get help from with leaving the country. On a Sunday afternoon he hit pay dirt.

*

Pastor Christopher from the Puget Sound area of Washington State was visiting Mongolia and helping Christian pastors with encouragement and direction. These young pastors coveted older, wiser men and kept Pastor Christopher busy whenever he visited.

Len Lancaster, Qui Ling and Rogette visited the church where Pastor Christopher was preaching and they invited him out to lunch after the service. However, Pastor Christopher was having lunch with three pastors and their families, so he invited this trio to join them even though no one seemed to know them. After a busy afternoon, Pastor Christopher finally had some time to talk with this family, the husband of which was obviously Asian/American.

In the course of talking, Pastor Christopher mentioned he had been in Air Force Intelligence a long time ago and this gave Len Lancaster the opening he needed.

"Eighteen months ago, I was serving as an undercover intelligence operative when I got caught, interrogated and imprisoned. I escaped with the help of my wife and have made it this far with my family. I need to get back to the U.S., but need an invitation from someone from there to speed the paperwork involving my passport, and the lack of a passport for my wife and daughter. Once in the U.S. I can reestablish contact with my handlers with less fear of being found and kidnapped or killed than I can here." Pastor Christopher could see this man was seriously looking for help.

"Give me a name, someone who can vouch for you, and I will be glad to help you," Pastor Christopher found himself liking this father.

"A former governor of Alaska will recognize the name 'Len Lancaster' and will tell you I died mysteriously while running against him for the governorship many years ago. My handlers faked the accident and my death as a cover for me to go covert into China. Ask him what we said to each other after one of the debates. We shook hands and he said 'May the best man win.' I said, 'Only time will tell who is right and who is wrong.' Hopefully he will remember what we both said."

"I will do that," Pastor Christopher said, "in the meantime, do you need protection?"

Len Lancaster handed the pastor a card with their apartment address on it. "This is where we are staying. We've had no problems yet."

"Okay, I'm planning on leaving Mongolia in two days. As soon as I make contact with the former governor to my satisfaction, we'll go together and buy tickets for you three and go through customs." Pastor Christopher was ready to escort this family to freedom if their story checked out.

The next day Pastor Christopher connected by phone with the former governor and confirmed what he needed to know without letting on that Len Lancaster was alive. The following day they finalized the paper work to get the family on board the same flight as Pastor Christopher and in his custody. As the 767 was safely in the air and out over the ocean, Pastor Christopher shared an experience with Len Lancaster and his wife and child.

"The reason I'm over here at all is a gentleman from our church died. On his death bed he said he left a large amount of money to the church to use as missionary funds. 'Go bring the good news to those who are hungry to hear, and help whoever you can.' Those were his exact words. I do believe I am fulfilling his request even now."

# 6

Mongolia. Joe Cornish was looking at his coffee mug. Eyeing Jonathan he asked, "Do you have operatives in Mongolia?"

Jonathan thought for a moment, "No, not specifically. Generally, I have acquaintances and friends who live or visit there for missionary or business purposes, and some who do both. I got that mug from a pastor friend that helps pastors in Mongolia, and he also has an eye for business."

"Mongolia is democratic, is it not?" Joe Cornish asked.

"Yes, for about fifteen years, oh...it's probably closer to twenty now," answered Jonathan, "It's surrounded by Communists." Jonathan's phone made an unusual noise. He stood and excused himself, "That is an alarm that signals I have a call on my satellite phone. Please excuse me for a couple minutes."

Joe Cornish's mind was tracking like a bloodhound. Jennifer could see Mongolia had captured her husband's attention. Joe noticed it, too.

Joe Cornish was talking more to himself than not, "One democratic country surrounded by Communists. Anybody in that area that was not a Communist who found himself in trouble would go to Mongolia for help. If Len Lancaster was replaced by an imposter and is imprisoned somewhere, we now know where he would go if he escaped. The question is then, how apt is he to escape? Again we need Tom's analysis, or Jonathan's knowledge."

Joe added, "We need someone in Mongolia ASAP."

Sharon jumped in, "Hey, I'm going to China; I could visit Mongolia."

Joe Cornish continued, "Although a democratic country, what could Mongolia provide, help-wise, besides some protection? The government would not want to step into an international incident. If you were on the run, leaving the area would be easiest from a democratic country. How many ways are there to go from Mongolia to another democratic country without stepping on Communist soil?" Everyone was following and they all said, "Just flying," at the same time.

Jonathan then emerged from his office. He had a stunned look and Sharon bounced up and into his arms, "What is it, honey?"

Jonathan's face changed slightly toward a smile. He stood at the table, "My pastor friend just called from Seattle. He just returned from Mongolia. He asked if the name 'Len Lancaster' meant anything to me. I told him he was the subject of numerous meetings I've been involved with in the last twenty-four hours."

"Pastor Christopher told me he has in tow: Len Lancaster, his Chinese wife, and their young daughter. They all just landed in Seattle. He's asking me what to do with them."

Everyone was stunned. Joe Cornish had his phone to his ear, "Tony, what's your security situation?"

"We're back to normal, sir. We know we found all the bombs because we apprehended the partner and he pushed the button before we got control of him. The only thing that blew was Henry's body, which we had in a dumpster."

Joe Cornish was shaking his head in amazement but continued, "Tony, we have a VIP family that just showed up at Sea-Tac. They escaped Communist China and are probably under a death threat. I need them safe and sound at Tony's Inn until we figure out what to do with them." Jonathan handed Joe Cornish a note. "You will…find them in the custody of a Pastor Christopher in a room at the airport called…believe it or not…the Air Force Security Lounge. He is a Chinese/American named Len Lancaster, his Chinese wife, and their daughter. There is no known imminent danger, but you know what to do. This guy is way past valuable. And Tony, take ten thousand cash and pass it on to the Pastor for his trouble. He really did us a timely favor."

"I'm on it boss, no worries. I'll keep you posted," Tony hung up, as had Joe Cornish who already had Tom's number dialed in.

"Tom, change of plans again. Leave Gretchen up there, and join PC on the flight south. However, I want you to connect with Tony when you land. Tom, we were just handed Len Lancaster in the flesh from Mongolia. He's at Sea-Tac in protective custody as we speak. Tony will have him at the Inn by the time you get there. Plan on spending the night at the Inn, then you and PC escort them here to Montana tomorrow."

"My God," was all Tom could say.

"Jonathan said Len works for him, so he's a professional, but they are probably exhausted. Ask questions, but don't probe too hard; he'll want to debrief here with Jonathan, and you and I can be in on that. Have Tony make sure they have new clothes and whatever they need."

"Yes, sir. See you tomorrow," Tom couldn't even imagine what things Len Lancaster would have to say.

*

Tom was a man of action. He would keep his phone on, but he wasn't going to sit around and wait for the jet. He grabbed PC away from her computer and headed for the Anchorage newspaper. As soon as he saw the girl he had taken to lunch, he remembered her name. Tina. She bounced up as soon as she saw Tom at the counter.

"Hi, hey, you didn't tell me you are the guy writing all those cool stories for the Seattle Times. I hope I was helpful..." she paused because PC was standing with Tom, "I mean the information I gave you, did it help?"

"Hi, Tina! Yes, you were great. I have my assistant here pouring over it and I wanted her to meet you!" PC didn't say anything until Tom kicked her lightly in the leg behind their backs.

"Yes. Tina. You really helped us out. Tom's perspective has changed since you and he..."

Tom quickly ended that line of thought, "Well, we need your help again. We want to be able to add a story to your paper, exclusively. We are working on it now and at the right time we want to run it. Who here at the paper should we talk to?"

"Oh, just me. I'll take care of you. I can get that done. You tell me the day before you want it run and I'll see that it gets in. Front page if you want."

"Tina, if you get the story on the front page, I'll add your name along with mine in the byline."

Now she smiled from ear to ear. You could see she wanted to jump and pump her fist, "Wow, no worries. I can get my editor to insert something, and a story with your name and mine would prove my value. Just let me know, Tom. I'll get it done," she gave him her number again and smiled at PC.

"Thanks, Tina. We'll be in touch," Tom took PC by the arm and breezed out the door.

"Oh, she's real cute. I bet she and her editor see eye to eye on insertions..."

"Tina's fitting right into our master plan. Come on, baby. We've got a story to write."

As soon as Tom and PC got back to the car, he drove and dictated. PC took notes. At the house they continued. By the time the doorbell rang they had the story filled out and on the computer. PC went to grab their luggage as Tom answered the door.

As they approached the house, Jeff and Matty noticed the new security lights were working. At the door, Jeff made introductions.

"Hey, Tom, we landed a half hour ago. The plane is probably ready for you guys. Tom, this is Matty. Matty, Tom is our resident journalist. He and his wife, PC are worth way more than we pay them."

Tom smiled and shook hands with Matty, "Matty, it's my pleasure. Jeff, the only guy up here I'm worried about is Roger, the former Governor of Alaska. I think his safety is important to us. I've written down the addresses of both his house and chalet."

Matty spoke up, "Here, I'll take that. If he's important, consider him protected. Who else up here?"

Tom grabbed the luggage from PC, "Well, just Jack and Gretchen. I'm taking my troubles with me," he took PC by the hand.

She looked at Matty and Jeff and said, "Bye." Matty and Jeff looked at each other and then went in to explore the house.

# 7

The flight down to Boeing Field went smoothly. Tom called Tony as soon as they stepped off the plane. The family was safely at Tony's Inn. Tom and PC arrived after a cab ride and joined Tony, Millie, James, Wallie, Alexander, Joni, Archie, and the Lancaster family at the dinner table. Tony was his gregarious self and insisted on making the introductions.

"Welcome, one and all. Welcome to Tony's Inn. I'm Tony. I'm a bad guy who's been given a second chance and, believe me, I'm going to prove that second chances are a good thing. James here is my business partner. His wife, Wallie, and my wife, Millie, are sisters, if you hadn't noticed. Alexander and Joni will make your stay better than you expected, and Archie is a cop friend on furlough. Welcome to Tom and PC, who just flew in from Alaska. Tom is a nosy journalist who treats us better than we deserve in print and in person. And his wife is just plain gorgeous." PC kicked Tom in the leg under the table for not announcing that fact to everyone first. Millie stomped on Tony's foot for doing it, and Len Lancaster was having trouble assimilating humor and comfort into daily life again.

"Ouch!" Tom said.

"Ouch!" Tony said. "Uh...and it is my pleasure to introduce Len Lancaster, Qui Ling, his wife, and Rogette, their beautiful daughter. These folks recently escaped Communist China. Friends, welcome!"

Tony sat down and motioned dinner to be served.

"Mr. Lancaster," Tom began.

"Please, call me Len." Len had a bit of an accent, having spoken mostly Chinese for quite a few years.

"Len, I had the privilege a few days ago of speaking about you with Roger, the former governor of Alaska. He expressed fond memories of you."

"Thank you, Tom. My feelings for Roger are quite the same. Is he in good health?"

"Yes, he was swimming laps when I first met him. I have the sense that he was good for Alaska in his day."

"Then I made the right decision to exit the race."

"I believe your contribution to Alaska is yet to unfold and my money says it's priceless."

"Let's hope so. Tom, maybe when the time is right, you could introduce me and my family to the former governor. I'd love to talk with him. We named our daughter after him."

"It would be my pleasure. Let's hope the opportunity arises."

*

As the evening progressed, Len began to relax as the feeling of safety overtook the apprehension of years of undercover work. PC took Qui Ling and Rogette by the hands and showed them the indoor pool area. By ten o'clock the family was safely in bed. Tom and PC got caught up on all that had happened at Tony's Inn including the marriage of Matty and Cindy.

After breakfast the next morning, James and Wallie took the family clothes shopping, with Archie and Alexander along for protection and to carry packages. Alexander noticed a pickpocket and two undercover store detectives. Archie noticed the clerk. He made a mental note to come back here on his own and do some shopping.

By noon they were ready to leave for Montana. Joni had the family stand between Tony and Millie and James and Wallie, and took a picture that would hang in the VIP case in the entry of Tony's Inn.

The flight to Montana and the conversation were pleasant. Len asked about the latest world events. Tom asked about Len's early years with Jonathan, and if he had a real interest in politics or was his candidacy just a cover. As the plane began descending, PC promised to entertain Qui Ling and Rogette to make sure they enjoyed their stay while the men talked.

When the wheels touched down and stopped rolling, a welcoming party of Jonathan and Sharon, Joe and Kandee, and Joe and Jennifer Cornish stood waiting to greet them. When the five descended the stairs from the jet, Sharon and Kandee stepped forward. Kandee handed Qui Ling and Rogette red roses, while Sharon stood before them and spoke in beautiful Chinese. She recited a formal welcome that took about thirty seconds. It was one that most Chinese youngsters had memorized at an early age. When Qui Ling heard it, her face changed to sheer delight as she heard her language spoken so beautifully, in a verse that she had dearly loved as a young girl. Len Lancaster smiled as if an expensive gift had been given to them. When Sharon finished, Qui Ling wrapped her arms around Sharon and hugged and laughed and cried a bit, as it was the most pleasant thing that had happened to them in two years. Len shook hands with Jonathan, then they hugged. As they all followed their host and hostess into the ranch house, Kandee and PC latched onto each other and would not let go. The two friends had not seen each other for too long.

The coolness of the late afternoon on the Montana hilltop disappeared as they sat semi-circle before a roaring fire in the large fireplace. Hot tea was served, followed by a traditional Chinese dinner overseen by Sharon. The newly arrived family blessed their hosts by eating heartily and enjoying speaking Chinese.

Soon it was apparent that jet lag was taking its toll, so the family went to bed early. The next morning would begin with the debriefing of Len Lancaster.

# 8

Senator William J. Williamsford of California, soon to be former senator because of his recuperation, was awakened at 4 AM by a phone call from the east coast. An Arizona friend, who worked as a lobbyist in Washington, D.C., was actually on the Senator's payroll as a covert intelligence man.

"Jay, sorry to wake you. Things are popping. The Chinese Ambassador has been burning the midnight oil with the Senate Majority Leader. What's going to be proposed is the sale of mineral rights on Federal Lands. Now everyone thinks range lands and desert and mountains, but there will be no language in the bill differentiating the land under say, the Pentagon, the Whitehouse, the Capital building. It's all included. No money would be exchanged. It would reduce our Federal debt with the Chinese."

"Okay, Fred, this is what we expected," Jay Williamsford said evenly.

"Yes, sir, but here's what we didn't expect. The bill will not pass the Senate. The failure will be blamed on the minority party. The President of the United States will then deem it necessary for national security to write an executive order to make it happen. Since no money changes hands, the House is technically sidelined. The executive order will be challenged and the Senate's role of advice and consent will come into play. It is at that point that the votes in the Senate will be there to approve the President's order."

"My God," Jay was hearing about chess pieces being placed. It was almost happening to fast to put up an effective defense. "Fred, we need to make a move that's not expected. Something that will make them stop and rethink."

"Yeah, Jay. Good thinking. I'm all ears!"

"Any ideas at all?" Jay asked Fred.

"Vote the bums out!" Fred and Jay both chuckled. The answer was the correct one. There just wasn't enough time. "Jay, they've got it scheduled first thing next month."

"Okay. Thanks, Fred, keep at it. I've got some ideas. Let's stay closely in touch," Jay Williamsford hung up. He dialed a number that set off an alarm of soft, classical music that gently woke up Janae. She recognized it as Jay wanting her assistance, but not in an emergency situation. She got up and got ready, then stopped at the kitchen for coffee. Janae gave the Senator a quick call.

"Hi, I'm bringing coffee in five minutes; want anything to eat?"

"Yeah, scramble us some eggs and cheese, and toast some of that homemade bread you and the girls made yesterday. Don't wake them, though; we've got business to discuss."

"Okay, be good till I get there!"

"I will. I've just got to figure out how to save the country."

"Oh, really. Isn't it someone else's turn?"

"Nope. It's you and me, my dearest, and our friends. Don't forget the salt and pepper."

Jay was finishing with his electric shaver when Janae joined him. She helped him wash his hair, clean up and change clothes, and get back into the super-wheelchair. At breakfast he filled her in on the early call. As they finished eating, he dialed Joe Cornish.

*

Joe and Jennifer Cornish were in the Central Time Zone and they were swimming in Jonathan's indoor pool at 5 AM. At 6 AM they were dry and making breakfast. Before eating, they paused and prayed together. That's when the phone rang.

"Yes."

"Good morning, Joe Cornish. This is Jay Williamsford from San Francisco. Our morning started early with some exploding news, so we thought we'd check on what was happening in Montana."

"Well, great to hear from you, Jay. We are going to debrief Len Lancaster this morning. He just got here after escaping from China with his wife and daughter. He's one of Jonathan's covert ops. He'll tell us if China's ready to take over the world yet."

"Well, it sounds like the majority party in the United States Senate is on the same track as the Chinese. We need to loosen a few rails or blow a bridge pretty quick if we have any hope of stopping this takeover."

"If you can put together a plan with the information you have, we will do the same. Let's connect this afternoon. How's Janae and the family?"

"We are all good. We'll do that from our end and call you back later today."

"Thank you, Jay," Joe Cornish hung up.

*

Jay and Janae looked at each other. Then Janae had a thought, "Remember when we eyed each other at the pool just as the earthquake was starting? The repercussions of that glance have grown into something strong without much effort on our part. We really just allowed ourselves to be carried along by a love that we recognized in a second, even though others are just now noticing it."

"Yes, I agree. That is true, Janae, very true..."

"Then let's find that thing in this political situation that is effortless, yet powerful."

Jay, having been in a political family and in political office of one kind or another for two decades, was drawing a blank. He had run and won election to precinct committeeman at the age of eighteen. Politics meant action. Action meant work. Effortlessness meant...? "What do you mean by effortlessness?"

"The work is already being done by someone else," Janae explained.

"Keep going."

"The only avenue we have open to us in which to apply power is in the Senate. The only power the Senate will have is in giving consent to the President's executive order. All of our efforts to dissuade that consent will fail. We need to ride that power, even though we are against it, and add to it something that they won't recognize as a road block, but will be just that."

"What could we possibly add that would make a huge change and yet no one would recognize it at its inception?"

"Something just like our love, Jay. To us the earthquake made a huge change in our lives, but no one noticed it. They were all noticing what they were focusing on."

"Okay. Again...what would that be...?" Jay paused for a moment, looked at Janae and recognized that slight mischievous smile that he was learning to love. "You have something in mind." Janae kept the smile and nodded her head.

The next hour was spent in explaining the art of effortlessly getting what you wanted while using the other person's hard work to accomplish it, and having the other person's plans befuddled as a consequence.

Janae's mischievous comment was, "Women do this all the time, Jay."

# 9

"State lands?" Joe Cornish asked.

"Yes, AND state lands; on federal AND state lands; not or, not and/or. It has to be mineral rights on federal AND state lands. If federal and state are linked together, legally they will have to be dealt with together. No one will ever get a majority of states to agree on anything, much less giving up state lands to satisfy a federal debt."

Jennifer Cornish was explaining to her husband what Janae had come up with and had explained to her over the phone while the guys were debriefing Len Lancaster. "It's brilliant because it's so simple. Our adversaries in the Senate will be focused on the federal lands, and adding state lands will just make it more lucrative to their way of thinking. They won't notice the poison pill, but once this passes, controversy will never end. Instead of partisan bickering, it will become a state's rights issue. We simply need to add two words to the bill and the ensuing in-fighting will enlighten the real intent of the bill's backers."

"Wow! Our Janae, she's... blossoming," Joe Cornish said, marveling.

"She's a woman who's been put into a new set of circumstances and it just happened to be a perfect fit. Sort of like what you caused to happen in my life," Jennifer had the beginnings of a smile.

"Oh, I plead guilty to that. I was sneaky and caught you at an emotional moment. You bit, and I've been the beneficiary of it ever since," Joe Cornish had the beginnings of a smile, also. Thinking back was a pleasant distraction.

*

The morning debriefing of Len Lancaster covered his first years in China.

As they took a quick break for lunch, Joe Cornish took the time to check in with all his contacts. The problems and solutions emanating from the mansion in San Francisco were exciting. In addition, Joe Cornish got an update from Seattle, and with Matty and Nicolus in Alaska together, anything could happen. Lunch was quick because everybody wanted to get back to Len Lancaster's story.

So was life when you were on the incoming tide of good.

The women were invited to sit in on the afternoon session, so Qui Ling, Sharon, and Jennifer joined their husbands, along with Joe and Tom. Kandee and PC were entertaining Rogette, while Cindy and Taylor were watching the farrier shoe the horses.

Len led out, "Consistent with my cover, I was holding classes in English, with a bent towards Bible study, in a coffee shop across the street from a government office. I chose that location because I wanted people to come that had some government connection. When they did, I had them practice English by speaking about their daily routine. Qui Ling also came to my class. As she began to participate, I quickly fell in love with her...because...well, there were many reasons. We began seeing each other at night. After a month we were sure enough of our love that she revealed who she was. She told me of her assignment from Chinese Intelligence to seduce and capture me for the purpose of replacing me with an imposter who would pass on less than accurate information.

Though we wanted to be together and free, we had to let her turn me in first, so as not to compromise her position. We made plans to meet again when her assignment was completed. It just hinged on me being able to escape, so we waited it out. It took a while, but the plan worked, and here we are." Len looked all around, sort of pleased with himself.

"Did your capture increase the amount of information you were able gather?" Jonathan asked, leading the debriefing.

"Yes, it sure ended up being that way. My captors thought their threat of punishment was why I cooperated, and I fomented that idea. I did not cause my captors problems, and it was not their intent to make me suffer, as long as I cooperated. That was one reason why my imposter was so convincing. I helped him act like me."

"So after some months, they asked if I wanted a woman. The prostitute I told them I wanted was the one I had working undercover for me as one of the general's lovers. They okayed it with a chuckle, because the general was feared because of his harshness, but no one really liked him. Before I got captured, we would be extremely careful about meeting. After my capture she was brought to me once a week as a reward for my cooperation. In reality I was learning much more than I had previously."

"My hope was that I could more easily escape by cooperating with my captors, than by trying to oppose them and somehow overpower them. Then I would gain my freedom, meet up with Qui Ling, and report back to you. So we waited patiently, and executed our plan. It just took time, and time was the one thing I had. So I used it to my advantage."

"Excellent," Joe Cornish inserted.

"Yes, very well done, Len. Especially with no guarantee you would be able to escape," Jonathan was pleased. "Now, what can we expect from the Chinese?"

"The Chinese Army is like any army, chomping at the bit to do something with the resources they have. The generals have plans of their own which involve the successful occupation of eastern

Russia, Alaska, and points south as they come available. But what nobody knows is, why are they doing it?"

Sharon was keeping an eye on Qui Ling. As a former sheriff, she was suspicious. As an admitted intelligence agent of the Chinese Army, Qui Ling should expect to be under suspicion. Sharon saw nothing unusual in her demeanor.

Joe jumped in with some speculation, "They are doing it because they can, and the accumulation of power is its own incentive. They have the numbers to do whatever they want."

Len continued, "All true. The Chinese Army is putting this all together covertly, not only from the U.S., but their own Chinese government knows very little of it. When they have everything in position covertly, they will make a splash when they initiate the invasion. However, the activity of the invasion of Alaska will provide cover for the quiet takeover of the government of China by the Chinese Army. Then they will be in position to do the negotiating with the U.S. on Alaska and the whole west coast as far as they are concerned. This has been well thought out, and has some cooperation from Washington, D.C., though I am not aware of the specifics of who is involved."

Sharon noticed a slight change in Qui Ling's expression when Len spoke of not knowing what U.S. officials were involved.

Joe Cornish was stunned into silence. Jonathan spoke, "The invasion of Alaska is cover for a coup by the Chinese Army of the Chinese government?"

"Yes, sir. That is one of the reasons for it, and someone in our administration thinks land for debt is a good idea, since the debt of the U.S. would be significantly reduced."

Joe Cornish decided to act as devil's advocate, to see what response he would get, "It is not an idea bereft of merit." He looked around.

Jennifer jumped in, "I guarantee you the present administration would take the debt reduction, leave the debt ceiling where it is, and use the available debt to fund all kinds of social programs.

The people of the United States would simply become indebted again with less land to trade away for it."

Jonathan took over again, "Okay, what is holding them back? Are they not ready yet? Where are they in the planning?"

"The Chinese Army agreed to wait for the U.S. to institute the Mineral Rights Act in Alaska, and in Washington, D.C. This would give a legal basis, after the invasion, for a compromise. Land for debt, with foreign ownership legal."

Joe Cornish suddenly turned stone-cold sober. Jonathan saw it, so did Jennifer. "Joseph, what's wrong? You have something," she said.

Joe Cornish was doing some serious thinking, "Somebody has bought us some time!"

Jonathan wasn't following. "What do you mean?"

Joe Cornish continued, "Whether for good or for bad, someone has bought us some time. Somebody convinced the Chinese Army to wait until the Senate bill goes through before they start their invasion. It could be, someone we aren't aware of is on our side and has bought desperately needed time in order to implement plans of their own to stop the invasion." Joe Cornish looked at Jennifer.

Jennifer thought for a moment and then said, "We need to talk to Jim." Joe Cornish was nodding his head.

Joe jumped in, "You're talking about your cousin, Jim? You've mentioned how big a help he was in Paraguay. Is he CIA?"

Jennifer nodded, "Yes, or some such thing."

Jonathan summarized, "So, we need to know if it's for good or for bad."

"Yes, for this reason," Joe Cornish explained. "If it's for the good of our country, we need to find out what plans whoever it is has in mind. They may be better than ours. We need to know so we don't do anything to hurt them. If it's for bad, we will use the time to implement our plans and strike with the full force of our covert operations."

Everyone then looked at Len Lancaster. Len, after a second, looked at his wife, Qui Ling. He nodded to her.

She acknowledged his nod, lowered her head to gather courage, and then looked up and spoke. "My father is high up in Chinese Army Intelligence. He went to school in America in his early twenties. He had a...romantic relationship with a girl student at the same school. Time has passed, but they have never forgotten each other. The girl is now in politics in the United States." Qui Ling stopped, not wanting to offer more information than was necessary. Everyone was blinking and thinking, as the potential importance of what she said set in.

Sharon spoke first, very kindly, "Qui Ling, do you know what political office she holds?"

"She is a senator in the United States Senate." Qui Ling spoke softly.

More wide-eyed blinking and thinking. This was beginning to sound too hard to believe.

Jennifer jumped in, "From what state?"

"She is a senator from the State of California," Qui Ling folded her hands in her lap and looked down at them.

Now everyone was shocked. The Senior Senator from California was a woman in her sixties who was a four-term senator. Surely she wasn't collaborating with the Chinese Army to take over Alaska and the west coast of the United States.

"You're talking about Senator Cassy Albright. She's been championing national causes for thirty years," Jennifer knew her history. Jay Williamsford had worked with Senator Albright many times. "This can't possibly be true."

Qui Ling raised her head at the suggestion of her being untruthful, "I wish for my father's sake none of this was true. I have a picture of my father and the girl student named Sandra from their college days." Qui Ling opened her purse, got out her wallet, and carefully pulled out an old picture. She passed it to Jennifer.

Jennifer looked at it and, though it was over forty years old, the resemblance of the youthful female student in the picture to Senator Cassy Albright was undeniable. "My God!" Jennifer passed the picture around. Each one looked. Then everyone looked at each other. Then everyone looked at Joe Cornish. He had a smile on his face. Jennifer recognized that smile. Her husband had a plan.

Jennifer addressed him, "My dear Joseph, have you so quickly solved the world's problems?"

"Senator Albright is our solution," Joe Cornish simply announced.

Tom hadn't said anything. He was just writing as fast as he could.

# 10

Nicolus, Nickolaea and Rolando were positioning the yacht just where they wanted it. They had docked and Nicolus went up to the office and negotiated two one-year slip leases, side by side. Then they maneuvered their yacht into position and tied it fast. Now they had a foothold in Anchorage.

Nicolus called Jack and told him they were in port.

"Hold on. We're coming with a truck. We'll be there soon and haul all the armaments to the house. See you in twenty minutes." Jack, along with Jeff and Matty, showed up in fifteen minutes with a truck and a car.

The cargo was either crated or in suitcases, and the men worked methodically so as not to draw undue attention. When the truck was all loaded, Jack and Matty drove it to the house. Jeff followed with Nicolus and Nickolaea in the car, and Rolando stayed on the yacht with the lady pilot.

At the house Gretchen was ready for them. She showed them where everything went, then turned to the task of dinner. Nickolaea monitored the area and stayed at the truck while the men unloaded.

When the moving of the armaments was completed, they sat down to a wonderful dinner. Conversation was about the beauty of Alaska and the business at hand for tomorrow. With plans laid, Nicolus and Nickolaea drove back to the yacht to spend the night. Everyone got a well-deserved rest.

*

When morning dawned, Nicolus and Nickolaea rose early and went for a walk around the marina area. When they got back, Nickolaea hugged her dad and she and Nicolus left for the safe house. Rolando and the lady pilot would stay aboard.

At the house, breakfast was ready. Nickolaea would stay with Gretchen and get acquainted with the security and communication gear, and the filing and storage of intel data. Jack and Matty drove around and found both of the former governor's houses, then stopped in Anchorage and bought Matty a four-wheel-drive Jeep. Jeff and Nicolus stayed at the house and checked and inventoried the armaments, and tested all the equipment for surveillance and communication.

As lunch time approached, they all arrived back at the house. After lunch, Jack and Jeff had a list of things to buy and do as they turned the house into a fort; a covert fort. Gretchen and Nickolaea went out for some shopping and coffee and got to know each other better.

Nicolus and Matty went hunting.

*

Joe Cornish, keeping in mind Jay and Janae's idea of inserting two words into the Mineral Rights Bill, began planning how to deal with a very powerful woman. Senator Cassy Albright had a long and successful career. Only in allowing the power of doing good to apply itself effortlessly to a given situation had Joe Cornish accomplished what he had. This was not a time to change course.

Joe Cornish had never met Senator Albright, but he needed her full attention. He could not mention Jay Williamsford and his involvement, but rather he needed the Senior Senator from California to go to the Junior Senator and request his assistance. The only way to convince Senator Albright that the hand that she was ready to play was actually a losing hand, was to let her get a peek at the winning hand. Once that happened, all her power would be redirected to the right cause. Joe Cornish took a deep breath and let it out slowly. This just might be fun.

*

Jay and Janae connected again with their Arizona friend. He was in D.C. doing what he was good at: talking with the underlings of the powerful people and giving them the ideas to casually present to their bosses about what would work best. They were all lawyers and wrote the bills in legalese. Their bosses had plenty to do without checking details and so trusted their younger, smarter teams. Two words would add a gateway of opportunity for the ones in power. When you worked for the ones in power, things went well for you, also, so the underlings were cooperative.

"Adding two words to the Mineral Rights Bill will not be hard. What else do you want me working on?"

"If you are successful with this small addition, we won't have to oppose the bill. Just keep at it and let me know any ideas you come up with. This should go smoothly. But as we know, smooth likes to develop wrinkles, so keep your eyes and ears open for them."

Then Jay called his men in Alaska.

"What have you found out about who is backing and funding the mineral rights sale bill?"

"The Chinese, but everything goes through the army. It's like the government is hands off while the Chinese Army runs everything."

"Is there a vote scheduled?"

"Yes, sir. First of the month."

"Is there anyone of importance standing up for the opposition to this bill?"

"Yes, sir. The governor is against it. She said she will not sign it if it passes and comes to her desk. She is part of the minority party. She was elected last year because the majority candidate was a known political hack with no spine of his own. This gal who won the Governorship is refreshingly blunt."

"Okay, I'm sending money to be put into the opposition account. This bill is touting prosperity for the working man. The opposite will happen if it's passed, but it's hard to get someone to vote against promised good fortune. Keep me posted."

Jay Williamsford put his phone down and looked at his bride to be. He was going to say 'I love you,' but his phone rang as soon as it hit the desk.

"Hello?"

"Jay, what can you tell me about Senator Cassy Albright?"

"Plenty," the next half hour was informative. Jay had been a new senator when she was halfway through her second term. She had been a big help. Joe Cornish listened carefully.

# 11

The best hunters were those who had a history of being hunted. Body guards and security people constantly protected their bosses from hunters, real or assumed, so Nicolus had the most experience in hunting. Matty, on the other hand, had more experience in killing.

Jack and Gretchen had seen the cargo ships with Chinese markings, coming and going since they were up here. They followed the container hauling trucks to a huge site, fenced and gated, belonging to a Chinese Construction conglomerate. This is where Nicolus and Matty came to hunt.

Matty was dressed as a workman and lingered behind Nicolus who was dressed in a business suit and carried a briefcase. Nicolus parked outside and walked up to the gate as other workmen flashed their ID's and walked right in. Nicolus announced to the guard that he was FBI and that his job was to check security, not inspect cargo. The guard got on the phone briefly and then pointed for Nicolus to head to the door labeled "Office." Matty cruised right in during the small disturbance along with other workers.

Nicolus's bearing brought everyone in the office to attention. Nicolus closed the door behind him and cast a cold look around the office. Mostly Chinese, some American secretaries. He casually held up his fake ID as he spoke.

"FBI. Your boss, please." An office door opened and a Chinese woman stepped out. Behind her was the boss.

"I work for the Federal Bureau of Investigation. I analyze security. The FBI wants to know if your security is able to withstand attempts to steal explosives you might have in storage in connection with construction. You might not know it, but this facility is a target for terrorists looking for explosives."

The woman whispered to the boss. The boss looked at Nicolus. He didn't want to have anything to do with him, and just gestured with his arm and turned back into his office. The woman smiled and said, "I will be glad to answer all your questions, sir."

*

Matty entered the worker's area where the men could get lunch, booze, and women during their breaks. He tried the side door that said "Janitor." Inside he put on a safety vest, grabbed a clipboard, hard hat and safety goggles. He also found a pair of chain cutters and walked out like he was in charge.

Outside he headed for the rows of containers lined up three tall. On the other side of these were containers with nothing stacked on top. Too heavy. Matty stopped at the first one and snapped the chain with the cutters. He opened the door to a gun barrel that was attached to a Chinese tank. Matty took a picture of the tank with his phone, then closed the half-door that had the numbers on it and took another picture. This time he had the numbers of the container and half the tank in the same picture. Then he closed the other door and refastened the chain. Matty was able to do this to six other containers randomly chosen before he froze in his tracks.

"Hey, what is this man doing?" Nicolus's voice was loud and harsh.

The lady and two security men with her stared at Matty. She said, "He's with inspections," then to Matty, "ID, quickly." Matty just turned around, stood dumbly and said nothing.

"Hey, I recognize this man," Nicolus said as he drew his gun. "Turn around and put your hands on the container." Matty complied. "Now search him," Nicolus said this to the two security men. Out came the chain cutters, the clipboard with unimportant papers on it and a phone. No wallet or ID.

"Where is your ID?" one of the men demanded.

Nicolus spoke next, "I recognize this man from his wanted poster. Do you gentlemen have handcuffs?" Handcuffs were produced and Matty was cuffed behind his back.

"I'm from the FBI and you, sir, are under arrest." He took the cutters, the clipboard and the phone as evidence. Then to the three security people he said, "Scour the premises; he might have an accomplice. I'm taking this one out to my car. Thank you, ma'am, for your assistance." Nicolus grabbed Matty by the arm and the two headed for the main gate. The woman and her two helpers scattered, not sure what they were looking for, but glad to be helping the FBI. They certainly didn't want the FBI to become suspicious. The guard at the gate just stared as Nicolus and Matty walked out to the Jeep and Nicolus opened the back door. He assisted Matty into the back seat, making sure he didn't bump his head in so doing. They drove away. When they saw no one was following them they pulled into a fast food restaurant and parked.

"Get anything?" Nicolus asked as he leaned over and unlocked the cuffs.

"Yeah, plenty. Let's get back to the house and load them onto the computer. But first, take a left at the next light and we'll drive by the former governor's house." Five minutes later they could see red and blue lights flashing from the former governor's driveway. Fire, Aid, and Sheriff vehicles were everywhere. "Keep going," Matty said as he retrieved his phone from the front seat and dialed the house. "Jeff, what's going on with the former governor?"

"We were monitoring the police band and a 911 call came from his house. Apparently the maid found him drowned in his pool."

"Damn. We're heading home with some good pictures," Matty hung up and shook his head. He didn't like promising to protect someone and then failing.

*

Jonathan was speaking, "Well, you two deserve some time off. Please relax. This is your home for the near future. You'll be safe here."

Then Len spoke, "Sir, Qui Ling has something more." They were all enjoying dinner together, but the seriousness of the conversation continued.

Joe Cornish perked up along with everyone else.

"Please," Jonathan responded, "If you are comfortable, please continue."

Qui Ling put her fork down and dabbed at her mouth with her napkin. "My father told Sandra Albright that if he ever had a serious message to convey to her, it would be brought to her personally by me."

Jonathan looked at Joe Cornish who had a Christmas morning look on his face. He bubbled over, "Jonathan, we'll have you and Sharon, and Len and Qui Ling visit the Senator and let her know the latest from China."

"Which is?"

"Good question. Let's put our heads together."

# 12

In Washington, D.C. two words were being added to a five thousand word document. Quick private insertions were the norm in this town from the President on down. Power, money, and sex were the three wheels that rolled along under the whole mechanism. The four points of the compass were lies, rumors, innuendoes, and bribes. The prizes were ambassadorships, judgeships, cabinet positions, and contracts. The caffeine was partisan zeal, the grease was favors, the safety net was who you knew, and the hole in the safety net was sometimes murder. The puzzling question was, why did so many people spend their time, money, and honor to get to Washington, D.C., and once there, desperately figure out how to stay?

And this was the best the world had to offer. In the history of the world, more people from more countries had risked everything they owned to come to America and be a part of the freedom that was so eloquently announced in the Declaration of Independence.

If good people just pointed in the right direction, bad people would still lead the way. It took more than pointing or knowing the way. It took walking in that direction, but the effort was difficult and sometimes dangerous. That was why, Joe Cornish had found out, you had to join in the tide that was going toward good and flow along with it. He was still learning, but working hard effortlessly was fun. If someone wanted to put Joe Cornish out to pasture, fine. But if the decision was up to him, he would move in that great tidal wave of good and ride one wave to the next wave, and to the next. It was way too fun to just stop.

*

Nicolus and Matty got back to the house and put the pictures onto the computer. Jack, Gretchen, and Jeff were stunned. Nickolaea just smiled.

"How did you get these pictures?" Jack asked.

"I used my phone camera."

"I know you used your phone camera, but... are these from the construction storage yard that has razor wire and armed guards at the gate?"

"Bingo, your intel was good."

"Okay, but... I can't for the life of me... wait... how many people died for you to get these?"

"Oh, come on. I didn't have that much fun today. We just walked in, took the pictures and walked back out."

"That would be impossible."

"Well, there were a few more details than that, but results are what's important. Anyway, what more do we know about the former governor's death?"

"The maid did it," Nickolaea was matter of fact and had never seen the movie Clue. She was serious.

Nicolus looked at her and smiled. Everyone else was surprised at how serious she sounded. Gretchen asked kindly, "How do you know?"

"I watched her being interviewed on TV."

"And something she said didn't fit?"

"She was lying," Nickolaea was as confident as predicting the sun coming up tomorrow.

"Was she lying to protect the killer or do you think she was the killer?"

"If I knew for sure, I'd kill whoever it was," Matty interjected, just wanting everybody to know he took his work seriously.

"If we knew that the former governor was murdered, and we knew who did it," Jack looked at Gretchen, "we would know more about who our enemies are."

"Are you saying it was the maid who actually killed him?" Gretchen asked Nickolaea again carefully.

"Yes."

Nicolus entered the conversation, "We'll get the proof tomorrow and be back by noon. Meanwhile these pictures should be passed on to Joe Cornish and Jonathan, along with the sad news of the death of the former governor."

"I can do that," Gretchen said, freeing up Nickolaea.

"Thank you, we'll go and prepare for tomorrow," Nicolus reached for Nickolaea's hand but paused and looked at Matty. "Do you suppose a quick look at the former governor's chalet would produce anything?"

"Yeah, I'll go do that. See you tomorrow." Nicolus, Nickolaea and Matty all left. Gretchen got to work on the computer. Jeff and Jack resumed their work of fortifying the fort.

*

Alaska was preparing a message for Montana. Montana was preparing a message for one part of California. Another part of California was preparing a message for Washington, D.C.. Washington, D.C. was preparing a message for China, and China was preparing a message for the world: We are in charge!

Pictures of proof of the invasion already taking place would get Senator Albright's attention. Putting them in the Anchorage newspaper would stop her in her tracks, and Joe Cornish had just the right message from Qui Ling to get the Senior Senator from California to do his bidding.

The Junior Senator from California made another call to his friend in D.C.

"Fred, what's the latest?"

"It has been typed up with the two word addition in it. Nobody has said anything yet. Monday is the first, and the process will begin."

"Okay, find out all you can. Who is voting against it, who is voting for it, and what the numbers are."

"Yes, sir."

*

The Chinese Ambassador to the United States was not sleeping well. He had composed and sent a note to his contact in the Chinese Army. He didn't try to be optimistic; the Army Intelligence officer would see right through him. He gave the bill a fifty/fifty chance of passage, and a late change in the wording looked helpful. He hadn't heard back with instructions yet.

His secretary, in bed next to him, was trying to relax him but it wasn't working. His weekly report to his superiors in the Chinese Government said nothing of what he was up to. He went over his options again. If the coup succeeded, he would be brought back to China and probably be made Secretary of State. If it failed, he would deny any involvement. If it succeeded, but did not last, he would defect and ask for asylum in the U.S. He was not going back to a firing squad. Now he needed sleep. Morning was four hours away. He turned his attention to his secretary.

*

On the other side of the world, the Chinese Army Intelligence officer had no superiors, as far as he was concerned. His master plan was unfolding and soon everyone would recognize his unsurpassed intelligence. His daughter was missing, but her last message indicated she was heading to the U.S. to personally deliver a message from him to his West Coast contact. The message: Thank you. He had no further need of her assistance. It would be signed with a bullet.

The intel officer was very pleased with his daughter. He had no idea how she would get into the U.S., but he knew she would accomplish it. He had trained her himself.

The mind-numbing politics of the U.S. was not going to control him. Wait, compromise, wait some more, compromise, then wait. Sorry, he had work to do and waiting didn't fit in. The U.S. was an overweight, gluttonous fool. It's overspending had collapsed into bankruptcy, but nobody dared say it out loud in the U.S. or in China. Well, he would stop the nonsense. The Chinese leaders were dithering and soon China would be on the opposite side of bankruptcy. They would hold the debt of a country who could not repay it. Arrogance had to have something to back it up, and the U.S. had nothing. He had his intelligence, and an operational army to back it up.

In school, he had majored in history. His lover had majored in economics. They dreamed of ruling the world, she delivering the U.S., and he delivering China. She was about to do that, and that was all he needed her for. He had plenty of young lovers. This was his time, his alone.

*

The phone was ringing in Joe Cornish's ear.

"Good afternoon, Senator Albright's office. How may I direct your call?"

"My name is Joe Cornish. I'm in charge of Special Investigations for the FBI, Seattle Office. I have an urgent message for the Senator's ears only."

"Yes, sir. Please hold while I connect you."

Jonathan, Len, and their wives had just lifted off in Jonathan's jet to LAX. They had a Sunday afternoon meeting scheduled with Senator Cassy Albright. The jet would land this evening and the four would get a good night's sleep and enjoy a leisurely morning while preparing for their afternoon meeting.

"Agent Cornish, I don't believe we've met, but I know you by reputation. How may I help you?"

"Madame Senator, please forgive my urgency. We have intercepted intel which points to a Chinese Intelligence agent in route to visit you with an important message."

"I...don't...have any dealings with the Chinese except, of course, with regard to business involving the State of California."

"Again, Madame Senator, please forgive me. The messenger is the daughter of a high ranking Chinese Army Intelligence officer. We have reason to believe her message to you personally will be short and sweet. A smile and a bullet."

The line was silent for a few seconds, "Sir...I don't...are you saying my life is in danger?"

"Yes, Madame Senator. Do you have any appointments tonight or tomorrow?"

"I'm leaving for Washington tomorrow evening. Just before that I have some former missionaries visiting with a gift for me, and one to pass on to the President. I really don't see how..."

"What country were the missionaries in?"

"Pardon me?"

"Are they from China, Madame Senator?"

"I...yes, I believe they were in China."

"Okay, please think very seriously about doing exactly what I am going to suggest to you. From my perspective your future depends on it. Four people are going to visit you. The first couple are covert operatives who are working for me. The other couple is a former missionary who married a woman in China. She is actually the daughter of the Army Intel guy. Her job is to kill you. Her husband is not aware of it. My operatives will stop her at the right time, trust me, and then will show you some astounding pictures which I assure you are real and recently taken."

"Agent Cornish, I'm not certain..."

"Madame Senator, it is not my job to convince you of the importance of this. You could simply cancel the appointment, but then she would still be out there. I can vouch for the planning and the timing of this operation. I am interested in exposing and catching a foreign agent, faking her death, and then interrogating her. Your cooperation will be held in the strictest confidence."

"Well...I am putting myself in your hands, but your reputation precedes you. Do I just invite them in when they call?"

"Yes, ma'am. Just be your gracious self. My operatives, Jonathan and Sharon, will do the rest. Feel free to call me at this number when it is all over."

"Thank you, Agent Cornish. I like the idea of helping the FBI."

"Thank you, Madame Senator. Again, my apologies for the urgency of this call." Joe Cornish hung up.

*

The Jeep, with Matty driving, neared the former governor's chalet. There was a moving van in the driveway and workers were moving the contents of the house into the van. They were Chinese. Matty went by and turned around. On his way back he noticed no markings on the moving van. Matty stopped at the small café in the town of Hope and ordered lunch. He took his time and was rewarded a few hours later. The moving van left and headed back towards Anchorage. Matty followed. It was beginning to get dark.

*

The next day Nicolus and Nickolaea announced themselves as security experts from the company who installed and handled the former governor's security alarm system at the house. They were let in by the policeman guarding the main door. The kitchen computer and the security computer had already been taken by the police in the investigation. Upstairs in the spare bedroom sat a computer that had not been used for a while. It only took Nickolaea ten minutes to get in to where she wanted to go. Part of the security video had been deleted. Nickolaea sifted through the computer's trash bin and found it. Sure enough, it showed the maid swimming with the former governor, and with a swift, professional move, rendered him unconscious. Then it showed her holding his head under water.

The police would not find the gap in the video until the investigation took its course. Nickolaea emailed the video to a coffee shop email address close to the safe house. On the way home they stopped for coffee and emailed the video to the safe house's email address. Then they erased it from the coffee shop account so a casual look would show nothing. By noon they were at the safe house computer looking at the video carefully in slow motion. The maid was looking over and saying something after she killed the former governor. Someone else was in the pool area, but was smart enough to stay out of the camera's way. A copy of this video could be used by that someone to blackmail the maid.

"This is amazing," Gretchen said, "what do we do with it?"

"We hang on to the evidence until it becomes useful and use the revelations to help us identify and thwart our enemies." Nickolaea was definitely in the game.

"The chalet got cleaned out and it was all brought to the construction storage yard...Damn it. Someone is running all this from inside Alaska, and I want whoever it is," Matty, as usual, wanted revenge. He wanted to break up the offensive plays that were being run.

"I've got an idea," Nicolus usually did.

# 13

Senator Cassy Albright was trying to order things in her mind. The vision of her former lover and of world domination had been drawn out by time and circumstance over the many years since their college days. The indiscretions and ideals of youth were altered by understanding and wisdom. Altered, but not gone. They had communicated many times over the years and a visit from his daughter was the signal of the beginning of their dream. It was quite understandable that love affairs had to end, but visions kept on. The absence of sex didn't mean the absence of love. Once committed to, love never ended.

What in the world would entice an FBI man to scare her with a story of assassination by the hand of the messenger she had been hoping to hear from for so many years? The idea that her committed goal of joining with her former lover in the reorganization of the world, starting with the east coast of his world and the west coast of her world, would be suddenly ended by a bullet from him was ludicrous. It wasn't even possible.

His daughter would embrace her since they had met before, and assure her of the moving into gear of the plan that two lovers of such deep and passionate commitment had begun years before. This was the beginning, not the end.

She could understand the FBI investigating and even trying to stop the reorganization. But trying to convince her that her life-long partner in vision, if not in love, would turn against her, even abandon her, even kill her, was not possible.

She would recognize the girl as soon as she opened the door. If it wasn't his daughter, then it would be an assassin. But probably one of the FBI's making. She would have her own bodyguard present. So let them come.

*

Sunday morning and Sunday afternoon were taken up with the business of moving the office of the Senior Senator from California back to the east coast. The buzz from the motion detector at the entrance to the driveway announced the arrival of her last appointment. The Senator stood inside the door with her six foot five inch bodyguard who came complete with bullet-proof vest and two concealed weapons. The closing of car doors outside prompted her to open the front door of her house. The two couples which met her eyes gave a picture of calmness and unhurriedness. Her tension eased a bit. The Senator's eyes quickly found and focused on the young Chinese woman. Yes, it was her.

"Qui Ling, you have come to me!" Cassy Albright stepped toward them, reaching for the daughter of her former lover, and for the feeling that all was well. Her bodyguard stayed right with her, one of his hands in his jacket pocket. Qui Ling also reached out and the two embraced, under the intense scrutiny of the bodyguard.

"My dear friend, Sandra. You have never left my thoughts and prayers. May I present my husband, Len," Len Lancaster shook the hand of the Senator.

"Madame Senator, it is my privilege to suddenly be a part of a friendship that my wife has mentioned many times."

"Welcome, Len. Please, let's step into the house."

The six entered the house and the door was closed. Now, if there was any shooting to be done, the bodyguard had reasonable cause in defending the house.

Len continued, "May I present our dear friends, Jonathan and Sharon. We are all friends with, and work closely with, FBI Agent Joe Cornish. Has he spoken with you?"

The Senator was a bit taken aback, thinking this would be more cloak and dagger. "Yes, I spoke with him yesterday. Shall we sit down with some coffee and talk?" They moved to the living room where coffee was being served.

"Qui Ling, it is so good to see you, and you are so beautiful!"

"Dear Sandra, I have news other than that of a husband and the beauty he brings me. I have news of my father which may not be what you are hoping for."

The bodyguard tensed, and the Senator's heart turned anxious again.

"My father thinks I am in the United States to accomplish the task he has entrusted to me. It was and is a task which I abhor and would die first rather than complete," she sipped her coffee and then lowered her cup onto the saucer in her lap. "He has aged, and with age has grown impatient. He has already started the invasion he dreams of and has sent me here to end your life once the legalities in Washington, D.C. are in place. Even these words in my mouth taste bad and I wish I did not have to say them. However, it is my wish that I could join you in stopping him instead. I am a fugitive from China, even though my father doesn't know it yet. I want to live with my new husband in my new country, and I place great value in the continuation of my friendship with you."

Now, great betrayal, and the wonderful taste of great friendship swirled around in the Senator's heart, mind, and mouth. She gulped some coffee and tried to get rid of the bad part of the taste. Her bodyguard surveyed the four for the first sign of unease or anxiety. He should have insisted on searching them.

"My dear…I hardly know…what to say."

"Madame Senator," Len Lancaster began, "if we may show you pictures which we had operatives in Alaska take, they may help clarify." He took out an envelope and laid out pictures on the coffee table. "These were taken in a Chinese construction company storage yard in Anchorage, the day before yesterday."

As the Senator bent over to look, the bodyguard kept looking at the four. "These seem to be tanks in shipping containers."

"Yes, and we investigated the numbers on the containers and researched their past. All were shipped from China in the past few months to Alaska."

"These tanks are in Alaska now?"

"Yes, ma'am. These six pictures are of approximately ten percent of the containers in the storage yard, and they were randomly taken." Len was careful not to be too convincing, but informational, "The longer weapons sit, the more maintenance they require."

The Senator looked up, not at Len, but at Qui Ling.

"Who does your father answer to these days?" she asked slowly.

"He answers to no one."

"Why would he send you to kill me?"

"Because after the legalities are in place he won't need you anymore. It is that way in my country. If you gain the ruling hand, you must kill off the ones who helped you attain it or they will overthrow you. You must involve younger, needier people who can be controlled by fear. My dear Sandra, I am now expendable, also. I appeal to you for help."

The Senator slowly looked down. The disaster she would not consider was now overtaking her. Yet a small bloom was growing out of the ashes. How could she not help this dear girl who had willingly chosen to help instead of harm her? "How can I help…?"

*

Nicolus's idea was simple. The sheriff's car was the first one in the driveway when he and Matty drove by the other day. Comparing the timing of its arrival with the time of the 911 call, it was an almost miraculous response. The sheriff had to have been the one the maid was talking to as she killed the former governor. He knew to stay out of the view of the surveillance camera near the pool. The sheriff in Anchorage was not elected but appointed by the mayor. That implicated the mayor. The mayor of Anchorage, who was Chinese/American, had been in office for twelve years and was starting his fourth term. Nicolus would go visit the mayor, and Matty would target him at the least indication of the release of the tanks. Jack and Gretchen would find the sheriff's off-duty watering hole, and Gretchen would offer herself to him as a distraction. Once distracted, the sheriff would be caught by Jack and Jeff, and offered freedom from his mess in order to clear his slate and start over. With the sheriff heading in the right direction, he would be able to identify other bad apples involved. The mayor would have his choice, Matty or freedom. A conference call with Joe Cornish solidified the plan.

# 14

The junior senator from California, Jay Williamsford, was preparing Janae for Washington, D.C. to take her seat as his replacement. Jay was also monitoring the mineral rights ownership debate. So far the two additional words had not been noticed.

Julie and Janet, the senator's two girls were helping take charge of their father's recovery. They would intensely miss Janae, but as soon as their father could travel, the three planned to go to D.C. and see her.

As Janae left for the East Coast, she realized that the importance of the work ahead as a senator could be overwhelming, but she knew the plans and strategies were being decided on by someone smarter than her. She was not being asked to do a job she could not do. It would be effortless and fun. She just had to be herself, which she could do, and this brought her peace.

Jennifer left the comforting presence of her husband for the career opportunity of a lifetime, and she was ready for it. As Chief of Staff for Senator Emily J. Halvorson, Janae to her friends, Jennifer would be in charge in a man's world. With the encouragement and wisdom from her husband and the others, this would be fun. The first order of business upon her arrival in Washington, D.C. would be the rescue the western hemisphere from an attack from the eastern hemisphere. Then wade into the other affairs of state. As a former district attorney, she knew how both politics and law enforcement worked. As a lawyer she was comfortable with details. As a champion of good there was lots of work to do, and then, of course there was the social side of being in the nation's capital. Jennifer and Janae would dazzle Washington, D.C. with their beauty and grace.

Joe and Kandee were leaving for the Province of British Columbia in western Canada to work with the Royal Canadian Mounted Police. Bill Buckingham, Joe Cornish's contact there, would have Canada ready for any attack.

Tom and PC would stay close to Joe Cornish, publishing story after story of the ongoing fight against the forces of bad-guy-dom. Tom's journalistic nose had gotten them into this spot and keeping it on course would gain him a Pulitzer in reporting. What bigger story was there than a coup in China, and the Chinese Army taking over legal ownership of Alaska, possibly British Columbia, and maybe even the whole west coast of the United States. Well, someone had to report it, and his wife, PC, was a huge comfort and help.

*

"Your help can be most effective by talking with Joe Cornish," Len Lancaster had one more item to show to Senator Cassy Albright. "But just before we leave I'd like you to take a look at this video from the home of the former governor of Alaska. He was a force for good in Alaska and, as I'm sorry to show you, he was murdered." Len assembled his laptop and started the video. "This woman was the maid in the house."

The Senator was stunned and so was her bodyguard. She spoke slowly, "That woman applied in person yesterday for a position I needed to fill. I was thinking of hiring her."

Jonathan spoke softly, "You've met this woman?"

"Yes. Just yesterday," the Senator slowly said.

The bodyguard spoke this time, slowly also, "We needed a replacement because...one of the staff was killed in a car accident, just last week."

The Senator put her hand on the bodyguard's arm, "They were engaged."

Now everyone was stunned. They all looked at each other, all thinking the same thing.

The bodyguard came back to life first as the gate alarm sounded. He stood and walked to the window that showed the driveway, "We've got company."

Jonathan and Sharon jumped up and went to the window, "Do you recognize the car?"

"No."

"Let me take care of this..." Sharon started walking as she spoke, and she was out the door before Jonathan could protest. It was the sheriff deputy in her coming alive. She walked right up to the car as it slowly rolled up the driveway and into the circle. Chevy sedan, California plates, windows not heavily tinted. Two in front, two in back. As the window rolled down she spoke first, "May I help you with directions?" Concealed weapon bulges were visible under their suit coats. Four men. Large, dark hair, two Caucasian, two Asian.

"Thank you, miss, uh...we must have got the wrong driveway."

"This is the home of Senator Albright. It's pretty hard to get it confused, with the name out front and all. If you gentlemen will just pull up to the side over there, we're expecting a sheriff escort any second now to accompany the Senator to the airport."

"Please convey our apologies, we are in a hurry ourselves," the car rounded the circle and sped out of the driveway.

Jonathan and the bodyguard were at Sharon's side before the car disappeared. The bodyguard asked, "What did you say?!"

"I told them they were having a near death experience."

"My God. I'm tempted to believe you," was all Jonathan could say.

"Four big men with concealed weapons. Two Caucasian, two Asian. California plates. Get me a piece of paper and a pen." Jonathan produced them and Sharon wrote down the license plate number. Then she got on her phone. "Boss, this is Sharon Madison...good...yeah, but I'll always think of you as my boss... I'm on vacation and witnessed an attempted crime; could you run a plate for me?" She gave her former boss in Washington State the California plate number. "Thank you, sir. Anything I can do for you down here?...Sunshine? ...Okay, sending some up. Talk to you soon...yeah, bye."

"I'd sure like to follow that car, but we'd better finish up here," Sharon eyed Jonathan and they returned to the house. Inside Len, Qui Ling and the senator were talking.

"Anybody we know?" asked the senator.

"Four men carrying weapons," Sharon said to Senator Albright. Then the former sheriff deputy asked the bodyguard, "Can you get help?"

"Yes, I have a help line to the Secret Service." He got up and moved to the window again and made that call.

Then Jonathan spoke, "We must leave, Senator, but call Joe Cornish. He will tell you how your help will be ever so valuable in stopping this Chinese invasion. Will you call him?"

"Yes. Yes, I will call him right now. I might just send an assassination team to China myself." She had the beginnings of a wry smile.

"I volunteer!" yelled the bodyguard from the window. He was serious.

*

"Agent Cornish, this is Senator Cassy Albright calling."

"Yes, Senator, a delight to hear from you."

"I met with your wonderful people and I must admit to a certain amount of shame in my thoughts about this invasion business. I wondered if you had any thoughts as to how I could be helpful in stopping this attack?"

"Madame Senator, I have more regard for you than I have time to express. If you could contact the Junior Senator from California and convince him to work together with you for the passage of the mineral rights ownership bill being introduced tomorrow, it would be extremely valuable."

"I would…think we would want to work against it."

"Yes, except we inserted into the bill a poison pill that will cause endless controversy after the fact, and therefore buy us time to deal with this threat. If it fails, the President will simply use his executive order power and make it happen."

"I…need not ask how you inserted a…poison pill…no. I would be glad to help in this regard and in any other way possible. I believe I owe you for saving my life. I had visitors this afternoon, and your people drove them off. It's possible they were sent to kill me."

"Senator, I assume you have adequate protective services?"

"Yes, my bodyguard just called the Secret Service for additional help. Thank you."

"Thank you, Madame Senator, for your help. Call me any time," Joe Cornish hung up.

As that call ended, the Joe Cornish express was lifting off with Jonathan, Sharon, Len Lancaster and Qui Ling aboard. At twenty thousand feet, Sharon received a call that explained the plates she had asked about. They belonged to a rental car, and it was rented by a construction company in Anchorage. Sharon eyed Qui Ling. Things were heating up. Was there an explosion imminent?

# 15

Qui Ling either didn't enjoy flying or something else was up. Sharon could see it. She was near tears. Len was noticing also, and he could see the concern on Sharon's face.

Len leaned closer, "There's something you haven't said yet. You're holding on to it because you don't want it to be true."

Qui Ling turned and buried her face in Len's chest in shame. After a moment she said, "I told my dear Sandra that I was now expendable, too. I said the words, but the feelings are just now coming."

Everyone waited and listened. Qui Ling continued, "I have shamed my father and he is aware of it now. There is no forgiveness for this in my country."

Len held her, "In my arms, your protection is guaranteed. We have many friends here."

Sharon added, "Your husband is right, we will see to your care."

Qui Ling pushed away from her husband just enough to face Sharon, "Those four men…in that car…were there to kill *me*…not Sandra. They followed us to her house. They were not aware of whose house it was, just that *I* was there."

There was silence in the plane.

Sharon's countenance changed. Her eyes got real serious. She looked at Jonathan with a look he had not seen before. He shifted gears quickly.

"Buckle up," Jonathan said as he rose and went into the cockpit. "Emergency landing at the nearest airport!" Jonathan buckled himself into the copilot's seat.

Rocko, the ex-fighter pilot, knew just what to do. They were on the ground in ten minutes. Then he asked, "What's up?"

"Just a precaution, but we might have picked up an extra passenger back at LAX. One with an explosive personality. How do we check it out?"

Rocko was on the phone to the tower at the Salt Lake City Airport where he had put down. He rolled to the outer perimeter and shut down. Everyone got off as fire trucks came screaming in. An aid car packed the four in and got out of there. Rocko stayed and led the search. As a bomb squad truck arrived, Rocko noticed something on the inside of the extended door covering for the nose wheel. Rocko motioned for the others to stay back, as he went in for a closer inspection. One of the firefighters in full gear went with him.

It was a box. It didn't have an alarm clock taped to it, and it wasn't ticking, but it was humming. Rocko looked it over and decided it was held in place magnetically. He put both hands on it and pulled it out. Then he stood and walked it over to the bomb squad truck and carefully put it into the armored bucket, where the explosion would go straight up. Then he went back to searching again. An hour later, Rocko was satisfied that he knew every inch of his jet again. The passengers were called back and loaded again, and they left Salt Lake City, heading north to Montana.

Jonathan explained to everyone as they settled in for the rest of the flight, "Rocko found a bomb that was timed to go off as we landed in Montana." Everybody just shook their heads.

Qui Ling actually looked a bit better, "My father is here directing things. He must be in Alaska."

*

It was easy for Gretchen to become a hard working executive woman who dressed up pretty after work and tried to find some entertainment. She walked into the exclusive bar that a handful of retired law enforcement guys owned.

The sheriff of this area of Alaska was big, but not fat, and he was quite handsome in his uniform. He sat at the bar surrounded by a group of guys and gals like bees buzzing around a beehive. Gretchen moved in her loveliest way through the crowd and sat a couple of stools away from the sheriff. When the bartender saw her, he moved from the sheriff to Gretchen, along with just about everyone's eyes. As soon as the sheriff noticed her, he looked around to see if she was accompanied by anyone. Gretchen ordered a glass of Chardonnay and then let out a quiet sigh. Feeling the gaze of the sheriff, she turned and looked into his big eyes.

The sheriff's blood pressure went up a few dozen points, which was normal for most men when Gretchen's gaze hit them. He swallowed and turned on his professional charm, "How are you this evening, ma'am?"

Gretchen held his eye for about three seconds and then turned to her glass of wine. When she looked back at the sheriff, the confidence had faded to a bit more of a helpless look. Then she smiled that smile that was noticeably fake. At that point the hook was set in the Sheriff. A stunningly beautiful woman with a confused countenance. "I...I'm...I'm good. I'm just trying to lose a guy I met last night. He's been calling me at work all day, and...I thought if I came in here..."

"Yes, ma'am," the Sheriff was trying to calm himself and sound professional. "You point him out to me if he comes in and I'll take care of him. And when your evening is done I'd be glad to escort you home; I'm off duty."

Gretchen put her hand to her mouth and looked back at her glass. She quickly reached for her drink and sipped, "Thank you, Sheriff," then she looked back at him and a bit more forcefully said, "Thank you."

Any guy who offers his assistance to a beautiful woman and is rewarded with a 'thank you' full of sincerity, has to be careful. If he's had a few drinks, it's harder. The sheriff, having just finished off his second beer, had been bending forward to see around the two people between him and Gretchen. Now he rose to his feet, slightly bumping into a couple of hangers-on unintentionally. "Ma'am, I'm Sheriff Daniel Deane," he took a step toward her and offered his hand. "Please, call me Dan."

Gretchen turned and held out her hand fully facing the sheriff. He gently took her hand and she asked, "Your name is Dan?"

"Yes, ma'am."

Gretchen smiled and sort of looked down at the sheriff's gun, "Nice to meet you, Dan...my name is Danielle..." then she raised her eyes to his, "My friends call me Dannie." Gretchen had her phone in her other hand and pushed a button on it without being noticed.

"Dannie, this is my pleasure. Will you join me at a table?" He kept hold of her hand and led her to a side table.

Before they were able to sit down, the door opened and in walked Jack. He looked around and when he spotted Gretchen he stopped and stared at her. Gretchen remained standing at the table and stared back at Jack. The sheriff noticed and whispered, "Is that him?"

Gretchen's hand went to her mouth and she nodded and whispered back, "Yes."

"Sit here, I'll take care of this," the sheriff then turned his gaze on Jack and went straight over to him.

Jack was smaller than the sheriff. "Good evening, Sheriff."

"Sir, I'd like to speak with you privately. Would you join me outside?" He stood directly in Jack's path to Gretchen.

"Yes, sir, Sheriff, but may I talk to that woman first?" Jack had to lean around the sheriff and point.

"No. Step outside." That professional law enforcement voice left no room for debate. He took Jack's arm, turned him around, and escorted him outside. "Stand here, bend over and place your hands on the hood of my car."

Jack did it but said, "Sheriff, you don't understand."

"Shut up, and don't move." The sheriff carefully searched Jack, took his wallet, cuffed him, and put him in the back seat of his patrol car. Then he got into the front seat. Looking into the wallet he said, "Okay, Jack, you are not under arrest, but I have the right to detain you and question you. You don't have to answer. The woman you were pointing to has complained that you have been following her today. What's the deal?"

"She has five hundred dollars of mine and I want it back," Jack was cooperating.

The sheriff, having heard it all before, rolled his eyes and said, "How did she get five hundred dollars from you?"

"She's a con. She came up to me at another bar last night and asked for help. She said her husband came home for dinner with a young blonde on his arm. She left and said she had nowhere to stay and needed money to fly down to LA where her daughter was."

"So you willingly gave her money."

"Yes, I did. Wouldn't you have?"

The sheriff shook his head as he was thinking, "Listen, I'll go in and see about your money. You stay put." He got out of the car, but looked back at Jack before he closed the door, "Just stay calm."

Sheriff Daniel Deane entered the bar and sat down at the table. Very carefully he asked, "Dannie, what happened last night with your husband?"

Gretchen produced a guilty look, then slowly said, "He came home with another woman. Brought her right into our home. So…I left."

"This man said you asked him for help and he gave you five hundred dollars. Is that true?"

"No…I took the five hundred from his drawer before I left."

"Left from where?"

"The house."

"What house?"

"Our house," The sheriff wasn't following. "The man out there is my husband, and I took the money from his underwear drawer before I left."

"Dannie, the man out in my car is your husband? Why didn't you tell me that before?"

"Because…he didn't want me anymore…and you were so nice to offer your help…and…"

"Okay, will you go out with me and talk with him? I'll help you get this straightened out."

Gretchen nodded and they went out to the patrol car. The sheriff put her in the front passenger seat.

"Jack, is Dannie your wife?"

"Yes, Gretchen is my wife. You looked at my ID, please look at hers." Gretchen handed her ID to Sheriff Daniel Deane.

"Okay, Jack and Gretchen, you have the same last name." He looked at Gretchen, "Would you kindly explain what's going on?"

Jack began, "Sheriff, you informed me that you had the right to question me. Now you have asked me a question. I ask you to listen patiently while I answer your question."

"Go ahead."

"Gretchen and I are husband and wife. We work as covert operatives for the FBI, Seattle Office of Special Investigations. We were tasked with meeting with the sheriff of this county about an important matter, privately. We have accomplished that." Jack glanced at Gretchen and then back to the sheriff.

Sheriff Deane squinted and pursed his lips, "Okay…keep going."

Jack continued, "Our boss at the FBI is presenting evidence to a grand jury tomorrow about the invasion of the Chinese Army into Alaska. Part of the evidence proves the involvement of you and the mayor in this affair."

Sheriff Deane had a stunned look on his face now, and sweat began to form under his uniform, "You're not making sense..."

"Our contact with you is a courtesy from the FBI to give you this one chance, right now, to unhook from this affair and live for the rest of your life free, under the custody of the FBI. If you do not take this offer, you will face the penalties for treason." Jack stopped to let what he said have its impact.

Sheriff Daniel Deane was wide-eyed and suddenly felt caged in his own patrol car. He was looking slightly down, but his eyes were going back and forth between Jack and Gretchen. "You can't prove..." then he caught himself, paused, and then said, "Go on, I'm listening."

Gretchen took over, "Dan, you can live free from prosecution and prison starting now, by simply agreeing to help us and the FBI to curtail this invasion."

Jack added, "Our boss thought that you might understand, whereas he was less positive about the mayor."

Sheriff Deane's mind was running in circles now, looking for a way out. At the mention of the mayor, he blurted out, "You're right about the mayor! He's a damn politician, and they've offered him the Governorship of the new Province of Alaska...look...I didn't like this from the start. But the Chinese guy running it offered a lot, and he's already killed people when they gave the wrong answer." The sheriff was shaking his head. In less than two minutes he had been disarmed even though he was the only one with a gun. In a soft voice he said, "Tell me what to do."

"Gretchen will ride with you. Follow me to our safe house and we will explain more, and show you how you can help. First, please take these cuffs off me." Jack turned his back side to the sheriff who leaned back and unlocked the cuffs.

Jack wanted to get out, but Sheriff Deane said, "Hold on. This Chinese guy is all business. He's very dangerous and he might even have me under surveillance."

"Okay. Noted. Let's do it this way. You lead with your lights flashing, I'll follow you, and Gretchen will tell you were to go. That way it will look like you're doing your job."

"Yeah, good," Sheriff Daniel Deane got out and opened the back door. Jack got out and into his own car. Then the sheriff drove away, with Gretchen next to him, into his new life.

# 16

Rocko made a smooth landing at the ranch's runway in the hills above the Big Horn River. His passengers were glad to be home safely. They were met by Joe Cornish, Tom and PC, and two-year-old Rogette. While Rocko tended to his flying machine, the rest went into the ranch house and enjoyed the warmth and safety of dinner at home, and an evening of telling their story. Joe Cornish listened attentively and Tom wrote as fast as he could. Rogette wouldn't sit anywhere but on her mommy's lap, and there she fell asleep.

*

Tony's Inn in Seattle saw more activity than usual. George, from Southern California, was sending operatives and armaments north for its fortification. It was becoming a way station for those being sent on to Alaska for covert missions. Tony, Millie, James, Wallie, Alexander and Joni, all had their hands full. Joe Cornish had gotten Archie a position in the growing police department in Nome, Alaska, and his communications were extremely valuable.

*

Sheriff Daniel Deane was making sure he didn't lose the car following him. He had his flashing lights on, but not his siren. He had his uniform on, was doing the job he loved, and pretty much everyone who saw his patrol car coming knew who he was.

Gretchen, in the passenger seat, was directing him to the safe house. The sheriff felt good. He had a beautiful woman beside him. The few minutes of mostly silence between them was sweet, but he was bubbling to say what he felt. So he finally did, "I have to say this, Gretchen. You are a very beautiful woman."

"Yeah, and I'm a law enforcement officer, too! How cool is that?" Gretchen was beautiful, and felt beautiful, but what she liked best was that she was on the side of good, and the more she worked, the more good got done. Plus, the success they were having seemed to come with very little effort expended.

The sheriff replied, "It's a great combination. But I've got to tell you, these guys are really bad guys."

"I don't doubt it a bit, but I've got a couple of bad guys for you to meet who are now good guys, and I'd put them up against anyone, anytime, Sheriff."

"This I've got to see. Please, call me Dan."

"Okay, Dan. Turn here."

*

Joe Cornish hung up. Jack had just called and explained the outcome of their contact with Sheriff Daniel Deane of Anchorage.

Sitting with everyone in Montana, he said, "Who wants to go to Alaska?"

Tom dropped his pencil because PC kicked him in the leg. "Uh...we do, sir...we do." He looked at PC to make sure he had covered everything.

"Perfect. We'll leave in the morning." Joe Cornish then dialed Tony in Seattle, "Tony, my yacht is going to Alaska as soon as you can load it with armaments and personnel ready for ops in Alaska."

"Yes, sir. We'll load tonight and she'll be ready to sail in the morning."

"Perfect. Listen, Tony, I need your input. Jack and Gretchen just turned the sheriff in the Anchorage area. He was apparently helping the Chinese invasion with some reluctance. Jack's going to introduce the sheriff to Nicolus and Matty and put their heads together to plan how to meet this challenge. Do you see any problem with that... I guess what I mean is, I'd like you to be there, too. Can Seattle spare you and Millie for a bit?"

"Yeah, the others can run things just fine. We'll ride up on the yacht."

"Well, I'd rather have you join Tom, PC and myself on the jet so we can talk some more. We'll probably touch down at Boeing Field about ten tomorrow morning, and then fly on to Anchorage. Will that work?

"Yes, sir. That will work fine. We'll be there waiting at 10 AM."

Joe Cornish hung up, dialed his men on his yacht and updated them.

After taking care of business he said, "Well then, dear friends, the world is secure for another moment. Jonathan, I'll leave this dear family in your capable hands and take Tom and PC with me to Anchorage. I'm sure we can find some trouble to start up there."

PC jumped in, "Oh good, I like getting into trouble."

Tom just looked at her. Then he stood and took her hand, saying, "Okay, troublemaker, let's head for bed."

Joe Cornish was up and off to bed, too. As he walked to his room, he dialed the number of Jay Williamsford in San Francisco and filled him in on the call that he could be expecting from his fellow senator, Cassy Albright. Then for the next hour he sat in his room making more calls and working on plans for the next few weeks.

# 17

The next morning was early as usual for Joe Cornish. He talked with Jennifer in the nation's capital while he walked in the cool morning light of the Montana dawn. Planning, walking, talking, praying, thinking, planning; it was a routine for him that he enjoyed because he was doing good and the need was everywhere. As he applied his routine to events at hand, he savored the eye-opening thoughts and ideas he came up with. Good seemed to break out when given the opportunity. He looked forward to setting foot in Alaska again.

With breakfast over, he, Tom and PC boarded his jet and took off for Seattle. Joe Cornish spoke with Tom and PC about the possibilities of events in the next few days. He wanted to let them know what to expect so they would have an idea of what to write in their weekly story for the Seattle Times.

PC thought there was something wrong when she felt the jet slow down, but they were just starting the descent into Boeing Field. Tony and his wife, Millie, scampered up the stairs with some luggage and got belted in as the plane lined up to take off again. Millie and PC managed to get a hug in before takeoff.

"I'm encouraged with the way things are going and the speed at which they are happening. We are simply trying to keep up. The overall good that is making headway into some very dark areas in this adventure we call our country, is amazing. And we get to be a part of it. Bad guys will step in, when good guys hesitate."

"Wow. Can I quote you on that?" Tom knew a good line when he heard one.

"No, you know you can't quote me. But yes, use the phrase and the ideas. We want to do two things through your stories. Show good people what can be done, and show bad people what has been done. Just don't use our names, except for yours in the bylines."

"Girls, there will be you two and Jeff to run the household. Everything from food and laundry to communications and security. Gretchen and Nickolaea will help you get acquainted with everything, but they will be out in the field some, too. Tony, you and I will assess Sheriff Deane and decide whether he can work with Nicolus and Matty, or not. Then our job is to plan and execute a surgical strike into the heart of the invasion and make sure it hurts."

Tony asked, "Do we know what or who the main target is?"

"Qui Ling is quite sure her father is running things in Alaska and Sheriff Deane has met him. We don't know his name, but he has already killed for not getting his way. The sheriff's life may already be in danger, which is why we must move fast. Our plans should somehow follow this line of thinking: Sheriff Deane will be our forward man, Nicolus, our delivery guy, and Matty, our assassin or demolition man, whichever is needed."

"The Chinese have used patience to grow in strength. We will pierce their strength, and by doing so, we will add to the burden of their patience. A dictatorial tyrant will, at that point, do something foolish and our job is to exploit that weakness into the very heart of the invasion."

"How will we know what and where?" Tom asked.

"They will present those answers to us. We just need to have our eyes open. Now Tom, I think we need to run the story you have prepared in the local paper as soon as we can."

"Okay, if I get it done this afternoon, it should be in the paper two mornings later." Tom saw PC was about to chime in, so he kept going, "We'll monitor it until it happens."

"Perfect. Tony, any thoughts?"

"Only one. We imported some heroin from a Chinese Army guy once. I wonder if it's the same guy?"

"What was his name?" Joe Cornish asked.

"Same deal. No name. But he was ruthless. He came after some of my rivals who had tried to short him. This guy was all business."

"Would he or his men recognize you or Nicolus or Matty?"

"No, I don't think so. He always used an intermediary. Always the same gal."

Now Joe Cornish's mind came to a screeching halt. He looked at Tony, "You've met Qui Ling and heard her talk."

"Yeah, I thought the same thing at first, but I'm sure it's not her. But I wonder if she has a sister."

Joe Cornish had his phone out and in thirty seconds was talking to Jonathan. Using the speaker phone the group in Montana listened as Joe Cornish framed the question as delicately as he could.

Qui Ling answered readily, "That would be my cousin. She goes wherever my father goes. I think they are... lovers. I was trained in covert intelligence, she was trained in ruthless murder. She acts as my father's bodyguard and assassin."

"Qui Ling, thank you for that information. And I must ask you, could you turn her by talking to her? Does she secretly want out like you did?" Joe Cornish wanted to give Qui Ling a moment to think about this.

"No," She answered without hesitation.

"You sound very positive."

"Yes. My cousin murdered my mother at my father's request. She is obsessed with him. I would say it is my cousin who is running the woman who killed the former governor. The accident in California killing Senator Albright's staff member was probably a murder, also."

"How can we identify your cousin?"

"You can't. She alters her appearance. I myself would only recognize her by her voice."

"But she recognizes you," Joe Cornish wanted to be clear.

"Yes."

"Okay, thank you, Qui Ling. Jonathan, I leave her in your capable hands."

"Joe, I heard from my men in China this morning. The Vice President of China has disappeared. It's not public knowledge yet, but the President has cancelled appointments and is holed up in anticipation of trouble."

"My God! Okay, thank you, Jonathan. Keep me posted."

# 18

Sheriff Daniel Deane flipped off his lights as Gretchen pointed him onto a residential street. Motion detector lights went on as they pulled into a driveway and Jack pulled in next to them. As they got out and approached the house, more lights automatically went on. The yard was hedged all around with high shrubbery and the house appeared to have new windows. The front door had a bullet-proof glass door where the screen door had been. Jeff opened the front door from inside and watched as Gretchen keyed in the code on the key pad of the glass door. Sheriff Deane followed Gretchen in as Jack checked the driveway one last time before he came in and shut the door.

In the kitchen, Gretchen made introductions, "Sheriff Daniel Deane, this is our base. Jeff here is currently in charge of this facility. Nicolus and Nickolaea are excellent at whatever they put their hands to, and Matty is just plain dangerous. We're glad he's on our side. The sheriff goes by Dan. Dan, please have a seat at the kitchen table with us. This is where we think, plan, eat, and brag."

Matty took over, "Dan, you and me come from opposite sides of the track, but I've been given a second chance, so now I see us as being on the same side. If we work together, your life will be as important to me as my own."

Nickolaea had gotten up and was putting mugs of coffee in front of everyone as Nicolus spoke, "Dan, my wife is a gift I didn't deserve. It's the same with the second chance I was given; it was a gift I still don't deserve. Freedom is something you can't buy, but as a gift it is priceless. We would all welcome your participation in stopping this invasion, if a second chance seems good to you."

Then Jeff spoke up, "Dan, I've been an undercover operative since I was nineteen. I owe any success, not to mention my life, to Joe Cornish who works for the FBI. You'll meet him soon. Good guys don't come any better."

Then Jack added, "Yeah, I talked to Joe Cornish on my way over and he's coming up tomorrow. He wants to meet with you, Dan. By the way, Gretchen was one of Joe Cornish's undercover operatives at the strip club I operated. She talked me into turning, and I owe her and Joe Cornish my very life. The owner of the club shot my two brothers, but we managed to turn him, too. He'll be up tomorrow with Joe Cornish."

"My God. I've never seen such fast and thorough rehabilitation before. I'm what...I guess you'd call a...dirty cop. You've probably never seen one of them before." Sheriff Deane was starting to ease a bit.

Matty chimed in, "Oh, I had twenty of them on my payroll down in San Diego. One of them came with me. He's undercover in the Nome police department as we speak."

"Nome? That place is like the wild west. I knew the sheriff there. He got voted out and I never saw him again. I want you to know, this Chinese guy is bad news."

"Well, I just want a chance to shake his hand. If I get that chance, I'll squeeze the life out of him. The last thing he'll see is me, grinning." Matty just wanted everyone to know what his idea was.

Nickolaea spoke as she sat down, "There is a time for killing and a time for second chances. Let's hope he's smart, and knows the difference."

Sheriff Deane thought for a moment, "I...know of twelve different murders that he has committed himself...he doesn't deserve a second chance."

"Yes," said Nicolus, "we never deserved it either. But when we were offered it, we all grabbed it like a Christmas present and haven't looked back. Dan, your immediate problem is, he's going to find out you are missing and come looking for you. You can't go anywhere without some of us with you. How about family?"

"Oh," he quickly glanced over at Gretchen and back again, "I never had time to get married. My folks got hit head-on by a drunk. They both died. I was belted into a car seat in back, and the doctors pulled me through. I got fostered around and fell in love with hard work enough to put myself through college and the police academy. It doesn't seem that long ago, but it's because I really like being a sheriff. Time flies. Just don't let me catch you drunk behind a wheel."

"Okay," Nicolus was thinking, "Where can we put your sheriff car so no one will find it?"

"Oh, yeah. I didn't think of that, but I know the perfect place. Somebody follow me and bring me back."

"My wife and I will follow you," Nicolus said. "Matty, they might be out there ready to attack as soon as we leave."

"Right. I got it covered. You call me if you get in trouble."

*

Nicolus and Nickolaea followed Dan to the sheriff's office and he parked in his usual place. They parked across the street as he got out and walked into the building. He never came back out that door, but after a half hour Nickolaea saw him coming up from behind them dressed in plain clothes. He tapped on the rear door, slid in and ducked down. "Go ahead," Dan said. "The Chevy Blazer over to the left thinks I'm still inside."

Nicolus drove around a while and made sure he was not being followed. Then they went to the safe house. "Any trouble?" Nicolus asked as they entered and closed the door.

"Nope. Not a peep," Matty said. He had a knife out and was sharpening it.

"Okay, we might have gotten away clear. Let's all get some sleep. Remember, we're at war, and we've got to sleep when we can. I'll take first watch. Nickolaea, I'll come and get you at 3AM." Nicolus gave Dan a cell phone. "Sleep with it in your hand or under you. If it vibrates, it means we're under attack. Jack and Gretchen will show you your room and where the weapons are." Nicolus held his hand out and said, "Welcome."

For the first time in a long time, Dan felt good about himself even though he had changed out of his uniform.

# 19

Tom and PC were the first ones off the corporate jet when it landed in chilly Anchorage. They carted their luggage through the airport and found the taxi lineup. Tom gave the driver the destination and off they went. They were on a mission for Joe Cornish.

When the taxi pulled over, PC was the first to notice, "Hey, this isn't..."

Tom interrupted to keep her from saying 'the newspaper.' "Thanks, driver. Now listen," Tom waved three one hundred dollar bills in the driver's face to get his attention off PC. "You have our luggage. We might be fifteen minutes or two hours. I will call your cell and tell you where and when to pick us up." Tom jotted down the driver's phone number. "Just don't forget us, okay?" Tom dropped the money in the driver's lap.

"Yes, sir. You are my only customer until you say differently."

Tom got out with his briefcase and helped PC out. She looked at the motel they were in front of and said, "Can't wait, huh?" Tom grabbed her hand and walked toward the motel. Halfway across the parking lot he glanced around and saw the taxi was still there.

"Just follow my lead and pretend you're in love with me."

"Sorry, Charlie. I don't do either of those things: follow or pretend."

"Oh, you're in for a treat then. First times are always fun," Tom escorted her in the door of the motel office.

"May I help you?"

"Hi. We'd like a room with a king-size bed." Tom looked out the window and saw the taxi was gone. "But we're late for an appointment," Tom held up his briefcase, "so will this hold it for us?" He dropped two one hundred dollar bills on the desk, wheeled PC around and headed for the door.

"I'll need a name, sir!"

"Tom. We'll get the key when we get back." The door closed behind them and they headed out to the street and up the sidewalk.

"What are we doing?" PC asked with just a bit of an attitude.

"My dear, have you forgotten?" Tom was glancing around and keeping up the pace as if they were being watched. "You're married to the smartest and soon to be richest journalist in the world." Then he put his arm around her as if they were lovers on a stroll, and said softly, "We've got to figure we are at war. We don't want a taxi report of us being dropped off at the newspaper office with this story coming out."

"Where's the newspaper building?"

"Four or five blocks up. We need the exercise."

The taxi driver went directly to a coffee hangout for cabbies. He flashed the three bills at his friends and laughed, "He said he'd be fifteen minutes or two hours." He raised his coffee cup in a toast and said, "Here's to two hours, buddy. You had a handful of woman with you!"

*

Joe Cornish, Tony and Millie were met at the airport by Jeff in the new Jeep wagon. He arrived just after Tom and PC left. Joe Cornish helped load luggage and then said, "A tour of the city, my good man, and then how about lunch at one of the clubs." Tony perked up with surprise.

Jeff interjected, "Sir, we have lunch ready at the house."

"Jeff, I'd like to include Tom and PC in as much as we can. They are on a mission of about two hours duration. I want to pick them up before we go to the safe house, so we have a two hour window. Could you perhaps call and tell everyone we'll be delayed and to go ahead and have lunch? And tell them we'll bring dinner back with us for tonight." Jeff had his phone out and to his ear. Life was always an adventure with Joe Cornish.

After a short tour of the city, Jeff pulled into the biggest strip club in Anchorage. Tony and Millie were excited, so Joe Cornish gave them some instructions, "Let's go in separately, and act like we don't know each other. That will give me time with Jeff. You two check the place out and have lunch. See what you can see. Most importantly, see if you recognize anyone or see anyone who might recognize you. When you see Jeff and I leave, you guys leave, too. Have fun."

Tony and Millie did just that. After an hour and a half they had an eyeful and a wonderful lunch. When they saw Joe Cornish and Jeff paying their bill, they waited a bit and then did the same. As Jeff drove around waiting for a call from Tom, Joe Cornish quizzed Tony and Millie, "Anything interesting?"

"No surprises. They run a well-organized club. There wasn't anything wildly wrong, and I wouldn't change anything in a drastic way. I didn't see one person I recognized, either." Tony looked at Millie.

"Yeah, nice place. I chatted with some of the girls in the restroom. They don't mind working here." She looked at Tony, "I saw a girl who is a younger sister to one of the girls in San Diego."

"Which one?"

"You remember Candace? She was kind of…big."

"Oh, okay. I remember."

Joe Cornish then said, "Millie, did she recognize you?"

"No, she was dancing."

"Would she if you introduced yourself to her?"

"Uh... no, she wouldn't recognize me, but she would remember who I was... you know, by reputation."

Joe Cornish looked at Tony, "Man, it would be nice to have some eyes and ears on the inside. Millie, what do you think the chances are that you could talk to her and turn her to our side, but still have her work there?"

"No need. I can go in and talk to her based on my acquaintance with her sister. You'd be surprised what us girls talk about. I'll find out if she's having fun, or if she has it bad, or what. It'll take me a couple of times over three or four days. I would enjoy it."

Joe Cornish sort of shrugged and looked at Tony, "Wow! Okay, perfect. Thank you, Millie." Then his phone rang.

*

Tom and PC entered the newspaper building, "How come I can never remember that girl's name?"

"It's Tina, and it's because there is something more vivid that you remember about her."

"Oh, yeah, Tina. Okay, here we go." They walked in and up to the counter.

Tina jumped up with a big grin, "Hi Tom, hi PC. Tell me what's cooking?"

"It's hot, Tina. How soon can you get it in?"

"Tomorrow's paper is already put to bed unless the world ends or something. The next day your article will be on the front page. Am I good or what?"

Tom had his hand on PC's arm and began to squeeze as she was about to speak. "Great, Tina, and if you get it on the front page, put your name in the byline with mine." Tom opened his briefcase and handed the printed story to her.

"Gee, Tina, do you really think your editor can get it in?" PC was trying to cause trouble.

"Oh, yeah. I just invite him over and cook for him."

"Yeah, I can picture…"

"Thanks, Tina. See you soon." Tom had PC turned around and out the door before she could cause any more trouble.

"Well, that went well." They walked back toward the motel and Tom called the taxi driver as they got there, "We're on the sidewalk, waiting."

Two minutes later the taxi screeched to a halt and the driver got out and opened the rear door for them.

"Perfect timing. Now drop us off at the airport, please." Ten minutes later Tom and PC were loading their luggage onto a cart and waving goodbye to a happy cabbie. Tom then phoned Joe Cornish, "We're in front of the airport."

"Okay, go ahead and rent a car. We'll meet you there and follow you to the safe house."

# 20

Not long after that, the Jeep wagon and a rented Ford sedan pulled up to the Alaska safe house. Everything looked normal. As soon as Tom and PC got out, the front door opened and Jack, Nicolus, and Matty came out and helped get all the luggage into the house in one trip. Then they gathered in the big kitchen.

Joe Cornish shook hands with Nicolus and Nickolaea because it had been a while since he had seen them. He also shook hands with Jack, and Gretchen gave him a huge hug. She then introduced Sheriff Daniel Deane to the ones who hadn't met him. After handshakes, Millie went right up to Matty and gave him a big hug. She said, "That's from Cindy and so is this," she handed Matty an envelope with a letter in it. Matty looked at it. On the front it said 'To my Matty,' and on the back it said 'Don't forget, I love you.' Matty had to turn away and go look out the window. His thoughts were of the hell he had put that girl through before they met Joe Cornish, and somehow she wanted him to know she loved him. He muscled back the tears that wanted to come, folded the envelope and stuffed it into his back pocket. He went around and checked every window before he sat down at the big table with everyone else.

"Well, Sheriff Deane, I hope we are not scaring you." Joe Cornish began.

"Sir, my new friends here have all been telling me what an important event being given a second chance has been to them. With me it's still sinking in, but I'll tell you this, I give you permission to shoot me in the back if I get riled up and try to go back, because that will be what is waiting for me if I do."

"Sheriff, I congratulate you on your decision and on your courage." Joe Cornish was simple and serious. He continued, "Tom and PC have written a story exclusively for the Anchorage newspaper that will come out the day after tomorrow. It will be the catalyst for action. Millie noticed at lunch today at the club, a sister of a friend that she can get information out of. This could be very valuable."

"With this story coming out, we are looking for our enemy to make a blunder of big enough proportions for us to drive a spear into the heart of this invasion, and at least make it hurt. Then, from the consequences of that spear, we stay on offense and strike over and over where we see openings until the invasion crumbles."

"What if we encounter these tanks in the street?" Tony had seen the pictures.

"We won't be engaging them. We are the guerrillas, good guerrillas. The enemy will hand us victory after victory without being aware of it. Some of these battles have already begun and the enemy doesn't have a clue. Washington, D.C. is the scene of one of those battles. Jeff will be leaving soon to pick up Taylor in Montana and join Janae and Jennifer in D.C. They have their hands full already because what's going on there is vital to our success here. Jonathan has a team in China monitoring events there, and ready to do whatever might be helpful. Tony's Inn in Seattle is sending up a steady stream of arms and covert operatives to join the work force up here as our eyes and ears. Joe and Kandee are in Canada helping them to prepare for an invasion. The newspaper story will help them."

"Sheriff Deane is the ace up our sleeve that no one knows we have. Sheriff, your knowledge of the town, contacts you have, and the fact that you've met the invasion's boss will all prove important in their own time. Our job is to use your expertise, but keep you safe at the same time."

The sheriff commented, "So far it's working."

"Okay, I have a few important details before we break up and the cooks decide on what to do for dinner since I said I would bring dinner and I forgot."

"Not a problem, boss!" Gretchen reassured everyone.

"Thank you. We've gotten three vital pieces of information in the last few days. Len Lancaster, his wife and child who just escaped from China are safely tucked away in Montana. We've gotten two big things from them. First, this invasion into Alaska is a cover for the Chinese Army to take over the Chinese government." Everybody's jaw dropped. "Secondly, Len's wife Qui Ling, who is the daughter of the Chinese Army general, says her cousin is the general's bodyguard and is as ruthless as anyone we've ever encountered."

Sheriff Deane jumped in, "I've met her. She scared the...she scared me."

Nicolus glanced at Nickolaea, and the slightest smile was forming on her face. Matty snickered, but was getting antsy. All he could see was someone's hands going for his Cindy's throat and he wanted to take them on right now.

Joe Cornish continued, "The last item came in this morning. Jonathan's men in China found out that the Chinese Vice President is missing and the President himself has cancelled all his appointments and is expecting trouble. Nobody else knows this."

Now there was silence in the room as the enormity of the situation became more apparent.

"Ladies and gentlemen, I guarantee you we are on the winning side. How long it will take and how many lives will be affected are yet to be known. But we are undercover, and as such have the best shot at tripping and crippling this menace. Perhaps the United States Army might join in, if needs be."

Everyone pondered this and the "tip of the sword" situation they were in.

Then Joe Cornish changed the mood, "Ladies, if you would see to dinner and security, I'd like to speak to the men for a few minutes."

Nickolaea headed for the security room, Gretchen, PC, and Millie for the kitchen appliances.

Jack, Jeff, Nicolus, Matty, Tony, and Tom escorted Joe Cornish and Sheriff Daniel Deane into the library and sat down. Jack had anticipated Joe Cornish's arrival and had a bottle of merlot ready. He poured everyone a glass.

"Thank you, Jack. Gentlemen, as a team we all work together toward one goal, yet each of us has unique abilities to contribute as well. As things proceed in the next few days, we will each step up when necessary to apply those specialties, while we do all we can to support and defend one another. We cannot afford to lose even one of our ladies, so we must accompany them and treat them as our most valuable asset. Their intuition and unique perspective are invaluable. We do not know if this facility has been compromised or if we are still a secret, hence our security. Our teamwork will not keep trouble from happening, but it will lessen its impact on our operation."

"With Tom's story hitting the newsstands in about thirty hours, intel is our most important job right now. Tony, we need a list of all the covert operatives that have been sent up from Seattle, and their phone numbers. We need to speak with each one in the next 24 hours."

"Yes, sir. I'll get those from James."

"Matty, we need to hear from Archie in Nome. Is he alright? Can he hang in there? What is happening?"

"Yes, sir, that one's mine."

"Jack, you and Gretchen go with Millie tomorrow as she makes contact with the girl she recognized at the club. This could be a gold mine."

"Got it, sir."

"Jeff, as much as I need you here, I'd sleep better if I knew you were in Washington, D.C. with Taylor, keeping an eye on Jennifer and Janae. No use letting that jet sit. You might as well get ready and leave whenever you want. You will be vital to us because you will be acquainted with both Anchorage and D.C."

"Yes, sir."

"Sheriff Deane, believe it or not, you will be the hub. You will be called on for information as we are out on missions. You will understand and make sense of seemingly unrelated details coming in. You will also be the last defense if this base comes under attack. Plus, your authority will be important as the invasion fails and we go back to the way things were. We are all extremely glad you're here."

"I'm glad, too, sir."

"Well then, let me dismiss you all to whatever you have to do, so I can make some phone calls. Oh, and Tom, could you stay for a second?" Tom sat back down as the others left.

"Tom, I want to be the first person to read the paper with your story in it. Try to find out where the carriers meet to get their papers. Buy a half dozen from the single copy guy or from any carrier that will sell you some if single copy shows up late."

"Got it."

"What do you think will happen when the story gets out?"

"I've been trying to think that through," Tom said. "Illegal Chinese tanks in storage on Alaskan soil. The mayor and law enforcement in the Anchorage area have all been bought out or scared into silence. Uh...the governor's good. She won't be bought or silenced. She could, and probably would, call out the National Guard. Some of them will call in sick. Putting National Guard up against Chinese Professional Army would be suicide, but the governor will probably be out there leading the way."

"Where would the first skirmish take place?"

"Well, the best bet is the gates of the Chinese construction storage yard."

"I think you're right, but the Chinese aren't going to let their strength get bottled up behind a fence. So...they would have to have a force outside the perimeter, far enough away from the gate to come in behind an attacking army and crush them."

"Hmm. You're right!"

"I have some phone calls to make. Would you get Matty and Nicolus and sit back down with Sheriff Deane? Go through this with them and see if either of them know a place from which the enemy could make a surprise attack."

"Yes, sir."

"Thanks, Tom. I'll be out in a while."

# 21

At dinner, Joe Cornish had that bit of a smile on his face that said, 'I've got some good news, but I'm going to make you wonder what it is for a while.'

He had been talking with Jennifer in D.C. and she was celebrating, "Our opposition wanted the bill to fail while looking like they were working hard to get it passed. We wanted it to pass, but we were proceeding like we wanted it to fail, but behind the scenes we lined up enough votes to get it passed."

"You mean it already passed?"

"Yes, my dear Joseph. Nobody focused on the two words Jay managed to get inserted into the bill. I have no idea how he did that, by the way, and it passed on the first vote. Joseph, you should have seen the opposition's faces. All their work seemed to collapse in on itself, like when they show a building being demolished in slow motion. All we did was sit and watch!"

"Well done, my princess. Having you with Janae in Washington, D.C. is almost worth every moment I have to be away from you. Almost, mind you."

Joe Cornish had listened for half an hour to all the details from his wife until she finally got settled down. Now he was relating them to the team at the dinner table.

Tom asked the first question because he wanted to get it precisely correct so he could write the story. "Giving foreign entities the right to buy the mineral rights underneath the federal land they already have the right to buy, would open the door to domination by that foreign entity. However, we inserted the words, 'AND STATE' between the word 'federal' and the word 'lands.' So foreign entities would have the right to buy state lands, along with the mineral rights under them, also."

Gretchen jumped in, "And this would cause endless problems because no state would ever agree to such federal legislation telling them what to do."

Tom tugged back, "Yeah, except the bill has already passed. If the President signs it, the only course for changing it would be through the courts, after the fact. The years it would take to get a case in front of the Supreme Court to argue the law's constitutionality would render the effort useless. We'd all be speaking Chinese by then."

Everyone looked at Joe Cornish who was cutting his pork chop and enjoying every bite. He was also enjoying everyone's input. The smile was still there.

PC added, "If Janae and Jennifer are involved, we're on the right track."

"Thank you, my dear ones. You are all on the right track. Keep going," Joe Cornish surprisingly said with his mouth half full.

Everyone looked back to Tom.

"Then...you're talking...a constitutional amendment," Tom had to think for a moment.

PC inserted, "Like the Bill of Rights!"

"Yeah..." Tom agreed, "the first ten amendments were called the Bill of Rights...there's been...twenty-seven, I think, that have been ratified...but...how are you going to get a supermajority of both houses of Congress to agree to propose the amendment that would stop the bill that the Senate just passed?"

"Mmm. Very good. The dinner, and the conversation. Tom, think back to December of 1933." Joe Cornish loved drawing out of people whatever was there.

"Uh...that would be prohibition...or rather the repeal of prohibition."

"And," Joe Cornish added slowly with determination, "the prohibiting of violations of state laws regarding alcohol by the federal government."

"Whoa, I didn't know that was in there...so...," Tom loved this, too, "so...an amendment that not only repeals this bill, but forbids it from ever happening again."

"Yes. Unless another constitutional amendment changes it."

"Okay, this is good. But...we still need 'how.'" Tom looked around the room and stopped at Gretchen, hoping for a clue.

Joe Cornish did the same thing. Then everyone, including Gretchen, burst out laughing.

"Sorry, that's the extent of my expertise," Gretchen admitted.

PC jumped in again, "Keep talking. Nickolaea and I will serve dessert. But don't say anything too important until we get back!" The two got up and dished up blueberry cobbler and ice cream.

"And coffee, thank you," Joe Cornish said lifting his cup.

Then he continued, but in a digressive fashion since the girls were busy getting dessert. He put his cup down and stood, and began pacing around the table, "If...you will allow me, I'd like to share with you a bit of my past." Tom reached for his notebook and pen.

Joe Cornish was looking at the floor as he paced, "In college, I majored in history and religion. I wasn't overly smart, the two just fit together well. They both have mysteries to be solved. My dealing with these mysteries enhanced and brought to the surface my enjoyment of investigation. Going into law enforcement provided a way to make a living while doing what I loved. My knack at investigation led me to the Seattle Office of the FBI where, for some reason, dead-end cases seemed to accumulate. Nobody else wanted to deal with them, so 'voila,' I was given a free hand to do what I loved."

"Now, if you'll indulge me a bit further, I'll give you a brief history of history." Tom looked around. All seemed fascinated, but he sensed this topic would soon be over everyone's head.

"History starts with the Almighty. Now, being almighty, nothing gets past Him, nothing surprises Him, in fact, He is the establishment of all things. His singularity produced a most daring and all-encompassing feat: the rescuing of mankind from our own mess. The torturous murder of His only heir, His son, at our hand, legally bought for Himself the salvation of the objects of His love, us."

"If you remember your Bible, the Old Testament testified to the old agreement between the Almighty and us, with hints of a new agreement to come. The New Testament testifies to the new agreement between the Almighty and us, based on the purchasing power of the innocent blood of his Son. It makes the old agreement obsolete. Not distinctively, but inclusively."

The girls were putting dessert in front of everyone.

"Now, we move forward to the year 1776. An old world and a new world existed. On July 4th, the new world declared a new agreement between government and people. Government, being the expression of God's authority, and the people, the object of His love. Leaning on the Almighty for wisdom was the operative and enduring idea."

"Both of these new agreements, in their own time, legally ended tyranny and birthed freedom. Fears had flourished under the old agreements, and people used these old fears to try to tarnish freedom. It was thought that freedom from the penalty of wrong doing through God's forgiveness would bring more wrong doing, and freedom from the punishment of Kings, Queens, and dictators would bring chaos. After all, people couldn't govern themselves. However, these doubts have been thoroughly demolished when leaning on the Almighty for wisdom was the focus. Our country has waxed and waned in the enjoyment of freedom, according to the clearness of our vision of the effectiveness of the Almighty's daring feat."

"The nailing down in words of this new arrangement in the late 1700's, was the Constitution of the United States. It took a confederation of individual colonies, joined by limited agreements for defense and economy, and created a federal or central government which had member states. The fears of repression, familiar under the old agreements, always brought doubts in some minds about the new. So a way to amend the Constitution was included, which helped with the doubts, in order to get the proposed constitution passed."

Now Joe Cornish sat back down as the girls were seated again.

He continued, "Article Five of the Constitution of the United States of America provides two ways to propose an amendment to the constitution, and the same two ways to ratify a proposed amendment. The first and most commonly used way is the supermajority of both houses of Congress. This way won't work in our case, since the Senate just voted on and passed this particular bill, as Tom has wisely deduced."

"The second way is for a supermajority of the states, that being two-thirds majority, to convene and make a proposal called an Article Five Convention Proposal. This type of proposal has never been done in the history of our country. The ratification for this second way would need the agreement of three-quarters of the states. This has only been done once in the history of our country, to my knowledge. In 1933, the first way was used to propose the repeal of prohibition, and the second way was used to ratify it."

This hung in the air as dessert and coffee began to be enjoyed by everyone except Tom. He was still staring at Joe Cornish. Then he looked around the table and then down at his dessert as his mind was playing catch up with all that Joe Cornish had said.

"We..." Tom started, almost to himself, "we would be making history... who...I mean how...I mean, so what's our next step?"

"Mmm. Wow, who made this?" Joe Cornish exclaimed.

Millie, Gretchen, and PC looked at Nickolaea.

Joe Cornish smiled, "Nicolus, your wife is indeed a gift." The beam on Nicolus's face might have been enhanced by a few tears quickly welling up.

"Yes, sir, she is indeed," Nicolus muttered. As he looked at Nickolaea, one of those tears escaped. Nicolus looked back down and took another bite while the tear dropped into his lap. He could not remember shedding a tear, even as a boy. All he could think of was what a great debt he had built up and how it was all taken away when he was offered, and he simply agreed to, a second chance. And Nickolaea was...she was a gift on top of a pardon. Nicolus would never go back. Ever.

Joe Cornish continued, "Dear family, I love you all. Now, as we speak...and eat, Janae and Jennifer are working to secure a signed statement from governors to agree to convene an Article Five Convention proposing the repeal of this law and the prohibition of the federal government from legislating laws concerning the use of state lands. How many governors do you suppose will sign this?"

Gretchen chimed in, "All of them!"

Tom added, "Even Alaska's. She'll probably be the first!"

"Yes, hopefully so." Joe Cornish now took a moment to think, "Tom brings up a good thought." He looked at Nicolus and Matty, "Do you think we could provide some covert protection for Alaska's governor?"

The conversation after the meal wove back and forth covering many pertinent topics. The more they talked, the more peace everyone had. The planning, with a defensive posture and an offensive outlook, would keep them a step ahead of their enemy. This would create confusion in the enemy's ranks. This confusion would open up targets that were easy to hit. Success for the good guys would bring confidence, and defeat for the bad guys would bring discouragement. The feeling that was settling over the little family in Anchorage, assembled for the doing of good, was: This will work.

*

After things broke up, Sheriff Deane took Tony and Millie aside and asked which lady they had recognized at the club.

Millie answered, "I don't know her name, but I recognized her as the sister of one of the girls in the San Diego club."

"I wouldn't mind going and finding out, because I've either dated or arrested most of them."

"Dan, you'd be dead before the night was out. Millie and I will go and she'll talk with her. We'll get the scoop on her."

"Okay, sounds good," The sheriff was disappointed, but understood the wisdom of it.

Presently Tony, Millie, and Matty left for the club. PC and Gretchen cleaned up the kitchen, and Joe Cornish helped with the dishes.

Jack, Dan, Nicolus, and Nickolaea checked security and caught up with the communications that were coming in from operatives, as well as news events they were monitoring around the world.

Tom was still at the table, writing furiously.

# 22

It was time. The patient wait had paid off. It was time to take off the waiting like a coat and throw it to the ground. The sun with its warmth and glory was now present. And it was about time, because the Chinese Army had no equals. Waiting past the time for action was what cowards did. Taking your rightful place in the world by your own hard work was natural. If someone didn't see it, they weren't worth having around.

Qui Ling's father was called 'the General' by most. His bodyguard called him 'my lover.' He had enjoyed many lovers. When he tired of them he simply killed them. His bodyguard, though, was family, a gift a family should rightfully give to a member who brought glory to their name. He would always keep her at his side.

It was morning and the General dialed his phone, "It is time to move. The plans are all in place. It is our time. Give the word to go." He ended the call, kissed the bodyguard, and watched her get dressed while he enjoyed his coffee and first cigarette. Tonight he would dine in the governor's Anchorage mansion.

*

Before going to bed, Dan and Nicolus had talked about the governor while Nickolaea had given Dan a short haircut. This morning as he shaved, he left the beginnings of a beard. He and Nicolus were going out early, before the sun was even lightening the dark horizon. The temperature around Anchorage was thirty two degrees and it had been raining. They would drive carefully.

Dan wore a hat and a coat with the collar turned up. He rode in the passenger seat and eyed his city the way he would if he was in his sheriff's car. The streets were still pretty much deserted, and as they slowed to go by the gate of the Chinese construction storage yard, they saw smoke rising in the cool air inside the yard.

Nicolus heard a dull roar and said, "Roll down your window."

Dan did and the sound of many tanks warming up poured in. He rolled it back up quickly. Not seeing anyone on watch, they kept a slow pace, noticing whatever they could.

"Tanks warming up. Okay, where would they stage a backup force to deal with an attack here on the gate?"

"Turn here and head up the hill." A mile later, almost to the top of the hill, they saw more smoke. "It's the bus barn for the city buses. They're warming up."

"The city buses are probably under the mayor's jurisdiction. Let's go make sure of what we see."

"Yeah, you're right." When they turned onto the street that went by the front gate of the bus barn, the gate was open and a tank was sitting in the opening warming up. "Damn," Dan said, "easy does it, but let's get the hell out of here." Nicolus kept going, and apparently nobody saw them. "Man, we've got to get back to the house and warn everyone."

Nicolus had another idea, "Call the house phone. Nickolaea will answer. Tell her what we saw and that we are going to check on the governor before we head back." Dan did. "Now direct me to the governor's mansion." Dan instructed him as they drove.

A few blocks away from the mansion, Dan exclaimed, "Damn! Pull over."

They both rolled down their windows. Exhaust smoke and dull roars met their ears and noses, "My God, they're at the gate to the mansion. They're going to start with the governor!" Dan's first thought was to call dispatch. Then he shook his head and looked at Nicolus, "We're here, want to do something?"

"Yep," Nicolus was assessing the situation. "If I was in charge of the Chinese Army, I would surround the property with tanks, but put the most power into a frontal assault. Our best bet is to check out the back where they are weakest."

"Okay, turn around and we'll get a few streets back and carefully sneak up from behind," Dan suggested.

Ten minutes later they were five blocks away from the back of the mansion and on foot. They had tactical gear on, including vests, grenades, silenced automatic weapons and handguns. They had knives strapped to each leg and mic and ear pieces in case they got separated. They each took one side of the street and paralleled each other as they crept ever closer. Two blocks away they heard an explosion on the front side of the mansion.

Nicolus whispered into his mic, "Okay, they've blown the front gate. This is real. We shoot to kill."

"Roger."

As they neared the street bordering the backyard of the mansion, they looked both ways. To the left was a tank pointed at the mansion, with a soldier standing in the open hatch, focusing on the mansion. Dan followed Nicolus as they ran up to the tank. The engine noise covered the sound of their approach and Nicolus kept going. Leaping up, he grabbed the soldier out of the hatch and dragged him to the ground. A quick shot under the armor killed the soldier as the next one popped out of the hatch and aimed his gun at Nicolus. Dan was up on the tank and made the same maneuver Nicolus had. As a third soldier appeared, Nicolus was back on the tank and stayed with what worked. On the ground with three dead soldiers, Dan whispered, "How many guys does a tank have?"

"Three, I think. Let's go find out," They climbed up onto the tank and Nicolus quickly brushed his hand over the hole and no shots came. He eased a flashlight down into the hole and turned it on. Nothing. He peered into the hole and decided it was empty, "Come on."

Inside the tank they looked around; it appeared quite modern. "You know how to drive one of these?" Dan decided to ask.

"Of course I do. Where I come from you learn it in high school." Dan looked at Nicolus and wondered whether to believe him or not. "Okay, we've got a driver/spotter seat, and a shooter seat. I'll drive, you shoot." Nicolus closed the hatch, sat in the driver's seat and looked at the controls, "Yeah, just like in high school."

Dan sat in the shooter seat and looked over his controls, "Okay, it looks doable. Looks like we've got a dozen shots or more. Plus it looks like we've each got a machine gun above us."

"Okay, keep the gun pointed forward until I tell you. I'm turning left and going till I see a tank. Then we fire and go to the next one."

"Roger."

Nicolus looked out the view portal and the tank began to move. Sure enough, there was another tank at the corner of the property. Nicolus lined up on it and stopped. "Lower your gun a little…Okay…ready to fire?

"Ready."

"Fire!"

Nicolus watched the top third of the tank explode while Dan ejected the hot, spent shell out the back of the tank and slammed in the next shot. "Damn good shooting Sheriff. Let's find the next one." Nicolus moved up the side street and aimed at the next tank, "Ready to fire?"

"Ready."

"Fire!"

This tank was starting to turn its gun toward them when it blew up. "I like the way you shoot. Next." The tank lurched forward. According to the pattern, the next one was at the corner. It was already turning its gun on Nicolus and Dan, and so was the next tank beyond it around the corner. Nicolus kept going until he had the first tank in between him and the second tank, "Ready to fire?"

"Ready."

"Fire!"

Before the first tank could turn his gun far enough, it blew.

"Give me another shot, same place. As soon as you're ready, pull the trigger." Boom! The second tank hesitated, not wanting to shoot its brother. It exploded, too, although Nicolus couldn't see it for all of the smoke. "Hang on!"

Nicolus slammed his tank into reverse and backed up, then drove forward in a semicircular motion around the burning tanks. All he could see out his view portal were more tanks, "Turn your gun twenty degrees to the right." Nicolus nosed right up to the side track of the next tank and kept going in first gear, pushing the tank in front of him. His gun had slid under the other tank's gun and prevented it from turning. "Ready to fire?"

"Ready."

Another foot of push and Nicolus's barrel was aimed at the lead tank inside the gate. He gauged it so that if he missed he wouldn't hit the mansion, "Fire!"

The first tank inside the gate blew and blocked access to the mansion. "Okay, gun back to where it was." Nicolus reversed the tank a few yards, as Dan turned the barrel back. "Ready to fire?"

"Ready."

When the barrel was forward again Nicolus said, "Fire!" The tank he had been pushing blew up. "Okay, let's get the hell out of here, unless you want to take a shot at driving."

"I'm with you!" Dan yelled. Nicolus turned on a dime and headed back where they had come from. Shells were whistling by. They were being shot at. Moving fast, they turned up the street they had walked down, then into an alley and shut the tank down. "Let's move!"

Nicolus and Dan climbed out and shut the hatch. They ran up the alley to the next street and up toward their car. The first tank following them screeched to a halt just past the alley and backed up. It turned its barrel, aimed and fired, blowing up the tank Nicolus and Dan had vacated. It gave the two enough time to get to the car and move it back another five blocks.

"Okay, let's hoof it down and see if we can rescue the Governor."

"What?! We just got clean away with multiple kills! Don't you think we should pull back and call in back up?"

"Nope. Joe Cornish says if you're on a roll, just keep going until you're done or something or someone stops you."

"Oh...Okay, I'm with you."

"You're right, though. I should call Matty. He'll never forgive me if I don't." They were jogging now, another street over, back toward the mansion.

Nicolus speed dialed the house, "Babe, wake up Matty and hand him the phone."

"Are you alright?"

"Yeah, just having some fun. Babe, what Joe said last night, it's true. It's how I feel."

"I know."

"After I talk to Matty, call your dad and tell him to lay low. There are bullets flying out here."

"You're my love, be safe...here's Matty."

"Yeah?"

"Matty, me and Dan are out here taking fire. Get the Jeep wagon and find the intersection of Walrus and Colorado. Our car is there. We're going to try to rescue the governor and her family. We are ten blocks down from the car, but be ready, we'll be coming out hot. Give the phone back to Nickolaea, but don't say anything."

"I'm on my way."

# 23

Nicolus and Dan entered into the fray again. Confusion was reigning so they made it to the fence in back of the mansion and cut a hole in it. They crossed the yard with hand guns drawn as dawn was breaking. At the corner of the three story building, they holstered their guns and climbed up the drain pipe to the flat roof. Carefully surveying the roof, they saw no one. They climbed onto the roof and snuck forward to the front corner.

There must have been fifty men milling around on the grounds in front of the mansion, but apparently no one had entered the building. They looked like they were waiting for orders, or their orders were only to secure the grounds.

"Go to the other corner. We'll walk toward each other throwing grenades into the yard. At the middle we turn around and go back, gunning down anything that moves."

"Gotcha," Dan moved low and made it to the corner.

"Go," Nicolus said into his mic. They each used all six of their grenades by the time they met. They turned around and went back to their corners low, slow, and firing. Not much up front moved when they were done.

"Let's find a roof access." They each searched their side until they found a square trap door in the back middle of the roof. Nicolus pulled a small pry bar from his leg pocket and worked at the door until it opened. They both entered and dropped down into the darkness. Dan's flashlight found the door. Nicolus opened it and listened. Nothing. Then he yelled out, "FBI, we're here to rescue the governor." Nothing. They moved into the hall and to the staircase. Again Nicolus yelled and then listened. This time he heard something. They inched their way down the stairs, handguns drawn. Half way down, Nicolus yelled again and the governor stepped out at the bottom of the stairs. Nicolus stopped and raised his gun barrel toward the ceiling.

"Governor, my boss is Joe Cornish of the Seattle Office of the FBI. He sent me to rescue you and anyone with you. Is anyone hurt?"

"No. Thank God, no one's hurt. Could I borrow your automatic rifle for a few minutes?"

"Ma'am, as soon as I get you to safety, you'll be the boss. How many are with you?"

"Four all together and the dog."

"The dog stays. Let's group at the back door."

"The dog stays, with me. It's small, but it knows how to attack."

"Roger, let's move." Nicolus knew better than to argue.

At the first floor back door, three minutes later, the governor's husband, two boys, and the governor with the dog in her arms, were ready.

Dan peeked out the window and saw men, "I count five, maybe more."

"Okay. Dan, one of us takes the family to the corner room and out the window, through the fence, and up to the car. Matty should be there. The other one opens this door, to draw any fire and create a diversion for the escape." Nicolus got out his phone and speed dialed Matty.

"Yeah."

"Matty, you here?"

"Yeah, I'm at the car, loaded and ready."

"Good. Come down ten blocks to the east side of the mansion. We'll be coming out the right corner window and through the fence. It will be Dan and four others. I'll be at the back door in the middle of the building, drawing fire. Shoot anything you see except us."

"Aw, I hate restrictions. Give me five," Matty was moving as he put his phone away.

"Matty will attack from the back in five minutes. I hate waiting."

Dan agreed. So did the governor.

"Okay, move into position, and tell me when you're ready."

The governor's phone began to ring.

"Don't answer it," Nicolus was serious. The governor heard it in his voice. "They can locate where you are in the house if you answer it."

"Should I turn it off?"

"No, just leave it alone till we get clear."

"But you used your phone."

"Yeah, but they don't know my number. They knew yours somehow."

"Maybe it was the State Patrol seeing if I was okay."

"Maybe it was. But you are *not* okay. You are under attack and they will understand that you might have a good reason to not answer."

"Okay, I'm sorry. Thank you for coming to get us."

"Are you comfortable using a gun?"

"Damn right I am," She pulled a Berretta out of her purse. Nicolus looked at her husband. He pulled a .38 out of his pocket.

"Okay, one of ours will be across the street. Don't shoot him, me, or Dan. Other than that, shoot whatever moves. Dan, give me your rifle. I'll use both to cover you. Move into position."

Now there was banging on the front door. Reinforcements must have come. Nicolus decided it was good news. He'd let as many in the front door as possible before going out the back.

"In position. The window is up. Someone is breaking in the front," Dan whispered into the mic.

"Yeah, I know. Get ready."

The whole front door and jamb fell in with a loud bang. But no gunfire. "Go when you hear me start to shoot."

Nicolus opened the back door and started to shoot. First he stood, then he knelt and reloaded and shifted to the other gun to give the first one a few seconds to cool down. He moved to the right along the building and fired at the muzzle flashes. Just before he got to the opposite corner from where the escape was hopefully taking place, Nicolus jumped into a cement walled window well. He reloaded and then switched guns again. He was taking a lot of fire.

Dan eased out the window first. The gunshots were all being directed away from them. The family all got out and together they moved across the yard, crouching low. Dan saw movement in some shrubs and shot three shots. A Chinese soldier fell out.

He looked at the governor's husband and said, "Go through the hole in the fence first. Don't be afraid to use your gun except on the big guy over there across the street. Once we are all through, we'll head for him together."

A bullet zinged over their heads. "Go!" Dan turned, squatted down and aimed his hand gun. From around the corner of the mansion, two men were advancing. It was a long shot, but he aimed and emptied his gun. Then he reloaded and dove through the fence.

"We're clear," said the husband.

"Okay, let's go." As soon as they started across the street, Matty started firing toward the bad guys who had Nicolus pinned down.

They made it across the street and Matty yelled, "Keep going!"

They huddled and then the governor's husband led the way with a brisk walk. The governor kept the boys close and hung onto the dog. Dan took up the rear, constantly looking around for trouble.

The little Alaskan first family was making it to safety.

Matty waded into the fray with an automatic rifle in each hand. He shot up the shrubs and the trees and crouched down at the fence to reload. Before firing again, he called out, "Nicolus!"

"Yeah, I'm coming over."

"Go!" Just as Nicolus started across the yard, fire came from the back door. Matty turned and unloaded in that direction. When he was empty, Nicolus was at his side. He fired as Matty reloaded. Then they both crossed the street and kept going. Nobody followed, so they jogged up the slight incline for ten blocks. They got to Dan and the family just as they were reaching the car.

Nicolus directed as they got to the cars, "Dan, you drive; Matty rides shotgun. I'll follow close behind with the family. Dan, take the back roads if there are any."

"Yeah, I've got a route all figured."

"Sheriff Deane!" The governor exclaimed, "I didn't know it was you!"

"Yes, ma'am. I'll give you the whole story at the house."

"What house?"

"You'll see." Off they went. They made it through the back roads, but they could see tanks when they looked down toward the city. When they arrived at the safe house they all got out and inside to safety.

# 24

It was still morning, and the smell of tank engine exhaust and spent gunpowder mixed with fog and drizzle all over the Anchorage area. Confusion was reigning among the citizens because all law enforcement, fire, and aid units had been ordered to stand down.

Alaska's first family was tucked into a king-size bed in the quickly vacated master bedroom of the safe house. They were given pajamas of various sizes in exchange for their clothes which went immediately into the washing machine, as they were the only clothes they had. Cleaned up, with pajamas on, and under the covers, except for the dog who was on top, they all soon conked out, as most of the night had been sleepless and stress-filled.

Juneau was the capital of Alaska, but the governor spent most of her time in and around Anchorage, where the action was. Most of the time it was a smart move. Once in a while it wasn't, unless you wanted to be a leader of whatever happened and not just an office holder. Nobody questioned this governor's desire, or resolve.

*

When the General was informed that the governor had escaped his well-planned scenario, and the ambush of the National

Guard and their annihilation had not materialized, he pulled his gun and shot the messenger. Then he ordered the mayor into his office. A moment later the mayor was escorted in by the General's bodyguard and directed to stand next to the dead messenger.

"You will announce martial law and find the governor for me. Your alternative is a spot on the floor next to the messenger."

"Yes, sir. No worries. Set-backs are a part of war."

The General pulled his gun and aimed, "What did you say?"

"Yes, sir...I said yes, sir," the mayor backed out of the office. The bodyguard closed the door and walked to the General, unbuttoning the first two buttons of her shirt. She sat on the General's lap and pulled his head to her bosom.

The General breathed deeply of her perfumed body, and then looked up at her, "The sheriff is missing. He fancied you. Find him and bring him to me. Use seduction or use the point of a knife, I care not which. I want him standing in front of me, alive." The bodyguard gently took the General's chin and kissed his lips. Then she got up, buttoned up and left.

*

In China, the General's brother was also a general, but he was two years younger and knew how the chain of command worked. When he got the word, 'go,' he went into the next room and shot the Vice President. Then, back in his office, he called for a meeting with the President. However, no one in the President's office answered the phone. It just kept ringing.

The President of China had told his staff he was secluding himself in his office and they should all go home and pray to their ancestors for help. Then he had taken his two bodyguards and his Chief of Staff and exited the back of the building. In two armored vehicles, he and his entourage traveled up into the mountains.

The President had always had suspicions of an Army coup and had prepared a mountain retreat, which closely resembled a fort. No one was aware of it because he had contracted with a Mongolian construction company to build it. The location was in the hills above Erenhot, China, close to the Mongolian border. Here he took his stand.

A small covert force of the Mongolian Army was his protection. His plan was simple. If the coup crumbled he would stay there until it was safe to return to the capitol. If the coup was successful, he would flee to the Mongolian capital and, together with the democratically elected President of Mongolia, stand against the advances of the Chinese Army. The United States would not allow a democratic state to be demolished by a Communist army.

So, the Chinese President could not be located. This infuriated the General's little brother because he knew his older brother would not stand for it. He hoped things were going so well in Alaska that this setback would be of no consequence.

So went the thinking of tyrants who use murder as a policy.

*

In Nome, business was pretty much normal. But "normal" was the harried effort to finish the airport enlargement, to make Nome a world class port, and to continue the ever increasing import of construction containers from China by plane and ship. This was all being done without the cooperation of the weather.

Archie, the dirty cop from San Diego, was working undercover in the Nome police department. Together with a handful of operatives working construction, he found that the radio stations from Anchorage were offline, as were their cell phones. He needed a satellite phone. No news from the safe house in Anchorage was not good news. Even with no news or new direction, they kept working and collecting intel. It was cold, hard work, but they played after work to blend in, and that warmed them up. Archie couldn't believe the lucky break he had stumbled into. He would never go back to his old life.

*

Jeff and the jet had left the Anchorage airport just hours before the airport had been shut down. He was landing in Montana to collect Taylor, give Cindy a hastily written note from Matty, report to Jonathan and Sharon, pack, and head to Washington, D.C.. The satellite phones between Jonathan's ranch base and the safe house in Anchorage were working well. Jonathan filled Jeff in on what he had missed. Wow! He had made it out just in time. Jeff shook his head in amazement at the ability of Joe Cornish to see ahead and plan accordingly.

When he and Taylor were all loaded into the jet, Jeff made sure he had the letter from Joe Cornish to Jennifer on his person. Communication was as important to the good guys as bullets were to the bad guys. And Taylor and Jeff were more important to each other than anything.

*

Joe Cornish was manning the communication and security room with Nickolaea when the guys and the First Family of Alaska arrived. Jack and Gretchen took over the care of the family and Nicolus, Matty, and Dan stacked all the weapons they had used on tables in the garage area. There they cleaned and restored everything to fighting readiness.

Joe Cornish, along with Tom and his notebook, stepped into the garage and let the guys tell their story. He realized he was witnessing his covert family doing what they were best at when it needed to be done, without being told. Nobody was expected to do something they did not know how to do.

"Excellent. Just excellent. You guys deserve the Congressional Medal of Honor. Maybe someday you'll get it. Our next move is to get the governor out of Alaska, ASAP, before things tighten up even more. I'm thinking Rolando's yacht would be the best way out, but we would need to scout out the marina first."

Nicolus looked up from his work at the mention of his father-in-law.

"I'm thinking a guy and gal together would be less suspicious. Nicolus, do you and Nickolaea want to make contact with Rolando and see if it is possible?"

"Yes, definitely. That's a good idea." He stopped what he was doing and left to get cleaned up. Nickolaea brought a plate of breakfast in to him as he was dressing. Shortly they were on their way to the marina in the rented car.

The city was definitely under the influence of the Chinese Army. If martial law was in effect, it was not quite organized yet. Nicolus and Nickolaea made it to her father's yacht and were welcomed aboard. After a few moments of explanation, Nicolus left Nickolaea to help her father and the lady pilot get the yacht ready to sail while he headed back to the safe house.

With clean clothes and breakfast ready, Jack and Gretchen gently woke up the First Family of Alaska. They were sleepy, but realized their ordeal was not yet over. They quickly dressed and sat down at the big kitchen table.

"Please," started the governor, "let me thank you again, Agent Cornish, for sending a team to rescue us. I do believe you saved our lives and possibly that of Alaska. What is the latest?"

"It was our pleasure to do what needed to be done. Communications are all down except for our satellite phone. We believe martial law has been imposed. We have operatives out now to see to what extent the Chinese Army has taken over."

"Very good. What are our plans to take our land back?" The governor asked, ready for action.

"Governor, our intel tells us the general in charge is ruthless. Rescuing you has stung him enough to make him mad. This will lead to him making mistakes, and we will take advantage of each one. But your lives are still in danger and when our location is found out, this safe house will come under attack. We have a small window of time to get you and your family to safety."

"I'm not heading for safety, sir. I'm going to..."

"Forgive me, Governor," Joe Cornish interrupted. "Alaska's communications are down. Your state needs you to give a first-hand account of the situation to the President of the United States, and formally request emergency aid. The assistance of the U. S. Army will not be sent without your request or agreement. Our intel tells us the Army, Navy, and Air Force bases in Alaska have been compromised. Canada is already moving forces to their Alaskan border and are waiting to assist. Only the President can request a foreign country to enter our borders with their armed forces, and only you can tell him it needed to be done yesterday. Ma'am, with all due respect, we need you to head up the cavalry and come to our rescue. In the meantime, I promise I'll hold the fort till you come."

Now the governor took a deep breath, "Sir, you seem to have the situation pegged." With the beginnings of a smile, she added, "Tell us what to do."

"Well, we're waiting on intel, but the plan is to get you and your family to the marina and aboard one of our yachts. Out on the ocean you can call in and get this process started with less chance of being found than if you called from here. Then head for Seattle or wherever you're instructed to go to make your formal request. We have packed a few items for you since you had no time or chance to bring anything with you. Now, please eat and we'll await the response from our intel team. We may have to move quickly as soon as he gets back."

"Thank you again, Agent Cornish, and thank you to all your team."

*

Ten minutes later, Nicolus pulled into the driveway and went into the garage first. "Pack everything back up. We've got to roll." Then he reported to Joe Cornish, "Sir, if we are going to go, we've got to go now. If we..."

"Nicolus, your word is all I need. You and Nickolaea go with them on the yacht to see to the family's safety. Go out into the ocean where she can call the President and get help started. Take her wherever they want to meet her, and then get to Seattle. Stop at Tony's Inn and see that things are good there. Use their satellite phone to call me, and we'll go from there. I'm thinking you two might connect with Joe and Kandee in Vancouver and travel north to try to cross back into Alaska from Canada. If you're successful, notice what there is to notice and we'll try to connect, back here if possible."

Joe Cornish then handed Nicolus an envelope full of money, and turned to the family in the kitchen, "Okay, Governor. I'm going to put you back into the hands of Nicolus, Nickolaea, and Matty, and squeeze you all into one vehicle to go down to the marina. God speed, and I'm sure we'll be talking again."

# 25

Nicolus, with Matty riding shotgun and the family in the back seat, rolled easily through Anchorage in the direction of the marina. Tanks, trucks with soldiers, and Humvee-type vehicles zoomed by in all directions. They weren't in a panic, and weren't stopping every car. It was like they all had a destination and were almost running into each other to get there. The word "professional" did not come to mind. As Nicolus expected, the marina had a tank and some trucks parked in front that weren't there an hour ago. Nicolus slowed to a stop and noticed Nickolaea standing with the soldier in charge, waving and jumping up and down as animated as he had ever seen her. He realized it was an act and said, "Okay, I think we are family or friends meeting to go fishing. We are all excited and glad to see Nickolaea. We'll just hope we're not recognized. Everybody out."

"See officer, here they are! Hi everybody!" Nickolaea was shouting, "We're going fishing and we're going to have a blast!" The Chinese officer could speak and understand English, but didn't even notice Nickolaea's accent.

"Hi, honey!" Nicolus yelled and waved. "We're here!"

The governor, not one to be shy, got into the act. She ran ahead and into Nickolaea's arms, "Ohhh, it's been so long! So good to see you."

"Ohhh, look how big the boys have gotten," Nickolaea exclaimed, then turned to the governor's husband and gave him a hug, too.

Then the husband chimed in, "Now you promised us fish. Are they going to bite in this chilly weather?"

"Oh yes, but you're right. Let's get on the boat, out of this weather. I'm going to bring some coffee back to the men here!"

That brought in the officer, "No, just go ahead and go. There is a six o'clock curfew, so you must make it back by then. And you can't leave this jeep here."

"No worries, officer," Matty explained. "I'm just seeing them safely aboard and then I'll get the Jeep out of here." Nicolus just smiled like a dumb tourist. It was hard to act that way, but he couldn't believe what he was seeing Nickolaea do, so he tried his best.

Ten minutes later Matty had the lines untied and was strolling back up the dock waving back at them. He got into the Jeep and left.

Matty decided to take a ride around town on his way back.

The airport was a clogged mess, with every passenger being checked and no flights even lined up on the tarmac to take off. The newspaper building didn't exist anymore. It must have taken a direct hit from a tank or two. So much for tonight's story. Traffic was moving, what there was of it, but Chinese Army personnel were everywhere. Matty decided to pull into the club if it was still there. Sure enough, this was where the Chinese brass were headquartered, so to speak.

Matty parked and quietly walked in and sat at the bar. As Matty held his hand up with one finger raised, a woman brushed her hands over his shoulder and sat down beside him.

"Buy me a drink?" she asked.

Matty was going to say 'beat it,' but when he looked her in the eye he recognized the same girl he had met last night that Millie had talked to. He raised a second finger and nodded to the bartender.

"Thank you, honey," the girl said out loud, then leaned in and whispered, "Get me out of here, please."

Matty handed the bartender a twenty and grabbed the two opened bottles in one hand and the girl's hand in the other. They quietly walked out. Matty handed the bottles to a soldier and said, "Here, you need this more than I do." The soldier either didn't understand him or was thirsty. They got into the Jeep and left for the house.

"Those damn Chinese are taking turns with every female in there. Thank you for taking me with you. Do you know where Millie is?"

# 26

Sheriff Daniel Deane still felt like the sheriff, but the title carried no significance anymore since the Chinese Army proclaimed and enforced martial law. They seemed very adept at police action. They were controlling the greater Anchorage area, and most of the other towns and bases which made up the State of Alaska.

After last night's daring and successful rescue of the governor and her family, Dan was wondering about the Chinese Army's ability to bring war. He and Nicolus had probably killed close to one hundred Chinese soldiers and destroyed at least six tanks, seven if you count the one they borrowed and then abandoned just before it was hit. They, and the family they rescued, took no casualties or injuries. Maybe the Chinese Army was great at controlling, but not so good at attacking and gaining ground.

In any event, he wanted his town back and the key was to kill the General. And he knew what the General looked like. He'd just have to get by the bodyguard.

Dan was thinking all this as he was finishing cleaning up the garage. He heard a car enter the driveway and he peeked out the window. It was Matty and...Chrissy. Matty was bringing Chrissy into the house with him. She was the gal Tony said he, Millie, and Matty had talked to last night, the one Millie sort of knew. Dan had never dated her, but the one time he had arrested her, he had liked her. He had decided in the back of his mind that someday he might pursue her. Then he stopped thinking and said out loud, though no one heard him, "Now why would I want to marry a prostitute?" Then, thinking some more he realized, if ten beautiful women were his choice, there was something about Chrissy. He would still choose her. He had declined to mention that to Matty or the others though because it wasn't important.

Dan looked away from the window, but saw movement out of the corner of his eye at the last second. He looked back out the window. Someone could have dashed up the driveway as the house door was opening and hid behind the car. It was probably a dog. He looked the area over again and glanced at Matty's back as he was going in the door. Again, as he was looking away, he saw movement out of the corner of his eye. Looking at the door again in that split second, he saw someone else's back side go in and close the door.

"What the hell was that?" he said, in a whisper to himself. It was...a female body, not Matty's. His next thought brought cold sweat from his pores. The bodyguard? The General's female bodyguard? What...how...the General must need something real bad...or...someone. Then things started making sense. She was here for him. Dan knew what the General looked like. He was her target.

Okay, he had to settle down and think rationally. He was being hunted. He would stealthily turn the tables and sneak in, line up a shot and kill her without saying a word. He checked his holstered gun. It was clean and loaded. But then another thought hit him which brought more scared, cold sweat. If the General wanted him, she would have to bring him back alive. And that's what he needed, one shot face to face with the General.

Dan closed his eyes. My God, that would be suicide. Even if he killed the General, he'd be dead, too. And he wanted to live. Especially now, since he had walked away from his treason and was given a second chance, he wanted to live. All of a sudden this second chance thing was as important as the others had said it was. And if he lived, he wanted to live with Chrissy. No...no, he had to keep his mind clear.

Dan pulled his gun. He moved to the inside door of the garage and eased it open enough to peer out. He could just barely see into the kitchen. The bodyguard was smaller than Matty, but she had one arm around his middle and her hand had something in it. Her other hand had a gun pointed at everyone else. He couldn't see who all was there, but Matty was frozen. It was a stand-off. She must be holding a grenade.

The General's bodyguard/assassin was speaking, "I am not afraid to die with you today. If I come back without him, I will die anyway. I will count to three and then shoot whoever I choose. If he does not come out, I will continue until all of you are dead and then I will be free to hunt him down...One..."

"Why are you afraid of your third option?" Joe Cornish did what came naturally, offering a second chance at life.

"What third option? Your tricks will not work. Two." A slight smile began on Jack's face. He had gone through this before. He glanced at Tony. Tony was glancing at him with the same thought.

"You'll have to extend your count to five or I will not have a chance to explain," Joe Cornish was cool, calm, and in charge.

The bodyguard had her gun trained on Joe Cornish because he was the one doing the talking.

Jack took a step toward her and said, "You'd better listen; you will never regret it."

"Three," the bodyguard moved the gun slightly and pulled the trigger. Jack took the bullet in his chest.

Gretchen screamed, Matty grabbed the hand that held the grenade with both his hands and squeezed tight. Tony was already in flight toward her gun as she was turning it to Matty's head. Matty bent over, lifting her off her feet. Tony's hands reached the gun as it went off. It might have even been his grasp that made it go off, but Matty's head bent down enough and Tony's grasp tilted the gun up enough to direct the bullet through Matty's scalp, not his head.

As Matty hit the floor, Joe Cornish dove and grasped the grenade hand as Matty's grasp lightened. Matty's last conscious move was to push back so his body pinned the bodyguard to the floor. Tony was able to wrestle the gun from her hand, which immediately went down to her leg for her knife. She managed to get it out, but Dan appeared and stomped on her wrist, holding it to the floor.

Joe Cornish wrestled a better grasp than the bodyguard, and took over control of the grenade. He rolled away from her looking at the grenade.

The bodyguard's upper arm and shoulder were pinned under Matty, but from her elbow to her finger tips she was searching Matty for another weapon. Her other hand tilted the knife and burrowed it into Dan's foot. He winced, but mashed his other foot into the fingers holding the knife and put all his weight into it. He audibly heard bones crack.

The bodyguard's other hand found a gun in Matty's waistband, pulled it out and fired. The bullet grazed Chrissy in the leg as she was just standing there frozen. She collapsed back into PC, which was a smart idea, since PC was a nurse. At the sight of the gun, Millie stepped forward and stomped onto the woman's forearm.

The bodyguard got one more shot off in the direction of Joe Cornish before Tony put the muzzle of the gun he had taken away from her into her gun hand and shot. The bullet went through her hand into the floor. Then Tony pushed Millie away and rolled away himself with both guns.

But the bodyguard wasn't finished. She swung her leg up and kicked Dan hard in his lower spine. He fell forward into the wall and onto the floor in pain. Then she got herself out from under Matty using mostly her legs, and managed to stand up. She was desperately trying to get another grenade out with her wrists and hold it up to her teeth to pull the pin. Her mangled hands just got in the way and the grenade dropped to the floor, pin still secure.

Seeing Tony on the floor with two guns, she took one step and launched herself right down onto him. Her head aimed for Tony's chin and landed squarely where aimed, but Tony got two shots off before blacking out from the quick hit; they went into her gut and chest. Then they lay motionless, Tony unconscious with the bodyguard on top.

Millie was having none of that. She went berserk and reached down with two hands to drag the woman off, yelling, "Get off my husband, you Chinese bitch!"

The two slugs had gone through the bodyguard's vest at point blank range, but were deflected enough to only wound her and knock the wind out of her. Turning her over sucked the wind back into her lungs and she let out a terrible yelp of pain as she lifted both legs to viciously kick Millie. Millie saw them coming and dove at her legs like a cornerback trying to tackle a much more powerful running back. She landed on top of the woman's legs and stayed there, wrapped around her.

PC having quickly ministered to Chrissy, saw and heard Millie's attack, and rushed over to help. She sat down on the bodyguard's chest, which pushed the air out again and left her stunned for a few more seconds. That was long enough for Tom to come over, pull PC off, and bend over to back hand the bodyguard as hard as he could across her face.

"Ooouch!" Tom dearly paid for it, but it put the assassin out of commission. He stood up holding his hand and yelled to PC, "Take my belt off and cross her ankles and put a tourniquet around them." She did. Tom looked around for something else, then looked down and unbuckled the bodyguard's belt and pulled it off. He turned her over onto her stomach and placed both hands behind her back, crossed at the wrists. He looked at PC who was not afraid of seeing blood and said, "Take this belt and do the same here." She did.

Then Tom surveyed the situation. Jack was in Gretchen's arms, alive, but not looking good. She had taken off her shirt, wadded it up, and was pressing it onto the wound. Joe Cornish was getting up with the grenade in one hand and picking up the other grenade with his other hand. He said, "I'll be right back." He disappeared out the door. Millie was bending over, hugging Tony, trying to revive him. Chrissy was on her back holding a towel firmly on her wound as PC had instructed her. She was going into shock. PC had another towel to Matty's head and was holding it there as she looked around at all her patients to see who needed her next. Dan was looking around trying to shake the cobwebs. Eyeing Tom and the bodyguard, he tried to get up.

"Tom, help me up and get my belt off," Tom did. "We've got to hog tie her." Tom took off Dan's belt and slid it under the bodyguard's belted wrists. Then he bent her legs back at the knees and slipped the belt under the ankle belt. He drew it tight enough to fit the buckle in the first hole. She let out a grunt.

"That looks uncomfortable," Tom observed.

"Exactly," Dan muttered and stumbled over to a chair.

PC then went into full force, "Tom, hold this on Matty's head." She let go and went to Jack and Gretchen. "Dan, get a blanket from the bedroom and keep Chrissy warm. Put pressure on that leg wound."

"Okay," Dan grunted and stumbled to his task with renewed vigor because it was for Chrissy. His lower back felt like someone hit it full tilt with a sledge hammer.

Joe Cornish came back in the door, "No accomplices, and grenades are disarmed. What can I do?"

PC looked at him and instructed, "Get a chair and sit here on the other side of me." PC noticed he was bleeding from the arm.

Joe Cornish sat down and looked at Jack, "How is he?"

"Give me your arm." PC dabbed some blood away and looked at the wound, then tied a towel around it. "There is a box of first aid stuff in the bathroom. Get it and drag it in to me. Don't use your wounded arm. You're going to be my nurse."

PC provided her expertise to her little family. After about an hour she sat back down and surveyed things with Tom, Joe Cornish, Gretchen, and Dan.

"The bullet went all the way through Jack. That's the best news. There would be a lot more blood loss if an artery had been hit, so that's good news. He probably has a collapsed lung, though.

He needs a hospital and antibiotics, but we'll keep him still and warm until then. He's fifty/fifty, Gretchen, and that's darn good for a gunshot wound to the chest." Gretchen had both hands up to her face, with tears of panic and joy alternating.

"We got Chrissy bandaged up. Let's move her into a bed and keep her warm. Matty stays in that arm chair with his bandaged head higher than the rest of his body. Don't let him get up; let's get a blanket on him, too. Tony might have a broken jaw and probably whiplash. Somehow we've got to keep him down and sedated. He's in their bedroom and Millie's watching him. I gave him, Jack, and Matty shots of morphine, which will keep them for a while, but we've got to keep an eye on them. Dan, I want to give you some morphine, too. You need to stay immobile."

"No way!" Dan replied. "We could still be under attack! She might have called in our location before she came in. We have got to have at least one man at the front door with enough fire power for ten, in case more trouble comes. Keeping them outside will be three quarters of the battle. I'll set that up and take first watch. At least one person has to sleep."

Joe Cornish said, "May I suggest Tom and PC put Chrissy into bed, and as everyone is stable for the moment, PC, you lay down beside Chrissy and rest. You'll probably have to take sleep whenever you can. I'll keep an eye on everyone till we need you."

"Tom, go into your room and conk out. You, me, and Dan will take turns sleeping. One sleeps, one helps PC and cooks, etc., and one stays on guard on the equipment and at the front door. Try to sleep a couple of hours if possible, but if you can't sleep, get up and trade with the next guy. And let's push the couch parallel with Jack so Gretchen can rest next to him."

"Okay, I can live with that," PC said. "What about her?"

PC had bandaged the bodyguard's hands and the two holes on her stomach and chest which weren't deep. She had dried blood on her chin and blood in her mouth. She was very uncomfortable, but hadn't said anything even though her mouth was uncovered.

Dan looked at her and said, "Lady, don't even think about peeing on the carpet. Just let me know and I'll drag you out onto the lawn."

The bodyguard looked from Dan over to Joe Cornish, but she said nothing. Joe Cornish looked at her and said, "You can talk."

It hurt every time she breathed, "Please take the one rope off."

"Since we have the guns now, I think I'll do that," Joe Cornish bent down and tightened the belt a bit to undo it. She grunted with pain. Then her legs were let go and she rolled onto her side and tried to exercise her legs slightly to regain circulation.

"Tie my hands in front of me so I can lay on my back, and yes, I have to pee...please!"

"Did you call in our location?"

"No, I didn't...I should have...Please!"

Gretchen spoke, "I'll help her pee. Boss, you stand at the bathroom door with a gun. Tom, you guys take care of Chrissy and sleep."

Joe Cornish looked at the bodyguard, "Are you going to be good with that?"

"Yes...please!"

Joe Cornish nodded at Gretchen and she untied the belt at the bodyguard's feet, and helped her up. She couldn't stand on her own, so Gretchen helped her into the bathroom. Joe Cornish stood at the half closed door. After she was done, she could almost walk, so they returned to the kitchen. Gretchen retied her feet, then untied her hands, let her flex her arms a bit and retied them in front of her. She lay down on the floor on her back, in considerable pain, and closed her eyes.

# 27

The lady pilot was doing the best she could. Motoring down Cook Inlet away from Anchorage, she battled intermittent fog and steady rain. When they got out into the Gulf of Alaska, the waves grew from a storm front. Nevertheless, she headed southwest out into the ocean, monitoring their surroundings by sight and by radar.

Nickolaea and Rolando were keeping Alaska's First Family warm, comfortable, and settled.

Nicolus was setting up the satellite phone near the governor, and when he was ready, asked, "Who do you want to call?"

"The junior senator from Alaska," the governor dug out her phone to get the number for him. She discovered her cell phone was working now, so she dialed the senator's office in D.C., "This is the governor of Alaska. Get me the senator, immediately."

After a moment, the junior senator came on the line, "Governor?"

"Mark, the Chinese have taken over. I've escaped and am on a yacht out in the Gulf. I need to get to safety and talk to the President."

"Uh...what...uh...yes, we...uh...hang on Governor, don't hang up. Give me a minute." The junior senator knew what to do, he just had to calm himself down and do it. Thirty seconds later, he spoke again, "Governor, early this morning the President instructed a carrier heading for port in Everett, Washington to turn up toward Alaska instead. They are monitoring the international

Mayday channel as they go, so turn to that channel and call for help. They will intercept you and you can talk to the President from the carrier."

"Thanks, Mark. I'm thinking the senior senator might be involved, so don't tell him I contacted you. 'Bye." The governor hung up and yelled up to the pilot, "Put out a call for help on the international Mayday channel. There should be an aircraft carrier around nearby."

"Yes, Ma'am." It only took a minute, and the pilot yelled back, "Ma'am, they're only five miles away. We'll snug up to them and they will lift you all up in a bucket. Put on some warm clothes, it's nasty out there."

An hour later, the ability of the U.S. Navy to do whatever it takes, had the First Family of Alaska safe on board, warm, and the governor explaining to the President of the United States what the situation was, what needed to happen, and how to do it.

The lady pilot of the yacht pulled away from the carrier with Nicolus by her side. "Can you get us back to Anchorage?" Nicolus asked.

"Yes...but..."

"Just drop us off at a dock and then get Rolando back to Seattle. Can you do that in this weather?"

"Yes."

Two hours later Nicolus and Nickolaea stepped off onto an out of the way dock, just outside Anchorage, with parkas covering their assault gear. They walked up to the house connected with the dock. A man with a shotgun met them at the door.

"Don't come any closer," the man yelled down the sights of the gun.

"FBI assault team, sir. I need your four by four. I can pay for it."

The man slowly lowered his gun and stared at them. Nicolus offered him the envelope full of money that Joe Cornish had given him, but the man handed him the keys instead.

"Don't need the money, son. Take the Jeep...Just give 'em hell."

Nicolus and Nickolaea were on the road in a few minutes with the heat on, heading for the safe house.

*

Neither the governor, nor the sheriff, were standing in front of him. The General felt like shooting someone again. He strolled out of his office, gun in hand, and walked down to the mayor's office. The mayor was on the phone, but hung up at the sight of the General.

"I've got everybody looking, sir, but the governor has vanished."

The General raised his gun and shot the mayor in the forehead. "That's okay," he said, "I'll find her myself," and walked back out. He walked down the hall with his gun still out, letting it cool a bit before holstering it. Down the stairs to the main level, his lieutenants fell in with him as he walked to his armored Humvee.

"Move my office to the governor's mansion." One of his aides stepped away to take care of it. The General opened the back of his vehicle and got out a shotgun and plenty of shells, then they were underway with a Humvee of soldiers following.

The governor's mansion had an army of carpenters fixing and tidying the place up. When the General arrived, a late lunch was all ready for him. He sat down with his lieutenants and raised his wine glass, "Gentlemen, a week from tonight we will be dining in the governor's mansion in Vancouver, Canada."

# 28

"What third option?" The bodyguard had fallen asleep for a while and awoke as PC was checking everybody. PC gave her some water as Joe Cornish came in. "What third option?"

"Live free, instead of die hard. You're a little late."

"Tell me what you mean," she grunted.

"Change sides. Help us stop the invasion. Live free in my custody. In America, if you want."

"You cannot protect me."

"I haven't killed you."

"Why?"

"It's called a second chance, a do over, a mulligan. It's a chance to do something good instead of something bad. It's only for those who don't deserve it. You qualify, big time."

"The General will torture me."

"We've already saved him the trouble."

"You cannot stop him."

"We've stopped his best."

The bodyguard licked her lips to say more, but hesitated.

"You and your boss are murderers. You can only advance when good people compromise or give up, scared. Your boss is a monster."

"So am I."

"Start doing good now, and you will be on the side of good. Your dead ancestors, who you pray to, will see you and help."

"My ancestors would have nothing to do with me."

"What about your cousin?"

"What cousin?"

"Qui Ling."

"My General's daughter is gone and cannot be found."

"She is under my protection. I will take you to her when the invasion is stopped."

"Who are you?"

"I'm your only chance at life."

Now the bodyguard closed her eyes again. Joe Cornish got up to check Matty's head bandage.

"We've got company!" Dan blurted out as he first heard, and then saw a car pull into the driveway.

"Who? How many?" Joe Cornish gave Matty a gun and moved to the door, staying low.

"I don't recognize the Jeep. It looks like two. They're getting out...It's Nicolus and Nickolaea! They must have run into trouble."

"Nicolus doesn't run into trouble," Joe Cornish observed. He opened the front door wide enough to yell, "We were ambushed. Make sure no one's following you."

Nickolaea stopped, turned around, and crouched with her gun drawn all in one smooth move. Nicolus walked to the street and looked around, then came back, and they moved inside. "Whose car is out on the street?"

"Come on in and I'll introduce you. We're glad you came back. Everyone okay?"

"Yes, sir. We delivered everyone to an aircraft carrier that's just down in the Gulf. Rolando's going to Seattle to check on things there." He eyed Dan, Matty, and Jack. "Where's Tony?"

"He's in the bedroom with Millie's; he's got a broken jaw. Jack took the bullet meant for me, Matty's got a new crease on his head, Dan's back might be cracked, and Chrissy took a stray bullet in the leg. PC and Gretchen are nursing us back to health, and Tom's sleeping."

Nickolaea looked around, "Who is Chrissy?"

*

In China, the coup was going smoothly, except for finding the President. All the newspapers, TV, and radio stations were shut down, and Army Intelligence took over their control. Communication networks were being monitored to a degree not realized by those using them, so it kept Intelligence informed of what was happening in all areas of the country. Those bent on resisting the takeover didn't know how closely their communications, and therefore their actions, were being monitored.

The business of business took a two day holiday. Banking, stock market, and especially postal and package deliveries, all stopped for their own various reasons. Quick changes always bring uncertainty. Uncertainty causes some to take their money out of the bank and guard it themselves. Even the Chinese Army could not survive a run on the banks. The stock market usually plunges with quick change, but recovers shortly after with some people making a lot of money. Especially those who knew what was going on, like the Army's brass. Letters and packages were the biggest problem. Even with all of the technology, a letter written in code, or a package containing coded items, could not be controlled. A holiday was needed.

The General's younger brother was quite pleased with the smooth flow of things. It would only leave one thing for the General to be angry about, and the President would soon be found. Of all the rumors swirling around, the dumbest was that the President was hiding in a fort on the Mongolian border being guarded by a contingent of the Mongolian Army. But all rumors had to be investigated, so a platoon was sent north.

China was transforming quietly before the world's eyes. With the Army in charge, the people could be controlled for their own good. That was how civilization worked.

*

To the north and east, in The Peoples Republic of Alaska, things were smoothing out, also. The General could work around the missing governor, but if his bodyguard came back without the sheriff, he would eliminate her. Authority had to be maintained. Lovers were plentiful, bodyguards less so, but he could damn well take care of himself. Incompetence had to be cut off. It was how civilization worked. The family would understand.

By the time the compromisers in Washington, D.C. had compromised, and the ownership swap of land for debt had been accomplished, he would have ships in every port from Vancouver, British Columbia to the Mexican border unloading tanks and armaments. The stupid American politicians would agree to anything to save their soft, safe way of life. Even giving up part of their country. The General shook his head in disgust, but he was smiling.

And who would come to America's defense, the Japanese? Japan was the bone he had thrown to the North Koreans. One word from him and Korea would be unified again, with Japan as icing on the cake. After it was all said and done, he would eliminate the North Korean leaders and install his own men.

The next move was to deal with the pesky Canadians. There was only one main road down into British Columbia worth worrying about. If a massive frontal invasion of men and tanks moved south on that road, the Canadian Army would have to move north to confront them before they reached Vancouver. At that point the tanks in the Port of Vancouver would deploy and crush the Canadian Army from the rear.

China was on the move, rising to the top as it had many times over many thousands of years. It just took the right man at the top. Such a man deserved the perks associated with the risk. The former Alaskan governor had an interesting wine cellar, and most of the girls at the big club downtown were eager to please. This was how an ordered society worked. He would make sure of that.

# 29

Pastor Christopher was enjoying being home again with family and friends. His hilltop home was in a modest community overlooking part of Puget Sound.

He was standing out at the mailbox, rereading a letter that had just arrived. It was from one of his dear pastor friends in Mongolia. He had just gotten back from being with them and expected it to be a thank you note, however, the contents of the letter proved to be different. A slight puff of wind brought his attention back to where he was, and he hurriedly closed the mailbox and headed back into the house to his study. He handed his wife the rest of the mail and said, "Sure," to the offer of a cup of coffee. Sitting down in his desk chair he reread the letter again, slowly.

A moment later, with a soft knock on the door, his wife entered with coffee and sat by his side.

"They want you back so soon?" she leaned over and whispered, seeing the return address on the envelope.

Pastor Christopher silently eyed his wife, then took a sip of the coffee. His mind was trying to grasp what his eyes were reading, "They want me to pass on a message to the President."

"What? What president?"

"The President of the United States."

"What? You hate the President of the United States!"

"No, I don't. I dislike his policies."

"The pastors of Mongolia want you to pass on a message to the President?"

"The President of Mongolia asked the pastors if they knew someone trustworthy enough to handle getting a top secret message from him to the President of the United States."

Now she was stunned, "You were…in Air Force Intelligence… before we were married. Did you handle top secret stuff back then?"

"Yes."

The pastor's wife got up and closed the study door all the way and closed the mini-blinds on the window. She sat back down and whispered, "What's the message?"

Pastor Christopher smiled, "That's what I can't figure out. It makes no sense." He held the letter so she could see the last two paragraphs.

"It's…like a…fairytale. It must be coded."

Pastor Christopher looked at his wife with astonishment, then dug out his wallet. "Honey, you are amazing!"

"Yes. This we know. But what are you talking about?"

"Almost six years ago now, when I first visited Mongolia and met with some of the pastors there, one laughingly gave me a piece of paper with a key to a code written on it so we could communicate, since his English was poor. We all laughed, but he insisted I put it in my wallet. I…wonder if I…" Slowly he lifted a folded piece of paper from his wallet.

For the next few minutes they sat side by side applying the key to the coded paragraphs. Then they sat upright again and stared at each other. Pastor Christopher reached for his phone and dialed his lawyer.

*

Nicolus came out of Tony's bedroom, and quietly closed the door. "I think the hospitals are still operating. Nickolaea, Gretchen, and I will take Jack there. Then we'll..."

"Take me...with you," the bodyguard's voice was still shaky, but she opened her eyes. "I can get us past the guards. They will not question me. They can rebandage my wounds and then I will go with you." She looked over at PC and said, "Thank you for saving my life."

Nicolus had not spoken to her and wasn't about to. He looked at Joe Cornish.

Joe Cornish was eyeing the bodyguard, "If we agree to take you along, you cannot change your mind without dying. I will kill you myself."

"I have no wish to die...if there is a chance to live."

Nicolus had heard this before. It was similar to what Nickolaea had said to him when they were offered a second chance. Thinking back, he remembered he had been only a second away from shooting Joe Cornish dead. Since that hesitation caused by his wife's words, he had never been more happy or more filled with peace. "Where do you think I am going after the hospital?"

"We must...go to the governor's mansion... the General will only stay there a few nights."

"Can you get us in to him?" Nicolus asked.

"No. The men around him have orders to kill me on sight."

"You have a plan?" Joe Cornish continued the thought.

The bodyguard slowly turned her head and eyed Gretchen, "Only she... would have a chance to...kill my General."

Gretchen slowly turned her head away from Jack. PC was the only other woman in the room. Gretchen realized the bodyguard was looking at her.

*

"Harkness, Schaeffer, and Polamberly. How may I direct your call?"

"Peter Schaeffer, please. Tell him it's Pastor Christopher."

"Thank you, sir. One moment."

"Pastor Christopher, you're a nice break in my day."

"Peter, a serious matter has come up and I need to talk privately with someone I trust. Your name is at the top of my list. Please tell me now if you are unable to meet with me."

"I am able. Where and when?"

"My house, the sooner the better."

"I'm on my way. Is this a personal matter? I want to be prepared."

"Peter, do you remember me telling you I was in Air Force Intelligence a long time ago?"

"Yes, I do," Peter Schaeffer answered. There was no reply; the phone was silent. "I'm on my way."

*

The small platoon that got sent north to the southern border of Mongolia to check the rumor about the President of China, felt like they had the afternoon off. They stopped along the way to fortify themselves with adult beverages for the big battle. They were pretty much drunk when they parked the Humvee and walked with weapons shouldered to the big door of the walled fortress. When the big doors began to open out toward them, they backed up, right into the arms of the Mongolians who appeared behind them and escorted them inside. They were disarmed, brought into a room, and given food and drink. When they were full, they were given a place to sleep. In the morning, after a big breakfast, they all wondered at their good fortune. They agreed they would not be treated any better if they were in the house of the President of China himself. Presently that very person entered the room.

The soldiers were all wide eyed and suddenly feared for their lives.

"I have treated you fairly after your long journey. I will not let you shoot or arrest me. Will you join me?"

The least of rank in the platoon looked at the others and then spoke out, "Aren't you the President of China?"

"Yes, I am."

The soldier said, "I'm already on your side."

"Glad to hear it. Anybody else?"

They all looked at each other and raised their hands.

"Good. Report to this man here. He is the general." The president went back to his office, twelve men richer.

*

At the end of the day the General's brother was given the final report regarding the mission to find and capture the President of China. He shook his head at the failure, and dismissed the platoon who hadn't checked in as probably too drunk to find their way home, not to mention their phones. He settled down to a night of frolic and sleep. He was now the second most important man in China, and he might as well start acting like it.

# 30

Nicolus, Joe Cornish, Jack and Gretchen, along with the bodyguard, drove the back roads to the hospital in Anchorage. Gretchen knew the way.

Jack was the first to get care in the emergency room, then the bodyguard, and then Joe Cornish had his arm tended to. Jack was admitted to the hospital, the bodyguard was treated and released, and Joe Cornish was told to go home and keep the arm immobile.

Gretchen kissed Jack good bye as he was wheeled into surgery. She didn't know if it was for the night, or forever.

When the four got back into Nicolus's Jeep, the bodyguard helped Gretchen out of her clothes and into an outfit she had brought in a suitcase from the house. She instructed Gretchen on her hair and makeup, and then pulled a bottle of perfume from her pocket. She liberally dabbed it between Gretchen's breasts, then whispered something in her ear.

At a familiar spot ten blocks behind the governor's mansion, Nicolus stopped the Jeep and got dressed in his tactical gear as he had the previous time. He then moved on foot toward the mansion.

Joe Cornish took his life in his hands and let the bodyguard drive from there. She drove toward the mansion, and right up to the front gate. The sentry leveled his gun at them, but she barked orders at him. After looking into the back seat at Gretchen, the sentry opened the gate for them and then called ahead. At the front door, Joe Cornish jumped out and opened the door for Gretchen. She was dressed in a very revealing and appealing outfit, but she walked and talked all business. Inside the door she eyed the officers who guarded access to the General. They were all stunned by her beauty. The last two officers standing at the General's door leveled their guns and spoke in Chinese, motioning for her to raise her hands and prepare to be searched.

"I don't understand your gibberish," Gretchen said loudly. "And I will not raise my hands for you. Get out of my way."

The General heard a woman's voice and thought it might be his bodyguard. He opened the door and there in front of him was Gretchen in all her fullness.

He was stunned momentarily, but caught himself. "Who are you?" he bellowed.

She stepped right up to him so he could smell her perfume. In a soft, respectful voice she said, "I am a gift, as you can tell, from the one who loves you. She was wounded today fulfilling her mission and will come to you tomorrow with her prey."

The General drew her into his office and closed the door, "How do I know you did not kill her and take the perfume from her?"

Gretchen took a small step closer and slowly raised both her hands. She carefully took his head in her hands and gently lowered his nose into her bosom. He breathed deeply, then straightened and held Gretchen at arm's length.

"Please dine with me."

For the next hour the General drank in Gretchen's beauty and her elegance in social graces. He was used to women fawning over him, but this woman was different. He engaged her in conversation and Gretchen did the best she could, sticking to subjects she knew and keeping her answers vague. She enjoyed the Alaskan Salmon and drank only half as much as the General did. After dinner he put on music and asked her to dance. This was something Gretchen was good at, and so she impressed the half-drunk General.

When they were arm in arm, she whispered to him that she had visited here before at the invitation of a former governor. He had shown her the exquisite view from the roof and had undressed her and made love to her up there on a mattress covered by a mosquito net. Had the General seen the view from up there yet?

No, he hadn't.

She took him by the arm, led him out into the hall, pretending she was remembering eight years ago. As she led the way according to the directions Nicolus had given her, Gretchen was acting excited and a bit giggly, which was making the General excited. At the door to the room where the opening to the roof was, she looked at him, then at the two officers with them.

"They come with me wherever I go. Just forget they are here."

She snuggled close to him and whispered, "Okay, if you say so."

Gretchen opened the door, but one of the guards went in first, turning on the light. As the others came in, he stood up a ladder under the trap door in the ceiling. The guard went up first, unlatched the door, and opened it. He then lifted himself up and out onto the roof. Once on the roof he looked around and then said, "Come up."

The four reached the roof and walked around to the front of the building, looking for the view.

"Here," she said, "is where the governor showed me his great strength."

The General grabbed Gretchen and kissed her fiercely on her lips, neck and bosom. The two sharp hollow sounds didn't even register in the General's mind, but the two thuds on each side of him did. He stopped and looked down at the guards, then at Gretchen. She was the last sight he saw as Nicolus's gun butt came crashing down on the back of his head.

"Are you alright?" Nicolus asked Gretchen.

"I'll get over it."

"Okay, retrace your steps, search his room quickly for any obvious clues that would be helpful, and walk right out and into the Jeep." Nicolus helped her into the opening in the roof. She retraced her steps, not sneaking, but dancing and flowing as if she was drunk and in love, in case anyone saw her.

Nicolus injected the General with a syringe full of morphine, then put a vest on him and zipped it up. Next he put a rope under the vest from waist to neck in the back and carried him to the back edge of the roof. Hoisting the General over the side of the roof, he gently belayed him down to the ground. As he climbed down the drain pipe, he heard a guard dog approaching. Nicolus drew his silenced handgun and shot the attacking dog. A moment later the handler came around the corner of the mansion and Nicolus shot him, also. The man dropped on top of his dog. Leaving no time for more company, Nicolus grabbed the General and drug him across the lawn. He gently pushed the General through the hole in the perimeter fence which he had recut on his way in. Then he hoisted the General onto his back and walked across the street, up two blocks, and into the alley.

Gretchen searched the General's office and then walked out blowing kisses at the officers as she went. The first one turned to go check on his boss, so she stopped him with her hand to his cheek and said, "He is sleeping, don't you dare disturb him." She lowered her hand, dragging it across his chest, and kept going out the door and down the front steps. She forced herself not to hurry. At the rear door of the Jeep she stopped and bellowed, "Open this door for me."

A wide-eyed Joe Cornish jumped out and opened the door. They both jumped in and the bodyguard drove out the gate.

When they rendezvoused with Nicolus, they hoisted the General into the back of the Jeep and changed the seating to men in front, women in back. By the time they reached the hospital, Gretchen was back in her other clothes. She walked into the hospital to be with Jack as if the greatest kidnapping in history was just a story, and had never actually happened. Nicolus continued through the back roads and soon they pulled into the driveway of the safe house.

# 31

Peter Schaeffer had been a Navy Seal for four years, twenty years ago. As he headed over the Narrows Bridge from Tacoma, he called one of his former team mates, "Jess, I might have a situation needing our help. See who's available within the next two weeks, okay?" Fifteen minutes later he pulled into Pastor Christopher's driveway.

"Peter, thank you. Come on in," the pastor said, greeting him at the door.

He hugged the Pastor's wife as they sat down in the study with coffee and cookies, hot out of the oven. "Are you in any immediate danger?"

"No, but read this letter."

Peter read it twice. "Do you have the key to the code?"

"Yes. I think we decoded it correctly. It reads: 'I am in the mountains south of your border. Send a secret note by hand messenger to the President of the United States. Send me aid through Mongolia only. If he would stop the Chinese Army, I know how.'" Pastor Christopher looked at his lawyer, "It's signed, 'The President of China.' I got it in the regular mail from a pastor friend in Mongolia."

They explained more as the lawyer looked at the letter again, front and back, and at the envelope and stamps.

Looking at the pastor and his wife, he said, "There is no way to authenticate this. The President of Mongolia is simply using people he trusts. Those people turned to you."

"And we've turned to you, Peter. How do I show this to the President? A president I didn't vote for and don't support?"

"Only the Ambassador from Mongolia can ask to see the president and reasonably expect to see him within a week. We need the President of Mongolia to direct his Ambassador to the U.S. to make an appointment with the President of the United States and have you and I present with him at that meeting. I can alert those in the Secret Service whom I trust, to let them know you and I are coming. All you can do is send a letter back to your pastor friend, regular mail, and have him send that particular message to the President of Mongolia. Let's compose the letter right now and I'll mail it in Tacoma."

Pastor Christopher was thinking aloud, "This means the Chinese move in Alaska is a diversion for a silent coup in China. The Chinese Government is not really behind the Alaska move."

"I'd say you're right. Know any good men in Alaska?"

*

In the driveway, Nicolus drove ahead enough so that the back of the Jeep was next to the side door into the garage. By the time they got out and had the back opened, Dan had the door open. They manhandled the General out of the Jeep and into the garage, where Tom and Dan had set up a single bed.

The General was awake, but groggy. He relaxed and fell asleep when he was laid on the bed. Joe Cornish went in and found PC. "How is everyone?"

"Everyone is good. Tony and Matty want to get up. You'll have to talk to them. Chrissy is content to sleep. Millie's got some dinner ready, and Dan..."

They stepped into the garage and Dan was talking to the General who was asleep. "...and I'm going to go out and take it back. I can outdraw and outshoot any of your...soldiers, so you better get out your phone and order a ship load of body bags..." He stopped when Joe Cornish followed PC into the garage. "I'm okay, no attacks while you were gone, no contacts. I'm ready for the next mission."

"I was hoping that was the case. PC will you check the General? We want to keep him comfortable and asleep."

"Sure, then I need to go see Gretchen and Jack."

Joe Cornish looked at her, not sure if she was serious. "Why?"

"We're out of medical supplies. I need a resupply. Either we steal an aid car, or I visit the hospital."

"Okay, let's huddle over dinner," he looked at the bodyguard.

"I'll watch him while you eat," she said. "Afterward someone can feed me. Handcuff one of his hands to the bed, and one of mine to this chair."

Dan pulled his cuffs and secured the General to the bed, then dug out a tie strap and reached for her.

"Not necessary," said Joe Cornish. "Let's go plan."

*

Morning brought chaos in the governor's mansion.

The officer who had taken Gretchen's advice and not checked on the General had broken down the door of his room only to find it empty. He searched the entire suite connected to the General's room and found nothing. He drew his gun and put it to his own head because he deserved to die, but hesitated only because he realized the General would want to do it himself. He took a deep breath and instituted a building-wide search.

The roof, yard, and fence behind the mansion yielded clues that the General had been taken. If there was any way to redeem himself, it would be to find and rescue the General. He quickly gave instructions for a systematic search and focused on the task with singular determination. He set himself up at the General's desk with all communications coming to him. As morning drug on, there were no more clues. The harried searching settled into a calm as the officer began to look around. He was in charge. If the General was not found or found dead, he would be in charge. He *was* in charge. The invasion had to proceed, and as the General's temporary replacement, it was his responsibility. He was temporarily in charge. *He* was in charge.

By afternoon the search had become a token effort, and by evening the invasion took top billing again. The officer was beginning to feel at home in the General's chair.

*

In China, the General's younger brother couldn't figure out why the General was not calling, demanding an update. He checked in with all his search parties who were looking for the President of China, so he could say he was up to date and handling the search personally. Then he called the General himself. An officer answered the call.

"Where is the General?" his younger brother demanded.

"Sir, we are searching for him." The officer said plainly.

The general in China hesitated. That was going to be *his* line. "What do you mean, 'searching'?"

The officer continued, "The General is missing and we are searching for him." His confidence was growing. "Have you found the President of China yet?"

"No, but we are searching." The little brother was flustered. He didn't know whether to be outraged or joyful. Now there was silence on both ends of the phone.

The officer spoke first, "I am in charge in Alaska, you are in charge in China. We are both doing our jobs."

"Yes," was all the little brother said. Then he lowered his voice and said, "Tell me what happened."

"We have evidence that the General was kidnapped, but we have not heard anything from anyone."

The general in China was trying to think. If he was second-in-command and first-in-command was missing, then *he* was first-in-command. He decided to be encouraging instead of demanding. "You are doing exactly as you should. I promote you to General-in-charge of Alaska."

The officer was feeling more confident by the minute but decided not to bite off more than he could chew, "Thank you, sir. We are on schedule."

"What is the schedule?"

The new General-in-charge of Alaska hesitated, "It is...to be in the governor's mansion in Vancouver, Canada in...six days."

The first-in-command in China hesitated, "My brother's plans are... ambitious," he said.

"Yes, sir. No room for mistakes or setbacks," damn, he shouldn't have used the word mistake. The new general held his breath.

The first-in-command noticed the two words. "Yes, but this is a setback we should stop and consider."

"Yes, sir. I agree."

Okay. He decided to go further, "The Chinese Government is not in favor of this invasion; the idea was my brother's."

"Yes, sir."

"The coup was not the idea of the Chinese Army until my brother was in charge."

"Yes, sir."

"I am not ready to rule China. Are you ready to conquer the west coast of North America?"

"No, sir."

The invasion of Alaska and points south by the Chinese Army ended right then and there.

"Then let us put our heads together and plan an orderly withdrawal back to China."

"Yes. Yes, sir. I agree. Sir, if the General...reappears, what should I do?"

"You will do to him what must be done and you will tell no one. Not even me."

# 32

Days had gone by and things were getting less, not more exciting. Joe Cornish had decided to let things ride since the tanks were being withdrawn. Nicolus and Nickolaea had carefully driven around and noticed that ships were being loaded with containers, rather than unloaded. The cell phones, TV, and radio were still not working.

The Anchorage newspaper used the presses of the Palmer Weekly News to produce their first newspaper in five days. Tom's story was on the front page, with a byline that included the fact that it had been scheduled to be printed the day that their offices were demolished. The facts and predictions of the story, having been proved true in the days following, sent Tom's career into orbit.

Jack had made it through his operation and was recovering. Joe Cornish and PC had visited Gretchen and Jack at the hospital twice, each time taking home much needed first aid supplies and medicines. At the safe house, everyone's injuries were mending. PC had administered the medicines and they had made the difference.

The plans for the General were still being formulated. At this point, they could not afford to have him awake and alert. Once a day, PC woke him up so he could use the bathroom. The bodyguard had helped him take a bath one day and he recognized her, but thought they were back in China. They put him back in bed with another dose of morphine before he woke up all the way.

Joe Cornish was up early the next day and went for a walk outside the house for the first time. He wondered what else had happened to cause the turn-around. Good men, Joe Cornish thought, good men and women were probably at the root of it, whatever it was. One person, doing one good thing, would begin the tides to turn and rivers to flow back uphill. He reminded himself not to be afraid in the future, but to look for the effortless seam running between good and bad that could even change the course of society. If things kept going like they were, he might find himself back at his desk in Seattle in a few weeks, looking into the next special investigation file on top of his inbox. He chuckled as he realized he kind of missed that rattle of the etched glass pane in the door to his office. The one that said: Joe Cornish, Special Investigations, FBI, Seattle Office.

# Epilogue

Pastor Christopher, his wife, and Peter Schaeffer the lawyer, accompanied the Ambassador from Mongolia to talk with the President of the United States. The meeting lasted half an hour. The top secret message was passed on to the President. He thanked the group, had pictures taken, and assured them it was already being looked into.

A month later, the White House announced that the invasion of Alaska, involving a rogue element of the Chinese Army and several international arms producing corporations, had been stopped. Up and down the west coast, the Chinese were sending construction containers by the hundreds, back to China. It was further announced through the White House Press Secretary, that the President, working with the President of Mongolia, had offered assistance to the leaders of China, but was refused.

A vote was taken in the United States Senate, regarding the Twenty-Eighth Amendment to the Constitution of the United States. It passed 100 to 0.

One of the senators had a big smile on her face. She looked at her chief of staff and admitted, "This is kind of fun! What's next?"

Now, read those three questions at the beginning again...

God will bless you as you formulate your answers!

DAK

Other Books by Deane Addison Knapp

THE GOLD MINE
What Would You Do?

An inspirational book about the value of God's love, THE GOLD MINE was displayed at the May 2015 Book Expo America at Javits Center, New York City.

Author's comments: God's love is the power that can change us from the inside out. An assurance of God's love for us (faith) comes easily when we value God's love accurately. This is not a how-to book, but an easy to read family story that will inspire readers to believe that God loves us way more than we think He does.

Think what might happen if you realigned your assessment of God's love for you with His reality. Take time to read THE GOLD MINE, then put a copy on your coffee table and send one to friends and relatives as a gift. See what they say. This could be way more fun than you've had in a long time.

DAK

Books Coming Soon By Deane Addison Knapp

The Transfer (a new story)........................................................2016

The Vancouver Office (sequel to The Seattle Office)................2017

The Hideout (sequel to The Transfer)......................................2018

Printed in the United States
By Bookmasters